PENGUIN CLASSICS

SERIES ADVISOR: PAUL POPLAWSKI

SELECTED STORIES

DAVID HERBERT LAWRENCE was born into a miner's family in Eastwood, Nottinghamshire, in 1885, the fourth of five children. His first novel, *The White Peacock*, was published in 1911. In 1912 Lawrence went to Germany and Italy with Frieda Weekley, the German wife of a professor at Nottingham University College, where Lawrence had studied; she divorced, and they were married on their return to England in 1914. Lawrence had published *Sons and Lovers* in 1913; but *The Rainbow*, completed in 1915, was suppressed, and for three years he could not find a publisher for *Women in Love*, which he first completed in 1917. After the First World War he travelled extensively in Europe, Australia, America and Mexico. He returned to Europe from America in 1925, and lived mainly in Italy and France. His last novel, *Lady Chatterley's Lover*, was published in 1928 but was banned in England and America. In 1930 he died in Vence, in the south of France, at the age of forty-four.

SUE WILSON taught on the postgraduate programme on D. H. Lawrence for several years at the University of Nottingham, where she was a Lecturer in Modern English Literature. She is currently a Senior Lecturer in Drama at Anglia Ruskin University in Cambridge.

LOUISE WELSH made her living for many years as a dealer in out-of-print and second-hand books. Her first novel, *The Cutting Room* (Canongate Books) is being translated into nineteen languages. The *Guardian* chose Louise as one of Britain's Best First Novelists of 2002 and 'a woman to watch' in 2003. She is a regular radio broadcaster, has published many short stories and contributed articles and reviews to most British broadsheets. Her second book, *Tamburlaine Must Die*, was published in August 2004. Louise lives in Glasgow.

PAUL POPLAWSKI is a Senior Lecturer at the University of Leicester. He is a member of the editorial board of the Cambridge Edition of Lawrence's Works and his recent publications include the revised third edition of *A Bibliography of D. H. Lawrence* (Cambridge, 2001), and *Encyclopedia of Literary Modernism* (Greenwood Press, 2003).

D. H. LAWRENCE

Selected Stories

Edited with Notes by SUE WILSON
With an Introduction by LOUISE WELSH

PENGUIN BOOKS

PENGUIN CLASSICS

Penguin Books Ltd, 80 Strand, London WC2R ORL, England
Penguin Group (USA) Inc., 375 Hudson Street, New York, New York 10014, USA
Penguin Group (Canada), 90 Eglinton Avenue East, Suite 700, Toronto, Ontario, Canada M4P 2Y3
(a division of Pearson Penguin Canada Inc.)
Penguin Ireland, 25 St Stephen's Green, Dublin 2, Ireland
(a division of Penguin Books Ltd)
Penguin Group (Australia), 250 Camberwell Road, Camberwell, Victoria 3124, Australia
(a division of Pearson Australia Group Pty Ltd)
Penguin Books India Pvt Ltd, 11 Community Centre, Panchsheel Park, New Delhi – 110 017, India
Penguin Group (NZ), 67 Apollo Drive, Mairangi Bay, Auckland 1310, New Zealand
(a division of Pearson New Zealand Ltd)
Penguin Books (South Africa) (Pty) Ltd, 24 Sturdee Avenue, Rosebank, Johannesburg 2196, South Africa

Penguin Books Ltd, Registered Offices: 80 Strand, London WC2R ORL, England

www.penguin.com

This collection first published in Penguin Classics 2007
4

The story texts copyright © the Estate of Frieda Lawrence Ravagli, 1983, 1987, 1990, 1995, 2007
Introduction copyright © Louise Welsh, 2007
Notes copyright © Sue Wilson, 2007
Chronology, Further Reading and A Note on the Texts copyright © Paul Poplawski, 2006, 2007
All rights reserved

The moral right of the introducer and the editor has been asserted

pp. xxxii–xxxvi constitute an extension of this copyright page

Set in 10.25/12.25pt Post Script Adobe Sabon
Typeset by Rowland Phototypesetting Ltd, Bury St Edmunds, Suffolk
Printed in England by Clays Ltd, St Ives plc

ISBN: 978-0-141-44165-8

www.greenpenguin.co.uk

Penguin Books is committed to a sustainable future
for our business, our readers and our planet.
The book in your hands is made from paper
certified by the Forest Stewardship Council.

Contents

Acknowledgements

This volume uses the texts established by the Cambridge University Press editions of D. H. Lawrence's short stories (with the exception of 'Vin Ordinaire': see A Note on the Texts). I am greatly indebted to the Cambridge editors: Michael Herbert, Christa Jansohn, Bethan Jones, Dieter Mehl, Bruce Steele, Lindeth Vasey and John Worthen. I am also particularly grateful to Linda Bree and Alison Powell of Cambridge University Press for supplying me with corrected proofs for the text of the story 'Things'.

The Explanatory Notes for each Cambridge edition were a valuable editorial resource, as were the notes prepared for the Penguin Twentieth-Century Classics and Oxford World's Classics editions of Lawrence's short stories. My thanks are due to Antony Atkins, Michael Bell, Keith Cushman, Brian Finney and N. H. Reeve.

I also wish to thank Laura Barber for initiating this project and Mariateresa Boffo and Marcella Edwards at Penguin for guiding me through it. Lindeth Vasey and Sally Boyles gave me essential advice at every stage; I am very grateful for their forbearance. Meticulous proofreading by Henry Maas and Stephen Ryan caught serious and silly errors that I was very relieved to have the chance to correct. I would also like to thank John Worthen and Paul Poplawski for all their generous and expert advice throughout the preparation of this edition.

S. W.
March 2006

Chronology

1885 11 September: David Herbert Lawrence born in Eastwood, Nottinghamshire, third son of Arthur John (coalminer) and Lydia Lawrence.

1898–1901 Attends Nottingham High School.

1901 October–December: Clerk at Nottingham factory of J. H. Haywood; falls ill.

1902–5 Pupil-teacher in Eastwood and Ilkeston; meets Chambers family, including Jessie, in 1902.

1905–6 Uncertificated teacher in Eastwood; starts to write poetry, shows it to Jessie.

1906–8 Studies for teaching certificate at University College, Nottingham; begins first novel *The White Peacock* in 1906.

1907 Writes first short stories; first published story, 'A Prelude', appears in the *Nottinghamshire Guardian* (under Jessie's name).

1908–11 Elementary teacher at Davidson Road School, Croydon.

1909 Jessie sends selection of Lawrence's poems to the *English Review*; Ford Madox Hueffer (editor) accepts five and recommends *The White Peacock* to a publisher. Writes 'Odour of Chrysanthemums' (–1911) and first play, *A Collier's Friday Night*.

1910 Engaged to Louie Burrows; death of his mother. First drafts of *The Trespasser* and 'Paul Morel' (later *Sons and Lovers*).

1911 *The White Peacock* published. Second draft of 'Paul Morel'; writes and revises short stories. 'Odour of Chrysanthemums' published. Third draft of 'Paul Morel' (–1912).

Falls seriously ill with pneumonia (November–December).

1912 Recuperates in Bournemouth; in February, breaks off engagement, returns to Eastwood and resigns teaching post. Meets Frieda Weekley (née von Richthofen), the wife of a professor at Nottingham University, and in May goes with her to Germany and then to Italy for the winter. *The Trespasser* published. Revises 'Paul Morel' into *Sons and Lovers*.

1913 Drafts Italian essays and starts to write 'The Sisters' (which will become *The Rainbow* and *Women in Love*). *Love Poems* published. April–June in Germany; writes 'The Prussian Officer' and other stories. *Sons and Lovers* published (May). Spends the summer in England with Frieda, then they return to Italy. Works on 'The Sisters'.

1914 *The Widowing of Mrs Holroyd* (play) published (USA). Finishes 'The Wedding Ring' (latest version of 'The Sisters') and returns to England with Frieda; her divorce finalised, they marry on 13 July. At the outbreak of war (August), Methuen & Co. withdraw from their agreement to publish 'The Wedding Ring'. War prevents return to Italy; lives in Buckinghamshire and Sussex. Rewrites 'The Wedding Ring' as *The Rainbow* (–1915).

1915 Writes 'England, My England'; works on essays for *Twilight in Italy*. Moves to London in August. *The Rainbow* is published in September but withdrawn in October, and prosecuted as obscene and banned a month later. Hopes to travel to USA with Frieda but at the end of December they settle in Cornwall (–October 1917).

1916 Rewrites the other half of 'The Sisters' material as *Women in Love*; it is finished by November but refused by several publishers (–1917). Reading American literature. *Twilight in Italy* and *Amores* (poems) published.

1917 Begins work on *Studies in Classic American Literature* (hereafter *Studies*). Revises *Women in Love*. Expelled from Cornwall with Frieda in October under Defence of the Realm Act; they return to London. Begins the novel *Aaron's Rod*. *Look! We Have Come Through!* (poems) published.

1918 Lives mostly in Berkshire and Derbyshire (–mid 1919). *New Poems* published; first versions of eight *Studies* essays published in periodical form (–1919). War ends (November). Writes *The Fox*.

1919 Revises *Studies* essays in intermediate versions. Revises *Women in Love* for Thomas Seltzer (USA). In November leaves for Italy.

1920 Moves to Sicily (February) and settles at Taormina. Publication of *Women in Love* in USA, *Touch and Go* (play), *Bay* (poems) and *The Lost Girl* in England.

1921 Visits Sardinia with Frieda and writes *Sea and Sardinia*. *Movements in European History* (textbook) and *Women in Love* published in England; *Psychoanalysis and the Unconscious* and *Sea and Sardinia* published in USA. Travels to Italy, Germany and Austria (April–September) and then returns to Taormina. Finishes *Aaron's Rod*, writes *The Captain's Doll* and *The Ladybird*, revises *The Fox*.

1922 February–September: Travels with Frieda to Ceylon, Australia and USA. *Aaron's Rod* published; writes *Kangaroo* in Australia. Arrives in Taos, New Mexico, in September; rewrites *Studies* (final version). *Fantasia of the Unconscious* and *England My England and Other Stories* published. Moves to Del Monte Ranch, near Taos, in December.

1923 *The Ladybird* (with *The Fox* and *The Captain's Doll*) published. Travels to Mexico with Frieda. *Studies* published in August (USA). Writes 'Quetzalcoatl' (early version of *The Plumed Serpent*). *Kangaroo* and *Birds, Beasts and Flowers* (poems) published. Rewrites *The Boy in the Bush* from Mollie Skinner's manuscript. Frieda returns to England in August; Lawrence follows in December.

1924 In France and Germany, then to Kiowa Ranch, near Taos. *The Boy in the Bush* published; writes 'The Woman Who Rode Away', *St. Mawr* and 'The Princess'. Death of his father. Goes to Mexico with Frieda.

1925 Finishes *The Plumed Serpent* in Oaxaca; falls ill, nearly dies and is diagnosed with tuberculosis. Returns to Mexico City and then to Kiowa Ranch. *St. Mawr Together with The Princess* published. Travels via London to Italy. *Reflections on the Death of a Porcupine* (essays) published; writes *The Virgin and the Gipsy* (–January 1926).

1926 *The Plumed Serpent* and *David* (play) published. Visits England for the last time; returns to Italy and writes first version of *Lady Chatterley's Lover*, then second version (–1927).

1927 Tours Etruscan sites with Earl Brewster; writes *Sketches of Etruscan Places*; writes first part of *The Escaped Cock* (second part in 1928). Suffers series of bronchial haemorrhages. *Mornings in Mexico* (essays) published. Starts third version of *Lady Chatterley's Lover*.

1928 *The Woman Who Rode Away and Other Stories* published. Finishes, revises and privately publishes third version of *Lady Chatterley's Lover* in limited edition (late June); distributes it through network of friends but many copies confiscated by authorities in USA and England. Travels to Switzerland for health, and then to Bandol in the south of France. *The Collected Poems of D. H. Lawrence* published; writes many of the poems for *Pansies*.

1929 Organises cheap Paris edition of *Lady Chatterley's Lover* to counter piracies. Typescript of *Pansies* seized by police in London. Travels to Spain, Italy and Germany; increasingly ill. Police raid exhibition of his paintings in London (July). Expurgated (July) and unexpurgated (August) editions of *Pansies* published; *The Escaped Cock* published. Returns to Bandol. Writes biblical commentary *Apocalypse* (– January 1930).

1930 2 March: Dies of tuberculosis at Vence, Alpes Maritimes, France, and is buried there. *Nettles* (poems), *Assorted Articles*, *The Virgin and the Gipsy* and *Love Among the Haystacks & Other Pieces* published.

1931 *Apocalypse* published.

1932 *Sketches of Etruscan Places* published (as *Etruscan Places*). *Last Poems* published.

1933–4 Story collections *The Lovely Lady* (1933) and *A Modern Lover* (1934) published.

1935 Frieda has Lawrence exhumed and cremated, and his ashes taken to Kiowa Ranch.

1936 *Phoenix* (compilation) published.

1956 Death of Frieda.

1960 Penguin Books publish the first unexpurgated English edition of *Lady Chatterley's Lover*, following the famous obscenity trial.

Introduction

Somewhere, tucked away in the forgotten recesses of a dusty storeroom in some gallery of modern art, there may be a lost Warhol screen print of D. H. Lawrence, his beard shifting from pink to blue to acid yellow. By 1960 Lawrence had been dead for thirty years, but his work seems as much a part of the era of newly won sexual freedom and class-consciousness as the pill. Philip Larkin (who claimed he always mowed his grass wearing a T-shirt depicting D. H. Lawrence) places him at the centre of the sexual revolution, juxtaposing *Lady Chatterley's Lover* with the trendiest pop group of the day:

> Sexual intercourse began
> In nineteen sixty-three
> (Which was rather late for me) –
> Between the end of the *Chatterley* ban
> And the Beatles' first LP.[1]

Lawrence explored an impressive breadth of forms and concerns in his short literary life. When he died at the age of forty-four he left behind eleven published novels, numerous anthologies of novellas, short stories and poetry, impressive collections of literary criticism and non-fiction, several plays and a massive body of correspondence.

This collection of stories encapsulates much of the breadth of concern that populates Lawrence's writing, but they are more than a mere introduction to greater works. In the words of literary critic Diana Trilling, if Lawrence 'had written nothing except his long and short stories, not even his novels, he would still have made a major contribution to modern fiction'.[2]

So why should our imaginary screen print be lost? Why doesn't it appear proudly alongside those of other iconic figures, Marilyn Monroe, David Bowie and Jackie Kennedy? Why indeed is Lawrence's work slipping from the school and university curriculum, falling from all but second-hand bookshop shelves, no longer the subject of 'major motion pictures' and television adaptations?

D. H. Lawrence's critics have always been at least as eminent and as passionate as his supporters. Asked to contribute to Berkeley's D. H. Lawrence fellowship fund Vladimir Nabokov paid up but announced, 'I dislike D. H. Lawrence as a writer and detest Taos.'[3]

Some of Lawrence's later vilification came from a feminist movement that was re-examining texts and discovering patriarchal attitudes embedded in them. Kate Millett brands Lawrence an 'overt racist' who would nevertheless use 'the lower-caste male . . . to master or humiliate the white man's own insubordinate mate'.[4] In other words she considers that Lawrence would overcome his disgust at people of colour if he could use them to control or debase an errant woman.

The poet Tony Hoagland is so fed up with Lawrence's detractors he resolves to address the next one he meets directly, telling him or her that they should be honoured to raise:

> just one of D. H. Lawrence's urine samples
> to your arid psychobiographic
> theory-tainted lips.[5]

The lack of sympathy towards Lawrence and his work that Hoagland deplores is not confined to critics. A resident of Lawrence's hometown, Eastwood, summed up a popular reaction towards Lawrence in the 1980s: 'We kicked him out o' Eastwood and we kicked him out o' England. We want no more of him here.'[6] Recently BBC Radio 4 visited the town as part of a programme marking the seventy-fifth anniversary of Lawrence's death. Some of the residents interviewed were still uncomfortable with the memory of Lawrence. 'The old men used to tell us how he would spy on courting couples,' said an elderly lady. This offers a fascinating insight into the way Lawrence was perceived by some in his hometown – not just as a sex maniac, but perhaps also as a man who caught the lives of residents so well that they felt that he had indeed spied on them. How otherwise could this insider/outsider know their lives so intimately?

The urge to explain and explore writers' lives through their fiction should generally be resisted. After all, they are making things up. But, for this writer at least, the temptation to look at Lawrence's life, especially the early years, through the filter of his works is irresistible. This introduction breaks no new ground in Lawrence studies, but it is an attempt to look beyond his life, to examine concerns that fuelled Lawrence's creative work and to acknowledge some of the social and philosophical influences that influenced his writing. Not every story in this volume makes an appearance in this short essay, which looks at the collection as a whole rather than piece by piece, but every story is a masterpiece in its own right.

D. H. Lawrence was born in Eastwood near Nottingham in 1885, the fourth child of Arthur and Lydia Lawrence. Arthur was a coalminer who had started in the pits at the age of ten. Lydia, more educated than her husband and with more genteel ambitions, had famously 'married beneath herself' and felt it keenly. She had aspirations for her children, especially Lawrence's gifted brother Ernest, which went beyond the dirty, dangerous occupation of their father. When Ernest died at the age of twenty-three, Lydia's hopes seem to have been transferred on to her youngest son David Herbert, known at home as Bert.

The tensions between his parents made a powerful impression on young Bert. Lydia Lawrence perceived her husband's trips to the public house as central to a feckless lack of ambition. Arthur Lawrence considered them a natural pastime; a means of washing away the pit dust while socialising with workmates who depended on each other for their lives in a dangerous environment. Lydia wanted her boys to achieve more than their father, while Arthur couldn't see why what had been good enough for him wasn't good enough for his sons.

Eastwood and Lawrence's early family life permeates much of his work. He described 'Odour of Chrysanthemums' as 'full of my childhood's atmosphere'.[7]

In this story, Elizabeth Bates, pregnant with her third child, is waiting for her husband Walter to return home from the mine, but suspects that he has gone to the local public house. As the night progresses she almost hopes that he *is* in the pub getting drunk, the only other reason for his lateness being an accident in the pit. Unable to dismiss her fear, but 'nursing her wrath to keep it warm', Elizabeth sets out for a neighbour's house to enquire if her husband has been seen. A fellow miner confirms Walter is not in the local and the alarm is raised when it is realised that no one saw him leave the pit. Some workmates return to check on him, but they are too late: he has been smothered behind a collapsed pit-roof. Elizabeth's husband is brought home, his body unmarked but lifeless.

Lawrence's 'Eastwood' writings have a hint of documentary about them. This is a fiction that engages with the most secret, internal emotions of its subjects, but it is also an illuminating slice of real life, a family at home glimpsed clearly for a second through the window of a passing train, a precursor to the socially aware docudramas of Ken Loach.

Lawrence recalled how he often wished that his father would die in the pit and it is tempting to see 'Odour of Chrysanthemums' partly as a recollection of that uncomfortable desire. A similar revisiting of the fantasy occurs in Lawrence's novel *Sons and Lovers*, as John Worthen points out:

> The young Paul Morel lying in bed at night, hating his father, has gone a whole journey deeper into rage than his siblings. He prays: 'Let him be killed at pit.' A late essay confirms this as a true memory of young Lawrence, awaiting his father's return and the dreaded row downstairs . . .[8]

Tucked within 'Odour of Chrysanthemums' is the possibility that it was suspicion and drink that killed Elizabeth's husband.

When asked if she saw her father coming home from the pit, young Annie

> became serious. She looked at her mother with large, wistful blue
> eyes.
>   'No, mother, I've never seen him. Why? Has he come up an'
> gone past to Old Brinsley? He hasn't, mother, 'cos I never saw
> him.' (78:22–6)

Perhaps if Elizabeth had listened to her daughter and raised the alarm earlier or indeed if his gang members had made sure he had exited the pit, her husband could have been saved. Perhaps the blame lies partly in Walter's habit of preferring drink to his family to such an extent that his lateness is not an initial cause for alarm. But Lawrence doesn't linger over these possibilities. Death has been with us all the way.

> 'It was chrysanthemums when I married him, and chrysan-
> themums when you were born, and the first time they ever
> brought him home drunk he'd got brown chrysanthemums in his
> button-hole.' (80:31–4)

What is there left to complete these landmarks except a death? Yet it would be wrong to see the miner's life as simply marriage, birth, work, drink and demise because there are also the chrysanthemums, a hardy evocation of nature and beauty – an evocation which runs throughout these short stories and much of the rest of Lawrence's work.

Lawrence was living at home in Eastwood when the national miners' strike began in February 1912. His early story 'The Miner at Home' is one of a series Lawrence wrote between February and April of that year, shortly after illness forced him to turn to writing full-time. It is a simple though accomplished short story already showing the observational skills and original-ity of expression of a great writer.

> He wore no coat, and his arms were freckled black. He stripped
> to the waist, hitched his trousers into the strap, and kneeled on

the rug to wash himself. There was a great splashing and
spluttering. The red firelight shone on his cap of white soap, and on
the muscles of his back, on the strange working of his red and
white muscular arms, that flashed up and down like individual
creatures. (44:13–19)

Lawrence's working-class characters are complex, intelligent
and sensitive; by no means the standard fictional portrayal of
the working class in Lawrence's time or indeed today. In 'Love
Among the Haystacks' a young man quotes a couplet in German
while stacking a haystack, in 'The Miner at Home' a miner
wrestles with his own reluctance to go on strike while trying to
persuade his wife that he should, in 'Adolf' a weary father
returning home from nightshift rescues an abandoned rabbit
for his children.

Language is of course at the root of Lawrence's writing.
Like fellow working-class poets Robert Burns[9] and John Clare,
Lawrence considered the lives of ordinary people good enough
for literature. He also wrote his characters' speech in the
language that he had grown up with.

'Tha sees,' he said, as he leaned on the pommel of his fork, 'tha
thowt as tha 'd done me one, didna ter?' He smiled as he spoke,
then fell again into his pleasant torment of musing. (4:3–5)

Modern writers such as James Kelman or Irvine Welsh do
not feel the need to employ standard English to narrate for
characters who speak in dialect, and the modern reader coming
to Lawrence's work may regret that he didn't express such tales
completely in the language of his subjects. The contrast can
give the impression of a narrator of 'superior' class or education
relaying the actions of people who seem sassy enough to talk
for themselves. Lawrence is sometimes portrayed as a writer
eager to leave his class behind, a precursor of John Lennon's
'Working Class Hero' who vents his frustration on the people
who formed him, calling them 'fucking peasants', unable to
understand why they too can't escape the restrictions of their
birth.

Lawrence had intended 'Adolf' (a short early sketch, it was never anthologised during his lifetime) for the *Athenaeum*. 'I will try to be pleasant and a bit old fashioned,'[10] Lawrence wrote to the editor. In the event 'Adolf' was rejected. Perhaps this self-conscious resolve to be old-fashioned accounts for the lack of Lawrence's usual bite. Or perhaps the realism and element of tension that Lawrence could not bring himself to quite banish accounts for the journal's refusal. The narrator's father, a miner, returns from nightshift just as his children rise, fresh and full of energy from bed.

> Then night met morning face to face, and the contact was not always happy. Perhaps it was painful to my father to see us gaily entering upon the day into which he dragged himself soiled and weary. (220:5–8)

Or perhaps it was Lawrence's use of profanity (albeit in French in this instance), for which he would later be so severely censured and censored, that decided the editor of the *Athenaeum* against accepting 'Adolf'. As the antisocial rabbit hops back into the wild,

> bob! bob! bob! goes the white tail, *merde! merde! merde!* it says to the pursuer. The rabbit can't help it. In his utmost extremity he still flings the insult at the pursuer. (227:25–8)

'Adolf' gives us a glimpse of Lawrence's irreverence; there are times when the whole world is *merde* to him too. It also perhaps gives us a flavour of Lawrence's sense of humour, which his friends frequently write of in their recollections of the man, but that often seems absent from his writings.

Lawrence's poor health made him unsuited to working in the mines and his intelligence, coupled with the support and determination of his family, enabled him to continue his education and gain work, initially as a clerk and later as a teacher in a board school.[11] Neither profession was to his taste, and the young Lawrence must have feared he would be caught in a life from which there was no means of escape. The chance of making a living from his writing was even slimmer than for young writers today.

Lawrence was keenly aware and deeply afraid of the fate life might hold for him. Trapped by birth and circumstance in an occupation he found unfulfilling, marriage would probably soon follow clinching him in a financial and social trap that would foster frustration. His only release from drudgery would be in physical and sexual expression and eventually death.

Such restrictions undercut the lives around him. His mother had escaped the poverty of her family home through marriage to a miner only to find herself committed to an unsatisfactory union. She maintained her education and stimulated her mind through church activities, but there would be no real escape for her from the restrictions of class, gender and poverty. As Lawrence reached adolescence and entered the world of work and education he could see the same pattern being replicated in his own life and that of his friends and siblings. A combination of zeitgeist, talent and poor health released Lawrence into full-time writing, but the life he might have had continued to inform his work.

Lawrence frequently writes from a female point of view. He was delighted when an early anonymous review of *The White Peacock* asked,

> To begin with, what is the sex of 'D. H. Lawrence'? The clever analysis of the wayward Lettie ... almost convince[s] us that it is the work of a woman ... if so, we must wonder greatly at the sympathetic understanding of the male point of view ...[12]

Young Lawrence had sisters and many female friends. He grew up in a world where women might address their husbands as 'master' or 'mester', but they worked as hard as men. Lawrence had ample examples of women's intelligence, but he was aware of the restrictions that society placed on them. For example, sex before marriage was a taboo that if discovered would result in automatic dismissal for a female teacher while men might escape with a warning. Women were not permitted to work after marriage and all economic freedom was lost to them as soon as they acknowledged or gave in to love or sexual desire. By filtering some of his stories through women's eyes Lawrence ups the ante. If it was difficult for him to realise his potential, how much more difficult must it be for women?

In 'The Last Straw', Fanny is a recently demobbed 'lady's maid, thirty years old, come back to marry her first love, a foundry worker, after having kept him dangling, off and on, for a dozen years' (230:10–12). Everything about Fanny's return is a comedown. She repeats the phrase in her head: 'What a come-down! What a come-down!' Her stylish luggage sits on the platform next to the cheerful train that will wait in the station for a tempting ten minutes after she alights, but there is no returning to the fine life she has left behind. 'She had come home—for good' and home is a kind of prison (231:11–12, 9).

Lawrence repeatedly portrays human relationships as a trap; Fanny has to marry for security and social status, but in Lawrence's stories society continually distorts the natural sexual impulse into a snare. In 'The Man Who Loved Islands' he writes,

> It was the automatism of sex that had caught him again. Not that he hated sex . . . But it had become mechanical, automatic, and he wanted to escape that. Automatic sex shattered him, and filled him with a sort of death. (302:11–15)

If love and marriage are tricky things for a man or woman of means they are much trickier propositions for those without financial advantage. But in Lawrence's world social standing can bring its own problems.

> *There must be more money*! *There must be more money*! The children could hear it all the time, though nobody ever said it aloud. They heard it at Christmas, when the expensive and splendid toys filled the nursery. Behind the shining modern rocking-horse, behind the smart doll's house, a voice would start whispering: There *must* be more money! There *must* be more money! (270:12–18)

Restriction of the self, whether it be sexual or social, is anathema to Lawrence.

Women were a constant source of inspiration and support in Lawrence's creative life. Firstly his mother, who after the death of Ernest, focused her ambitions on Lawrence. His friend Jessie Chambers also helped to nurture his artistic ambitions and talents. She shared his love of literature and encouraged Lawrence's writing, even reading first drafts after he had disappointed her by withdrawing his (admittedly reluctantly given) declarations of affection. Fellow teacher Helen Corke granted Lawrence access to her diaries detailing her unhappy love affair with a married man who eventually committed suicide. With her permission Lawrence used them to form the basis of his novel *The Trespasser*.

Ultimately there was Frieda, his wife, at the time of their meeting a married woman, six years older than Lawrence and the mother of three young children. If Lawrence had had any yearnings for respectability, his elopement with Frieda would have done for them. Her husband was a modern languages professor at Nottingham University College, where Lawrence's name remained a taboo for many years. But the obligation to be true to himself and the need to create drew Lawrence much more than a ticket to polite society ever could.

Frieda was originally from Germany and the prejudice and harassment that she and Lawrence experienced during the First World War were perhaps factors in helping him to realise what a catastrophe this first major modern war was. It was also a catalyst that sent the couple overseas, never to live permanently in Britain again.

The Lawrences' marriage was often difficult, sometimes violent, frequently poverty-stricken and uncomfortable, but as with any intense and difficult relationship it opened new emotions to the writer. The fact that Frieda came from a different class and country, was older than Lawrence and had experience of a different way of life expanded his horizons still further. The semi-voluntary exile the couple went into after the war expanded the range of experiences and observations available to fuel his intellect and his writing. Lawrence crossed continents, societies, classes and cultures. He could portray a Prussian officer as successfully as he could a Nottinghamshire mining family, a decadent sun-worshipper or a disillusioned gentleman gardener.

There are traces of a bitter wit in 'England, My England'. Evelyn is suited to a simple life of a man of the soil, but because he is a gentleman he cannot be trained for or permitted to follow his vocation. The income will never be enough to support his family in the manner to which they must become accustomed and Evelyn, though gently born, is not of independent means.

'England, My England' was written in 1915 and expresses a sense of rage with the First World War at a time when the majority of the country was still firmly behind the conflict. As the husband of a German wife Lawrence could have had no illusions. He and Frieda had returned to England to get married. They had intended to stay for a brief holiday, but were stranded by the outbreak of the conflict. They settled in Cornwall where Frieda's nationality led to open persecution and accusations of spying for the enemy. Eventually they were expelled from the county at only three days' notice, under the newly strengthened Defence of the Realm Act. Lawrence was to date his disenchantment with his homeland from this time. After the war, he never lived in England permanently again.

The couple were living on the Sussex estate of the Meynell family when Lawrence conceived 'England, My England'. The story offended his hosts and when Perceval Lucas, the husband of one of the Meynell daughters, was killed in France the following year, the story seemed horribly prescient. Lawrence, who had described 'England, My England' as 'a story about the Lucas's', briefly wished that it were at 'the bottom of the sea'.[13]

A heightened awareness of mortality invoked by the early death of his older brother, combined with his own serious illnesses and brushes with death, might help to explain Lawrence's prodigious output. Like that other short-lived, wandering writer Robert Louis Stevenson, Lawrence knew that his chances of making old bones were slim. There is an appreciation for life within his tales, and the theme of wasted existences and death is repeated in these short stories. Life is fragile. A moment's lapse or act of defiance can kill.

In 'Love Among the Haystacks' one brother shoves another from the top of a tall stack of hay. The fallen man narrowly misses a small knob of wood that might have killed him had his head glanced against it, disaster is averted and both young men meet mates, fall in love and get married. They are true to nature, true to themselves and to each other. The young orderly in 'The Prussian Officer' is not so fortunate. The young man's officer has conceived an attraction for him. But instead of acknowledging or acting on his desire the officer represses it, beating and abusing the younger man until he attacks his superior in turn. The result is the death of both men. Lawrence's portrayal of the violence that repression can create is all the more remarkable for its time, a period of institutional, social and legal persecution of homosexuals. A confused contemporary reviewer tried to explain the officer's savagery through the example of a criminal who when asked why

> he had thought it necessary to put a comparatively harmless female out of the way, made reply that he did not like the shape of her nose. In the same way, if hard pressed, the Prussian officer might have answered that he did not like the shape of the limber young fellow's body.[14]

The problem is of course that he liked it against his inclination.

Same sex desire is also hinted at in 'The Blind Man', another story set in wartime, and one with echoes of *Lady Chatterley's Lover*. Isabel and Maurice Pervin are living quietly in Maurice's farmstead awaiting the birth of their child. Maurice has been wounded in the war and returned without his sight, but the couple have adjusted to the change and live a quiet, countryside existence. On the whole they are happy, though occasionally assaulted by depression and ennui. On the evening on which the story is set, their near isolation is about to be broken by a visit from Isabel's old friend Bertie Reid. Bertie and Maurice have never got on, but life has changed in the years since they were last together and old enmity is to be set aside.

Magnetic forces of attraction and repulsion swing between the three protagonists. The newcomer in 'The Blind Man' is an outsider not because of his class, but because of his sexuality. Many of Lawrence's readers would have caught the coded description of Bertie:

> He was a bachelor . . . He lived in beautiful rooms overlooking the river, guarded by a faithful Scottish man-servant. And he had his friends among the fair sex – not lovers, friends. So long as he could avoid any danger of courtship or marriage, he adored a few good women with constant and unfailing homage . . . if they seemed to encroach on him, he withdrew and detested them. (212:29–36)

But Bertie is also an insider. He and Isabel are kin, they have been friends from childhood, they are also both Scottish while Maurice is English: 'He disliked the Scotch accent in Bertie's speech, and the slight response it found on Isabel's tongue' (210:5–7).

Lastly, Isabel and Bertie Reid can both see. 'The Blind Man' lacks the dramatic peaks of 'The Prussian Officer', but it is one of Lawrence's and perhaps English literature's most accomplished stories. The final quiet realisation of the isolation that can exist even within our deepest connections is as powerful as any violent act.

Lawrence's response to and respect for the natural world appears over and again in his work, but there also seems to be a recognition that one can slip too far into nature. Man is man, and the natural world is a thing apart. We have left whatever state of nature we might once have occupied. The workers in 'Love Among the Haystacks' appear to have a synergy with nature, but the boys are eager to return to a more civilised berth.

'The Man Who Loved Islands' is perhaps partly an expression of the Nietzschean concept of striving 'to become master over all space',[15] that is, his small island. But in the end it is the island that has dominance over the man. Nature becomes increasingly predatory, snow falls 'panther-like' and thunder mutters 'unsatisfied'.

Lawrence projects a world that will endure whether men and women exist or not. In 'Sun' Juliet makes a lover of the sun, bathing naked in its rays, but she will still have to submit to her husband's sexual demands. No matter how much freedom Juliet gains, her next child will be fathered by this soft, white man because she is tied to him by society if not by her nature.

Lawrence is a writer of wonderful descriptive powers. His dialogue rings true and is revealing of his characters, though he is not averse to 'telling' rather than 'showing'. In a lesser writer the effect might be irritating, but Lawrence can hold the tale. Sometimes the effect is one of a parable, told by a wryly humorous narrator. 'There was a man who loved islands. He was born on one, but it didn't suit him . . .' (286:4–5).

Britain was an island that couldn't hold Lawrence. He died in France in 1930 aged forty-four after a battle with tuberculosis. At the time of his death Lawrence was considered on a level with a pornographer. His was not a name to be spoken lightly in polite society. Obituaries, with the notable exception of E. M. Forster's, were almost universally unkind. A few devotees, such as his friends and fellow writers Catherine Carswell, Aldous Huxley and, later, the critic F. R. Leavis, kept Lawrence's flame alive. But ironically it was the *Chatterley* trial of 1960 that brought Lawrence's work to a wider audience. His new popularity was partly based on the same, supposedly scandalous subject matter that had condemned him in an earlier age, and which now contributed towards a new climate of sexual openness.

The link between Lawrence's fiction and sex persists in the modern imagination. In November 2005 on a trip to Toronto an advertisement jumped out at me from the pages of the free listings paper: 'CHATTERLEY Gorgeous 45 yr. old with Exotic Lingerie, Gents 35+ Preferred'.[16] This lingering association between his work and the more seedy side of sexuality would not have thrilled Lawrence, who was heard to mutter after a particularly damning review, 'Nobody *likes* being called a cesspool.'[17]

Lawrence has always been a writer who has engendered strong responses; he has been both celebrated and scorned.

A recent *Guardian* profile described his status as 'currently out of vogue; his work seen as period pieces'. It remains to be seen whether the twenty-first century will allow the critical pendulum to swing in his favour.

Louise Welsh

NOTES

1. Philip Larkin, *Collected Poems* (London: Faber and Faber, 2001), p. 167.
2. Diana Trilling, Introduction to *The Portable D. H. Lawrence* (London: Penguin Books, 1947; 1980), p. 1.
3. Vladimir Nabokov, *Selected Letters 1940–77*, ed. Dimitri Nabokov and Matthew J. Bruccoli (London: Vintage Books, 1991). Lawrence's ashes are buried in Taos, New Mexico. Socialite Mabel Dodge Luhan swapped a ranch in Taos in return for the original manuscript of *Sons and Lovers*.
4. Kate Millett, *Sexual Politics* (London: Rupert Hart-Davis, 1971; London: Virago, 1977), p. 39.
5. Tony Hoagland, *Donkey Gospel* (London: Graywolf Press, 1998).
6. Melvyn Bragg, 'D. H. Lawrence, the Country of His Heart', in *D. H. Lawrence 1885–1930, A Celebration*, ed. Andrew Cooper (Nottingham: D. H. Lawrence Society, 1985), p. 39.
7. D. H. Lawrence, *The Letters of D. H. Lawrence 1901–13*, vol. i, ed. James T. Boulton (Cambridge: Cambridge University Press, 1979), p. 471.
8. John Worthen, *D. H. Lawrence: The Life of an Outsider* (London: Penguin Books), p. 13.
9. Lawrence planned a 'Burns novel', writing of his proposed subject, 'He seems a good deal like myself': *Love Among the Haystacks and Other Stories*, ed. John Worthen (Cambridge: Cambridge University Press, 1987), p. xxxvii.
10. The *Athenaeum* (1828–1921) published many great writers, including T. S. Eliot, Thomas Hardy and Virginia Woolf. In 1921 it was incorporated into the *Nation*, which later merged with the *New Statesman*. The quotation comes from *England, My England and Other Stories*, ed. Bruce Steele (Cambridge: Cambridge University Press, 1990), p. xlix.
11. Board schools catered for five to ten year olds and were run by

locally elected school boards. They were a result of the 1870 Education Act.

12. *Morning Post*, 9 February 1911, reproduced in *D. H. Lawrence: The Critical Heritage*, ed. R. P. Draper (London: Routledge and Kegan Paul, 1970), p. 36.

13. *England, My England and Other Stories*, ed. Bruce Steele, p. xxxii.

14. Unsigned review in *Outlook* (1914), reproduced in *D. H. Lawrence: The Critical Heritage*, p. 82.

15. Friedrich Nietzsche, *The Will to Power* (New York: Vintage, 1968), p. 340.

16. *The Eye*, Toronto free listing paper, November 2005.

17. Worthen, *D. H. Lawrence: The Life of an Outsider*, p. xxiii.

Further Reading

CRITICAL STUDIES OF LAWRENCE'S WORK

The following is a selection of some of the best Lawrence criticism published since 1985.

Michael Bell, *D. H. Lawrence: Language and Being* (Cambridge University Press, 1992). Philosophically-based analysis of Lawrence's work.

Michael Black, *D. H. Lawrence: The Early Fiction* (Macmillan, 1986). Very close analytical approach to Lawrence's fiction up to and including *Sons and Lovers*.

James C. Cowan, *D. H. Lawrence: Self and Sexuality* (Ohio State University Press, 2002). Sensitive and intelligent psychoanalytical study.

Keith Cushman and Earl G. Ingersoll, eds., *D. H. Lawrence: New Worlds* (Fairleigh Dickinson University Press, 2003). Gathers essays about Lawrence and America.

Paul Eggert and John Worthen, eds., *Lawrence and Comedy* (Cambridge University Press, 1996). Collects essays concerning Lawrence's uses of satire and comedy.

David Ellis, ed., *Casebook on 'Women in Love'* (Oxford University Press, 2006). Essays of modern criticism.

David Ellis and Howard Mills, *D. H. Lawrence's Non-Fiction: Art, Thought and Genre* (Cambridge University Press, 1988). Collection which examines in particular Lawrence's writing of the 1920s.

Anne Fernihough, *D. H. Lawrence: Aesthetics and Ideology*

(Oxford University Press, 1993). Wide-ranging enquiry into the intellectual context of Lawrence's writing.

Anne Fernihough, ed., *The Cambridge Companion to D. H. Lawrence* (Cambridge University Press, 2001). Usefully wide-ranging collection.

Louis K. Greiff, *D. H. Lawrence: Fifty Years on Film* (Southern Illinois University Press, 2001). Detailed account and analysis of screen adaptations.

G. M. Hyde, *D. H. Lawrence* (Palgrave Macmillan, 1990). Brief but provocative account of all Lawrence's writing.

Earl G. Ingersoll, *D. H. Lawrence, Desire and Narrative* (University Press of Florida, 2001). Postmodern approach to the major fiction.

Paul Poplawski, ed., *Writing the Body in D. H. Lawrence: Essays on Language, Representation, and Sexuality* (Greenwood Press, 2001). Gathers modern essays.

N. H. Reeve, *Reading Late Lawrence* (Palgrave Macmillan, 2004). Especially finely written account of Lawrence's late fiction.

Neil Roberts, *D. H. Lawrence, Travel and Cultural Difference* (Palgrave Macmillan, 2004). Valuable post-colonial study of Lawrence's travel-related writings 1921–5.

Carol Siegel, *Lawrence Among the Women: Wavering Boundaries in Women's Literary Traditions* (University Press of Virginia, 1991). Important and wide-ranging feminist reassessment of Lawrence.

Jack Stewart, *The Vital Art of D. H. Lawrence* (Southern Illinois University Press, 1999). Insightful study of Lawrence and the visual arts.

Peter Widdowson, ed., *D. H. Lawrence* (Longman, 1992). Useful collection surveying contemporary theoretical approaches to Lawrence.

Linda Ruth Williams, *Sex in the Head: Visions of Femininity and Film in D. H. Lawrence* (Harvester Wheatsheaf, 1993). Feminist approach to selected works of Lawrence.

John Worthen and Andrew Harrison, eds., *Casebook on 'Sons and Lovers'* (Oxford University Press, 2005). Essays of modern criticism.

REFERENCE, EDITIONS, LETTERS
AND BIOGRAPHY

The standard bibliography of Lawrence's work is *A Bibliography of D. H. Lawrence*, 3rd edn., ed. Warren Roberts and Paul Poplawski (Cambridge University Press, 2001). A useful reference work is Paul Poplawski's *D. H. Lawrence: A Reference Companion* (Greenwood Press, 1996) which gathers material up to 1994 and includes comprehensive bibliographies for most of Lawrence's works; Poplawski's 'Guide to further reading' in the *Cambridge Companion to D. H. Lawrence* goes up to 2000.

Lawrence's letters – arguably including some of his very best writing – have been published in an eight-volume complete edition, edited by James T. Boulton and published by Cambridge University Press.

Lawrence's work has now been almost completely published in the Cambridge Edition; thirty-three volumes have appeared and are variously available in paperback and hardback. The edited texts from a number of the volumes have also been published by Penguin.

A biographical work on Lawrence still worth consulting is the magnificent three-volume *D. H. Lawrence: A Composite Biography*, ed. Edward Nehls (University of Wisconsin Press, 1957–9). Between 1991 and 1998, Cambridge University Press published a three-volume biography which remains the standard work: John Worthen, *D. H. Lawrence: The Early Years 1885–1912* (1991), Mark Kinkead-Weekes, *D. H. Lawrence: Triumph to Exile 1912–1922* (1996) and David Ellis, *D. H. Lawrence: Dying Game 1922–1930* (1998). The most recent single-volume modern biography is that by John Worthen, *D. H. Lawrence: The Life of an Outsider* (Penguin Books, 2005).

A Note on the Texts

The texts in this volume (except 'Vin Ordinaire') are those established for the Cambridge University Press editions listed below. Each edition contains an apparatus of all the changes made to the base-texts, a full discussion of the editorial decisions taken, and a detailed account of the history of textual transmission, including locations for all surviving manuscript and typescript sources.

England, My England and Other Stories, ed. Bruce Steele (Cambridge University Press, 1990): 'England, My England' (1915 version, printed as an appendix), 'The Horse-Dealer's Daughter', 'The Blind Man', 'Adolf', 'The Last Straw'.

Love Among the Haystacks and Other Stories, ed. John Worthen (Cambridge University Press, 1987): 'Love Among the Haystacks', 'The Miner at Home', 'New Eve and Old Adam'.

The Prussian Officer and Other Stories, ed. John Worthen (Cambridge University Press, 1983): 'The White Stocking', 'Odour of Chrysanthemums', 'The Prussian Officer'.

The Virgin and the Gipsy and Other Stories, ed. Michael Herbert, Bethan Jones and Lindeth Vasey (Cambridge University Press, 2006): 'Things'.

The Woman Who Rode Away and Other Stories, ed. Dieter Mehl and Christa Jansohn (Cambridge University Press, 1995): 'Sun', 'The Rocking-Horse Winner', 'The Man Who Loved Islands'.

*

'Love Among the Haystacks': the manuscript (in private hands) written by November 1911, and revised in 1913, is the base-text, slightly emended. A typescript prepared posthumously in 1930 became the source of the text published in the Nonesuch Press edition of *Love Among the Haystacks & Other Pieces* (November 1930).

'The Miner at Home': written by 14 February 1912; accepted
by the *Nation*, which sent proofs on 14 March and published
it on 16 March 1912. The story was collected in *Phoenix:
The Posthumous Papers of D. H. Lawrence*, ed. Edward
D. McDonald (New York: Viking, 1936). The base-text
and only-surviving original source is the first printing in
the *Nation*. The Cambridge text has been revised at 47:2:
gets' appen *emended to* gets 'appen.

'The White Stocking': first written in the autumn of 1907;
re-written in 1910 and revised in 1911 and 1913 (when it
was typed), and published by the American magazine the
Smart Set (October 1914). Lawrence re-wrote the story again
in July 1914, and revised it heavily in proof for Duckworth's
The Prussian Officer and Other Stories (November 1914).
The base-text is the final version printed in Duckworth's
volume. The Cambridge text has been revised at 64:29:
"Yes," *emended to* "Yes."

'Odour of Chrysanthemums': first written late 1909, and
revised in 1910 and 1911 on proof sheets from the *English
Review*, which published it in June 1911. Lawrence revised
the story again in the summer of 1914, re-writing the ending
completely, and also revised it heavily in proof for *The Prussian Officer and Other Stories*. The base-text is the final
version printed in Duckworth's volume, emended from the
1910–11 proofs.

'New Eve and Old Adam': written between mid-May and
10 June 1913, and perhaps revised in July 1914 when
Lawrence was revising stories for Duckworth, but first
published in the selection of short fiction *A Modern Lover*
published by Martin Secker (October 1934). The manuscript
(University of Tulsa) is the base-text, slightly emended. The
Cambridge text has been revised at:

97:28: stretched *emended to* sketched
107:10: house *emended to* home
107:14: semi-erotic *emended to* semi-erotic,
112:19: audience;— *emended to* audience;
112:30: braided *emended to* banded

119:36: touch-touch of *emended to* touch—touch—of
120:9: her, *emended to* her;

'Vin Ordinaire': written between May and June 1913; typed in July 1913 and perhaps revised in October; the base-text is the *English Review* publication (June 1914), and the story will be published in *The Vicar's Garden and Other Stories*, ed. N. H. Reeve (Cambridge University Press, forthcoming). It was re-written as 'The Thorn in the Flesh' in July 1914 and appeared in that form in *The Prussian Officer and Other Stories*. The *English Review* text has been revised at 133:36: as/as *emended to* as.

'The Prussian Officer' ['Honour and Arms']: written between May and June 1913; it was typed in July 1913, perhaps revised in October 1913, and printed in a shortened form, with Lawrence's title 'Honour and Arms', in the *English Review* (August 1914). The full text was published, with its title changed to 'The Prussian Officer' (without Lawrence's consent), in *The Prussian Officer and Other Stories*. The base-text is the final version printed in Duckworth's volume, emended from the manuscript (University of Texas at Austin).

'England, My England': first written in June 1915 and typed that summer; Lawrence revised the typescript and then proofs for the *English Review*. It may have been further revised but was also cut for publication in that magazine in October 1915. The base-text is a set of uncorrected *English Review* proofs (Nottinghamshire Archives) which, while lacking Lawrence's proof changes, include phrases and passages cut from the *English Review*. The story was re-written and extended in October 1921 and was published in Thomas Seltzer's *England My England and Other Stories* (October 1922; probably for typographical reasons, the title of Seltzer's volume omitted the comma before 'My' that exists in the story's title).

'The Horse-Dealer's Daughter': first written probably in January 1916 and revised in November and again in October 1921; it was published in the *English Review* (April 1922) and then included in *England My England and Other Stories*. The base-text here is the magazine printing.

'The Blind Man': first written November 1918, later heavily

revised, and published in the *English Review* in July 1920. Lawrence revised the text again very slightly in October 1921 for *England My England and Other Stories*. The base-text is the magazine printing, emended from Seltzer's volume. The Cambridge text has been revised at 202:33: note from *emended to* note came from.

'Adolf': written March 1919 and later corrected by Lawrence in typescript. It was published in the *Dial* (September 1920) and collected posthumously in *Phoenix* (1936). The base-text is the corrected typescript (University of Texas at Austin), slightly emended. The Cambridge text has been revised at 220:16: He like *emended to* He liked.

'The Last Straw' ['Fanny and Annie']: written in May 1919, typed (and probably revised) in July 1920. Lawrence corrected proofs for *Hutchinson's Story Magazine* (November 1921) and the story was reprinted in *England My England and Other Stories*. The base-text is the magazine version, emended from Seltzer's volume. Lawrence asked for the title to be changed to 'The Last Straw' in a letter to his English publisher Martin Secker of 29 December 1921.

'Sun': first written and typed in December 1925: this version was published by the *New Coterie* (Autumn 1926), and was also included in Secker's *The Woman Who Rode Away and Other Stories* (May 1928). In 1928, Lawrence wrote the story out afresh for the American collector Harry Crosby, altering it considerably while doing so. This version was published privately by the Black Sun Press in Paris (October 1928). The base-text is the 1928 manuscript (University of Texas at Austin). As this version of the story was originally published separately, its title is usually italicised, as in the Cambridge edition; however, for this edition the title is presented in roman type to conform to the style of the other stories.

'The Rocking-Horse Winner': written February 1926 and published in *Harper's Bazaar* (July 1926) and in Secker's *The Woman Who Rode Away and Other Stories*. The base-text is the manuscript (University of Nottingham), emended from the magazine version.

'The Man Who Loved Islands': first written June–July 1926

and then typed and extensively revised by Lawrence. The revised typescript was used for the text in the *Dial* magazine (July 1927), for which Lawrence corrected proofs, and it was also collected in Alfred Knopf's *The Woman Who Rode Away and Other Stories* (May 1928). It was not included in Secker's volume of that name because of the threat of legal action by the novelist Compton Mackenzie; it was first collected in Britain in Secker's *The Lovely Lady* (January 1933). The base-text is the revised typescript, emended from the *Dial* proofs (both at Yale University). The Cambridge text has been revised at 311:5: power the *emended to* power of the.

'Things': written late May 1927; the story was published in the *Bookman* (August 1928) and collected in Secker's *The Lovely Lady*. The base-text is the manuscript (University of Texas at Austin), emended from an uncorrected typescript (University of California at Berkeley) where the manuscript has been damaged. The Cambridge text has been revised at 313:9: Ah!—freedom! To be free to one's *emended to* Ah!—freedom! To be free to live one's.

Paul Poplawski

This selection of the stories of D. H. Lawrence draws on work written at all stages of his career and from all his published collections. Some of the most famous stories are included (for example, 'Love Among the Haystacks', 'Odour of Chrysanthemums' and 'The Rocking-Horse Winner') but this volume also brings together for the first time in this form three stories he wrote consecutively in May and June 1913 at the very height of his early career ('The Prussian Officer', 'Vin Ordinaire' and 'New Eve and Old Adam'). It also chooses unusual and compelling early versions of two stories, 'Vin Ordinaire' to complete the sequence above (a much bleaker and spare treatment of the scenario that became 'The Thorn in the Flesh' by July 1914) and the 'England, My England' of 1915, where personal negation and national self-destruction are drawn together with more urgency than in the longer version of 1921–2. Conversely, the exuberant and frank 'Sun' is included in its later and heavily revised form of 1928 to demonstrate Lawrence's remarkable ability to revisit and re-imagine his own writing.

Together this selection offers a range of work in settings as different as English hayfields in summer, miners' cottages, Bavarian landscapes, bohemian Paris, Sicilian villas and Italian palazzos; New York and New England exist to be left – and perhaps returned to, defeated. There is much more to be found than mere surface verisimilitude in these stories, but the diversity of place and time was one main principle of selection for the volume. It aims to offer a rich, varied and compact version of Lawrence's whole career as an imaginative writer.

Sue Wilson

Selected Stories

LOVE AMONG THE HAYSTACKS

The two large fields lay on a hillside facing south. Being newly cleared of hay, they were golden green, and they shone almost blindingly in the sunlight. Across the hill, half way up, ran a high hedge, that flung its black shadow finely across the molten glow of the sward. The stack was being built just above the hedge. It was of great size, massive, but so silvery and delicately bright in tone that it seemed not to have weight. It rose dishevelled and radiant among the steady, golden-green glare of the field. A little further back was another, finished stack.

The empty wagon was just passing through the gap in the hedge. From the far-off corner of the bottom field, where the sward was still striped grey with winrows, the loaded wagon launched forward, to climb the hill to the stack. The white dots of the hay-makers showed distinctly among the hay.

The two brothers were having a moment's rest, waiting for the load to come up. They stood wiping their brows with their arms, sighing from the heat and the labor of placing the last load. The stack they rode was high, lifting them up above the hedge tops, and very broad, a great slightly hollowed vessel into which the sunlight poured, in which the hot sweet scent of hay was suffocating. Small and inefficacious the brothers looked, half submerged in the loose, great trough, lifted high up as if on an altar reared to the sun.

Maurice, the younger brother, was a handsome young fellow of twenty one, careless and debonnair, and full of vigour. His grey eyes, as he taunted his brother, were bright and baffled with a strong emotion. His swarthy face had the same peculiar smile, expectant and glad and nervous, of a young man roused for the first time in passion.

"Tha sees," he said, as he leaned on the pommel of his fork, "tha thowt as tha 'd done me one, didna ter?" He smiled as he spoke, then fell again into his pleasant torment of musing.

"I thought nowt—tha knows so much," retorted Geoffrey, with the touch of a sneer. His brother had the better of him. Geoffrey was a very heavy, hulking fellow, a year older than Maurice. His blue eyes were unsteady, they glanced away quickly; his mouth was morbidly sensitive. One felt him wince away, through the whole of his great body. His inflamed self-consciousness was a disease in him.

"Ah but though, I know tha did," mocked Maurice. "Tha went slinkin' off—" Geoffrey winced convulsively—"thinking as that wor the last night as any of us 'ud ha'e ter stop here, an' so tha'd leave me to sleep out, though it wor thy turn——"

He smiled to himself, thinking of the result of Geoffrey's ruse.

"I didna go slinkin' off, neither," retorted Geoffrey, in his heavy, clumsy manner, wincing at the phrase. "Didna my feyther send me to fetch some coal—"

"Oh yes, oh yes—we know all about it. But tha sees what tha missed, my lad."

Maurice, chuckling, threw himself on his back in the bed of hay. There was absolutely nothing in his world, then, except the shallow ramparts of the stack, and the blazing sky. He clenched his fists tight, threw his arms across his face, and braced his muscles again. He was evidently very much moved, so acutely that it was hardly pleasant, though he still smiled. Geoffrey, standing behind him, could just see his red mouth, with the young moustache like black fur, curling back and showing the teeth in a smile. The elder brother leaned his chin on the pommel of his fork, looking out across the country.

Far away was the faint blue heap of Nottingham. Between, the country lay under a haze of heat, with here and there a flag of colliery smoke waving. But near at hand, at the foot of the hill, across the deep-hedged highroad, was only the silence of the old church and the castle farm, among their trees. The large view only made Geoffrey more sick. He looked away, to the wagons crossing the field below him, the empty cart like a big insect moving down hill, the load coming up, rocking like a ship, the brown head of the horse ducking, the brown knees lifted and planted strenuously. Geoffrey wished it would be quick.

"Tha didna think—"

Geoffrey started, coiled within himself, and looked down at the handsome lips moving in speech below the brown arms of his brother.

"Tha didna think '*er* 'd be theer wi' me—or tha wouldna ha' left me to it," Maurice said, ending with a little laugh of excited memory. Geoffrey flushed with hate, and had an impulse to set his foot on that moving, taunting mouth, which was there below him. There was silence for a time, then, in a peculiar tone of delight, Maurice's voice came again, spelling out the words, as it were:

> "Ich bin klein, mein Herz ist rein
> Ist niemand d'rin als Christ allein."

Maurice chuckled, then, convulsed at a twinge of recollection, keen as pain, he twisted over, pressed himself into the hay.

"Can thee thy prayers in German," came his muffled voice.

"I non want," growled Geoffrey.

Maurice chuckled. His face was quite hidden, and in the dark he was going over again his last night's experiences.

"What about kissing 'er under th' ear, Sorry," he said, in a curious, uneasy tone. He writhed, still startled and inflamed by his first contact with love.

Geoffrey's heart swelled within him, and things went dark. He could not see the landscape.

"An' there's just a nice two-handful of her bosom," came the low, provocative tones of Maurice, who seemed to be talking to himself.

The two brothers were both fiercely shy of women, and until this hay harvest, the whole feminine sex had been represented by their mother, in presence of any other women they were dumb louts. Moreover, brought up by a proud mother, a stranger in the country, they held the common girls as beneath them, because beneath their mother, who spoke pure English, and was very quiet. Loud-mouthed and broad tongued, the common girls were. So the two young men had grown up virgin but tormented.

Now again Maurice had the start of Geoffrey, and the elder brother was deeply mortified. There was a danger of his sinking into a morbid state, from sheer lack of living, lack of interest. The foreign governess at the vicarage, whose garden lay beside the top field, had talked to the lads through the hedge, and had fascinated them. There was a great elder bush, with its broad creamy flowers crumbling onto the garden path, and into the field. Geoffrey never smelled elder-flower without starting and wincing, thinking of the strange foreign voice that had so startled him as he mowed out with the scythe in the hedge bottom. A baby had run through the gap, and the Fräulein, calling in German, had come brushing down the flowers in pursuit. She had started so on seeing a man standing there in the shade, that for a moment she could not move: and then she had blundered onto the rake which was lying by his side. Geoffrey, forgetting she was a woman when he saw her pitch forward, had picked her up carefully, asking: "Have you hurt you?"

Then she had broken into a laugh, and answered in German, showing him her arms, and knitting her brows. She was nettled rather badly.

"You want a dock leaf," he said.

She frowned in a puzzled fashion.

"A do-ock leaf?" she repeated.

He had rubbed her arms with the green leaf.

And now, she had taken to Maurice. She had seemed to prefer himself at first. Now she had sat with Maurice in the moonlight, and had let him kiss her. Geoffrey sullenly suffered, making no fight.

Unconsciously, he was looking at the vicarage garden. There she was, in a golden brown dress. He took off his hat, and held up his right hand in greeting to her. She, a small golden figure, waved her hand negligently from among the potato rows. He remained arrested in the same posture, his hat in his left hand, his right arm upraised, thinking. He could tell by the negligence of her greeting that she was waiting for Maurice. What did she think of himself? Why wouldn't she have him?

Hearing the voice of the wagoner leading the load, Maurice rose. Geoffrey still stood in the same way, but his face was sullen, and his upraised hand was slack with brooding. Maurice faced up-hill. His eyes lit up and he laughed. Geoffrey dropped his own arm, watching.

"Lad!" chuckled Maurice. "I non knowed 'er wor there." He waved his hand clumsily. In these matters Geoffrey did better. The elder brother watched the girl. She ran to the end of the path, behind the bushes, so that she was screened from the house. Then she waved her handkerchief wildly. Maurice did not notice the manœuvre. There was the cry of a child. The girl's figure vanished, re-appeared holding a white childish bundle, and came down the path. There she put down her charge, sped up-hill to a great ash-tree, climbed quickly to a large horizontal bar that formed the fence there, and, standing poised, blew kisses with both her hands, in a foreign fashion that excited the brothers. Maurice laughed aloud, as he waved his red handkerchief.

"Well, what's the danger?" shouted a mocking voice from below. Maurice collapsed, blushing furiously.

"Nowt!" he called.

There was a hearty laugh from below.

The load rode up, sheered with a hiss against the stack, then sank back upon the scotches. The brothers ploughed across the mass of hay, taking the forks. Presently a big, burly man, red and glistening, climbed to the top of the load. Then he turned round, scrutinised the hillside from under his shaggy brows. He caught sight of the girl under the ash-tree.

"Oh that's who it is," he laughed. "I thought it was some such bird, but I couldn't see her."

The father laughed in a hearty, chaffing way, then began to teem the load. Geoffrey, on the stack above, received his great forkfuls, and swung them over to Maurice, who took them, placed them, building the stack. In the intense sunlight, the three worked in silence, knit together in a brief passion of work. The father stirred slowly for a moment, getting the hay from under his feet. Geoffrey waited, the blue tines of his fork glittering in expectation: the mass rose, his fork swung beneath it, there was a light clash of blades, then the hay was swept onto the stack, caught by Maurice, who placed it judiciously. One after another, the shoulders of the three men bowed and braced themselves. All wore light blue, bleached shirts, that stuck close to their backs. The father moved mechanically, his thick, rounded shoulders bending and lifting dully; he worked monotonously. Geoffrey flung away his strength. His massive shoulders swept and flung the hay extravagantly.

"Dost want to knock me ower?" asked Maurice angrily. He had to brace himself against the impact. The three men worked intensely, as if some will urged them. Maurice was light and swift at the work, but he had to use his judgment. Also, when he had to place the hay along the far ends, he had some distance to carry it. So he was too slow for Geoffrey. Ordinarily, the elder would have placed the hay as far as possible where his brother wanted it. Now, however, he pitched his forkfuls into the middle of the stack. Maurice strode swiftly and handsomely across the bed, but the work was too much for him. The other two men, clenched in their receive and deliver, kept up a high pitch of labor. Geoffrey still flung the hay at random. Maurice was perspiring heavily with heat and exertion, and was getting worried. Now and again, Geoffrey wiped his arm across his brow, mechanically, like an animal. Then he glanced with satisfaction at Maurice's moiled condition, and caught the next forkful.

"Wheer dost think thou'rt hollin' it, fool?" panted Maurice, as his brother flung a forkful out of reach.

"Wheer I'n a mind," answered Geoffrey.

Maurice toiled on, now very angry. He felt the sweat trickling down his body: drops fell into his long black lashes, blinding him, so that he had to stop and angrily dash his eyes clear. The veins stood out in his swarthy neck. He felt he would burst, or drop, if the work did not soon slacken off. He heard his father's fork dully scrape the cart-bottom.

"There, the last," the father panted. Geoffrey tossed the last light lot at random, took off his hat, and, steaming in the sunshine as he wiped himself, stood complacently watching Maurice struggle with clearing the bed.

"Don't you think you've got your bottom corner a bit far out," came the father's voice from below. "You'd better be drawing in now, hadn't you."

"I thought you said next load," Maurice called, sulkily.

"Ay! All right. But isn't this bottom corner—?"

Maurice, impatient, took no notice.

Geoffrey strode over the stack, and stuck his fork in the offending corner.

"What—here . . . ?" he bawled in his great voice.

"Ay—isn't it a bit loose?" came the irritating voice.

Geoffrey pushed his fork in the jutting corner, and, leaning his weight on the handle, shoved. He thought it shook. He thrust again with all his power. The mass swayed.

"What art up to, tha fool!" cried Maurice, in a high voice.

"Mind who tha 'rt callin' a fool," said Geoffrey, and he prepared to push again. Maurice sprang across, elbowed his brother aside. On the yielding, swaying bed of hay, Geoffrey lost his foot hold, and fell grovelling. Maurice tried the corner.

"It's solid enough," he shouted angrily.

"Ay—all right," came the conciliatory voice of the father— "you do get a bit of rest now there's such a long way to cart it," he added reflectively.

Geoffrey had got to his feet.

"Tha 'll mind who tha 'rt nudging, I can tell thee," he threatened heavily; adding, as Maurice continued to work, "An' tha non ca's him a fool again, dost hear?"

"Not till next time," sneered Maurice.

As he worked silently round the stack, he neared where his brother stood like a sullen statue, leaning on his fork-handle, looking out over the countryside. Maurice's heart quickened in its beat. He worked forward, until a point of his fork caught in the leather of Geoffrey's boot, and the metal rang sharply.

"Are ter going to shift thysen?" asked Maurice threateningly. There was no reply from the great block. Maurice lifted his upper lip like a dog. Then he put out his elbow, and tried to push his brother into the stack, clear of his way.

"Who are ter shovin'?" came the deep, dangerous voice.

"Thaïgh," replied Maurice, with a sneer.

And straightway the two brothers set themselves against each other, like opposing bulls, Maurice trying his hardest to shift Geoffrey from his footing, Geoffrey leaning all his weight in resistance. Maurice, insecure in his footing, staggered a little, and Geoffrey's weight followed him. He went slithering over the edge of the stack.

Geoffrey turned white to the lips, and remained standing, listening. He heard the fall. Then a flush of darkness came over him, and he remained standing only because he was planted. He had not strength to move. He could hear no sound from below, was only faintly aware of a sharp shriek from a long way off. He listened again. Then he filled with sudden panic.

"Feyther!" he roared, in his tremendous voice:

"Feyther! Feyther!"

The valley re-echoed with the sound. Small cattle on the hill-side looked up. Men's figures came running from the bottom field, and much nearer, a woman's figure was racing across the upper field. Geoffrey waited in terrible suspense.

"Ah-h!" he heard the strange, wild voice of the girl cry out. "Ah-h!"—and then some foreign wailing speech. Then "Ah-h!—Are you dea-ed!"

He stood sullenly erect on the stack, not daring to go down, longing to hide in the hay, but too sullen to stoop out of sight. He heard his oldest brother come up, panting:

"Whatever's amiss!" and then the laborer, and then his father.

"What *ever* have you been doing?" he heard his father ask, while yet he had not come round the corner of the stack. And then, in a low, bitter tone:

"Ehe, he's done for! I'd no business to ha' put it all on that stack."

There was a moment or two of silence, then the voice of Henry, the eldest brother, said crisply:

"He's not dead—he's coming round."

Geoffrey heard, but was not glad. He had as lief Maurice were dead. At least that would be final: better than meeting his brother's charges, and of seeing his mother pass to the sickroom. If Maurice was killed, he himself would not explain, no, not a word, and they could hang him if they liked. If Maurice were only hurt, then everybody would know, and Geoffrey could never lift his face again. What added torture, to pass along, everybody knowing. He wanted something that he could stand back to, something definite, if it were only the knowledge that he had killed his brother. He *must* have something firm to back up to, or he would go mad. He was so lonely, he who above all needed the support of sympathy.

"No, he's commin' to, I tell you he is," said the laborer.

"He's not dea-ed, he's not dea-ed," came the passionate, strange sing-song of the foreign girl. "He's not dead—no-o."

"He wants some brandy—look at the colour of his lips," said the crisp, cold voice of Henry. "Can you fetch some?"

"Wha-at?—Fetch—?." Fräulein did not understand.

"Brandy," said Henry, very distinct.

"Brrandy!" she re-echoed.

"You go, Bill," groaned the father.

"Ay, I'll go," replied Bill, and he ran across the field.

Maurice was not dead, nor going to die. This Geoffrey now realised. He was glad after all that the extreme penalty was revoked. But he hated to think of himself going on—. He would *always* shrink now. He had hoped and hoped for the time when he would be careless, bold as Maurice, when he would not wince and shrink. Now he would always be the same, coiling up in himself like a tortoise with no shell.

"Ah-h! He's getting better!" came the wild voice of the Fräulein, and she began to cry, a strange sound, that startled the men, made the animal bristle within them. Geoffrey shuddered as he heard, between her sobbing, the impatient moaning of his brother, as the breath came back.

The laborer returned at a run, followed by the vicar. After the brandy, Maurice made more moaning hiccuping noise.

Geoffrey listened in torture. He heard the vicar asking for explanations. All the muted, anxious voices replied in brief phrases.

"It was that other," cried the Fräulein. "He knocked him over—Ha!"

She was shrill and vindictive.

"I don't think so," said the father, to the vicar, in a quite audible but private tone, speaking as if the Fräulein did not understand his English.

The vicar addressed his children's governess in bad German. She replied in a torrent which he would not confess was too much for him. Maurice was making little moaning, sighing noises.

"Where's your pain, boy, eh?," the father asked, pathetically.

"Leave him alone a bit," came the cool voice of Henry. "He's winded, if no more."

"You'd better see that no bones are broken," said the anxious vicar.

"It wor a blessing as he should a dropped on that heap of hay just there," said the laborer. "If he'd happened to ha' catched hisself on this nog o' wood 'e wouldna ha' stood much chance."

Geoffrey wondered when he would have courage to venture down. He had wild notions of pitching himself headforemost from the stack: if he could only extinguish himself, he would be safe. Quite frantically, he longed not-to-be. The idea of going through life thus coiled up within himself in morbid self-consciousness, always lonely, surly, and a misery, was enough to make him cry out.—What would they all think when they knew he had knocked Maurice off that high stack.

They were talking to Maurice down below. The lad had recovered in great measure, and was able to answer faintly.

"Whatever was you doin'?" the father asked gently. "Was you playing about with our Geoffrey?—Ay, and where is he?"

Geoffrey's heart stood still.

"I dunno," said Henry, in a curious, ironic tone.

"Go an' have a look," pleaded the father, infinitely relieved over one son, anxious now concerning the other. Geoffrey could not bear that his eldest brother should climb up and question him in his high-pitched drawl of curiosity. The culprit doggedly set his feet on the ladder. His nailed boots slipped a rung.

"Mind yourself," shouted the overwrought father.

Geoffrey stood like a criminal at the foot of the ladder, glancing furtively at the group. Maurice was lying, pale and slightly convulsed, upon a heap of hay. The Fräulein was kneeling beside his head. The vicar had the lad's shirt full open down the breast, and was feeling for broken ribs. The father kneeled on the other side, the laborer and Henry stood aside.

"I can't find anything broken," said the vicar, and he sounded slightly disappointed.

"There's nowt broken to find," murmured Maurice, smiling.

The father started. "Eh?" he said, "Eh?," and he bent over the invalid.

"I say it's not hurt me," repeated Maurice.

"What were you doing?" asked the cold, ironic voice of Henry. Geoffrey turned his head away: he had not yet raised his face.

"Nowt as I know on," he muttered in a surly tone.

"Why!" cried Fräulein in reproachful tone. "I see him—knock him over!" She made a fierce gesture with her elbow. Henry curled his long moustache sardonically.

"Nay lass, niver," smiled the wan Maurice. "He was fur enough away from me when I slipped."

"Oh ah!" cried the Fräulein, not understanding.

"Yi," smiled Maurice indulgently.

"I think you're mistaken," said the father, rather pathetically, smiling at the girl as if she were 'wanting'.

"Oh no," she cried. "I see him."

"Nay lass," smiled Maurice quietly.

She was a Pole, named Paula Jablonowsky: young, only twenty years old, swift and light as a wild cat, with a strange, wild-cat way of grinning. Her hair was blonde and full of life, all crisped into many tendrils with vitality, shaking round her face. Her fine blue eyes were peculiarly lidded, and she seemed to look piercingly, then languorously like a wild cat. She had

somewhat Slavonic cheekbones, and was very much freckled.
It was evident that the vicar, a pale, rather cold man, hated her.

Maurice lay pale and smiling in her lap, whilst she cleaved
to him like a mate. One felt instinctively that they were mated.
She was ready at any minute to fight with ferocity in his defence,
now he was hurt. Her looks at Geoffrey were full of fierceness.
She bowed over Maurice and caressed him with her foreign-
sounding English.

"You say what you lai-ike," she laughed, giving him lordship
over her.

"Hadn't you better be going and looking what has become
of Marjery?," asked the vicar in tones of reprimand.

"She is with her mother—I heared her. I will go in a whai-ile,"
smiled the girl, coolly.

"Do you feel as if you could stand?" asked the father, still
anxiously.

"Ay, in a bit," smiled Maurice.

"You want to get up?" caressed the girl, bowing over him,
till her face was not far from his.

"I'm in no hurry," he replied, smiling brilliantly.

This accident had given him quite a strange new ease, an
authority. He felt extraordinarily glad. New power had come
to him all at once.

"You in no hurry," she repeated, gathering the meaning. She
smiled tenderly: she was in his service.

"She leaves us in another month—Mrs Inwood could stand
no more of her," apologised the vicar quietly to the father.

"Why, is she——?"

"Like a wild thing—disobedient and insolent."

"Ha!"

The father sounded abstract.

"No more foreign governesses for me."

Maurice stirred, looked up at the girl.

"You stand up?" she asked brightly. "You well?"

He laughed again, showing his teeth winsomely. She lifted
his head, sprung to her feet, her hands still holding his head,
then she took him under the arm-pits and had him on his feet
before anyone could help. He was much taller than she. He

grasped her strong shoulders heavily, leaned against her, and, feeling her round, firm breast doubled up against his side, he smiled, catching his breath.

"You see I'm all right," he gasped. "I was only winded."

"You all raïght?," she cried, in great glee.

"Yes, I am."

He walked a few steps after a moment.

"There's nowt ails me, father," he laughed.

"Quite well, you?" she cried in a pleading tone. He laughed outright, looked down at her, touching her cheek with his fingers.

"That's it—if tha likes."

"If I lai-ike!" she repeated, radiant.

"She's going at the end of three weeks," said the vicar consolingly to the farmer.

2.

While they were talking, they heard the far-off hooting of a pit.

"There goes th' loose 'a," said Henry, coldly. "We're *not* going to get that corner up today."

The father looked round anxiously.

"Now Maurice, are you sure you're all right?" he asked.

"Yes, I'm all right. Haven't I told you?"

"Then you sit down there, and in a bit you can be getting dinner out. Henry, you go on the stack. Wheer's Jim?—Oh, he's minding the horses. Bill, and you Geoffrey, you can pick while Jim loads."

Maurice sat down under the wych elm to recover. The Fräulein had fled back. He made up his mind to ask her to marry him. He had got fifty pounds of his own, and his mother would help him. For a long time he sat musing, thinking what he would do. Then, from the float he fetched a big basket covered with a cloth, and spread the dinner. There was an immense rabbit pie, a dish of cold potatoes, much bread, a great piece of cheese, and a solid rice pudding.

These two fields were four miles from the home farm. But

they had been in the hands of the Wookeys for several generations, therefore the father kept them on, and everyone looked
forward to the hay harvest at Greasley: it was a kind of picnic.
They brought dinner and tea in the milk-float, which the father
drove over in the morning. The lads and the laborers cycled.
Off and on, the harvest lasted a fortnight. As the highroad from
Alfreton to Nottingham ran at the foot of the fields, some one
usually slept in the hay under the shed to guard the tools. The
sons took it in turns. They did not care for it much, and were
for that reason anxious to finish the harvest on this day. But
work went slack and disjointed after Maurice's accident.

When the load was teemed, they gathered round the white
cloth, which was spread under a tree between the hedge and
the stack, and, sitting on the ground, ate their meal. Mrs
Wookey sent always a clean cloth, and knives and forks and
plates for everybody. Mr Wookey was always rather proud of
this spread, everything was so proper.

"There now," he said, sitting down jovially. "Doesn't this
look nice now—Eh?"

They all sat round the white spread, in the shadow of the
tree and the stack, and looked out up the fields as they ate. From
their shady coolness, the gold sward seemed liquid, molten with
heat. The horse with the empty wagon wandered a few yards,
then stood feeding. Everything was still as a trance. Now and
again, the horse between the shafts of the load that stood
propped beside the stack, jingled his loose bit as he ate. The
men ate and drank in silence, the father reading the newspaper,
Maurice leaning back on a saddle, Henry reading the *Nation*,
the others eating busily.

Presently "Helloa! Er's 'ere again!" exclaimed Bill. All looked
up. Paula was coming across the field carrying a plate.

"She's bringing something to tempt your appetite, Maurice,"
said the eldest brother ironically. Maurice was mid-way through
a large wedge of rabbit pie, and some cold potatoes.

"Ay, bless me if she's not," laughed the father. "Put that
away, Maurice, it's a shame to disappoint her."

Maurice looked round very shamefaced, not knowing what
to do with his plate.

"Gi'e it over here," said Bill. "I'll polish him off."

"Bringing something for the invalid?" laughed the father to the Fräulein. "He's looking up nicely."

"I bring him some chicken, hm!" She nodded her head at Maurice childishly. He flushed and smiled.

"Tha doesna mean ter bust 'im," said Bill.

Everybody laughed aloud. The girl did not understand, so she laughed also. Maurice ate his portion very sheepishly.

The father pitied his son's shyness.

"Come here and sit by me," he said. "Eh, Fräulein! Is that what they call you?"

"I sit by you, father," she said innocently.

Henry threw his head back and laughed long and noiselessly. She settled near to the big, handsome man.

"My name," she said, "is Paula Jablonowsky."

"Is what?" said the father, and the other men went into roars of laughter.

"Tell me again," said the father. "Your name—?"

"Paula."

"Paula? Oh—well, it's a rum sort of name, eh? His name—," he nodded at his son—

"Maurice—I know." She pronounced it sweetly, then laughed into the father's eyes. Maurice blushed to the roots of his hair.

They questioned her concerning her history, and made out that she came from Hanover, that her father was a shop-keeper, and that she had run away from home because she did not like her father. She had gone to Paris.

"Oh," said the father, now dubious. "And what did you do there?"

"In school—in a young ladies' school."

"Did you like it?"

"Oh no—no laïfe—no life!"

"What?"

"When we go out—two and two—all together—no more. Ah, no life, no life."

"Well, that's a winder!" exclaimed the father. "No life in Paris! And have you found much life in England?"

"No—ah no. I don't like it." She made a grimace at the vicarage.

"How long have you been in England?"

"Chreestmas—so."

"And what will you do?"

"I will go to London, or to Paris. Ah, Paris!!—Or get married!" She laughed into the father's eyes.

The father laughed heartily.

"Get married, eh? And who to?"

"I don't know. I am going away."

"The country's too quiet for you?" asked the father.

"Too quiet—hm!" she nodded in assent.

"You wouldn't care for making butter and cheese?"

"Making butter—hm!" She turned to him with a glad, bright gesture. "—I like it."

"Oh," laughed the father, "you would, would you."

She nodded vehemently, with glowing eyes.

"She'd like anything in the shape of a change," said Henry judicially.

"I think she would," agreed the father. It did not occur to them that she fully understood what they said. She looked at them closely, then thought, with bowed head.

"Hullo!" exclaimed Henry, the alert. A tramp was slouching towards them through the gap. He was a very seedy, slinking fellow, with a tang of horsey braggadocio about him. Small, thin, and ferrety, with a week's red beard bristling on his pointed chin, he came slouching forward.

"Han yer got a bit of a job goin'?" he asked.

"A bit of a job," repeated the father. "Why, can't yer see as we've a'most done?"

"Ay—but I noticed you was a hand short, an' I thowt as 'appen you'd gie me half a day."

"What, are *you* any good in a hay close?" asked Henry, with a sneer.

The man stood slouching against the haystack. All the others were seated on the floor. He had an advantage.

"I could work aside any on yer," he bragged.

"Tha looks it," laughed Bill.

"And what's your regular trade?" asked the father.

"I'm a jockey by rights. But I did a bit o' dirty work for a boss o' mine, an' I was landed. 'E got the benefit, I got kicked out. 'E axed me—an' then 'e looked as if 'e'd never seed me."

"Did he though!" exclaimed the father sympathetically.

"'E did that!" asserted the man.

"But we've got nothing for you," said Henry coldly.

"What does the boss say?" asked the man, impudent.

"No, we've no work you can do," said the father. "You can have a bit o' something to eat, if you like."

"I should be glad of it," said the man.

He was given the chunk of rabbit pie that remained. This he ate greedily. There was something debased, parasitic about him, which disgusted Henry. The others regarded him as a curiosity.

"That was nice and tasty," said the tramp, with gusto.

"Do you want a piece of bread 'n cheese?" asked the father.

"It'll help to fill up," was the reply.

The man ate this more slowly. The company was embarrassed by his presence, and could not talk. All the men lit their pipes, the meal over.

"So you dunna want any help?," said the tramp at last.

"No—we can manage what bit there is to do."

"You don't happen to have a fill of bacca to spare, do you?"

The father gave him a good pinch.

"You're all right here," he said, looking round. They resented this familiarity. However, he filled his clay pipe and smoked with the rest.

As they were sitting silent, another figure came through the gap in the hedge, and noiselessly approached. It was a woman. She was rather small, and finely made. Her face was small, very ruddy, and comely, save for the look of bitterness and aloofness that it wore. Her hair was drawn tightly back under a sailor hat. She gave an impression of cleanness, of precision and directness.

"Have you got some work?" she asked of her man. She ignored the rest. He tucked his tail between his legs.

"No, they haven't got no work for me. They've just gave me a draw of bacca."

He was a mean crawl of a man.

"An' am I goin' to wait for you out there on the lane all day?"

"You nedn't if you don't like. You could go on."

"Well, are you coming?" she asked contemptuously.

He rose to his feet in a ricketty fashion.

"You nedn't be in such a mighty hurry," he said. "If you'd wait a bit you might get summat."

She glanced for the first time over the men. She was quite young, and would have been pretty, were she not so hard and callous-looking.

"Have you had your dinner?" asked the father.

She looked at him with a kind of anger, and turned away. Her face was so childish in its contours, contrasting strangely with her expression.

"Are you coming?" she said to the man.

"He's had his tuck-in. Have a bit, if *you* want it," coaxed the father.

"What have you had?" she flashed, to the man.

"He's had all what was left o' th' rabbit pie," said Geoffrey, in an indignant, mocking tone, "and a great hunk o' bread an' cheese."

"Well, it was gave me," said the man.

The young woman looked at Geoffrey, and he at her. There was a sort of kinship between them. Both were at odds with the world. Geoffrey smiled satirically. She was too grave, too deeply incensed even to smile.

"There's a cake here though—you can have a bit o' that," said Maurice blithely.

She eyed him with scorn.

Again she looked at Geoffrey. He seemed to understand her. She turned, and in silence departed. The man remained obstinately sucking at his pipe. Everybody looked at him with hostility.

"We'll be getting to work," said Henry, rising pulling off his coat. Paula got to her feet. She was a little bit confused by the presence of the tramp.

"I go," she said, smiling brilliantly. Maurice rose and followed her sheepishly.

"A good grind, eh?" said the tramp, nodding after the Fräulein. The men only half understood him, but they hated him.

"Hadn't you better be getting off?," said Henry.

The man rose obediently. He was all slouching, parasitic
insolence. Geoffrey loathed him, longed to exterminate him.
He was exactly the worst foe of the hypersensitive; insolence
without sensibility, preying on sensibility.

"Aren't you goin' to give me summat for her?—it's nowt
she's had all day, to my knowin'. She'll 'appen eat it if I take it
'er—though she gets more than I've any knowledge of"—this
with a lewd wink of jealous spite. "And then tries to keep a
tight hand on me———" he sneered, taking the bread and cheese,
and stuffing it in his pocket.

3.

Geoffrey worked sullenly all afternoon, and Maurice did the
horse-raking. It was exceedingly hot. So the day wore on, the
atmosphere thickened, and the sunlight grew blurred. Geoffrey
was picking with Bill—helping to load the wagons from the
winrows. He was sulky, though extraordinarily relieved:
Maurice would not tell. Since the quarrel neither brother had
spoken to the other. But their silence was entirely amicable,
almost affectionate. They had both been deeply moved, so
much so that their ordinary intercourse was interrupted: but
underneath, each felt a strong regard for the other. Maurice
was peculiarly happy, his feeling of affection swimming over
everything. But Geoffrey was still sullenly hostile to the most
part of the world. He felt isolated. The free and easy intercom-
munication between the other workers left him distinctly alone.
And he was a man who could not bear to stand alone, he was
too much afraid of the vast confusion of life surrounding him,
in which he was helpless. Geoffrey mistrusted himself with
everybody.

The work went on slowly. It was unbearably hot, and everyone was disheartened.

"We s'll have getting-on-for another day of it," said the father
at tea-time, as they sat under the tree.

"Quite a day," said Henry.

"Somebody 'll have to stop, then," said Geoffrey. "It 'ud better be me."

"Nay lad, I'll stop," said Maurice, and he hid his head in confusion.

"Stop again tonight!" exclaimed the father. "I'd rather you went home."

"Nay, I'm stoppin'," protested Maurice.

"He wants to do his courting," Henry enlightened them.

The father thought seriously about it.

"I don't know——" he mused, rather perturbed.

But Maurice stayed. Towards eight o'clock, after sundown, the men mounted their bicycles, the father put the horse in the float, and all departed. Maurice stood in the gap of the hedge and watched them go, the cart rolling and swinging downhill, over the grass stubble, the cyclists dipping swiftly like shadows, in front. All passed through the gate, there was a quick clatter of hoofs on the roadway under the lime trees, and they were gone. The young man was very much excited, almost afraid, at finding himself alone.

Darkness was rising from the valley. Already, up the steep hill the cart-lamps crept indecisively, and the cottage windows were lit. Everything looked strange to Maurice, as if he had not seen it before. Down the hedge a large lime tree teemed with scent that seemed almost like a voice speaking. It startled him. He caught a breath of the over-sweet fragrance, then stood still, listening expectantly.

Up hill, a horse whinneyed. It was the young mare. The heavy horses went thundering across to the far hedge.

Maurice wondered what to do. He wandered round the deserted stacks restlessly. Heat came in wafts, in thick strands. The evening was a long time cooling. He thought he would go and wash himself. There was a trough of pure water in the hedge bottom. It was filled by a tiny spring that filtered over the brim of the trough down the lush hedge bottom of the lower field. All round the trough, in the upper field, the land was marshy, and there the meadow-sweet stood like clots of mist, very sickly smelling in the twilight. The night did not darken, for the moon was in the sky, so that as the tawny colour drew off the heavens they remained pallid with a dimmed moon. The purple bell-flowers in the hedge went black, the ragged robin turned its pink to a faded white, the meadow-sweet gathered light as if it were phosphorescent, and it made the air ache with scent.

Maurice kneeled on the slab of stone bathing his hands and arms, then his face. The water was deliciously cool. He had still an hour before Paula would come: she was not due till nine. So he decided to take his bath at night instead of waiting till morning. Was he not sticky, and was not Paula coming to talk to him? He was delighted the thought had occurred to him. As he soused his head in the trough, he wondered what the little creatures that lived in the velvetty silt at the bottom would think of the taste of soap. Laughing to himself, he squeezed his cloth into the water. He washed himself from head to foot, standing in the fresh, forsaken corner of the field, where no one could see him by daylight, so that now, in the veiled grey tinge of moonlight, he was no more noticeable than the crowded flowers. The night had on a new look: he never remembered to have seen the lustrous grey sheen of it before, nor to have noticed how vital the lights looked, like live folk inhabiting the silvery spaces. And the tall trees, wrapped obscurely in their mantles, would not have surprised him had they begun to move in converse. As he dried himself, he discovered little wander-ings in the air, felt on his sides soft touches and caresses that were peculiarly delicious: sometimes they startled him, and he laughed as if he were not alone. The flowers, the meadow-sweet particularly haunted him. He reached to put his hand over their fleeciness. They touched his thighs. Laughing, he gathered them and dusted himself all over with their cream dust and fragrance. For a moment he hesitated in wonder at himself: but the subtle glow in the hoary and black night reassured him. Things never had looked so personal and full of beauty, he had never known the wonder in himself before.

At nine o'clock he was waiting under the elder bush, in a state of high trepidation, but feeling that he was worthy, having a sense of his own wonder. She was late. At a quarter past nine she came, flitting swiftly, in her own eager way.

"No she would *not* go to sleep," said Paula, with a world of wrath in her tone. He laughed bashfully. They wandered out into the dim, hillside field.

"I have sat—in that bedroom—for an hour, for hours," she cried indignantly. She took a deep breath: "Ah, breathe!" she smiled.

She was very intense, and full of energy.

"I want—" she was clumsy with the language—"I want—I should laïke—to run—there!" She pointed across the field.

"Let's run then," he said, curiously.

"Yes!"

And in an instant she was gone. He raced after her. For all he was so young and limber, he had difficulty in catching her. At first he could scarcely see her, though he could hear the rustle of her dress. She sped with astonishing fleetness. He overtook her, caught her by the arm, and they stood panting, facing one another with laughter.

"I could win," she asserted blithely.

"Tha couldna," he replied, with a peculiar, excited laugh. They walked on, rather breathless. In front of them suddenly appeared the dark shapes of the three feeding horses.

"We ride a horse?," she said.

"What, bareback?," he asked.

"You say?"—She did not understand.

"With no saddle?"

"No saddle—yes—no saddle."

"Coop lass!" he said to the mare, and in a minute he had her by the forelock, and was leading her down to the stacks, where he put a halter on her. She was a big, strong mare. Maurice seated the Fräulein, clambered himself in front of the girl, using the wheel of the wagon as a mount, and together they trotted up-hill, she holding lightly round his waist. From the crest of the hill they looked round.

The sky was darkening with an awning of cloud. On the left the hill rose black and wooded, made cosy by a few lights from cottages along the highway. The hill spread to the right, and tufts of trees shut round. But in front was a great vista of night, a sprinkle of cottage candles, a twinkling cluster of lights, like an elfish fair in full swing, at the colliery, an encampment of light at a village, a red flare on the sky far off above an iron foundry, and in the farthest distance the dim breathing of town-lights. As they watched the night stretch far out, her arms tightened round his waist, and he pressed his elbows to his side, pressing her arms closer still. The horse moved restlessly. They clung to each other.

"Tha doesna want to go right away?" he asked the girl behind him.

"I stay with you," she answered softly, and he felt her crouching close against him. He laughed curiously. He was afraid to kiss her, though he was urged to do so. They remained still, on the restless horse, watching the small lights lead deep into the night, an infinite distance.

"I don't want to go," he said, in a tone half pleading.

She did not answer. The horse stirred restlessly.

"Let him run," cried Paula, "fast!"

She broke the spell, startled him into a little fury. He kicked the mare, hit her and away she plunged downhill. The girl clung tightly to the young man. They were riding bareback down a rough, steep hill. Maurice clung hard with hands and knees. Paula held him fast round the waist, leaning her head on his shoulders, and thrilling with excitement.

"We shall be off, we shall be off," he cried, laughing with excitement, but she only crouched behind, and pressed tight to him. The mare tore across the field. Maurice expected every moment to be flung onto the grass. He gripped with all the strength of his knees. Paula tucked herself behind him, and often wrenched him almost from his hold. Man and girl were taut with effort.

At last the mare came to a standstill, blowing. Paula slid off, and in an instant Maurice was beside her. They were both highly excited. Before he knew what he was doing, he had her in his arms, fast, and was kissing her, and laughing. They did not move for some time. Then, in silence, they walked towards the stacks.

It had grown quite dark, the night was thick with cloud. He walked with his arm round Paula's waist, she with her arm round him. They were near the stacks when Maurice felt a spot of rain.

"It's going to rain," he said.

"Rain!" she echoed, as if it were trivial.

"I s'll have to put the stack-cloth on," he said gravely. She did not understand.

When they got to the stacks, he went round to the shed, to return staggering in the darkness under the burden of the immense and heavy cloth. It had not been used once during the hay harvest.

"What are you going to do?" asked Paula, coming close to him in the darkness.

"Cover the top of the stack with it," he replied. "Put it over the stack, to keep the rain out."

"Ah!" she cried. "Up there!" He dropped his burden.

"Yes," he answered.

Fumblingly, he reared the long ladder up the side of the stack. He could not see the top. "I hope it's solid," he said, softly.

A few smart drops of rain sounded drumming on the cloth. They seemed like another presence. It was very dark indeed between the great buildings of hay. She looked up the black wall, and shrank to him.

"You carry it up there?" she asked.

"Yes," he answered.

"I help you?," she said.

And she did. They opened the cloth. He clambered first up the steep ladder, bearing the upper part, she followed closely, carrying her full share. They mounted the shaky ladder in silence, stealthily.

4.

As they climbed the stacks a light stopped at the gate on the highroad. It was Geoffrey, come to help his brother with the cloth. Afraid of his own intrusion, he wheeled his bicycle silently towards the shed. This was a corrugated iron erection, on the opposite side of the hedge from the stacks. Geoffrey let his light go in front of him, but there was no sign from the lovers. He thought he saw a shadow slinking away. The light of the bicycle lamp sheered yellowly across the dark, catching a glint of rain-drops, a mist of darkness, shadow of leaves and strokes of long grass. Geoffrey entered the shed—no one was there. He walked slowly and doggedly round to the stacks. He had passed the wagon, when he heard something sheering down upon him. Starting back under the wall of hay, he saw the long ladder slither across the side of the stack, and fall with a bruising ring.

"What wor that?" he heard Maurice, aloft, ask cautiously.

"Something fall," came the curious, almost pleased voice of the Fräulein.

"It wor niver th' ladder," said Maurice. He peered over the side of the stack. He lay down, looking.

"It is an' a'!" he exclaimed. "We knocked it down with the cloth, dragging it over."

"We fast up here?," she exclaimed with a thrill.

"We are that—without I shout and make 'em hear at the vicarage."

"Oh no," she said quickly.

"I don't want to," he replied, with a short laugh. There came a swift clatter of rain-drops on the cloth. Geoffrey crouched under the wall of the other stack.

"Mind where you tread—here, let me straighten this end," said Maurice, with a peculiar intimate tone, a command and an embrace. "We s'll have to sit under it. At any rate we shan't get wet."

"Not get wet!" echoed the girl, pleased, but agitated.

Geoffrey heard the slide and rustle of the cloth over the top of the stack, heard Maurice telling her to "Mind!"

"Mind!" she repeated. "Mind! You say 'Mind!'."

"Well, what if I do!" he laughed. "I don't want you to fall over th' side, do I?" His tone was masterful, but he was not quite sure of himself.

There was silence a moment or two.

"Maurice!" she said, plaintive.

"I'm here," he answered, tenderly, his voice shaky with excitement, that was near to distress. "There, I've done. Now should we sit under this corner."

"Maurice!" she was rather pitiful.

"What? You'll be all right," he remonstrated, tenderly indignant.

"I be all raïght," she repeated, "I be all right, Maurice?"

"Tha knows tha will—I canna ca' thee Powla. Should I ca' thee Minnie?" It was the name of a dead sister.

"Minne!" she exclaimed in surprise.

"Ay, should I?"

She answered in full-throated German. He laughed shakily.

"Come on—come on under. But do yer wish you was safe in th' vicarage? Should I shout for somebody?" he asked.

"I don't wish, no!" She was vehement.

"Art sure?," he insisted, almost indignantly.

"Sure—I quite sure." She laughed.

Geoffrey turned away at the last words. Then the rain beat heavily. The lonely brother slouched miserably to the hut, where the rain played a mad tattoo. He felt very miserable, and jealous of Maurice.

His bicycle lamp, downcast, shone a yellow light on the stark floor of the shed or hut with one wall open. It lit up the trodden earth, the shafts of tools lying piled under the beam, beside the dreary grey metal of the building. He took off the lamp, shone it round the hut. There were piles of harness, tools, a big sugar box, a deep bed of hay—then the beams across the corrugated iron, all very dreary and stark. He shone the lamp into the night: nothing but the furtive glitter of rain-drops through the mist of darkness, and black shapes hovering round.

Geoffrey blew out the light and flung himself onto the hay. He would put the ladder up for them in a while, when they would be wanting it. Meanwhile he sat and gloated over Maurice's felicity. He was imaginative, and now he had something concrete to work upon. Nothing in the whole of life stirred him so profoundly, and so utterly, as the thought of this woman. For Paula was strange, foreign, different from the ordinary girls: the rousing, feminine quality seemed in her concentrated, brighter, more fascinating than in anyone he had known, so that he felt most like a moth near a candle. He would have loved her wildly—but Maurice had got her. His thoughts beat the same course, round and round: what was it like when you kissed her, when she held you tight round the waist; how did she feel towards Maurice, did she love to touch him; was he fine and attractive to her; what did she think of himself— she merely disregarded him, as she would disregard a horse in a field; why should she do so, why couldn't he make her regard himself, instead of Maurice: he would never command a woman's regard like that, he always gave in to her too soon: if only some woman would come and take him for what he was worth, though he was such a stumbler and showed to such disadvantage, ah, what a grand thing it would be; how he would kiss her. Then round he went again in the same course, brooding almost like a madman. Meanwhile the rain drummed deep on the shed, then grew lighter and softer. There came the drip, drip of the drops falling outside.

Geoffrey's heart leaped up his chest, and he clenched himself, as a black shape crept round the post of the shed and, bowing, entered silently. The young man's heart beat so heavily, in plunges, he could not get his breath to speak. It was shock, rather than fear. The form felt towards him. He sprang up, gripped it with his great hands, panting

"Now then!"

There was no resistance, only a little whimper of despair.

"Let me go," said a woman's voice.

"What are you after?" he asked, in deep, gruff tones.

"I thought 'e was 'ere," she wept despairingly, with little, stubborn sobs.

"An' you've found what you didn't expect, have you?"

At the sound of his bullying she tried to get away from him.

"Let me go," she said.

"Who did you expect to find here?" he asked, but more his natural self.

"I expected my husband—him as you saw at dinner. Let me go."

"Why, is it you?" exclaimed Geoffrey. "Has he left you?"

"Let me go," said the woman sullenly, trying to draw away. He realised that her sleeve was very wet, her arm slender under his grasp. Suddenly he grew ashamed of himself: he had no doubt hurt her, gripping her so hard. He relaxed, but did not let her go.

"An' are you searching round after that snipe as was here at dinner?" he asked. She did not answer.

"Where did he leave you?"

"I left him—here. I've seen nothing of him since."

"I s'd think it's good riddance," he said. She did not answer. He gave a short laugh, saying:

"I should ha' thought you wouldn't ha' wanted to clap eyes on him again."

"He's my husband—an' he's not goin' to run off, if I can stop him."

Geoffrey was silent, not knowing what to say.

"Have you got a jacket on?" he asked at last.

"What do you think?—You've got hold of it."

"You're wet though, aren't you?"

"I shouldn't be dry, comin' through that teemin' rain.—But 'e's not here, so I'll go."

"I mean," he said humbly, "are you wet through?"

She did not answer. He felt her shiver.

"Are you cold?" he asked, in surprise and concern.

She did not answer. He did not know what to say.

"Stop a minute," he said, and he fumbled in his pocket for his matches. He struck a light, holding it in the hollow of his large, hard palm. He was a big man, and he looked anxious. Shedding the light on her, he saw she was rather pale, and very weary looking. Her old sailor hat was sodden and drooping with rain. She wore a fawn-coloured jacket of smooth cloth. This jacket was black-wet where the rain had beaten—her skirt hung sodden, and dripped onto her boots. The match went out.

"Why you're wet through," he said.

She did not answer.

"Shall you stop in here while it gives over?" he asked. She did not answer.

"'Cause if you will, you'd better take your things off, an' have th' rug. There's a horse rug in the box."

He waited, but she would not answer. So he lit his bicycle lamp, and rummaged in the box, pulling out a large brown blanket, striped with scarlet and yellow. She stood stock still. He shone the light on her. She was very pale, and trembling fitfully.

"Are you that cold?" he asked in concern. "Take your jacket off, and your hat, and put this right over you."

Mechanically, she undid the enormous fawn-coloured buttons, and unpinned her hat. With her black hair drawn back from her low, honest brow, she looked little more than a girl, like a girl driven hard with womanhood by stress of life. She was small, and natty, with neat little features. But she shivered convulsively.

"Is something a-matter with you?" he asked.

"I've walked to Bulwell and back," she quivered, "looking for him—an' I've not touched a thing since this morning." She did not weep—she was too dreary-hardened to cry. He looked at her in dismay, his mouth half open: 'Gormin'' as Maurice would have said.

"'Aven't you had nothing to eat!" he said.

Then he turned aside to the box. There, the bread remaining was kept, and the great piece of cheese, and such things as sugar and salt, with all table utensils: there was some butter.

She sat down drearily on the bed of hay. He cut her a piece of bread and butter, and a piece of cheese. This she took, but she ate listlessly.

"I want a drink," she said.

"We 'aven't got no beer," he answered. "My father doesn't have it."

"I want water," she said.

He took a can and plunged through the wet darkness, under the great black hedge, down to the trough. As he came back he saw her in the half-lit little cave sitting bunched together. The soaked grass wet his feet—he thought of her. When he gave her a cup of water, her hand touched his, and he felt her fingers hot and glossy. She trembled so she spilled the water.

"Do you feel badly?" he asked.

"I can't keep myself still—but it's only with being tired and having nothing to eat."

He scratched his head contemplatively, waited while she ate

her piece of bread and butter. Then he offered her another
piece.

"I don't want it just now," she said.

"You'll have to eat summat," he said.

"I couldn't eat any more just now."

He put the piece down undecidedly on the box. Then there
was another long pause. He stood up with bent head. The
bicycle, like a restful animal, glittered behind him, turning
towards the wall. The woman sat hunched on the hay, shivering.

"Can't you get warm?" he asked.

"I shall by an' by—don't you bother. I'm taking your seat—
are you stopping here all night?"

"Yes."

"I'll be goin' in a bit," she said.

"Nay, I non want you to go. I'm thinkin' how you could get
warm."

"Don't you bother about me," she remonstrated, almost
irritably.

"I just want to see as the stacks is all right. You take your
shoes an' stockin's an' *all* your wet things off: you can easy
wrap yourself all over in that rug, there's not so much of you."

"It's raining—I s'll be all right—I s'll be going in a minute."

"I've got to see as the stacks is safe. Take your wet things
off."

"Are you coming back?" she asked.

"I mightn't, not till morning."

"Well, I s'll be gone in ten minutes, then. I've no rights to be
here, an' I s'll not let anybody be turned out for me."

"You won't be turning me out."

"Whether or no, I shan't stop."

"Well, shall you if I come back?" he asked. She did not
answer.

He went. In a few moments, she blew the light out. The rain
was falling steadily, and the night was a black gulf. All was
intensely still. Geoffrey listened everywhere: no sound save the
rain. He stood between the stacks, but only heard the trickle of
water, and the light swish of rain. Everything was lost in blackness. He imagined death was like that, many things dissolved

in silence and darkness, blotted out, but existing. In the dense blackness he felt himself almost extinguished. He was afraid he might not find things the same. Almost frantically, he stumbled, feeling his way, till his hand touched the wet metal. He had been looking for a gleam of light.

"Did you blow the lamp out?" he asked, fearful lest the silence should answer him.

"Yes," she answered humbly. He was glad to hear her voice. Groping into the pitch dark shed, he knocked against the box, part of whose cover served as table. There was a clatter and a fall.

"That's the lamp, an' the knife, an' the cup," he said. He struck a match.

"Th' cup's not broke." He put it into the box.

"But th' oil's spilled out o' th' lamp. It always was a rotten old thing." He hastily blew out his match, which was burning his fingers. Then he struck another light.

"You don't want a lamp, you know you don't. And I s'll be going directly, so you come an' lie down an' get your night's rest. I'm not taking any of your place."

He looked at her by the light of another match. She was a queer little bundle, all brown, with gaudy border folding in and out, and her little face peering at him. As the match went out she saw him beginning to smile.

"I can sit right at this end," she said. "You lie down."

He came and sat on the hay, at some distance from her. After a spell of silence:

"Is he really your husband?" he asked.

"He is!" she answered grimly.

"Hm!" Then there was silence again.

After a while: "Are you warm now?"

"Why do you bother yourself?"

"I don't bother myself—do you follow him because you like him?" He put it very timidly. He wanted to know.

"I don't—I wish he was dead"—this with bitter contempt. Then doggedly "But he's my husband."

He gave a short laugh.

"By Gad!" he said.

Again, after a while:

"Have you been married long?"

"Four years."

"Four years—why, how old are you?"

"Twenty three."

"Are you turned twenty three?"

"Last May."

"Then you're four month older than me." He mused over it. They were only two voices in the pitch-black night. It was eerie. Silence again.

"And do you just tramp about?" he asked.

"He reckons he's looking for a job. But he doesn't like work in any shape or form. He was a stable man when I married him, at Greenhalgh's, the horse dealers, at Chesterfield, where I was housemaid. He left that job when the baby was only two month, and I've been badgered about from pillar to post ever sin'. They say a rolling stone gathers no moss——"

"An' where's the baby."

"It died when it was ten month old."

Now the silence was clinched between them. It was quite a long time before Geoffrey ventured to say, sympathetically,

"You haven't much to look forward to."

"I've wished many a score time when I've started shiverin' an' shakin' at nights, as I was taken bad for death. But we're not that handy at dying." He was silent.

"But whatever shall you do?," he faltered.

"I s'll find him, if I drop by th' road."

"Why?" he asked, wondering, looking her way, though he saw nothing but solid darkness.

"Because I shall. He's not going to have it all his own road."

"But why don't you leave him?"

"Because he's *not goin' to have it all his own road*."

She sounded very determined, even vindictive. He sat in wonder, feeling uneasy, and vaguely miserable on her behalf. She sat extraordinarily still. She seemed like a voice only, a presence.

"Are you warm now?" he asked, half afraid.

"A bit warmer—but my feet—!" She sounded pitiful.

"Let me warm them with my hands," he asked her. "I'm hot enough."

"No thank you," she said, coldly.

Then, in the darkness, she felt she had wounded him. He was writhing under her rebuff, for his offer had been pure kindness.

"They're 'appen dirty," she said, half mocking.

"Well—mine is—an' I have a bath a'most every day," he answered.

"I don't know when they'll get warm," she moaned to herself.

"Well then, put them in my hands."

She heard him faintly rattling the match box, and then a phosphorescent glare began to fume in his direction. Presently he was holding two smoking, blue-green blotches of light towards her feet. She was afraid. But her feet ached so, and the impulse drove her on, so she placed her soles lightly on the two blotches of smoke. His large hands clasped over her instep, warm and hard.

"They're like ice!" he said, in deep concern.

He warmed her feet as best he could, putting them close against him. Now and again convulsive tremors ran over her. She felt his warm breath on the balls of her toes, that were bunched up in his hands. Leaning forward, she touched his hair delicately with her fingers. He thrilled. She fell to gently stroking his hair, with timid, pleading finger-tips.

"Do they feel any better?" he asked, in a low voice, suddenly lifting his face to her. This sent her hand sliding softly over his face, and her finger-tips caught on his mouth. She drew quickly away. He put his hand out to find hers, in his other palm holding both her feet. His wandering hand met her face. He touched it curiously. It was wet. He put his big fingers cautiously on her eyes, into two little pools of tears.

"What's a matter?" he asked, in a low, choked voice.

She leaned down to him, and gripped him tightly round the neck, pressing him to her bosom in a little frenzy of pain. Her bitter disillusionment with life, her unalleviated shame and degradation during the last four years, had driven her into loneliness, and hardened her till a large part of her nature was caked and sterile. Now she softened again, and her spring might be beautiful. She had been in a fair way to make an ugly old woman.

She clasped the head of Geoffrey to her breast, which heaved and fell, and heaved again. He was bewildered, full of wonder. He allowed the woman to do as she would with him. Her tears fell on his hair, as she wept noiselessly; and he breathed deep as she did. At last she let go her clasp. He put his arms round her.

"Come and let me warm you," he said, folding her up on his knee, and lapping her with his heavy arms against himself. She was small and 'câline'. He held her very warm and close. Presently she stole her arms round him.

"You *are* big," she whispered.

He gripped her hard, started, put his mouth down, wanderingly, seeking her out. His lips met her temple. She slowly, deliberately turned her mouth to his, and with opened lips, met him in a kiss, his first love kiss.

5.

It was breaking cold dawn when Geoffrey woke. The woman was still sleeping in his arms. Her face in sleep moved all his tenderness: the tight shutting of her mouth, as if in resolution to bear what was very hard to bear, contrasted so pitifully with the small mould of her features. Geoffrey pressed her to his bosom: having her, he felt he could bruise the lips of the scornful, and pass on erect, unabateable. With her to complete him, to form the core of him, he was firm and whole. Needing her so much, he loved her fervently.

Meanwhile the dawn came like death, one of those slow, livid mornings that seem to come in a cold sweat. Slowly, and painfully, the air began to whiten. Geoffrey saw it was not raining. As he was watching the ghastly transformation outside, he felt aware of something. He glanced down: she was open eyed, watching him: she had golden brown, calm eyes, that immediately smiled into his. He also smiled, bowed softly down and kissed her. They did not speak for some time. Then:

"What's thy name?" he asked curiously.

"Lydia," she said.

"Lydia!" he repeated, wonderingly. He felt rather shy.

"Mine's Geoffrey Wookey," he said.

She merely smiled at him.

They were silent for a considerable time. By morning light, things look small. The huge trees of the evening were dwindled to hoary, small, uncertain things, trespassing in the sick pallor of the atmosphere. There was a dense mist, so that the light could scarcely breathe. Everything seemed to quiver with cold and sickliness.

"Have you often slept out?" he asked her.

"Not so very," she answered.

"You won't go after *him*?" he asked.

"I s'll have to," she replied, but she nestled in to Geoffrey. He felt a sudden panic.

"You mustn't," he exclaimed, and she saw he was afraid for himself. She let it be, was silent.

"We couldn't get married?" he asked, thoughtfully.

"No."

He brooded deeply over this. At length:

"Would you go to Canada with me?"

"We'll see what you think in two months' time," she replied quietly, without bitterness.

"I s'll think the same," he protested, hurt.

She did not answer, only watched him steadily. She was there for him to do as he liked with; but she would not injure his fortunes, no, not to save his soul.

"Haven't you got no relations?" he asked.

"A married sister at Crich?"

"On a farm?"

"No—married a farm-laborer—but she's very comfortable. I'll go there, if you want me to, just till I can get another place in service."

He considered this.

"Could you get on a farm?" he asked wistfully.

"Greenhalgh's was a farm."

He saw the future brighten: she would be a help to him. She agreed to go to her sister, and to get a place of service,—until

Spring, he said, when they would sail for Canada. He waited for her assent.

"You will come with me then?" he asked.

"When the time comes," she said.

Her want of faith made him bow his head: she had reason for it.

"Shall you walk to Crich or go from Langley Mill to Ambergate? But it's only ten mile to walk. So we can go together up Hunt's Hill—you'd have to go past our lane-end, then I could easy nip down an' fetch you some money—" he said, humbly.

"I've got half a sovereign by me—it's more than I s'll want."

"Let's see it," he said.

After a while, fumbling under the blanket, she brought out the piece of money. He felt she was independent of him. Brooding rather bitterly, he told himself she'd forsake him. His anger gave him courage to ask:

"Shall you go in service in your maiden name?"

"No."

He was bitterly wrathful with her—full of resentment.

"I bet I s'll niver see you again," he said, with a short, hard laugh. She put her arms round him, pressed him to her bosom, while the tears rose to her eyes. He was reassured, but not satisfied.

"Shall you write to me tonight?"

"Yes, I will."

"And can I write to you—who shall I write to?"

"Mrs Bredon."

" 'Bredon'!" he repeated bitterly.

He was exceedingly uneasy.

The dawn had grown quite wan. He saw the hedges drooping wet down the grey mist. Then he told her about Maurice.

"Oh, you *shouldn't*!" she said. "You should ha' put the ladder up for them, you *should*."

"Well—I don't care."

"Go and do it now—and I'll go."

"No, don't you. Stop an' see our Maurice, go on, stop an' see him—then I s'll be able to tell him."

She consented in silence. He had her promise she would not

go before he returned. She adjusted her dress, found her way to the trough, where she performed her toilet.

Geoffrey wandered round to the upper field. The stacks loomed wet in the mist, the hedge was drenched. Mist rose like steam from the grass, and the near hills were veiled almost to a shadow. In the valley, some peaks of black poplar showed fairly definite, jutting up. He shivered with chill.

There was no sound from the stacks, and he could see nothing. After all, he wondered were they up there. But he reared the ladder to the place whence it had been swept, then went down the hedge to gather dry sticks. He was breaking off thin dead twigs under a holly tree when he heard, on the perfectly still air: "Well I'm dashed!"

He listened intently. Maurice was awake.

"Sithee here!" the lad's voice exclaimed.

Then, after a while, the foreign sound of the girl:

"What—oh, thair!"

"Ay, th' ladder's there, right enough."

"You said it had fall down."

"Well, I heard it drop—an' I couldna feel it nor see it."

"You said it had fall down—you lie, you liar."

"Nay, as true as I'm here—"

"You tell me lies—make me stay here—you tell me lies——."
She was passionately indignant.

"As true as I'm standing here—," he began.

"Lies!—lies!—lies!" she cried. "I don't believe you, never. You *mean*, you *mean*, *mean*, *mean*!!"

"A' raïght, then!" he was now incensed, in his turn.

"You are bad, mean, mean, mean."

"Are yer commin' down?" asked Maurice coldly.

"No—I will not come with you—mean, to tell me lies."

"Are ter commin down?"

"No, I don't want you."

"A' raïght then!"

Geoffrey, peering through the holly tree, saw Maurice negotiating the ladder. The top rung was below the brim of the stack, and rested on the cloth, so it was dangerous to approach. The Fräulein watched him from the end of the stack, where the cloth

thrown back showed the light, dry hay. He slipped slightly,—
she screamed. When he had got onto the ladder, he pulled
the cloth away, throwing it back, making it easy for her to
descend.

"Now are ter comin?" he asked.

"No;" she shook her head violently, in a pet.

Geoffrey felt slightly contemptuous of her. But Maurice
waited.

"Are ter comin?" he called again.

"No," she flashed, like a wild cat.

"All right, then I'm going."

He descended. At the bottom, he stood holding the ladder.

"Come on, while I hold it steady," he said.

There was no reply. For some minutes he stood patiently
with his foot on the bottom rung of the ladder. He was pale,
rather washed-out in his appearance, and he drew himself
together with cold.

"Are ter commin', or aren't ter?" he asked at length.

Still there was no reply.

"Then stop up till tha'rt ready," he muttered, and he went
away. Round the other side of the stacks he met Geoffrey.

"What, are thaïgh here?" he exclaimed.

"Bin here a' naïght," replied Geoffrey. "I come to help thee
wi' th' cloth, but I found it on, an' th' ladder down, so I thowt
tha'd gone."

"Did ter put th' ladder up?"

"I did a bit sin."

Maurice brooded over this, Geoffrey struggled with himself
to get out his own news. At last he blurted:

"Tha knows that woman as wor here yis'day dinner—'er
come back, an' stopped i' th' shed a' night, out o' th' rain."

"Oh—ah!" said Maurice, his eye kindling, and a smile crossing his pallor.

"An' I s'll gi'e her some breakfast."

"Oh ah!" repeated Maurice.

"It's th' man as is good-for-nowt, not her," protested
Geoffrey. Maurice did not feel in a position to cast stones.

"Tha pleases thysen," he said, "what ter does." He was very

quiet, unlike himself. He seemed bothered and anxious, as Geoffrey had not seen him before.

"What's up wi' thee?" asked the elder brother, who in his own heart was glad, and relieved.

"Nowt," was the reply.

They went together to the hut. The woman was folding the blanket. She was fresh from washing, and looked very pretty. Her hair, instead of being screwed tightly back, was coiled in a knot low down, partly covering her ears. Before, she had deliberately made herself plain-looking: now she was neat and pretty, with a sweet, womanly gravity.

"Hello, I didn't think to find you here," said Maurice, very awkwardly, smiling. She watched him gravely without reply. "But it was better in shelter than outside, last night," he added.

"Yes," she replied.

"Shall you get a few more sticks," Geoffrey asked him. It was a new thing for Geoffrey to be leader. Maurice obeyed. He wandered forth into the damp, raw morning. He did not go to the stack, as he shrank from meeting Paula.

At the mouth of the hut, Geoffrey was making the fire. The woman got out coffee from the box: Geoffrey set the tin to boil. They were arranging breakfast when Paula appeared. She was hat-less. Bits of hay stuck in her hair, and she was white-faced— altogether, she did not show to advantage.

"Ah—you!" she exclaimed, seeing Geoffrey.

"Hello!" he answered. "You're out early."

"Where's Maurice?"

"I dunno, he should be back directly."

Paula was silent.

"When have you come?" she asked.

"I come last night, but I could see nobody about. I got up half an hour sin', an' put th' ladder up ready to take the stack-cloth up."

Paula understood, and was silent. When Maurice returned with the faggots, she was crouched warming her hands. She looked up at him, but he kept his eyes averted from her. Geoffrey met the eyes of Lydia, and smiled. Maurice put his hands to the fire.

"You cold?" asked Paula tenderly.

"A bit," he answered, quite friendly, but reserved. And all the while the four sat round the fire, drinking their smoked coffee, eating each a small piece of toasted bacon, Paula watched eagerly for the eyes of Maurice, and he avoided her. He was gentle, but would not give his eyes to her looks. And Geoffrey smiled constantly to Lydia, who watched gravely.

The German girl succeeded in getting safely into the vicarage, her escapade unknown to anyone save the housemaid. Before a week was out, she was openly engaged to Maurice, and when her month's notice expired, she went to live at the farm.

Geoffrey and Lydia kept faith one with the other.

THE MINER AT HOME

Like most colliers, Bower had his dinner before he washed himself. It did not surprise his wife that he said little. He seemed quite amiable, but evidently did not feel confidential. Gertie was busy with the three children, the youngest of whom lay kicking on the sofa, preparing to squeal, therefore she did not concern herself overmuch with her husband, once having ascertained, by a few shrewd glances at his heavy brows and his blue eyes, which moved conspicuously in his black face, that he was only pondering.

He smoked a solemn pipe until six o'clock. Although he was really a good husband, he did not notice that Gertie was tired. She was getting irritable at the end of the long day.

"Don't you want to wash yourself?" she asked, grudgingly, at six o'clock. It was sickening to have a man sitting there in his pit-dirt, never saying a word, smoking like a Red Indian.

"I'm ready when you are," he replied.

She laid the baby on the sofa, barricaded it in with pillows, and brought from the scullery a great panchion, a bowl of heavy red earthenware like brick, glazed inside to a dark mahogany color. Tall and thin and very pale, she stood before the fire holding the great bowl, her grey eyes flashing.

"Get up, our Jack, this minute, or I'll squash thee under this blessed panchion."

The fat boy of six, who was rolling on the rug in the firelight, said broadly:

"Squash me, then."

"Get up," she cried, giving him a push with her foot.

"Gi'e ower," he said, rolling jollily.

"I'll smack you," she said grimly, preparing to put down the panchion.

"Get up, theer," shouted the father.

Gertie ladled water from the boiler with a tin ladling can. Drops fell from her ladle hissing into the red fire, splashing on to the white hearth, blazing like drops of flame on the flat-topped steel fender. The father gazed at it all, unmoved.

"I've told you," he said "to put cold water in that panchion first. If one o' th' children goes an' falls in——"

"You can see as 'e doesn't, then," snapped she. She tempered the bowl with cold water, dropped in a flannel and a lump of soap, and spread the towel over the fender to warm.

Then, and only then, Bower rose. He wore no coat, and his arms were freckled black. He stripped to the waist, hitched his trousers into the strap, and kneeled on the rug to wash himself. There was a great splashing and spluttering. The red firelight shone on his cap of white soap, and on the muscles of his back, on the strange working of his red and white muscular arms, that flashed up and down like individual creatures.

Gertie sat with the baby clawing at her ears and hair and nose. Continually she drew back her face and head from the cruel little baby-clasp. Jack was hanging on to the kitchen door.

"Come away from that door," cried the mother.

Jack did not come away, but neither did he open the door and run the risk of incurring his father's wrath. The room was very hot, but the thought of a draught is abhorrent to a miner.

With the baby on one arm, Gertie washed her husband's back. She sponged it carefully with the flannel, and then, still with one hand, began to dry it on the rough towel.

"Canna ter put th' childt down an' use both hands," said her husband.

"Yes; an' then if th' childt screets, there's a bigger to-do than iver. There's no suitin' some folk."

"The childt 'ud non screet."

Gertie plumped it down. The baby began to cry. The wife rubbed her husband's back till it grew pink, whilst Bower quivered with pleasure. As soon as she threw the towel down:

"Shut that childt up," he said.

He wrestled his way into his shirt. His head emerged, with black hair standing roughly on end. He was rather an ugly man, just above medium height, and stiffly built. He had a thin black moustache over a full mouth, and a very full chin that was marred by a blue seam, where a horse had kicked him when he was a lad in the pit.

With both hands on the mantelpiece above his head, he stood looking in the fire, his whitish shirt hanging like a smock over his pit trousers.

Presently, still looking absently in the fire, he said:

"Bill Andrews was standin' at th' pit top, an' give ivery man as 'e come up one o' these."

He handed to his wife a small, whitey-blue paper, on which was printed simply:

"February 14th, 1912.

"To the Manager—

"I hereby give notice to leave your employment fourteen days from above date.

"Signed——."

Gertie read the paper, blindly dodging her head from the baby's grasp.

"An' what d'you reckon that's for?" she asked.

"I suppose it means as we come out."

"I'm sure!" she cried in indignation. "Well, *tha'rt* not goin' to sign it."

"It'll ma'e no diff'rence whether I do or dunna—t'others will."

"Then let 'em!" She made a small clicking sound in her mouth. "This 'ill ma'e th' third strike as we've had sin' we've been married; an' a fat lot th' better for it you are, arena you?"

He squirmed uneasily.

"No, but we mean to be," he said.

"I'll tell you what, colliers is a discontented lot, as doesn't know what they *do* want. That's what they are."

"Tha'd better not let some o' th' colliers as there is hear thee say so."

"I don't care who hears me. An' there isn't a man in Eastwood but what'll say as th' last two strikes has ruined the place. There's that much bad blood now atween th' mesters an' th' men as there isn't a thing but what's askew. An' what *will* it be, I should like to know!"

"It's not on'y here; it's all ower th' country alike," he gloated.

"Yes; it's them blessed Yorkshire an' Welsh colliers as does it. They're that bug nowadays, what wi' talkin' an' spoutin', they hardly know which side their back-side hangs. Here, take this childt!"

She thrust the baby into his arms, carried out the heavy bowlful of black suds, mended the fire, cleared round, and returned for the child.

"Ben Haseldine said, an *he's* a union man—he told me when he come for th' union money yesterday, as th' men doesn't *want* to come out—not our men. It's th' union."

"Tha knows nowt about it, woman. It's a' woman's jabber, from beginnin' to end."

"You don't intend us to know. Who wants th' Minimum Wage? Butties doesn't. There th' butties 'll be, havin' to pay seven shillin' a day to men as 'appen isn't worth a penny more than five."

"But the butties is goin' to have eight shillin', accordin' to scale."

"An' then th' men as can't work tip-top, an' is worth, 'appen, five shillin' a day, they get the sack: an' th' old men, an' so on. . ."

"Nowt o' th' sort, woman, nowt o' th' sort. Tha's got it off 'am-pat. There's goin' to be inspectors for all that, an' th' men 'll get what they're worth, accordin' to age, an' so on."

"An' accordin' to idleness an'—an' what somebody says about 'em. I'll back! There 'll be a lot o' fairness!"

"Tha talks like a woman as knows nowt. What does thee know about it?"

"I know what you did at th' last strike. And I know this much, when Shipley men had *their* strike tickets, not one in three signed 'em—so there. An' *tha'rt* not goin' to!"

"We want a livin' wage," he declared.

"Hanna you got one?" she cried.

"Han we?" he shouted. "Han we? Who does more chunterin' than thee when it's a short wik, an' tha gets 'appen a scroddy twenty-two shillin'? Tha goes at me 'ard enough then."

"Yi; but what better shall you be? What better *are* you for th' last two strikes—tell me that?"

"I'll tell thee this much, th' mesters doesna mean us to ha'e owt. They promise, but they dunna keep to it, not they. Up comes Friday night, an' nowt to draw, an' a woman fit to ha'e yer guts out for it."

"It's nowt but th' day-men as wants the blessed minimum wage—it's not butties."

"It's time as th' butties *did* ha'e ter let their men make a fair day's wage. Four an' sixpence a day is about as much as 'e's allowed to addle, whoiver he may be."

"I wonder what you'll say next. You say owt as is put in your mouth, that's a fac'. What are thee, dost reckon?—are ter a butty, or day man, or ostler, or are ter a mester?—for tha might be, ter hear thee talk."

"I nedna neither. It ought to be fair a' round."

"It ought, hang my rags, it ought! Tha'rt very fair to me, for instance."

"An' arena I?"

"Tha thinks 'cause tha gi'es me a lousy thirty shillin' reg'lar tha'rt th' best man i' th' Almighty world. Tha mun be waited on han' an' foot, an' sided wi' whativer tha' says. But I'm *not!* No, an' I'm not, not when it comes to strikes. I've seen enough on 'em."

"Then niver open thy mouth again if it's a short wik, an' we're pinched."

"We're niver pinched that much. An' a short wik isn't no shorter than a strike wik; put that i' thy pipe an' smoke it. It's th' idle men as wants the strikes."

"Shut thy mouth, woman. If every man worked as hard as I do——"

"He wouldn't ha'e as much to do as me; an' 'e wouldna. But *I've* nowt to do, as tha'rt flig ter tell me. No, it's th' idle men as wants th' strike. It's a union strike this is, not a men's strike. You're sharpenin' th' knife for your own throats."

"Am I not sick of a woman as listens to every tale as is poured into her ears. No, I'm not takin' th' kid. I'm goin' out."

He put on his boots determinedly.

She rocked herself with vexation and weariness.

THE WHITE STOCKING

I

"I'm getting up, Teddilinks," said Mrs. Whiston, and she sprang out of bed briskly.

"What the Hanover's got you?" asked Whiston.

"Nothing. Can't I get up?" she replied animatedly.

It was about seven o'clock, scarcely light yet in the cold bedroom. Whiston lay still and looked at his wife. She was a pretty little thing, with her fleecy, short black hair all tousled. He watched her as she dressed quickly, flicking her small, delightful limbs, throwing her clothes about her. Her slovenliness and untidiness did not trouble him. When she picked up the edge of her petticoat, ripped off a torn string of white lace, and flung it on the dressing-table, her careless abandon made his spirit glow. She stood before the mirror and roughly scrambled together her profuse little mane of hair. He watched the quickness and softness of her young shoulders, calmly, like a husband, and appreciatively.

"Rise up," she cried, turning to him with a quick wave of her arm—"and shine forth."

They had been married two years. But still, when she had gone out of the room, he felt as if all his light and warmth were taken away, he became aware of the raw, cold morning. So he rose himself, wondering casually what had roused her so early. Usually she lay in bed as late as she could.

Whiston fastened a belt round his loins and went downstairs in shirt and trousers. He heard her singing in her snatchy fashion. The stairs creaked under his weight. He passed down the narrow little passage, which she called a hall, of the seven and sixpenny house which was his first home.

He was a shapely young fellow of about twenty-eight, sleepy now and easy with well-being. He heard the water drumming into the kettle, and she began to whistle. He loved the quick way she dodged the supper cups under the tap to wash them for breakfast. She looked an untidy minx, but she was quick and handy enough.

"Teddilinks," she cried.

"What?"

"Light a fire, quick."

She wore an old, sack-like dressing-jacket of black silk pinned across her breast. But one of the sleeves, coming unfastened, showed some delightful pink upper-arm.

"Why don't you sew your sleeve up?" he said, suffering from the sight of the exposed soft flesh.

"Where?" she cried, peering round. "Nuisance," she said, seeing the gap, then with light fingers went on drying the cups.

The kitchen was of fair size, but gloomy. Whiston poked out the dead ashes.

Suddenly a thud was heard at the door down the passage.

"I'll go," cried Mrs. Whiston, and she was gone down the hall.

The postman was a ruddy-faced man who had been a soldier. He smiled broadly, handing her some packages.

"They've not forgot you," he said impudently.

"No—lucky for them," she said, with a toss of the head. But she was interested only in her envelopes this morning. The postman waited inquisitively, smiling in an ingratiating fashion. She slowly, abstractedly, as if she did not know anyone was there, closed the door in his face, continuing to look at the addresses on her letters.

She tore open the thin envelope. There was a long, hideous, cartoon valentine. She smiled briefly and dropped it on the floor. Struggling with the string of a packet, she opened a white cardboard box, and there lay a white silk handkerchief packed neatly under the paper lace of the box, and her initial, worked in heliotrope, fully displayed. She smiled pleasantly, and gently put the box aside. The third envelope contained another white packet—apparently a cotton handkerchief neatly folded. She shook it out. It was a long white stocking, but there was a little weight in the toe. Quickly, she thrust down her arm, wriggling her fingers into the toe of the stocking, and brought out a small box. She peeped inside the box, then hastily opened a door on her left hand, and went into the little, cold sitting-room. She had her lower lip caught earnestly between her teeth.

With a little flash of triumph, she lifted a pair of pearl ear-rings from the small box, and she went to the mirror. There, earnestly, she began to hook them through her ears, looking at herself sideways in the glass. Curiously concentrated and intent she seemed as she fingered the lobes of her ears, her head bent on one side.

Then the pearl ear-rings dangled under her rosy, small ears. She shook her head sharply, to see the swing of the drops. They went chill against her neck, in little, sharp touches. Then she stood still to look at herself, bridling her head in the dignified fashion. Then she simpered at herself. Catching her own eye, she could not help winking at herself and laughing.

She turned to look at the box. There was a scrap of paper with this posy:

> "Pearls may be fair, but thou art fairer.
> Wear these for me, and I'll love the wearer."

She made a grimace and a grin. But she was drawn to the mirror again, to look at her ear-rings.

Whiston had made the fire burn, so he came to look for her. When she heard him, she started round quickly, guiltily. She was watching him with intent blue eyes when he appeared.

He did not see much, in his morning-drowsy warmth. He gave her, as ever, a feeling of warmth and slowness. His eyes were very blue, very kind, his manner simple.

"What ha' you got?" he asked.

"Valentines," she said briskly, ostentatiously turning to show him the silk handkerchief. She thrust it under his nose. "Smell how good," she said.

"Who's that from?" he replied, without smelling.

"It's a valentine," she cried. "How do I know who it's from?"

"I'll bet you know," he said.

"Ted!—I don't!" she cried, beginning to shake her head, then stopping because of the ear-rings.

He stood still a moment, displeased.

"They've no right to send you valentines, now," he said.

"Ted!—Why not? You're not jealous, are you? I haven't the least idea who it's from. Look—there's my initial"—she pointed with an emphatic finger at the heliotrope embroidery—

> "E for Elsie,
> Nice little gelsie,"

she sang.

"Get out," he said. "You know who it's from."

"Truth, I don't," she cried.

He looked round, and saw the white stocking lying on a chair.

"Is this another?" he said.

"No, that's a sample," she said. "There's only a comic." And she fetched in the long cartoon.

He stretched it out and looked at it solemnly.

"Fools!" he said, and went out of the room.

She flew upstairs and took off the ear-rings. When she returned, he was crouched before the fire blowing the coals. The skin of his face was flushed, and slightly pitted, as if he had had small-pox. But his neck was white and smooth and goodly. She hung her arms round his neck as he crouched there, and clung to him. He balanced on his toes.

"This fire's a slow-coach," he said.

"And who else is a slow-coach?" she said.

"One of us two, I know," he said, and he rose carefully. She remained clinging round his neck, so that she was lifted off her feet.

"Ha!—swing me," she cried.

He lowered his head, and she hung in the air, swinging from his neck, laughing. Then she slipped off.

"The kettle is singing," she sang, flying for the teapot. He bent down again to blow the fire. The veins in his neck stood out, his shirt collar seemed too tight.

> "Doctor Wyer,
> Blow the fire,
> Puff! puff! puff!"

she sang, laughing.

He smiled at her.

She was so glad because of her pearl ear-rings.

Over the breakfast she grew serious. He did not notice. She became portentous in her gravity. Almost it penetrated through his steady good-humour to irritate him.

"Teddy!" she said at last.

"What?" he asked.

"I told you a lie," she said, humbly tragic.

His soul stirred uneasily.

"Oh ay?" he said casually.

She was not satisfied. He ought to be more moved.

"Yes," she said.

He cut a piece of bread.

"Was it a good one?" he asked.

She was piqued. Then she considered—*was* it a good one? Then she laughed.

"No," she said, "it wasn't up to much."

"Ah!" he said easily, but with a steady strength of fondness for her in his tone. "Get it out then."

It became a little more difficult.

"You know that white stocking," she said earnestly. "I told you a lie. It wasn't a sample. It was a valentine."

A little frown came on his brow.

"Then what did you invent it as a sample for?" he said. But he knew this weakness of hers. The touch of anger in his voice frightened her.

"I was afraid you'd be cross," she said pathetically.

"I'll bet you were vastly afraid," he said.

"I *was*, Teddy."

There was a pause. He was resolving one or two things in his mind.

"And who sent it?" he asked.

"I can guess," she said, "though there wasn't a word with it—except——"

She ran to the sitting-room and returned with a slip of paper.

> "Pearls may be fair, but thou art fairer.
> Wear these for me, and I'll love the wearer."

He read it twice, then a dull red flush came on his face.

"And *who* do you guess it is?" he asked, with a ringing of anger in his voice.

"I suspect it's Sam Adams," she said, with a little virtuous indignation.

Whiston was silent for a moment.

"Fool!" he said. "An' what's it got to do with pearls?—and how can he say 'wear these for me' when there's only one? He hasn't got the brain to invent a proper verse."

He screwed the slip of paper into a ball and flung it into the fire.

"I suppose he thinks it'll make a pair with the one last year," she said.

"Why, did he send one then?"

"Yes. I thought you'd be wild if you knew."

His jaw set rather sullenly.

Presently he rose, and went to wash himself, rolling back his sleeves and pulling open his shirt at the breast. It was as if his fine, clear-cut temples and steady eyes were degraded by the lower, rather brutal part of his face. But she loved it. As she whisked about, clearing the table, she loved the way in which he stood washing himself. He was such a man. She liked to see his neck glistening with water as he swilled it. It amused her and pleased her and thrilled her. He was so sure, so permanent, he had her so utterly in his power. It gave her a delightful, mischievous sense of liberty. Within his grasp, she could dart about excitingly.

He turned round to her, his face red from the cold water, his eyes fresh and very blue.

"You haven't been seeing anything of him, have you?" he asked roughly.

"Yes," she answered, after a moment, as if caught guilty. "He got into the tram with me, and he asked me to drink a coffee and a Benedictine in the Royal."

"You've got it off fine and glib," he said sullenly. "And did you?"

"Yes," she replied, with the air of a traitor before the rack.

The blood came up into his neck and face, he stood motionless, dangerous.

"It was cold, and it was such fun to go into the Royal," she said.

"You'd go off with a nigger for a packet of chocolate," he said, in anger and contempt, and some bitterness. Queer how he drew away from her, cut her off from him.

"Ted—how beastly!" she cried. "You know quite well——" She caught her lip, flushed, and the tears came to her eyes.

He turned away, to put on his necktie. She went about her work, making a queer pathetic little mouth, down which occasionally dripped a tear.

He was ready to go. With his hat jammed down on his head, and his overcoat buttoned up to his chin, he came to kiss her. He would be miserable all the day if he went without. She allowed herself to be kissed. Her cheek was wet under his lips, and his heart burned. She hurt him so deeply. And she felt aggrieved, and did not quite forgive him.

In a moment she went upstairs to her ear-rings. Sweet they looked nestling in the little drawer—sweet! She examined them with voluptuous pleasure, she threaded them in her ears, she looked at herself, she posed and postured and smiled, and looked sad and tragic and winning and appealing, all in turn before the mirror. And she was happy, and very pretty.

She wore her ear-rings all morning, in the house. She was self-conscious, and quite brilliantly winsome, when the baker came, wondering if he would notice. All the tradesmen left her door with a glow in them, feeling elated, and unconsciously favouring the delightful little creature, though there had been nothing to notice in her behaviour.

She was stimulated all the day. She did not think about her husband. He was the permanent basis from which she took these giddy little flights into nowhere. At night, like chickens and curses, she would come home to him, to roost.

Meanwhile Whiston, a traveller and confidential support of a small firm, hastened about his work, his heart all the while anxious for her, yearning for surety, and kept tense by not getting it.

II

She had been a warehouse girl in Adams' lace factory before she was married. Sam Adams was her employer. He was a bachelor of forty, growing stout, a man well dressed and florid, with a large brown moustache and thin hair. From the rest of his well-groomed, showy appearance, it was evident his baldness was a chagrin to him. He had a good presence, and some Irish blood in his veins.

His fondness for the girls, or the fondness of the girls for him, was notorious. And Elsie, quick, pretty, almost witty little thing—she *seemed* witty, although, when her sayings were repeated, they were entirely trivial—she had a great attraction for him. He would come into the warehouse dressed in a rather sporting reefer coat, of fawn colour, and trousers of fine black-and-white check, a cap with a big peak and a scarlet carnation in his button-hole, to impress her. She was only half impressed. He was too loud for her good taste. Instinctively perceiving this, he sobered down to navy blue. Then a well-built man, florid, with large brown whiskers, smart navy blue suit, fashionable boots, and manly hat, he was the irreproachable. Elsie was impressed.

But meanwhile Whiston was courting her, and she made splendid little gestures, before her bedroom mirror, of the constant-and-true sort.

"True, true till death——"

That was her song. Whiston was made that way, so there was no need to take thought for him.

Every Christmas Sam Adams gave a party at his house, to which he invited his superior work-people—not factory hands and labourers, but those above. He was a generous man in his way, with a real warm feeling for giving pleasure.

Two years ago Elsie had attended this Christmas-party for the last time. Whiston had accompanied her. At that time he worked for Sam Adams.

She had been very proud of herself, in her close-fitting, full-skirted dress of blue silk. Whiston called for her. Then she tripped beside him, holding her large cashmere shawl across her breast. He strode with long strides, his trousers handsomely strapped under his boots, and her silk shoes bulging the pockets of his full-skirted overcoat.

They passed through the park gates, and her spirits rose. Above them the Castle Rock loomed grandly in the night, the naked trees stood still and dark in the frost, along the boulevard.

They were rather late. Agitated with anticipation, in the cloak-room she gave up her shawl, donned her silk shoes, and looked at herself in the mirror. The loose bunches of curls on either side her face danced prettily, her mouth smiled.

She hung a moment in the door of the brilliantly lighted room. Many people were moving within the blaze of lamps, under the crystal chandeliers, the full skirts of the women balancing and floating, the side-whiskers and white cravats of the men bowing above. Then she entered the light.

In an instant Sam Adams was coming forward, lifting both his arms in boisterous welcome. There was a constant red laugh on his face.

"Come late, would you," he shouted, "like royalty."

He seized her hands and led her forward. He opened his mouth wide when he spoke, and the effect of the warm, dark opening behind the brown whiskers was disturbing. But she was floating into the throng on his arm. He was very gallant.

"Now then," he said, taking her card to write down the dances, "I've got carte blanche, haven't I?"

"Mr. Whiston doesn't dance," she said.

"I am a lucky man!" he said, scribbling his initials. "I was born with an *amourette* in my mouth."

He wrote on, quietly. She blushed and laughed, not knowing what it meant.

"Why, what is that?" she said.

"It's you, even littler than you are, dressed in little wings," he said.

"I should have to be pretty small to get in your mouth," she said.

"You think you're too big, do you!" he said easily.

He handed her her card, with a bow.

"Now I'm set up, my darling, for this evening," he said.

Then, quick, always at his ease, he looked over the room. She waited in front of him. He was ready. Catching the eye of the band, he nodded. In a moment, the music began. He seemed to relax, giving himself up.

"Now then, Elsie," he said, with a curious caress in his voice that seemed to lap the outside of her body in a warm glow, delicious. She gave herself to it. She liked it.

He was an excellent dancer. He seemed to draw her close in to him by some male warmth of attraction, so that she became all soft and pliant to him, flowing to his form, whilst he united her with him and they lapsed along in one movement. She was just carried in a kind of strong, warm flood, her feet moved of themselves, and only the music threw her away from him, threw her back to him, to his clasp, in his strong form moving against her, rhythmically, deliciously.

When it was over, he was pleased and his eyes had a curious gleam which thrilled her and yet had nothing to do with her. Yet it held her. He did not speak to her. He only looked straight into her eyes with a curious, gleaming look that disturbed her fearfully and deliciously. But also there was in his look some of the automatic irony of the *roué*. It left her partly cold. She was not carried away.

She went, driven by an opposite, heavier impulse to Whiston.

He stood looking gloomy, trying to admit that she had a perfect right to enjoy herself apart from him. He received her with rather grudging kindliness.

"Aren't you going to play whist?" she asked.

"Ay," he said. "Directly."

"I do wish you could dance."

"Well, I can't," he said. "So you enjoy yourself."

"But I should enjoy it better if I could dance with you."

"Nay, you're all right," he said. "I'm not made that way."

"Then you ought to be!" she cried.

"Well, it's my fault, not yours. You enjoy yourself," he bade her. Which she proceeded to do, a little bit irked.

She went with anticipation to the arms of Sam Adams, when the time came to dance with him. It *was* so gratifying, irrespective of the man. And she felt a little grudge against Whiston, soon forgotten when her host was holding her near to him, in a delicious embrace. And she watched his eyes, to meet the gleam in them, which gratified her.

She was getting warmed right through, the glow was penetrating into her, driving away everything else. Only in her heart was a little tightness, like conscience.

When she got a chance, she escaped from the dancing-room to the card-room. There, in a cloud of smoke, she found Whiston playing cribbage. Radiant, roused, animated, she came up to him and greeted him. She was too strong, too vibrant a note in the quiet room. He lifted his head, and a frown knitted his gloomy forehead.

"Are you playing cribbage? Is it exciting? How are you getting on?" she chattered.

He looked at her. None of these questions needed answering, and he did not feel in touch with her. She turned to the cribbage-board.

"Are you white or red?" she asked.

"He's red," replied the partner.

"Then you're losing," she said, still to Whiston. And she lifted the red peg from the board. "One—two—three—four—five—six—seven—eight——Right up there you ought to jump——"

"Now put it back in its right place," said Whiston.

"Where was it?" she asked gaily, knowing her transgression. He took the little red peg away from her and stuck it in its hole.

The cards were shuffled.

"What a shame you're losing!" said Elsie.

"You'd better cut for him," said the partner.

She did so, hastily. The cards were dealt. She put her hand on his shoulder, looking at his cards.

"It's good," she cried, "isn't it?"

He did not answer, but threw down two cards. It moved him more strongly than was comfortable, to have her hand on his shoulder, her curls dangling and touching his ears, whilst she was roused to another man. It made the blood flame over him.

At that moment Sam Adams appeared, florid and boisterous, intoxicated more with himself, with the dancing, than with wine. In his eye the curious, impersonal light gleamed.

"I thought I should find you here, Elsie," he cried boisterously, a disturbing, high note in his voice.

"What made you think so?" she replied, the mischief rousing in her.

The florid, well-built man narrowed his eyes to a smile.

"I should never look for you among the ladies," he said, with a kind of intimate, animal call to her. He laughed, bowed, and offered her his arm.

"Madam, the music waits."

She went almost helplessly, carried along with him, unwilling, yet delighted.

That dance was an intoxication to her. After the first few steps, she felt herself slipping away from herself. She almost knew she was going, she did not even want to go. Yet she must have chosen to go. She lay in the arm of the steady, close man with whom she was dancing, and she seemed to swim away out of contact with the room, into him. She had passed into another, denser element of him, an essential privacy. The room was all vague around her, like an atmosphere, like under sea, with a flow of ghostly, dumb movements. But she herself was held real against her partner, and it seemed she was connected with him, as if the movements of his body and limbs were her own movements, yet not her own movements—and oh, delicious! He also was given up, oblivious, concentrated, into the dance. His eye was unseeing. Only his large, voluptuous body gave off a subtle activity. His fingers seemed to search into her flesh. Every moment, and every moment, she felt she would give way utterly, and sink molten: the fusion point was coming when she would fuse down into perfect unconsciousness at his feet and knees. But he bore her round the room in the dance, and he seemed to sustain all her body with his limbs, his body, and his warmth seemed to come closer into her, nearer, till it would fuse right through her, and she would be as liquid to him, as an intoxication only.

It was exquisite. When it was over, she was dazed, and was scarcely breathing. She stood with him in the middle of the room as if she were alone in a remote place. He bent over her. She expected his lips on her bare shoulder, and waited. Yet they were not alone, they were not alone. It was cruel.

"'Twas good, wasn't it, my darling?" he said to her, low and delighted. There was a strange impersonality about his low, exultant call that appealed to her irresistibly. Yet why was she aware of some part shut off in her? She pressed his arm, and he led her towards the door.

She was not aware of what she was doing, only a little grain of resistant trouble was in her. The man, possessed, yet with a superficial presence of mind, made way to the dining-room, as if to give her refreshment, cunningly working to his own escape with her. He was molten hot, filmed over with presence of mind, and bottomed with cold disbelief.

In the dining-room was Whiston, carrying coffee to the plain, neglected ladies. Elsie saw him, but felt as if he could not see her. She was beyond his reach and ken. A sort of fusion existed between her and the large man at her side. She ate her custard, but an incomplete fusion all the while sustained and contained within the being of her employer.

But she was growing cooler. Whiston came up. She looked at him, and saw him with different eyes. She saw his slim, young man's figure real and enduring before her. That was he. But she was in the spell with the other man, fused with him, and she could not be taken away.

"Have you finished your cribbage?" she asked, with hasty evasion of him.

"Yes," he replied. "Aren't you getting tired of dancing?"

"Not a bit," she said.

"Not she," said Adams heartily. "No girl with any spirit gets tired of dancing.—Have something else, Elsie. Come—sherry. Have a glass of sherry with us, Whiston."

Whilst they sipped the wine, Adams watched Whiston almost cunningly, to find his advantage.

"We'd better be getting back—there's the music," he said. "See the women get something to eat, Whiston, will you, there's a good chap."

And he began to draw away. Elsie was drifting helplessly with him. But Whiston put himself beside them, and went along with them. In silence they passed through to the dancing-room. There Adams hesitated, and looked round the room. It was as if he could not see.

A man came hurrying forward, claiming Elsie, and Adams went to his other partner. Whiston stood watching during the dance. She was conscious of him standing there observant of her, like a ghost, or a judgment, or a guardian angel. She was also conscious, much more intimately and impersonally, of the body of the other man moving somewhere in the room. She still belonged to him, but a feeling of distraction possessed her, and helplessness. Adams danced on, adhering to Elsie, waiting his time, with the persistence of cynicism.

The dance was over. Adams was detained. Elsie found herself beside Whiston. There was something shapely about him as he sat, about his knees and his distinct figure, that she clung to. It was as if he had enduring form. She put her hand on his knee.

"Are you enjoying yourself?" he asked.

"*Ever* so," she replied, with a fervent, yet detached tone.

"It's going on for one o'clock," he said.

"Is it?" she answered. It meant nothing to her.

"Should we be going?" he said.

She was silent. For the first time for an hour or more an inkling of her normal consciousness returned. She resented it.

"What for?" she said.

"I thought you might have had enough," he said.

A slight soberness came over her, an irritation at being frustrated of her illusion.

"Why?" she said.

"We've been here since nine," he said.

That was no answer, no reason. It conveyed nothing to her. She sat detached from him. Across the room Sam Adams glanced at her. She sat there exposed for him.

"You don't want to be too free with Sam Adams," said Whiston cautiously, suffering. "You know what he is."

"How, free?" she asked.

"Why—you don't want to have too much to do with him."

She sat silent. He was forcing her into consciousness of her position. But he could not get hold of her feelings, to change them. She had a curious, perverse desire that he should not.

"I like him," she said.

"What do you find to like in him?" he said, with a hot heart.

"I don't know—but I like him," she said.

She was immutable. He sat feeling heavy and dulled with rage. He was not clear as to what he felt. He sat there unliving whilst she danced. And she, distracted, lost to herself between the opposing forces of the two men, drifted. Between the dances, Whiston kept near to her. She was scarcely conscious. She glanced repeatedly at her card, to see when she would dance again with Adams, half in desire, half in dread. Sometimes she met his steady, glaucous eye as she passed him in the dance. Sometimes she saw the steadiness of his flank as he danced. And it was always as if she rested on his arm, were borne along, upborne by him, away from herself. And always there was present the other's antagonism. She was divided.

The time came for her to dance with Adams. Oh, the delicious closing of contact with him, of his limbs touching her limbs, his arm supporting her. She seemed to resolve. Whiston had not made himself real to her. He was only a heavy place in her consciousness.

But she breathed heavily, beginning to suffer from the closeness of strain. She was nervous. Adams also was constrained.
A tightness, a tension was coming over them all. And he was
exasperated, feeling something counteracting physical magnet-
ism, feeling a will stronger with her than his own intervening
in what was becoming a vital necessity to him.

Elsie was almost lost to her own control. As she went forward
with him to take her place at the dance, she stooped for her
pocket-handkerchief. The music sounded for quadrilles. Everybody was ready. Adams stood with his body near her, exerting
his attraction over her. He was tense and fighting. She stooped
for her pocket-handkerchief, and shook it as she rose. It shook
out and fell from her hand. With agony, she saw she had taken
a white stocking instead of a handkerchief. For a second it lay
on the floor, a twist of white stocking. Then, in an instant,
Adams picked it up, with a little, surprised laugh of triumph.

"That'll do for me," he whispered—seeming to take possession of her. And he stuffed the stocking in his trousers
pocket, and quickly offered her his handkerchief.

The dance began. She felt weak and faint, as if her will were
turned to water. A heavy sense of loss came over her. She could
not help herself any more. But it was peace.

When the dance was over, Adams yielded her up. Whiston
came to her.

"What was it as you dropped?" Whiston asked.

"I thought it was my handkerchief—I'd taken a stocking by
mistake," she said, detached and muted.

"And he's got it?"

"Yes."

"What does he mean by that?"

She lifted her shoulders.

"Are you going to let him keep it?" he asked.

"I don't let him."

There was a long pause.

"Am I to go and have it out with him?" he asked, his face
flushed, his blue eyes going hard with opposition.

"No," she said, pale.

"Why?"

"No—I don't want you to say anything about it."

He sat exasperated and nonplussed.

"You'll let him keep it, then?" he asked.

She sat silent and made no form of answer.

"What do you mean by it?" he said, dark with fury. And he started up.

"No!" she cried. "Ted!" And she caught hold of him, sharply detaining him.

It made him black with rage.

"Why?" he said.

Then something about her mouth was pitiful to him. He did not understand, but he felt she must have her reasons.

"Then I'm not stopping here," he said. "Are you coming with me?"

She rose mutely, and they went out of the room. Adams had not noticed.

In a few moments they were in the street.

"What the hell do you mean?" he said, in a black fury.

She went at his side, in silence, neutral.

"That great hog, an' all," he added.

Then they went a long time in silence through the frozen, deserted darkness of the town. She felt she could not go indoors. They were drawing near her house.

"I don't want to go home," she suddenly cried in distress and anguish. "I don't want to go home."

He looked at her.

"Why don't you?" he said.

"I don't want to go home," was all she could sob.

He heard somebody coming.

"Well, we can walk a bit further," he said.

She was silent again. They passed out of the town into the fields. He held her by the arm—they could not speak.

"What's a-matter?" he asked at length, puzzled.

She began to cry again.

At last he took her in his arms, to soothe her. She sobbed by herself, almost unaware of him.

"Tell me what's a-matter, Elsie" he said. "Tell me what's a-matter—my dear—tell me, then——"

He kissed her wet face, and caressed her. She made no response. He was puzzled and tender and miserable.

At length she became quiet. Then he kissed her, and she put her arms round him, and clung to him very tight, as if for fear and anguish. He held her in his arms, wondering.

"Ted!" she whispered, frantic. "Ted!"

"What, my love?" he answered, becoming also afraid.

"Be good to me," she cried. "Don't be cruel to me."

"No, my pet," he said, amazed and grieved. "Why?"

"Oh, be good to me," she sobbed.

And he held her very safe, and his heart was white hot with love for her. His mind was amazed. He could only hold her against his chest that was white hot with love and belief in her. So she was restored at last.

III

She refused to go to her work at Adams' any more. Her father had to submit and she sent in her notice—she was not well. Sam Adams was ironical. But he had a curious patience. He did not fight.

In a few weeks, she and Whiston were married. She loved him with passion and worship, a fierce little abandon of love that moved him to the depths of his being, and gave him a permanent surety and sense of realness in himself. He did not trouble about himself any more: he felt he was fulfilled and now he had only the many things in the world to busy himself about. Whatever troubled him, at the bottom was surety. He had found himself in this love.

They spoke once or twice of the white stocking.

"Ah!" Whiston exclaimed. "What does it matter?"

He was impatient and angry, and could not bear to consider the matter. So it was left unresolved.

She was quite happy at first, carried away by her adoration of her husband. Then gradually she got used to him. He always was the ground of her happiness, but she got used to him, as to the air she breathed. He never got used to her in the same way.

Inside of marriage she found her liberty. She was rid of the responsibility of herself. Her husband must look after that. She was free to get what she could out of her time.

So that, when, after some months, she met Sam Adams, she was not quite as unkind to him as she might have been. With a young wife's new and exciting knowledge of men, she perceived he was in love with her, she knew he had always kept an unsatisfied desire for her. And, sportive, she could not help playing a little with this, though she cared not one jot for the man himself.

When Valentine's day came, which was near the first anniversary of her wedding day, there arrived a white stocking with a little amethyst brooch. Luckily Whiston did not see it, so she said nothing of it to him. She had not the faintest intention of having anything to do with Sam Adams, but once a little brooch was in her possession, it was hers, and she did not trouble her head for a moment, how she had come by it. She kept it.

Now she had the pearl ear-rings. They were a more valuable and a more conspicuous present. She would have to ask her mother to give them to her, to explain their presence. She made a little plan in her head. And she was extraordinarily pleased. As for Sam Adams, even if he saw her wearing them, he would not give her away. What fun, if he saw her wearing his ear-rings! She would pretend she had inherited them from her grandmother, her mother's mother. She laughed to herself as she went down town in the afternoon, the pretty drops dangling in front of her curls. But she saw no one of importance.

Whiston came home tired and depressed. All day the male in him had been uneasy, and this had fatigued him. She was curiously against him, inclined, as she sometimes was nowadays, to make mock of him and jeer at him and cut him off. He did not understand this, and it angered him deeply. She was uneasy before him.

She knew he was in a state of suppressed irritation. The veins stood out on the backs of his hands, his brow was drawn stiffly. Yet she could not help goading him.

"What did you do wi' that white stocking?" he asked, out of a gloomy silence, his voice strong and brutal.

"I put it in a drawer—why?" she replied flippantly.

"Why didn't you put it on the fire back?" he said harshly. "What are you hoarding it up for?"

"I'm not hoarding it up," she said. "I've got a pair."

He relapsed into gloomy silence. She, unable to move him, ran away upstairs, leaving him smoking by the fire. Again she tried on the ear-rings. Then another little inspiration came to her. She drew on the white stockings, both of them.

Presently she came down in them. Her husband still sat immovable and glowering by the fire.

"Look!" she said. "They'll do beautifully."

And she picked up her skirts to her knees, and twisted round, looking at her pretty legs in the neat stockings.

He filled with unreasonable rage, and took the pipe from his mouth.

"Don't they look nice?" she said. "One from last year and one from this, they just do. Save you buying a pair."

And she looked over her shoulders at her pretty calves, and at the dangling frills of her knickers.

"Put your skirts down and don't make a fool of yourself," he said.

"Why a fool of myself?" she asked.

And she began to dance slowly round the room, kicking up her feet half reckless, half jeering, in a ballet-dancer's fashion. Almost fearfully, yet in defiance, she kicked up her legs at him, singing as she did so. She resented him.

"You little fool, ha' done with it," he said. "And you'll backfire them stockings, I'm telling you." He was angry. His face flushed dark, he kept his head bent. She ceased to dance.

"I shan't," she said. "They'll come in very useful."

He lifted his head and watched her, with lighted, dangerous eyes.

"You'll put 'em on the fire back, I tell you," he said.

It was a war now. She bent forward, in a ballet-dancer's fashion, and put her tongue between her teeth.

"I shan't backfire them stockings," she sang, repeating his words, "I shan't, I shan't, I shan't."

And she danced round the room doing a high kick to the

tune of her words. There was a real biting indifference in her behaviour.

"We'll see whether you will or not," he said, "trollops! You'd like Sam Adams to know you was wearing 'em, wouldn't you? That's what would please you."

"Yes, I'd like him to see how nicely they fit me, he might give me some more then."

And she looked down at her pretty legs.

He knew somehow that she *would* like Sam Adams to see how pretty her legs looked in the white stockings. It made his anger go deep, almost to hatred.

"Yer nasty trolley," he cried. "Put yer petticoats down, and stop being so foul-minded."

"I'm not foul-minded," she said. "My legs are my own. And why shouldn't Sam Adams think they're nice!"

There was a pause. He watched her with eyes glittering to a point.

"Have you been havin' owt to do with him?" he asked.

"I've just spoken to him when I've seen him," she said. "He's not as bad as you would make out."

"Isn't he!" he cried, a certain wakefulness in his voice. "Them who has anything to do wi' him is too bad for me, I tell you."

"Why, what are you frightened of him for?" she mocked.

She was rousing all his uncontrollable anger. He sat glowering. Every one of her sentences stirred him up like a red-hot iron. Soon it would be too much. And she was afraid herself; but she was neither conquered nor convinced.

A curious little grin of hate came on his face. He had a long score against her.

"What am I frightened of him for?" he repeated automatically. "What am I frightened of him for? Why, for you, you stray-running little bitch."

She flushed. The insult went deep into her, right home.

"Well, if you're so dull——" she said, lowering her eyelids, and speaking coldly, haughtily.

"If I'm so dull I'll break your neck the first word you speak to him," he said, tense.

"Pf!" she sneered. "Do you think I'm frightened of you?" She spoke coldly, detached.

She was frightened, for all that, white round the mouth.

His heart was getting hotter.

"You *will* be frightened of me, the next time you have anything to do with him," he said.

"Do you think *you'd* ever be told—ha!"

Her jeering scorn made him go white hot, molten. He knew he was incoherent, scarcely responsible for what he might do. Slowly, unseeing, he rose and went out of doors, stifled, moved to kill her.

He stood leaning against the garden fence, unable either to see or hear. Below him, far off, fumed the lights of the town. He stood still, unconscious with a black storm of rage, his face lifted to the night.

Presently, still unconscious of what he was doing, he went indoors again. She stood, a small, stubborn figure with tight-pressed lips and big, sullen, childish eyes, watching him, white with fear. He went heavily across the floor and dropped into his chair.

There was a silence.

"*You're* not going to tell me everything I shall do, and everything I shan't," she broke out at last.

He lifted his head.

"I tell you *this*," he said, low and intense. "Have anything to do with Sam Adams, and I'll break your neck."

She laughed, shrill and false.

"How I hate your word 'break your neck'," she said, with a grimace of the mouth. "It sounds so common and beastly. Can't you say something else——"

There was a dead silence.

"And besides," she said, with a queer chirrup of mocking laughter, "what do you know about anything? He sent me an amethyst brooch and a pair of pearl ear-rings."

"He what?" said Whiston, in a suddenly normal voice. His eyes were fixed on her.

"Sent me a pair of pearl ear-rings, and an amethyst brooch," she repeated, mechanically, pale to the lips.

And her big, black, childish eyes watched him, fascinated, held in her spell.

He seemed to thrust his face and his eyes forward at her, as he rose slowly and came to her. She watched transfixed in terror. Her throat made a small sound, as she tried to scream.

Then, quick as lightning, the back of his hand struck her with a crash across the mouth, and she was flung back blinded against the wall. The shock shook a queer sound out of her. And then she saw him still coming on, his eyes holding her, his fist drawn back, advancing slowly. At any instant the blow might crash into her.

Mad with terror, she raised her hands with a queer clawing movement to cover her eyes and her temples, opening her mouth in a dumb shriek. There was no sound. But the sight of her slowly arrested him. He hung before her, looking at her fixedly, as she stood crouched against the wall with open, bleeding mouth, and wide-staring eyes, and two hands clawing over her temples. And his lust to see her bleed, to break her and destroy her, rose from an old source against her. It carried him. He wanted satisfaction.

But he had seen her standing there, a piteous, horrified thing, and he turned his face aside in shame and nausea. He went and sat heavily in his chair, and a curious ease, almost like sleep, came over his brain.

She walked away from the wall towards the fire, dizzy, white to the lips, mechanically wiping her small, bleeding mouth. He sat motionless. Then, gradually, her breath began to hiss, she shook, and was sobbing silently, in grief for herself. Without looking, he saw. It made his mad desire to destroy her come back.

At length he lifted his head. His eyes were glowing again, fixed on her.

"And what did he give them you for?" he asked, in a steady, unyielding voice.

Her crying dried up in a second. She also was tense.

"They came as valentines," she replied, still not subjugated, even if beaten.

"When, to-day?"

"The pearl ear-rings to-day——the amethyst brooch last year."

"You've had it a year?"

"Yes."

She felt that now nothing would prevent him if he rose to kill her. She could not prevent him any more. She was yielded up to him. They both trembled in the balance, unconscious.

"What have you had to do with him?" he asked, in a barren voice.

"I've not had anything to do with him," she quavered.

"You just kept 'em because they were jewellery?" he said.

A weariness came over him. What was the worth of speaking any more of it? He did not care any more. He was dreary and sick.

She began to cry again, but he took no notice. She kept wiping her mouth on her handkerchief. He could see it, the blood-mark. It made him only more sick and tired of the responsibility of it, the violence, the shame.

When she began to move about again, he raised his head once more from his dead, motionless position.

"Where are the things?" he said.

"They are upstairs," she quavered. She knew the passion had gone down in him.

"Bring them down," he said.

"I won't," she wept, with rage. "You're not going to bully me and hit me like that on the mouth."

And she sobbed again. He looked at her in contempt and compassion and in rising anger.

"Where are they?" he said.

"They're in the little drawer under the looking-glass," she sobbed.

He went slowly upstairs, struck a match, and found the trinkets. He brought them downstairs in his hand.

"These?" he said, looking at them as they lay in his palm.

She looked at them without answering. She was not interested in them any more.

He looked at the little jewels. They were pretty.

"It's none of their fault," he said to himself.

And he searched round slowly, persistently, for a box. He tied the things up and addressed them to Sam Adams. Then he went out in his slippers to post the little package.

When he came back she was still sitting crying.

"You'd better go to bed," he said.

She paid no attention. He sat by the fire. She still cried.

"I'm sleeping down here," he said. "Go you to bed."

In a few moments she lifted her tear-stained, swollen face and looked at him with eyes all forlorn and pathetic. A great flash of anguish went over his body. He went over, slowly, and very gently took her in his hands. She let herself be taken. Then as she lay against his shoulder, she sobbed aloud:

"I never meant——"

"My love—my little love——" he cried, in anguish of spirit, holding her in his arms.

ODOUR OF
CHRYSANTHEMUMS

I

The small locomotive engine, Number 4, came clanking, stumbling down from Selston with seven full waggons. It appeared round the corner with loud threats of speed, but the colt that it startled from among the gorse, which still flickered indistinctly in the raw afternoon, outdistanced it at a canter. A woman, walking up the railway-line to Underwood, drew back into the hedge, held her basket aside, and watched the footplate of the engine advancing. The trucks thumped heavily past, one by one, with slow inevitable movement, as she stood insignificantly trapped between the jolting black waggons and the hedge; then they curved away towards the coppice where the withered oak-leaves dropped noiselessly, while the birds, pulling at the scarlet hips beside the track, made off into the dusk that had already crept into the spinney. In the open, the smoke from the engine sank and cleaved to the rough grass. The fields were dreary and forsaken, and in the marshy strip that led to the whimsey, a reedy pit-pond, the fowls had already abandoned their run among the alders, to roost in the tarred fowl-house. The pit-bank loomed up beyond the pond, flames like red sores licking its ashy sides, in the afternoon's stagnant light. Just beyond rose the tapering chimneys and the clumsy black headstocks of Brinsley Colliery. The two wheels were spinning fast up against the sky, and the winding-engine rapped out its little spasms. The miners were being turned up.

The engine whistled as it came into the wide bay of railway-lines beside the colliery, where rows of trucks stood in harbour. Miners, single, trailing, and in groups, passed like shadows diverging home. At the edge of the ribbed level of sidings squat a low cottage, three steps down from the cinder track. A large, bony vine clutched at the house, as if to claw down the tiled roof. Round the bricked yard grew a few wintry primroses. Beyond, the long garden sloped down to a bush-covered brook-course. There were some twiggy apple trees, winter-crack trees, and ragged cabbages. Beside the path hung dishevelled pink chrysanthemums, like cloths hung on bushes. A woman came stooping out of the felt-covered fowl-house half-way down the garden. She closed and padlocked the door, then drew herself erect, having brushed some bits from her white apron.

She was a tall woman of imperious mien, handsome, with definite black eyebrows. Her smooth black hair was parted exactly. For a few moments she stood steadily watching the miners as they passed along the railway: then she turned towards the brook-course. Her face was calm and set, her mouth was closed with disillusionment. After a moment she called:

"John!" There was no answer. She waited, and then said distinctly:

"Where are you?"

"Here!" replied a child's sulky voice from among the bushes. The woman looked piercingly through the dusk.

"Are you at that brook?" she asked sternly.

For answer the child showed himself before the raspberry-canes that rose like whips. He was a small, sturdy boy of five. He stood quite still, defiantly.

"Oh!" said the mother, conciliated. "I thought you were down at that wet brook—and you remember what I told you——"

The boy did not move or answer.

"Come, come on in," she said more gently, "it's getting dark. There's your grandfather's engine coming down the line!"

The lad advanced slowly, with resentful, taciturn movement. He was dressed in trousers and waistcoat of cloth that was too thick and hard for the size of the garments. They were evidently cut down from a man's clothes.

As they went slowly towards the house he tore at the ragged

wisps of chrysanthemums and dropped the petals in handfuls along the path.

"Don't do that—it *does* look nasty," said his mother. He refrained, and she, suddenly pitiful, broke off a twig with three or four wan flowers and held them against her face. When mother and son reached the yard her hand hesitated, and instead of laying the flower aside, she pushed it in her apron band. The mother and son stood at the foot of the three steps looking across the bay of lines at the passing-home of the miners. The trundle of the small train was imminent. Suddenly the engine loomed past the house and came to a stop opposite the gate.

The engine-driver, a short man with round grey beard, leaned out of the cab high above the woman.

"Have you got a cup of tea?" he said in a cheery, hearty fashion.

It was her father. She went in, saying she would mash. Directly, she returned.

"I didn't come to see you on Sunday," began the little grey-bearded man.

"I didn't expect you," said his daughter.

The engine-driver winced; then, reassuming his cheery, airy manner, he said:

"Oh, have you heard then? Well—and what do you think——?"

"I think it is soon enough," she replied.

At her brief censure the little man made an impatient gesture, and said coaxingly, yet with dangerous coldness:

"Well, what's a man to do? It's no sort of life for a man of my years, to sit at my own hearth like a stranger. And if I'm going to marry again it may as well be soon as late—what does it matter to anybody?"

The woman did not reply, but turned and went into the house. The man in the engine-cab stood assertive, till she returned with a cup of tea and a piece of bread and butter on a plate. She went up the steps and stood near the footplate of the hissing engine.

"You needn't 'a brought me bread an' butter," said her

father. "But a cup of tea"—he sipped appreciatively—"it's very nice." He sipped for a moment or two, then: "I hear as Walter's got another bout on," he said.

"When hasn't he?" said the woman bitterly.

"I heered tell of him in the 'Lord Nelson' braggin' as he was going to spend that b—— afore he went: half a sovereign that was."

"When?" asked the woman.

"A' Sat'day night—I know that's true."

"Very likely," she laughed bitterly. "He gives me twenty-three shillings."

"Ay, it's a nice thing, when a man can do nothing with his money but make a beast of himself!" said the grey-whiskered man. The woman turned her head away. Her father swallowed the last of his tea and handed her the cup.

"Ay," he sighed, wiping his mouth. "It's a settler, it is——"

He put his hand on the lever. The little engine strained and groaned, and the train rumbled towards the crossing. The woman again looked across the metals. Darkness was settling over the spaces of the railway and trucks: the miners, in grey sombre groups, were still passing home. The winding-engine pulsed hurriedly, with brief pauses. Elizabeth Bates looked at the dreary flow of men, then she went indoors. Her husband did not come.

The kitchen was small and full of firelight; red coals piled glowing up the chimney mouth. All the life of the room seemed in the white warm hearth and the steel fender reflecting the red fire. The cloth was laid for tea; cups glinted in the shadow. At the back, where the lowest stair protruded into the room, the boy sat struggling with a knife and a piece of white wood. He was almost hidden in shadow, only his movement seemed visible. It was half past four. They had but to await the father's coming to begin tea. As the mother watched her son's sullen little struggle with the wood, she saw herself in his silence and pertinacity, she saw the father in her child's indifference to all but himself. She seemed to be occupied by her husband. He had probably gone past his home, slunk past his own door, to drink before he came in, while his dinner spoiled and wasted in waiting. She glanced at the clock, and took the potatoes to strain them in the yard. The garden and the fields beyond the brook were closed in uncertain darkness. When she rose with the saucepan, leaving the drain steaming into the night behind her, she saw the yellow lamps were lit along the highroad that went up the hill away beyond the space of the railway-lines and the field. Then again she watched the men trooping home, fewer now, and fewer.

Indoors the fire was sinking and the room was dark red. The woman put her saucepan on the hob, and set a batter pudding near the mouth of the oven. Then she stood unmoving. Directly, gratefully, came quick young steps to the door. Someone hung on the latch a moment, then a little girl entered, and began pulling off her outdoor things, dragging a mass of curls just ripening from gold to brown over her eyes with her hat.

Her mother chid her for coming late from school, and said she would have to keep her at home the dark winter days.

"Why, mother, it's hardly a bit dark. The lamp's not lighted, and my father's not home yet."

"No, he isn't. But it's a quarter to five! Did you see anything of him?"

The child became serious. She looked at her mother with large, wistful blue eyes.

"No, mother, I've never seen him. Why? Has he come up an' gone past to Old Brinsley? He hasn't, mother, 'cos I never saw him."

"He'd watch that," said the mother bitterly, "he'd take care as you didn't see him. But you may depend upon it, he's seated in the 'Prince o' Wales.' He wouldn't be this late."

The girl looked at her mother piteously.

"Let's have our teas, mother, should we?" said she. The mother called John to table.

She opened the door once more and leaned out to look across the darkness of the lines. All was deserted: she could not hear the winding-engines.

"Perhaps," she said to herself, "he's stopped to get some ripping done."

They sat down to tea. John, at the end of the table near the door, was almost lost in the darkness. Their faces were hidden from each other.

The girl crouched against the fender slowly moving a thick piece of bread before the fire. The lad, his face a dusky mark on the shadow, sat watching her who was transfigured in the hot red glow.

"I do think it's beautiful to look in the fire," said the child.

"Do you?" said her mother. "Why?"

"It's so red, and full of little caves—and it feels so nice, and you can fair smell it."

"It'll want mending directly," replied her mother. "And then if your father comes he'll carry on and say there never is a fire when a man comes home sweating from the pit.—A public house is always warm enough."

There was silence till the boy said complainingly: "Make haste, our Annie."

"Well, I am doing! I can't make the fire do it no faster, can I?"

"She keeps waflin it about so's to make 'er slow," grumbled the boy.

"Don't have such an evil imagination, child," replied the mother.

Soon the room was busy in the darkness with the crisp sound of crunching. The mother ate very little. She drank her tea determinedly, and sat thinking. When she rose her anger was evident in the stern unbending of her head. She looked at the pudding in the fender, and broke out:

"It *is* a scandalous thing as a man can't even come in to his dinner. If it's crozzled up to a cinder I don't see why I should care. Past his very door he goes to get to a public house, and here I sit with his dinner waiting for him——"

She went out. As she dropped piece after piece of coal on the red fire, the shadows fell on the walls, till the room was almost in total darkness.

"I canna see," grumbled the invisible John. In spite of herself, the mother laughed.

"You know the way to your mouth," she said. She set the dustpan outside the door. When she came again like a shadow on the hearth, the lad repeated, complaining sulkily:

"I canna see."

"Good gracious!" cried the mother irritably, "you're as bad as your father if it's a bit dusk!"

Nevertheless she took a paper spill from a sheaf on the mantelpiece and proceeded to light the lamp that hung from the ceiling in the middle of the room. As she reached up her figure displayed itself just rounding with maternity.

"Oh mother——!" exclaimed the girl.

"What?" said the woman, suspended in the act of putting the lamp-glass over the flame. The copper reflector shone handsomely on her, as she stood with uplifted arm, turning her face to her daughter.

"You've got a flower in your apron!" said the child, in a little rapture at this unusual event.

"Goodness me!" exclaimed the woman, relieved. "One would think the house was afire." She replaced the glass and waited a moment before turning up the wick. A pale shadow was seen floating weirdly on the floor.

"Let me smell!" said the child, still rapturously, coming forward and putting her face to her mother's waist.

"Go along, silly!" said the mother, turning up the lamp. The light revealed their suspense, so that the woman felt it almost unbearable. Annie was still bending at her waist. Irritably, the mother took the flowers from out of her apron band.

"Oh mother—don't take them out!" cried Annie, catching her hand, and trying to replace the sprig.

"Such nonsense!" said the mother, turning away. The child put the pale chrysanthemums to her lips, murmuring:

"Don't they smell beautiful!"

Her mother gave a short laugh.

"No," she said. "Not to me. It was chrysanthemums when I married him, and chrysanthemums when you were born, and the first time they ever brought him home drunk he'd got brown chrysanthemums in his button-hole."

She looked at the children. Their eyes and their parted lips were wondering. The mother sat rocking in silence for some time. Then she looked at the clock.

"Twenty minutes to six!" In a tone of fine bitter carelessness she continued: "Eh, he'll not come now till they bring him. There he'll stick! But he needn't come rolling in here in his pit-dirt, for *I* won't wash him. He can lie on the floor——Eh, what a fool I've been, what a fool! And this is what I came here for, to this dirty hole, rats and all, for him to slink past his very door. Twice last week—he's begun now——"

She silenced herself, and rose to clear the table.

While, for an hour or more, the children played subduedly, intent, fertile of invention, united in fear of their mother's wrath and in dread of their father's homecoming, Mrs Bates sat in her rocking-chair making a 'singlet' of thick, cream coloured flannel, which gave a dull wounded sound as she tore off the grey edge. She worked at her sewing with energy, listening to the children, and her anger wearied itself, lay down to rest, opening its eyes from time to time and steadily watching, its ears raised to listen. Sometimes, even her anger quailed and shrank, and the mother suspended her sewing, tracing the foot-steps that thudded along the sleepers outside; she would lift her head sharply to bid the children "hush," but she recovered herself in time, and the footsteps went past the gate, and the children were not flung out of their play-world.

But at last Annie sighed, and gave in. She glanced at her waggon of slippers, and loathed the game. She turned plain-tively to her mother:

"Mother!—"—but she was inarticulate.

John crept out like a frog from under the sofa. His mother glanced up.

"Yes," she said, "just look at those shirt sleeves."

The boy held them out to survey them, saying nothing. Then somebody called in a hoarse voice away down the line, and suspense bristled in the room, till two people had gone by outside, talking.

"It is time for bed," said the mother.

"My father hasn't come," wailed Annie plaintively.

But her mother was primed with courage:

"Never mind. They'll bring him when he does come—like a

log." She meant there would be no scene. "And he may sleep on the floor till he wakes himself. I know he'll not go to work tomorrow after this!"

The children had their hands and faces wiped with the flannel. They were very quiet. When they had put on their nightdresses, they said their prayers, the boy mumbling. The mother looked down at them, at the brown silken bush of intertwining curls in the nape of the girl's neck, at the little black head of the lad, and her heart burst with anger at their father, who caused all three such distress. The children hid their faces in her skirts, for comfort.

When Mrs Bates came down, the room was strangely empty, with a tension of expectancy. She took up her sewing and stitched for some time without raising her head. Meantime her anger was tinged with fear.

II

The clock struck eight and she rose suddenly, dropping her sewing on her chair. She went to the stairfoot door, opened it, listening. The children were evidently asleep. She went out, locking the door behind her.

Something scuffled down the yard, and she started, though she knew it was only the rats, with which the place was overrun. The night was very dark. In the great bay of railway-lines bulked with trucks there was no trace of light, only away back she could see a few yellow lamps at the pit-top, and the red smear of the burning pit-bank on the night. She hurried along the edge of the track, then, crossing the converging lines, came to the stile by the white gates, whence she emerged on the road. Then the fear which had led her shrank. People were walking up to New Brinsley; she saw the lights in the houses; twenty yards further on were the broad windows of the "Prince of Wales," very warm and bright, and the loud voices of men could be heard distinctly. What a fool she had been to imagine that anything had happened to him! He was merely drinking over there at the "Prince of Wales." She faltered. She had never yet been to fetch him, and she never would go. Yet, while she was out, she must get some satisfaction. So she continued her walk towards the long straggling line of houses standing blank on the highway. She entered a passage between the dwellings.

"Mr Rigley?—Yes! Did you want him? No, he's not in at this minute."

The raw-boned woman leaned forward from her dark scullery and peered at the other, upon whom fell a dim light through the blind of the kitchen window.

"Is it Mrs Bates?" she asked in a tone tinged with respect.

"Yes. I wondered if your Master was at home. Mine hasn't come yet."

"'Asn't 'e! Oh, Jack's been 'ome an' 'ad 'is dinner an' gone out. E's just gone for 'alf an 'our afore bed-time. Did you call at th' 'Prince of Wales'?"

"No——"

"No, you didn't like——! It's not very nice." The other woman was indulgent. There was an awkward pause. "Jack never said nothink about—about your Mester," she added.

"No!—I expect he's stuck in there!"

Elizabeth Bates said this bitterly, and with recklessness. She knew that the woman across the yard was standing at her door listening, but she did not care. As she turned away,

"Stop a minute! I'll just go an' ask Jack if 'e knows anythink," said Mrs Rigley.

"Oh, no—I wouldn't like to put——!"

"Yes, I will, if you'll just step inside an' see as th' childer doesn't come downstairs and set theirselves afire."

Elizabeth Bates, murmuring a remonstrance, stepped inside. The other woman apologised for the state of the room.

The kitchen needed apology. There were little frocks and trousers and childish undergarments on the squab and on the floor, and a litter of playthings everywhere. On the black American cloth of the table were pieces of bread and cake, crusts, slops, and a teapot with cold tea.

"Eh, ours is just as bad," said Elizabeth Bates. Mrs Rigley put a shawl over her head and hurried out, saying:

"I shanna be a minute."

The other sat noting with faint disapproval the general

untidiness of the room. Then she fell to counting the shoes of various sizes scattered over the floor. There were twelve. She sighed and said to herself, "No wonder!"—glancing at the litter. There came the scratching of two pairs of feet across the yard, and the Rigleys entered. Elizabeth Bates rose. Rigley was a big man, with very large bones. His head looked particularly bony. Across his temple was a blue scar, caused by a wound got in the pit, a wound in which the coal-dust remained blue like tattooing.

"'Asna 'e come whoam yit?" asked the man, without any form of greeting, but with deference and sympathy. "I couldna say wheer he is—'e's non ower theer!"—he jerked his head to signify the "Prince of Wales."

"'E's 'appen gone up to th' 'Yew,'" said Mrs Rigley.

There was another pause. Rigley had evidently something to get off his mind:

"Ah left 'im finishin' a stint," he began. "Loose-a' 'ad bin gone about ten minutes when we com'n away, an' I shouted, 'Are ter comin', Walt?' an' 'e said, 'Go on, Ah shanna be but a'ef a minnit,' so we com'n ter th' bottom, me an' Bower, thinkin' as 'e wor just behint us. Ah'd a ta'en a hoath as 'e wor just behint—an' 'ud come up i' th' next bantle——"

He stood perplexed, as if answering a charge of desertion of his mate. Elizabeth Bates, now again certain of disaster, hastened to reassure him:

"I expect 'e's gone to th' 'Yew Tree,' as you say. It's not the first time.—I've fretted myself into a fever before now. He'll come home when they carry him."

"Ay, isn't it a bit too bad!" deplored the other woman.

"I'll just step up to Dick's an' see if 'e *is* theer," offered the man, afraid of appearing alarmed, afraid of taking liberties.

"Oh, I wouldn't think of bothering you that far," said Elizabeth Bates, with emphasis. But he knew she was glad of his offer.

As they stumbled up the entry, Elizabeth Bates heard Rigley's wife run across the yard and open her neighbour's door. At this suddenly all the blood in her body seemed to switch away from her heart.

"Mind!" warned Rigley. "Ah've said many a time as Ah'd fill up them ruts in this entry, sumb'dy 'll be breakin' their legs yit."

She recovered herself and walked quickly along with the miner.

"I don't like leaving the children in bed, and nobody in the house," she said.

"No, you dunna!" he replied, courteously. They were soon at the gate of the cottage.

"Well, I shanna be many minnits. Dunna you be frettin' now, 'e'll be a' right," said the butty.

"Thank you very much, Mr Rigley," she replied.

"You're welcome!" he stammered, moving away. "I shanna be many minnits."

The house was quiet. Elizabeth Bates took off her hat and shawl, and rolled back the rug. She was in a hurry to tidy the house. Somebody would be coming, she knew. When she had finished, she sat down. It was a few minutes past nine. She was startled by the rapid chuff of the winding-engine at the pit, and the sharp whirr of the brakes on the rope as it descended. Again she felt the painful sweep of her blood, and she put her hand to her side, saying aloud, "Good gracious!—it's only the nine o'clock deputy going down," rebuking herself.

She sat still, listening. Half an hour of this, and she was wearied out.

"What am I working myself up like this for?" she said pitiably to herself, "I s'll only be doing myself some damage."

She took out her sewing again.

At a quarter to ten there were footsteps. One person! She watched for the door to open. It was an elderly woman, in a black bonnet and a black woollen shawl—his mother. She was about sixty years old, pale, with blue eyes, and her face all wrinkled and lamentable. She shut the door and turned to her daughter-in-law peevishly.

"Eh, Lizzie, whatever shall we do, whatever shall we do!" she cried.

Elizabeth drew back a little, sharply.

"What is it, mother?" she said.

The elder woman seated herself on the sofa.

"I don't know, child, I can't tell you!"—she shook her head slowly. Elizabeth sat watching her, anxious and vexed.

"I don't know," replied the grandmother, sighing very deeply. "There's no end to my troubles, there isn't. The things I've gone through, I'm sure it's enough——!" She wept without wiping her eyes, the tears running.

"But mother," interrupted Elizabeth, "what do you mean? What is it?"

The grandmother slowly wiped her eyes. The fountains of her tears were stopped by Elizabeth's directness. She wiped her eyes slowly.

"Poor child! eh, you poor thing!" she moaned. "I don't know what we're going to do, I don't—and you as you are—it's a thing, it is indeed!"

Elizabeth waited.

"Is he dead?" she asked, and at the words her heart swung violently, though she felt a slight flush of shame at the ultimate extravagance of the question. Her words sufficiently frightened the old lady, almost brought her to herself.

"Don't say so, Elizabeth! We'll hope it's not as bad as that; no, may the Lord spare us that, Elizabeth. Jack Rigley came just as I was sittin' down to a glass afore going to bed, an' 'e said, ''Appen you'll go down th' line, Mrs Bates. Walt's had an accident. 'Appen you'll go an' sit wi' 'er till we can get him home.' I hadn't time to ask him a word, afore he was gone. An' I put my bonnet on an' come straight down, Lizzie. I thought to myself, 'Eh, that poor blessed child, if anybody should come an' tell her of a sudden, there's no knowin' what'll 'appen to 'er.' You mustn't let it upset you, Lizzie—or you know what to expect. How long is it, six months—or is it five, Lizzie? Ay!"—the old woman shook her head—"time slips on, it slips on! Ay!"

Elizabeth's thoughts were busy elsewhere. If he was killed—would she be able to manage on the little pension and what she could earn?—she counted up rapidly. If he was hurt—they wouldn't take him to the hospital—how tiresome he would be to nurse!—but perhaps she'd get him away from the drink and his hateful ways. She would—while he was ill. The tears offered to come to her eyes at the picture. But what sentimental luxury was this she was beginning?—She turned to consider the children. At any rate she was absolutely necessary for them. They were her business.

"Ay!" repeated the old woman, "it seems but a week or two since he brought me his first wages. Ay—he was a good lad, Elizabeth, he was, in his way. I don't know why he got to be such a trouble, I don't. He was a happy lad at home, only full of spirits. But there's no mistake he's been a handful o' trouble, a handful o' trouble, he has! I hope the Lord'll spare him to mend his ways, I hope so, I hope so. You've had a sight o' trouble with him, Elizabeth, you have indeed. But he was a jolly enough lad wi' me, he was, I can assure you. I don't know how it is. . . ."

The old woman continued to muse aloud, a monotonous irritating sound, while Elizabeth thought concentratedly, startled once, when she heard the winding-engine chuff quickly and the brakes skirr with a shriek. Then she heard the engine more slowly, and the brakes made no sound. The old woman did not notice. Elizabeth waited in suspense. The mother-in-law talked, with lapses into silence.

"But he wasn't your son, Lizzie—an' it makes a difference. Whatever he was, I remember him when he was little, an' I learned to understand him and to make allowances. You've got to make allowances for them—"

It was half past ten, and the old woman was saying: "But it's trouble from beginning to end; you're never too old for trouble, never too old for that——" when the gate banged back, and there were heavy feet on the steps.

"I'll go, Lizzie, let me go," cried the old woman, rising. But Elizabeth was at the door. It was a man in pit-clothes.

"They're bringin' 'im, Missis," he said. Elizabeth's heart halted a moment. Then it surged on again, almost suffocating her.

"Is he—is it bad?" she asked.

The man turned away, looking at the darkness:

"The doctor says 'e'd been dead hours. 'E saw 'im i' th' lamp cabin."

The old woman, who stood just behind Elizabeth, dropped into a chair, and folded her hands, crying: "Oh, my boy, my boy!"

"Hush!" said Elizabeth, with a sharp twitch of a frown. "Be still, mother, don't waken th' children: I wouldn't have them down for anything!"

The old woman moaned softly, rocking herself. The man was drawing away. Elizabeth took a step forward.

"How was it?" she asked.

"Well, I couldn't say for sure," the man replied, very ill at ease. " 'E wor finishin' a stint, an' th' butties 'ad gone, an' a lot o' stuff come down atop 'n 'im."

"And crushed him?" cried the widow, with a shudder.

"No," said the man, "it fell at th' back of 'im. 'E wor under th' face, an' it niver touched 'im. It shut 'im in. It seems 'e wor smothered."

Elizabeth shrank back. She heard the old woman behind her cry:

"What?—what did 'e say it was?"

The man replied, more loudly: " 'E wor smothered!"

Then the old woman wailed aloud, and this relieved Elizabeth.

"Oh, mother," she said, putting her hand on the old woman, "don't waken th' children, don't waken th' children."

She wept a little, unknowing, while the old mother rocked herself and moaned. Elizabeth remembered that they were bringing him home, and she must be ready. "They'll lay him in the parlour," she said to herself, standing a moment pale and perplexed.

Then she lighted a candle and went into the tiny room. The air was cold and damp, but she could not make a fire, there was no fireplace. She set down the candle and looked round. The candle-light glittered on the lustre-glasses, on the two vases that held some of the pink chrysanthemums, and on the dark mahogany. There was a cold, deathly smell of chrysanthemums in the room. Elizabeth stood looking at the flowers. She turned away, and calculated whether there would be room to lay him on the floor, between the couch and the chiffonier. She pushed the chairs aside. There would be room to lay him down and to step round him. Then she fetched the old red table-cloth, and another old cloth, spreading them down to save her bit of carpet. She shivered on leaving the parlour; so, from the dresser drawer she took a clean shirt and put it at the fire to air. All the time her mother-in-law was rocking herself in the chair and moaning.

"You'll have to move from there, mother," said Elizabeth. "They'll be bringing him in. Come in the rocker."

The old mother rose mechanically, and seated herself by the fire, continuing to lament. Elizabeth went into the pantry for another candle, and there, in the little pent-house under the naked tiles, she heard them coming. She stood still in the pantry doorway, listening. She heard them pass the end of the house, and come awkwardly down the three steps, a jumble of shuffling footsteps and muttering voices. The old woman was silent. The men were in the yard.

Then Elizabeth heard Matthews, the manager of the pit, say: "You go in first, Jim. Mind!"

The door came open, and the two women saw a collier backing into the room, holding one end of a stretcher, on which they could see the nailed pit-boots of the dead man. The two carriers halted, the man at the head stooping to the lintel of the door.

"Wheer will you have him?" asked the manager, a short, white-bearded man.

Elizabeth roused herself and came away from the pantry, carrying the unlighted candle.

"In the parlour," she said.

"In there Jim!" pointed the manager, and the carriers backed round into the tiny room. The coat with which they had covered the body fell off as they awkwardly turned through the two doorways, and the women saw their man, naked to the waist, lying stripped for work. The old woman began to moan in a low voice of horror.

"Lay th' stretcher at th' side," snapped the manager, "an' put 'im on th' cloths. Mind now, mind! Look you now——!"

One of the men had knocked off a vase of chrysanthemums.

He stared awkwardly, then they set down the stretcher. Elizabeth did not look at her husband. As soon as she could get in the room, she went and picked up the broken vase, and the flowers.

"Wait a minute!" she said.

The three men waited in silence while she mopped up the water with a duster.

"Eh, what a job, what a job, to be sure!" the manager was saying, rubbing his brow with trouble and perplexity. "Never knew such a thing in my life, never! He'd no business to ha' been left. I never knew such a thing in my life! Fell over him clean as a whistle, an' shut him in. Not four foot of space, there wasn't—yet it scarce bruised him."

He looked down at the dead man, lying prone, half naked, all grimed with coal-dust.

"'Sphyxiated,' the doctor said. It *is* the most terrible job I've ever known. Seems as if it was done o' purpose. Clean over him, an' shut 'im in, like a mouse-trap"—he made a sharp, descending gesture with his hand.

The colliers standing by jerked aside their heads in hopeless comment.

The horror of the thing bristled upon them all.

Then they heard the girl's voice upstairs calling shrilly: "Mother, mother—who is it? Mother!—who is it?"

Elizabeth hurried to the foot of the stairs and opened the door:

"Go to sleep!" she commanded sharply. "What are you shouting about? Go to sleep at once—there's nothing——"

Then she began to mount the stairs. They could hear her on the boards, and on the plaster floor of the little bedroom. They could hear her distinctly:

"What's the matter now?—what's the matter with you, silly thing?"—her voice was much agitated, with an unreal gentleness.

"I thought it was some men come," said the plaintive voice of the child. "Has he come?"

"Yes, they've brought him. There's nothing to make a fuss about. Go to sleep now, like a good child."

They could hear her voice in the bedroom, they waited whilst she covered the children under the bedclothes.

"Is he drunk?" the girl asked, timidly, faintly.

"No! No—he's not! He—he's asleep."

"Is he asleep downstairs?"

"Yes . . . and don't make a noise."

There was silence for a moment, then the men heard the frightened child again:

"What's that noise?"

"It's nothing, I tell you, what are you bothering for?"

The noise was the grandmother moaning. She was oblivious of everything, sitting on her chair rocking and moaning. The manager put his hand on her arm and bade her "Sh—sh!!"

The old woman opened her eyes and looked at him. She was shocked by this interruption, and seemed to wonder.

"What time is it?"—the plaintive thin voice of the child, sinking back unhappily into sleep, asked this last question.

"Ten o'clock," answered the mother more softly. Then she must have bent down and kissed the children.

Matthews beckoned the men to come away. They put on their caps and took up the stretcher. Stepping over the body, they tiptoed out of the house. None of them spoke till they were far from the wakeful children.

When Elizabeth came down she found her mother alone on the parlour floor, leaning over the dead man, the tears dropping on him.

"We must lay him out," the wife said. She put on the kettle, then returned and kneeling at the feet, began to unfasten the knotted leather laces. The room was clammy and dim with only one candle, so that she had to bend her face almost to the floor. At last she got off the heavy boots, and put them away.

"You must help me now," she whispered to the old woman. Together they stripped the man.

When they arose, saw him lying in the naïve dignity of death, the women stood arrested in fear and respect. For a few moments they remained still, looking down, the old mother whimpering. Elizabeth felt countermanded. She saw him, how utterly inviolable he lay in himself. She had nothing to do with him. She could not accept it. Stooping, she laid her hand on him, in claim. He was still warm, for the mine was hot where he had died. His mother had his face between her hands, and was murmuring incoherently. The old tears fell in succession as drops from wet leaves; the mother was not weeping, merely her tears flowed. Elizabeth embraced the body of her husband, with cheek and lips. She seemed to be listening, inquiring, trying to get some connection. But she could not. She was driven away. He was impregnable.

She rose, went into the kitchen, where she poured warm water into a bowl, brought soap and flannel and a soft towel.

"I must wash him," she said. Then the old mother rose stiffly, and watched Elizabeth as she carefully washed his face, carefully brushing the big blonde moustache from his mouth with the flannel. She was afraid with a bottomless fear, so she ministered to him. The old woman, jealous, said:

"Let me wipe him!"—and she kneeled on the other side, slowly drying as Elizabeth washed, her big black bonnet sometimes brushing the dark head of her daughter. They worked thus in silence for a long time. They never forgot it was death, and the touch of the man's dead body gave them strange emotions, different in each of the women; a great dread possessed them both, the mother felt the lie was given to her womb, she was denied; the wife felt the utter isolation of the human soul, the child within her was a weight apart from her.

At last it was finished. He was a man of handsome body, and his face showed no traces of drink. He was blonde, full-fleshed, with fine limbs. But he was dead.

"Bless him," whispered his mother, looking always at his face, and speaking out of sheer terror. "The dear lad—bless him!" She spoke in a faint, sibilant ecstasy of fear and mother love.

Elizabeth sank down again to the floor, and put her face against his neck, and trembled and shuddered. But she had to draw away again. He was dead, and her living flesh had no place against his. A great dread and weariness held her: she was so unavailing. Her life was gone like this.

"White as milk he is, clear as a twelvemonth baby, bless him, the darling!" the old mother murmured to herself. "Not a mark on him, clear and clean and white, as beautiful as ever a child was made," she murmured with pride. Elizabeth kept her face hidden.

"He went peaceful, Lizzie—peaceful as sleep. Isn't he beautiful, the lamb? Ay—he must ha' made his peace, Lizzie. 'Appen he made it all right, Lizzie, shut in there. He'd have time. He wouldn't look like this if he hadn't made his peace. The lamb, the dear lamb. Eh, but he had a hearty laugh. I loved to hear it. He had the heartiest laugh, Lizzie, as a lad——"

Elizabeth looked up. The man's mouth was fallen back, slightly open, under the cover of the moustache. The eyes, half shut, did not show glazed in the obscurity. Life with its smoky burning gone from him, had left him apart and utterly alien to her. And she knew what a stranger he was to her. In her womb was ice of fear, because of this separate stranger with whom she had been living as one flesh. Was this what it all meant— utter, intact separateness, obscured by heat of living? In dread she turned her face away. The fact was too deadly. There had been nothing between them, and yet they had come together, exchanging their nakedness repeatedly. Each time he had taken her, they had been two isolated beings, far apart as now. He was no more responsible than she. The child was like ice in her womb. For as she looked at the dead man, her mind, cold and detached, said clearly: "Who am I? What have I been doing? I have been fighting a husband who did not exist. *He* existed all the time. What wrong have I done? What was that I have been living with? There lies the reality, this man."—And her soul died in her for fear: she knew she had never seen him, he had never seen her, they had met in the dark and had fought in the dark, not knowing whom they met nor whom they fought. And now she saw, and turned silent in seeing. For she had been wrong. She had said he was something he was not; she had felt familiar with him. Whereas he was apart all the while, living as she never lived, feeling as she never felt.

In fear and shame she looked at his naked body, that she had known falsely. And he was the father of her children. Her soul was torn from her body and stood apart. She looked at his

naked body and was ashamed, as if she had denied it. After all,
it was itself. It seemed awful to her. She looked at his face, and
she turned her own face to the wall. For his look was other
than hers, his way was not her way. She had denied him what
he was—she saw it now. She had refused him as himself.—And
this had been her life, and his life.—She was grateful to death,
which restored the truth. And she knew she was not dead.

And all the while her heart was bursting with grief and pity
for him. What had he suffered? What stretch of horror for this
helpless man! She was rigid with agony. She had not been able
to help him. He had been cruelly injured, this naked man, this
other being, and she could make no reparation. There were the
children—but the children belonged to life. This dead man had
nothing to do with them. He and she were only channels
through which life had flowed to issue in the children. She was
a mother—but how awful she knew it now to have been a wife.
And he, dead now, how awful he must have felt it to be a
husband. She felt that in the next world he would be a stranger
to her. If they met there, in the beyond, they would only be
ashamed of what had been before. The children had come, for
some mysterious reason, out of both of them. But the children
did not unite them. Now he was dead, she knew how eternally
he was apart from her, how eternally he had nothing more to
do with her. She saw this episode of her life closed. They had
denied each other in life. Now he had withdrawn. An anguish
came over her. It was finished then: it had become hopeless
between them long before he died. Yet he had been her husband.
But how little!

"Have you got his shirt, 'Lizabeth?"

Elizabeth turned without answering, though she strove to
weep and behave as her mother-in-law expected. But she could
not, she was silenced. She went into the kitchen and returned
with the garment.

"It is aired," she said, grasping the cotton shirt here and there
to try. She was almost ashamed to handle him; what right had
she or anyone to lay hands on him; but her touch was humble
on his body. It was hard work to clothe him. He was so heavy
and inert. A terrible dread gripped her all the while: that he

could be so heavy and utterly inert, unresponsive, apart. The horror of the distance between them was almost too much for her—it was so infinite a gap she must look across.

At last it was finished. They covered him with a sheet and left him lying, with his face bound. And she fastened the door of the little parlour, lest the children should see what was lying there. Then, with peace sunk heavy on her heart, she went about making tidy the kitchen. She knew she submitted to life, which was her immediate master. But from death, her ultimate master, she winced with fear and shame.

NEW EVE AND OLD ADAM

I

"After all," she said, with a little laugh, "I can't see it was so wonderful of you, to hurry home to me, if you are so cross when you do come."

"You would rather I stayed away?" he asked.

"I wouldn't mind."

"You would rather I had stayed a day or two in Paris—or a night or two?"

She burst into a jeering "pouf!" of laughter.

"You!" she cried. "You and Parisian Nights' Entertainments! What a fool you would look."

"Still," he said, "I could try."

"You *would*!" she mocked. "You would go dribbling up to a woman—'Please take me—my wife is so unkind to me'."

He drank his tea in silence. They had been married a year. They had married quickly, for love. And during the last three months there had gone on almost continuously that battle between them which so many married people fight, without knowing why. Now it had begun again. He felt the physical sickness rising in him. Somewhere down in his belly the big, feverish pulse began to beat, where was the inflamed place caused by the conflict between them.

She was a beautiful woman of about thirty, fair, luxuriant, with proud shoulders and a face borne up by a fierce, native vitality. Her green eyes had a curious puzzled contraction just now. She sat leaning on the table against the tea-tray, absorbed. It was as if she battled with herself in him. Her green dress reflected in the silver, against the red of the firelight. Leaning abstractedly forward, she pulled some primroses from the bowl, and threaded them at intervals in the plait which bound round her head in the peasant fashion. So, with her little starred fillet of flowers, there was something of the Gretchen about her. But her eyes retained the curious half-smile.

Suddenly her face lowered gloomily. She sank her beautiful arms, laying them on the table. Then she sat almost sullenly, as if she would not give in. She was looking away out of the window. With a quick movement she glanced down at her hands. She took off her wedding ring, reached to the bowl for a long flower-stalk, and shook the ring glittering round and round upon it, regarding the spinning gold, and spinning it as if she would spurn it. Yet there was something about her of a fretful, naughty child, as she did so.

The man sat by the fire, tired, but tense. His body seemed so utterly still because of the tension in which it was held. His limbs, thin and vigorous, lay braced like a listening thing, always vivid for action, yet held perfectly still. His face was set and expressionless. The wife was all the time, in spite of herself, conscious of him: as if the cheek that was turned towards him had a sense which perceived him. They were both rendered elemental, like impersonal forces, by the battle and the suffering.

She rose and went to the window. Their flat was the fourth, the top storey of a large house. Above the high-ridged, handsome red roof opposite was an assembly of telegraph wires, a square, squat framework, towards which hosts of wires sped from four directions, arriving in darkly sketched lines out of the white sky. High up, at a great height, a seagull sailed. There was a noise of traffic from the town beyond.

Then, from behind the ridge of the house-roof opposite a man climbed up into the tower of wires, belted himself amid the netted sky, and began to work, absorbedly. Another man, half hidden by the roof-ridge, stretched up to him with a wire. The man in the sky reached down to receive it. The other, having delivered, sank out of sight. The solitary man worked absorbedly. Then he seemed drawn away from his task. He looked round, almost furtively, from his lonely height, the space pressing on him. His eyes met those of the beautiful woman who stood in her afternoon gown, with flowers in her hair, at the window.

"I like you," she said, in her normal voice.

The husband in the darkening room with her looked round slowly and asked:

"Whom do you like?"

Receiving no answer, he resumed his tense stillness.

She remained watching at the window, above the small, quiet street of large houses. The man, suspended there in the sky, looked across at her and she at him. The city was far below. Her eyes and his met across the lofty space. Then, crouching together again into his forgetfulness, he hid himself in his work. He would not look again. Presently he climbed down, and the tower of wires was empty against the sky.

The woman glanced at the little park at the end of the clean, grey street. The diminished, dark-blue form of a soldier was seen passing between the green stretches of grass, his spurs giving the faintest glitter to his walk.

Then she turned hesitating from the window, as if drawn by her husband. He was sitting still motionless, and detached from her, hard: held absolutely away from her by his will. She wavered, then went and crouched on the hearthrug at his feet, laying her head on his knee.

"Don't be horrid with me!" she pleaded, in a caressing, languid, impersonal voice.

He shut his teeth hard, and his lips parted slightly with pain.

"You know you love me," she continued, in the same heavy, sing-song way.

He breathed hard, but kept still.

"Don't you?" she said, slowly, and she put her arms round his waist, under his coat, drawing him to her. It was as if flames of fire were running under his skin.

"I have never denied it," he said, woodenly.

"Yes," she pleaded, in the same heavy, toneless voice. "Yes. You are always trying to deny it." She was rubbing her cheek against his knee softly. Then she gave a little laugh, and shook her head. "But it's no good." She looked up at him. There was a curious light in her eyes, of subtle victory. "It's no good, my love, is it?"

His heart ran hot. He knew it was no good his trying to deny he loved her. But he saw her eyes, and his will remained set and hard. She looked away into the fire.

"You hate it that you have to love me," she said, in a pensive voice through which the triumph flickered faintly. "You hate it that you love me—and it is petty and mean of you. You hate it that you can't stay away from me. You hate it that you had to hurry back to me from Paris."

Her voice had become again quite impersonal, as if she were talking to herself.

"At any rate," he said, "it is your triumph."

She gave a sudden, bitter-contemptuous laugh.

"Ha!" she said. "What is triumph to me, you fool. You can have your triumph. I should be only too glad to give it you."

"And I to take it."

"Then take it," she cried, in hostility. "I offer it you often enough."

"But you never mean to part with it."

"It is a lie. It is you, you, who are too paltry to take a woman. How often do I fling myself at you—!"

"Then don't—don't—"

"Ha—and if I don't—I get nothing out of you. Self!—self!—that is all you are."

His face remained set and expressionless. She looked up at him. Suddenly she drew him to her again, and hid her face against him.

"Don't kick me off, Pietro, when I come to you," she pleaded.

"You *don't* come to me," he answered stubbornly.

She lifted her head a few inches away from him and seemed to listen, or to think.

"What do I do then?" she asked, for the first time quietly.

"You treat me as if I were a piece of cake, for you to eat when you wanted."

She rose from him with a mocking cry of scorn, that yet had something hollow in its sound.

"Treat you like a piece of cake, do I!" she cried. "I, who have done all I have for you—!"

There was a knock, and the maid entered with a telegram. He tore it open.

"No answer," he said, and the maid softly closed the door.

"I suppose it is for you," he said, bitingly, rising and handing her the slip of paper.

She read it, laughed, then read it again, aloud:

"'Meet me Marble Arch 7.30—theatre—Richard.' Who is Richard?" she asked, looking at her husband rather interested. He shook his head.

"Nobody of mine," he said. "Who is he?"

"I haven't the faintest notion," she said, flippantly.

"But," and his eyes went bullying, "you *must* know."

She suddenly became quiet, and jeering, took up his challenge.

"Why must I know?" she asked.

"Because it isn't for me, therefore it must be for you."

"And couldn't it be for anybody else?" she sneered.

"'Moest, 14 Merrilies Street'," he read, decisively.

For a second she was puzzled into earnestness.

"Pah, you fool," she said, turning aside. "Think of your own friends," and she flung the telegram away.

"It is not for me," he said, stiffly and finally.

"Then it is for the man in the moon—I should think *his* name is Moest," she added, with a pouf of laughter against him.

"Do you mean to say you know nothing about it?" he asked.

"'Do you mean to say'," she mocked, mouthing the words, and sneering. "Yes I do mean to say, poor little man."

He suddenly went hard with disgust.

"Then I simply don't believe you," he said coldly.

"Oh—don't you believe me," she jeered, mocking the touch of sententiousness in his voice. "What a calamity—the poor man doesn't believe!"

"It couldn't possibly be any acquaintance of mine—" he said slowly.

"Then hold your tongue," she cried harshly. "I've heard enough of it."

He was silent, and soon she went out of the room. In a few minutes he heard her in the drawing-room, improvising furiously. It was a sound that maddened him; something yearning, yearning, striving, and something perverse, that counteracted the yearning. Her music was always working up towards a certain culmination, but never reaching it, falling away in a jangle. How he hated it. He lit a cigarette, and went across to the side board for whisky and soda. Then she began to sing. She had a good voice, but she could not keep time. As a rule it made his heart warm with tenderness for her, hearing her ramble through the songs in her own fashion, making Brahms sound so different by altering all his time. But today he hated her for it. Why the devil couldn't she submit to the natural laws of the stuff!

In about fifteen minutes she entered laughing. She laughed as she closed the door, and as she came to him where he sat.

"Oh," she said, "you silly thing, you silly thing! Aren't you a stupid clown?"

She crouched between his knees and put her arms round him. She was smiling into his face, her green eyes, looking into his, were bright and wide. But somewhere in them, as he looked back, was a little twist that could not come loose to him, a little cast, that was like an aversion from him, a strain of hate for him. The hot waves of blood flushed over his body, and his heart seemed to dissolve under her caresses. But at last, after many months, he knew her well enough. He knew that curious little strain in her eyes, which was waiting for him to submit to her, and then would spurn him again. He resisted her while ever it was there.

"Why don't you let yourself love me?" she asked, pleading, but a touch of mockery in her voice. His jaw set hard.

"Is it because you are afraid?"

He heard the slight sneer.

"Of what?" he asked.

"Afraid to trust yourself?"

There was silence. It made him furious that she could sit there caressing him and yet sneer at him.

"What *have* I done with myself?" he asked.

"Carefully saved yourself from giving all to me, for fear you might lose something."

"Why should I lose anything?" he asked.

And they were both silent. She rose at last and went away from him to get a cigarette. The silver box flashed red with firelight in her hands. She struck a match, bungled, threw the stick aside, lit another.

"What did you come running back for?" she asked, insolently, talking with half-shut lips because of the cigarette. "I told you I wanted peace—I've had none for a year. And for the last three months you've done nothing but try to destroy me."

"You have not gone frail on it," he answered sarcastically.

"Nevertheless," she said, "I am ill inside me. I am sick of you—sick. You make an eternal demand, and you give nothing back. You leave one empty." She puffed the cigarette in feminine fashion, then suddenly she struck her forehead with a wild gesture. "I have a ghastly, empty feeling in my head," she said. "I feel I simply *must* have rest—I must."

The rage went through his veins like flame.

"From your labours?" he asked, sarcastically, suppressing himself.

"From you—from *you*!" she cried, thrusting forward her head at him. "You, who use a woman's soul up, with your rotten life.—I suppose it is partly your health, and you can't help it," she added, more mildly. "But I simply can't stand it—I simply can't, and that is all."

She shook her cigarette carelessly in the direction of the fire. The ash fell on the beautiful asiatic rug. She glanced at it, but did not trouble. He sat, hard with rage.

"May I ask how I use you up, as you say?" he asked.

She was silent a moment, trying to get her feeling into words. Then she shook her hand at him passionately, and took the cigarette from her mouth.

"By—by following me about—by not leaving me *alone*. You give me no peace.—*I* don't know what you do, but it is something ghastly."

Again the hard stroke of rage went down his veins.

"It is very vague," he said.

"I know," she cried. "I can't put it into words—but there it is.—You—you don't love. I pour myself out to you, and then—there's nothing there—you simply aren't there."

He was silent for some time. His jaw had set hard with fury and hate.

"We have come to the incomprehensible," he said.—"And now, what about Richard?"

It had grown nearly dark in the room. She sat silent for a moment. Then she took the cigarette from her mouth and looked at it.

"I'm going to meet him," her voice, mocking, answered out of the twilight.

His heart went molten, and he could scarcely breathe.

"Who is he?" he asked, though he did not believe the affair to be anything at all, even if there were a Richard.

"I'll introduce him to you when I know him a little better," she said. He waited.

"But who is he?"

"I tell you, I'll introduce him to you later."

There was a pause.

"Shall I come with you?"

"It would be like you," she answered, with a sneer.

The maid came in, softly, to draw the curtains and turn on the light. The husband and wife sat silent.

"I suppose," he said, when the door was closed again, "you are wanting a Richard for a rest?"

She took his sarcasm simply as a statement.

"I am," she said. "A simple, warm man who would love me without all these reservations and difficulties. That is just what I do want."

"Well, you have your own independence," he said.

"Ha," she laughed. "You needn't tell me that. It would take more than you to rob me of my independence."

"I meant your own income," he answered quietly, while his heart was plunging with bitterness and rage.

"Well," she said, "I will go and dress."

He remained without moving, in his chair. The pain of this

was almost too much. For some moments the great, inflamed pulse struck through his body. It died gradually down, and he went dull. He had not wanted to separate from her at this point of their union: they would probably, if they parted in such a crisis, never come together again. But if she insisted, well then, it would have to be. He would go away for a month. He could easily make business in Italy. And when he came back, they could patch up some sort of domestic arrangement, as most other folk had to do.

He felt dull and heavy inside, and without the energy for anything. The thought of having to pack and take a train to Milan appalled him, it would mean such an effort of will. But it would have to be done, and so he must do it. It was no use his waiting at home. He might stay in town a night, at his brother-in-law's, and go away the next day. It were better to give her a little time to come to herself. She was really impulsive. And he did not really want to go away from her.

He was still sitting thinking, when she came downstairs. She was in costume and furs and toque. There was a radiant, half wistful, half perverse look about her. She was a beautiful woman, her bright, fair face set among the black furs.

"Will you give me some money?" she said. "There isn't any."

He took two sovereigns, which she put in her little black purse. She would go without a word of reconciliation. It made his heart set hard again.

"You would like me to go away for a month?" he said, calmly.

"Yes," she answered, stubbornly.

"All right then, I will. I must stop in town for tomorrow, but I will sleep at Edmund's."

"You could do that, couldn't you?" she said, accepting his suggestion, a little bit hesitating.

"If you want me to."

She knitted her brow, and put up her face pathetically.

"I'm so *tired*!" she lamented.

But there was exasperation and hate in the last word, too.

"Very well," he answered.

She finished buttoning her glove.

"You'll go, then?" she said, suddenly brightly, turning to depart. "Goodbye."

He hated her for the flippant insult of her leavetaking.

"I shall be at Edmund's tomorrow," he said.

"You will write to me from Italy, won't you?"

He would not answer the unnecessary question.

"Have you taken the dead primroses out of your hair?" he asked.

"I haven't," she said.

And she unpinned her hat.

"Richard *would* think me cracked," she said, picking out the crumpled, creamy fragments.

"Lovable and pathetic," he answered, sarcastic and bitter.

She strewed the withered flowers carelessly on the table, set her hat straight.

"Do you *want* me to go?" he asked, again, rather yearning.

She knitted her brows. It irked her to resist the appeal. Yet she had in her breast a hard, repellant feeling for him. She had loved him, too. She had loved him dearly. And—he had not seemed to realise her. So that now she *did* want to be free of him for a while. Yet the love, the passion she had had for him clung about her. But she did want, first and primarily, to be free of him again.

"Yes," she said, half pleading.

"Very well," he answered.

She came across to him, and put her arms round his neck. Her hatpin caught his head, but he moved, and she did not notice.

"You don't mind very much, do you, my love?" she said caressingly.

"I mind all the world, and all I am," he said.

She rose from him, fretted, miserable, and yet determined.

"I *must* have some rest," she repeated.

He knew that cry. She had had it, on occasions, for two months now. He had cursed her, and refused either to go away or to let her go. Now he knew it was no use.

"All right," he said. "Go and get it from Richard."

"Yes."—She hesitated. "Goodbye," she called, and was gone.

He heard her cab whirr away. He had no idea whither she was gone—but probably to Madge, her friend.

He went upstairs to pack. Their bedroom made him suffer. She used to say, at first, that she would give up anything rather than her sleeping with him. And still they were always together. A kind of blind helplessness drove them to one another, even when, after he had taken her, they only felt more apart than ever. It had seemed to her that he had been mechanical and barren with her. She felt a horrible feeling of aversion from him, inside her, even while physically she still desired him. His body had always a kind of fascination for her. But had hers for him? He seemed, often, just to have served her, or to have obeyed some impersonal instinct for which she was the only outlet, in his loving her. So at last she rose against him, to cast him off. He seemed to follow her so, to draw her life into his. It made her feel she would go mad. For he seemed to do it just blindly, without having any notion of her herself. It was as if she were sucked out of herself by some non-human force. As for him, he seemed only like an instrument for his work, his business, not like a person at all. Sometimes she thought he was a big fountain pen which was always sucking at her blood for ink.

He could not understand anything of this. He loved her—he could not bear to be away from her. He tried to realise her and to give her what she wanted. But he could not understand. He could not understand her accusations against him. Physically, he knew, she loved him, or had loved him, and was satisfied, or had been satisfied by him. He also knew that she would have loved another man nearly as well. And for the rest, he was only himself. He could not understand what she said about his using her and giving her nothing in return. Perhaps he did not think of her, as a separate person from himself, sufficiently. But then he did not see, he could not see that she had any real personal life, separate from himself. He tried to think of her in every possible way, and to give her what she wanted. But it was no good, she was never at peace. And lately there had been growing a breach between them. They had never come together without his realising it, afterwards. Now he must submit, and go away.

And her quilted dressing gown—it was a little bit torn, like most of her things—and her pearl-backed mirror, with one of the pieces of pearl missing—all her untidy, flimsy, lovable things, hurt him as he went about the bedroom, and made his heart go hard with hate, in the midst of his love.

2

Instead of going to his brother-in-law's, he went to an hôtel for the night. It was not till he stood in the lift with the attendant at his side that he began to realise that he was only a mile or so away from his own home, and yet further away than any miles could make him. It was about nine o'clock. He hated his bedroom. It was comfortable, and not ostentatious: its only fault was the neutrality necessary to an hôtel apartment. He looked round. There was one semi-erotic, Florentine picture of a lady with cats' eyes, over the bed. It was not bad. The only other ornament on the walls was the notice of hours and prices of meals and rooms. The couch sat correctly before the correct little table, on which the writing sachet and inkstand stood mechanically. Down below, the quiet street was half illuminated, the people passed sparsely, like stunted shadows. And of all times of the night, it was a quarter past nine. He thought he would go to bed. Then he looked at the white-and-glazed doors which shut him off from the bath. He would bath to pass the time away—in the bath-closet everything was so comfortable and white and warm—too warm: the level, unvarying heat of the atmosphere, from which there was no escape anywhere, seemed so hideously hôtel-like; this central-heating forced a unity into the great building, making it more than ever like an enormous box with incubating cells. He loathed it. But at any rate the bath-closet was human, white and business-like and luxurious.

He was trying, with the voluptuous warm water, and the exciting thrill of the shower-bath, to bring back the life into his dazed body. Since she had begun to hate him, he had gradually lost that physical pride and pleasure in his own physique which the first months of married life had given him. His body had gone meaningless to him again, almost as if it were not there. It had wakened up, there had been the physical glow and satisfaction about his movements, of a creature which rejoices in itself; a glow which comes on a man who loves and is loved passionately and successfully. Now this was going again. All the life was accumulating in his mental consciousness, and his body felt like a piece of waste. He was not aware of this. It was instinct which made him want to bathe. But that, too, was a failure. He went under the shower-spray with his mind occupied by business, or some care of affairs, taking the tingling water almost without knowing it, stepping out mechanically, as a man going through a barren routine. He was dry again, and looking out of the window, without having experienced anything during the last hour.

Then he remembered that she did not know his address. He scribbled a note and rang to have it posted.

As soon as he had turned out the light, and there was nothing left for his mental consciousness to flourish amongst, it dropped, and it was dark inside him as without. It was his blood, and the elemental male in it, that now rose from him: unknown instincts and unperceived movements out of the depths of his physical being rose and heaved blindly. The darkness almost suffocated him, and he could not bear it, that he was shut in this great, warm building. He wanted to be outside, with space springing from him. But again, the reasonable being in him knew it was ridiculous, and he remained staring at the dark, having the horrible sensation of a roof low down over him; whilst that dark, unknown being, which lived below all his consciousness in the eternal gloom of his blood, heaved and raged blindly against him.

It was not his thoughts that represented him. They spun like straws or the iridescence of oil on a dark stream. He thought of her, sketchily, spending an evening of light amusement with the symbolical Richard. That did not mean much to him. He did not really speculate about Richard. He had the dark, powerful sense of her, how she wanted to get away from him and from the deep, underneath intimacy which had gradually come between them, back to the easy, everyday life, where one knows nothing of the underneath, so that it takes its way apart from the consciousness. She did not want to have the deeper part of herself in direct contact with or under the influence of any other intrinsic being. She wanted, in the deepest sense, to be free of him. She could not bear the close, basic intimacy into which she had been drawn. She wanted her life for herself. It was true, her strongest desire had been previously to know the contact through the whole of her being, down to the very bottom. Now it troubled her. She wanted to disengage her roots. Above, in the open, she would give. But she must live perfectly free of herself, and not, at her source, be connected with anybody.——She was using this symbolical Richard as a spade to dig him away from her. And he felt like a thing whose roots are all straining on their hold, and whose elemental life, that blind source, surges backwards and forwards darkly in a chaos, like something which is threatened with spilling out of its own vessel.

This tremendous swaying of the most elemental part of him continued through the hours, accomplishing his being, whilst superficially he thought at random of the journey, of the Italian he would speak, how he had left his coat in the train, and the rascally official interpreter had tried to give him twenty lire for a sovereign—how the man in the hat-shop in the Strand had given him the wrong change—of the new shape in hats, and the new felt—and so on. Underneath it all, like the sea under a pleasure-pier, his elemental, physical soul was heaving in great waves through his blood and his tissue, the sob, the silent lift, the slightly-washing fall away again. So his blood, out of whose darkness everything rose, being moved to its depths by her revulsion, heaved and swung towards its own rest, surging blindly to its own re-settling.

Without knowing it, he suffered that night almost more than he had ever suffered during his life. But it was all below his consciousness. It was his life itself at storm, not his mind and his will engaged at all.

In the morning he got up, thin and quiet, without much

movement anywhere, only with some of the clearness of after-storm. His body felt like a clean, empty shell. His mind was limpidly clear. He went through the business of the toilet with a certain accuracy, and at breakfast, in the restaurant, there was about him that air of neutral correctness which makes men seem so unreal.

At lunch there was a telegram for him. It was like her to telegraph.

"Come to tea, my dear love."

As he read it, there was a great heave of resistance in him. But then he faltered. With his consciousness, he remembered how impulsive and eager she was when she dashed off her telegrams, and he relaxed. It went without saying that he would go.

3

When he stood in the lift going up to his own flat, he was almost blind with the hurt of it all. They had loved each other so much, in this his first home. The parlour-maid opened to him, and he smiled at her, affectionately. In the golden-brown and cream-coloured hall—Paula would have nothing heavy or sombre about her—a bush of rose-coloured azaleas shone, and a little tub of lilies twinkled naïvely.

She did not come out to meet him.

"Tea is in the drawing-room," the maid said, and he went in while she was hanging up his coat. It was a big room, with a sense of space, and a spread of whitey carpet—almost the colour of unpolished marble—and grey and pink border; of pink roses on big white cushions, pretty Dresden China, and deep, chintz-covered chairs and sofas which looked as if they were used freely. It was a room where one could roll in soft, fresh comfort, a room which had not much breakable in it, and which seemed, in the dusky spring evening, fuller of light than the streets outside.

Paula rose, looking queenly and rather radiant, as she held out her hand. A young man, whom Peter scarcely noticed, rose on the other side the hearth.

"I expected you an hour ago," she said, looking into her

husband's eyes. But though she looked at him, she did not see him. And he sank his head.

"This is another Moest," she said, presenting the stranger. "He knows Richard, too."

The young man, a German of about thirty, with a clean-shaven aesthetic face, long black hair brushed back a little wearily or bewildered from his brow, and inclined to fall in an odd loose strand again, so that he nervously put it back with his fine hand, looked at Moest and bowed. He had a finely cut face, but his dark blue eyes were strained, as if he did not quite know where he was. He sat down again, and his pleasant figure took a self-conscious attitude, of a man whose business it was to say things that should be listened to. He was not conceited or affected—naturally sensitive and rather naïve; but he could only move in an atmosphere of literature and literary ideas; yet he seemed to know there was something else, vaguely, and he felt rather at a loss. He waited for the conversation to move his way, as inert an insect waits, for the sun to set it flying.

"Another Moest," Paula was pronouncing emphatically. "Actually another Moest, of whom we have never heard, and under the same roof with us."

The stranger laughed, his lips moving nervously over his teeth.

"You are in this house?" Peter asked surprised.

The young man shifted in his chair, dropped his head, looked up again.

"Yes," he said, meeting Moest's eyes as if he were somewhat dazzled. "I am staying with the Lauriers, on the second flat."

He spoke English slowly, with a quaint, musical quality in his voice, and a certain rhythmic enunciation.

"I see, and the telegram was for you?" said the host.

"Yes," replied the stranger, with a nervous little laugh.

"My husband," broke in Paula, evidently repeating to the German what she had said before, for Peter's benefit this time, "was quite convinced I had an *affaire*"—she pronounced it in the French fashion—"with this terrible Richard."

The German give his little laugh, and moved, painfully self-conscious, in his chair.

"Yes," he said, glancing at Moest.

"Did you spend a night of virtuous indignation," Paula laughed to her husband, "imagining my perfidy?"

"I did not," said her husband. "Were you at Madge's?"

"No," she said. Then, turning to her guest: "Who is Richard, Mr Moest?"

"Richard," began the German, word by word, "is my cousin." He glanced quickly at Paula, to see if he were understood. She rustled her skirts, and arranged herself comfortably, lying, or almost squatting, on the sofa by the fire. "He lives in Hampstead."

"And what is he like?" she asked, with eager interest.

The German gave his little laugh. Then he moved his fingers across his brow, in his dazed fashion. Then he looked, with his beautiful blue eyes, at his beautiful hostess.

"I—" he laughed again nervously—"He is a man whose parts—are not very much—very well known to me. You see," he broke forth, and it was evident he was now conversing to an imaginary audience; he grasped at the air with his hand, and his eyes had the blind look of one thinking hard—"I cannot easily express myself in English.—I—I never have talked it. I shall speak, because I know nothing of modern England, a kind of Renaissance English."

"How lovely!" cried Paula. "But if you would rather, speak German. We shall understand sufficiently."

"I would rather hear some Renaissance English," said Moest.

Paula was quite happy with the new stranger. She listened to descriptions of Richard, shifting animatedly on her sofa. She wore a new dress, of a rich red tile colour, glossy and long and soft, and she had threaded daisies, like buttons, in the banded plait of her hair. Her husband hated her for these familiarities. But she was beautiful too, and warm-hearted. Only, through all her warmth and kindliness, lay, he said, at the bottom, an almost feline selfishness, a coldness.

She was playing to the stranger—nay, she was not playing, she was really occupied by him. The young man was the favorite disciple of the most famous present-day German poet and 'Meister'. He himself was occupied in translating Shakspere.

Having been always a poetic disciple, he had never come into touch with life save through literature, and for him, since he was a rather fine-hearted young man with a human need to live, this was a tragedy. Paula was not long in discovering what ailed him, and she was eager to come to his rescue.

It pleased her, nevertheless, to have her husband sitting by, watching her. She forgot to give tea to anyone. Moest, and the German, both helped themselves, and the former attended also to his wife's cup. He sat rather in the background, listening, and waiting. She had made a fool of him with her talk to this stranger of "Richard"; lightly and flippantly she had made a fool of him. He minded, but was used to it. Now she had absorbed herself in this dazed, starved, literature-bewildered young German, who was, moreover, really lovable, evidently a gentleman. And she was seeing in him her mission—"Just as," said Moest bitterly to himself, "she saw her mission in me, a year ago. She is no woman. She's got a big heart for everybody, but it must be like a common room: she's got no private, sacred heart, except perhaps for herself, where there's no room for a man in it."

At length the stranger rose to go, promising to come again.

"Isn't he adorable!" cried Paula, as her husband returned to the drawing-room. "I think he is simply adorable."

"Yes!" said Moest.

"He called this morning to ask about the telegram.—But poor devil, isn't it a shame, what they've done to him!"

"What who have done to him?" her husband asked, coldly, jealous.

"Those literary creatures.—They take a young fellow like that, and stick him up among the literary gods, like a mantel-piece ornament, and there he has to sit, being a minor ornament, while all his youth is gone.—It is criminal."

"He should get off the mantel-piece then," said Moest.

But inside him his heart was black with rage against her. What had she, after all, to do with this young man, when he himself was being smashed up by her. He loathed her pity and her kindliness, which was like a charitable institution. There was no core to the woman. She was full of generosity and bigness and kindness, but there was no heart in her, no security, no place for one single man. He began to understand now syrens and sphinxes and the other Greek fabulous, female things. They had not been created by fancy, but out of bitter necessity of the man's human heart to express itself.

"Ha!" she laughed, half contemptuous. "Did *you* get off your miserable starved isolation by yourself?—you didn't. You had to be fetched down, and I had to do it."

"Out of your usual charity," he said.

"But you can sneer at another man's difficulties," she said.

"Your name ought to be Panacea, not Paula," he replied.

He felt furious and dead against her. He could even look at her without the tenderness coming. And he was glad. He hated her. She seemed unaware. Very well, let her be so.

"Oh, but he makes me so miserable, to see him!" she cried. "Self-conscious, can't get into contact with anybody, living a false literary life like a man who takes poetry as a drug.—One *ought* to help him."

She was really earnest and distressed.

"Out of the frying-pan into the fire," he said.

"I'd rather be in the fire any day, than in a frying-pan," she said, abstractedly, with a little shudder. She never troubled to see the meaning of her husband's sarcasms.

They remained silent. The maid came in for the tray, and to ask him if he would be in to dinner. He waited for his wife to answer. She sat with her chin in her hands, brooding over the young German, and did not hear. The rage flashed up in his heart. He would have liked to smash her out of this false absorption.

"No," he said to the maid. "I think not. Are you at home for dinner, Paula?"

"Yes," she said.

And he knew by her tone, easy and abstracted, that she intended him to stay too. But she did not trouble to say anything.

At last, after some time, she asked:

"What did you do?"

"Nothing—went to bed early," he replied.

"Did you sleep well?"

"Yes thank you."

And he recognised the ludicrous civilities of married people, and he wanted to go. She was silent for a time. Then she asked, and her voice had gone still and grave:

"Why don't you ask me what I did?"

"Because I don't care—you just went to somebody's for dinner."

"Why don't you care what I do? Isn't it your place to care?"

"About the things you do to spite me?—no!"

"Ha!" she mocked. "I did nothing to spite you. I was in deadly earnest."

"Even with your Richard."

"Yes," she cried. "There *might* have been a Richard. What did you care?"

"In that case you'd have been a liar and worse, so why should I care about you then?"

"You *don't* care about me," she said, sullenly.

"You say what you please," he answered.

She was silent for some time.

"And did you do absolutely nothing last night?" she asked.

"I had a bath and went to bed."

Then she pondered.

"No," she said, "you don't care for me—"

He did not trouble to answer. Softly, a little china clock sang six.

"I shall go to Italy in the morning," he said.

"Yes."

"And," he said, slowly, forcing the words out, "I shall stay at the Aquila Nera at Milan—you know my address."

"Yes," she answered.

"I shall be away about a month. Meanwhile you can rest."

"Yes," she said, in her throat, with a little contempt of him and his stiffness.

He, in spite of himself, was breathing heavily. He knew that this parting was the real separation of their souls, marked the point beyond which they could go no further, but accepted the marriage as a comparative failure. And he had built all his life on his marriage. She accused him of not loving her. He gripped the arms of his chair. Was there something in it? Did he only want the attributes which went along with her, the peace of heart which a man has in living to one woman, even if the love between them be not complete; the singleness and unity in his life that made it easy; the fixed establishment of himself as a married man with a home; the feeling that he belonged to somewhere, that one woman existed—not was paid, but *existed*,—really to take care of him; was it these things he wanted, and not her? But he wanted her for these purposes— her, and nobody else. But was that not enough for her. Perhaps he wronged her—it was possible. What she said against him was in earnest. And what she said in earnest he had to believe, in the long run, since it was the utterance of her being. He felt miserable and tired.

When he looked at her, across the gathering twilight of the room, she was staring into the fire and biting her finger nail, restlessly, restlessly, without knowing. And all his limbs went suddenly weak, as he realised that she suffered too, that something was gnawing at her. Something in the look of her, the crouching, dogged, wondering look, made him faint with tenderness for her.

"Don't bite your finger nails," he said quietly, and obediently, she took her hand from her mouth. His heart was beating quickly. He could feel the atmosphere of the room changing. It had stood aloof, the room, like something placed round him, like a great box. Now everything got softer, as if it partook of the atmosphere, of which he partook himself, and they were all one.

His mind reverted to her accusations, and his heart beat like a caged thing against what he could not understand. She said he did not love her. But he knew that, in his way he did. In his way—but was his way wrong? His way was himself, he thought, struggling. Was there something wrong, something missing in his nature, that he could not love? He struggled madly, as if he were in a mesh, and could not get out. He did not want to believe that he was deficient in his nature. Wherein was he deficient? It was nothing physical. She said he could not come out of himself, that he was no good to her, because he could not get outside himself. What did she mean? Get outside himself! It seemed like some acrobatic feat, some slippery contortionist trick. No, he could not understand. His heart flashed hot with resentment. She did nothing but find fault with him. What did she care about him, really, when she could taunt him with not being able to take a light woman when he was in Paris.— Though his heart, forced to do her justice, knew that for this she loved him, really.

But it was too complicated and difficult, and already, as they sat thinking, it had gone wrong between them, and things felt twisted, horribly twisted, so that he could not breathe. He must go. He could dine at the hôtel and go to the theatre.

"Well," he said, casually, "I must go. I think I shall go and see 'The Black Sheep'."

She did not answer. Then she turned and looked at him with a queer, half bewildered, half perverse smile that seemed conscious of pain. Her eyes, shining rather dilated and triumphant, and yet with something heavily yearning behind them, looked into his. He could not understand, and, between her appeal and her defiant triumph, he felt as if his chest were crushed so he could not breathe.

"My love," she said, in a little singing, abstract fashion, her lips somehow sipping towards him, her eyes shining dilated: and yet he felt as if he were not in it, himself.

His heart was a flame that prevented his breathing. He gripped the chair like a man who is going to be put under torture.

"What?" he said, staring back at her.

"Oh my love!" she said softly with a little, intense laugh on her face, that made him pant. And she slipped from her sofa and came across to him, quickly, and put her hand hesitating on his hair. The blood struck like flame across his consciousness, and the hurt was keen like joy, like the releasing of something that hurts as the pressure is relaxed and the movement comes, before the peace. Afraid, his fingers touched her hand, and she sank swiftly between his knees, and put her face on his breast. He held her head hard against his chest, and again and again the flame went down his blood, as he felt her round, small, nut of a head between his hands pressing into his chest where the hurt had been bruised in so deep. His wrists quivered as he pressed her head to him, as he felt the deadness going out of him; the real life, released, flowing into his body again. How hard he had shut it off, against her, when she hated him. He was breathing heavily with relief, blindly pressing her head against him. He believed in her again.

She looked up, laughing, childish, inviting him with her lips. He bent to kiss her, and as his eyes closed, he saw hers were shut. The feeling of restoration was almost unbearable.

"Do you love me?" she whispered, in a little ecstasy.

He did not answer, except with the quick tightening of his arms, clutching her a little closer against him. And he loved the silkiness of her hair, and its natural scent. And it hurt him that the daisies she had threaded in should begin to wither. He resented their hurting her by their dying.

He had not understood. But the trouble had gone off. He was quiet, and he watched her from out of his sensitive stillness, a little bit dimly, unable to recover. She was loving to him, protective, and bright, laughing like a glad child too.

"We must tell Maud I shall be in to dinner," he said.

That was like him—always aware of the practical side of the case, and the appearances. She laughed a little little bit ironically—why should she have to take her arms from round him, just to tell Maud he would be in to dinner?

"I'll go," she said.

He drew the curtains and turned on the light in the big lamp that stood in a corner. The room was dim, and palely warm. He loved it dearly.

His wife, when she came back, as soon as she had closed the door, lifted her arms to him in a little ecstasy, coming to him. They clasped each other close, body to body. And the intensity of his feeling was so fierce, he felt himself going dim, fusing into something soft and plastic between her hands. And this connection with her was bigger than life or death. And at the bottom of his heart was a sob.

She was gay and winsome, at the dinner. Like lovers, they

were just deliciously waiting for the night to come up. But there
remained in him always the slightly broken feeling which the
night before had left.

"And you won't go to Italy," she said, as if it were an
understood thing.

She gave him the best things to eat, and was solicitous for his
welfare—which was not usual with her. It gave him deep, shy
pleasure. He remembered a verse she was often quoting as one
she loved. He did not know it for himself:

> "On my breasts I warm thy foot-soles
> Wine I pour, and dress thy meats;
> Humbly, when my lord disposes
> Lie with him on perfumed sheets—"

She said it to him sometimes, looking up at him from the
pillow. But it never seemed real to him. She might, in her sudden
passion, put his feet between her breasts. But he never felt like
a lord, never more pained and insignificant than at those times.
As a little girl, she must have subjected herself before her dolls.
And he was something like her lordliest plaything. He liked
that too. If only——.

Then, seeing some frightened little way of looking at him,
which she had, the pure pain came back. He loved her, and it
would never be peace between them, she would never belong
to him, as a wife. She would take him and reject him, like a
mistress. And perhaps for that reason he would love her all the
more: it might be so.

But then, he forgot. Whatever was or was not, now she loved
him. And whatever came after, this evening he was the lord.
What matter if he were deposed tomorrow, and she hated him!

Her eyes, wide and candid, were staring at him a little bit
wondering, a little bit forlorn. She knew he had not quite come
back. He held her close to him.

"My love," she murmured consolingly. "My love."

And she put her fingers through his hair, arranging it in little,
loose curves, playing with it and forgetting everything else. He
loved that dearly, to feel the light lift and touch—touch—of her

finger-tips making his hair, as she said, like an Apollo's. She lifted his face to see how he looked, and, with a little laugh of love, kissed him. And he loved to be made much of by her. But he had the dim, hurting sense, that she would not love him tomorrow, that it was only her great need to love that exalted him tonight. He *knew* he was no king: he did not feel a king, even when she was crowning and kissing him.

"Do you love me?" she asked, playfully whispering.

He held her fast and kissed her; while the blood hurt in his heart-chambers.

"You know," he answered, with a struggle.

Later, when he lay holding her with a passion intense like pain, the words blurted from him:

"Flesh of my flesh—Paula!—Will you——?"

"Yes my love," she answered, consolingly.

He bit his mouth with pain. For him it was almost an agony of appeal.

"But Paula—I mean it—flesh of my flesh—a wife—?"

She tightened her arms round him without answering. And he knew, and she knew that she put him off like that.

4

Two months later, she was writing to him in Italy: "Your idea of your woman is that she is an expansion, no, a *rib* of yourself, without any existence of her own. That I am a being by myself is more than you can grasp.—I wish I could absolutely submerge myself in a man—and *so I do*, I *always* loved you.————

"You will say 'I was patient.' Do you call that patient, hanging on for your needs, as you have done? The innerest life you have *always* had of me, and you held yourself aloof because you were afraid.

"The unpardonable thing was you told me you loved me.— Your *feelings* have hated me these three months, which did not prevent you from taking my love and every breath from me.— Underneath you undermined me, in some subtle, corrupt way that I did not see because I believed you, when you told me you loved me.——

"The insult of the way you took me these last three months
I shall never forgive you. I honestly *did* give myself, and always
in vain and rebuffed. The strain of it all has driven me quite
mad.

"You say I am a tragédienne, but I don't do any of your
perverse undermining tricks. You are always luring one into the
open like a clever enemy, but you keep safely under cover all
the time.———

"This practically means, for me, that life is over, my belief in
life.—I hope it will recover, but it never could do so with you—
——"

To which he answered: "If I kept under cover it is funny, for
there isn't any cover now.—And you can hope, pretty easily,
for your own recovery apart from me. For my side, without
you, I am done.—But you lie to yourself. You *wouldn't* love *me*,
and you won't be able to love anybody else—except generally."

VIN ORDINAIRE

I.

A wind was blowing, so that occasionally the poplars whitened as if a flame ran up them. The sky was blue and broken among moving clouds. Patches of sunshine lay on the level fields, and shadow on the rye and the vineyards. In the distance, very blue, the cathedral bristled against the sky, and the houses of the city piled up to her.

The barracks were a collection of about a dozen huts of corrugated iron, that sweltered like Dutch ovens on the hot summer plain, but were gay with nasturtiums climbing ambitiously up. The soldiers were always outside, either working in the patch of vegetable garden, or sitting in the shade, when not at drill in the yard enclosed by the wire fence.

Now the huts were deserted, the beds pushed up, everything tidy. Bachmann went to his cupboard for the picture postcard which he usually sent to his mother on Wednesday afternoon. Then he returned, to sit on the bench under the lime tree, that was sweet with blossom. Green-bladed flowers, like tiny wrecked aeroplanes, lay scattered in a circle on the ground, and the bench under the tree, shaken down by the wind. Another soldier was writing: three more were talking, their conversation full of the dirty language they always used.

Bachmann addressed his card, but could not think of anything to say to his mother. His brain was quite empty. The postcard lay on the bench before him, he held the pencil in his fingers suspended. He was a long-backed, limber youth of twenty-two, and his clumsy uniform could not quite conceal the grace of his figure. His face was tanned by the sun, and yet had a certain fair-skinned delicacy, showing the colouring of his cheeks. His moustache was reddish, and continually he stroked it with his left hand, as he sat and stared at the postcard.

"Dear Mother"—that was all he had written. And in a few more minutes he would have to set off. He stared at the "Liebe Mutter." Then suddenly he began to write: "I am just off to the drill, climbing the fortifications. The walls go clean up from the water." He stopped. "I can tell you, it is exciting." He stopped again. Then, a little pale, he continued: "The frost has got most of the cherries. Heidelberg cherries are 80 a pound. But they are all right here. Are ours all right?" The postcard was filled. He signed himself with love, got a stamp out of his purse, and stuck it on. Then, apprehensively, he looked round. He had handsome, rather prominent blue eyes, the colour of speedwell. His manner of lounging was somewhat voluptuous and sprawling, as if he were too full of life to do a thing meagrely.

His comrades were assembling in the yard. He put the post-card into his pocket and joined them, laughing. No one would have guessed that his heart was gnawed inside him with appre-hension. He moved with indifference and a little abandon, martial also, since he was a soldier. There was something young and conceited about him, something swagger and generous. The men treated him with a familiarity of affection, but they handled him rather cautiously for all that. He was easily the most noticeable among them, the most handsome, the best proportioned, quite un-German in his gracefulness of bearing and remark: also a little given to showing off.

Presently the sergeant appeared. He was a strongly-built, rather heavy man of forty. But it was evident he had gone to pieces. His head stuck forward, dropped a little between his straight, powerful shoulders. His face, once handsome and full of character, had relaxed, so that all its lines hung sullenly. The dark eyes were heavy underneath. It was the face of a passion-ate, ruined, hateful man. His duties were only intervals in his drinking.

He gave his orders briefly, evidently not one to waste words, and the little company moved down the white road. The vines on either side were dusty, the poppies at the edge of the corn blown to pieces, whilst the tall rye bowed deeply, and deeply again, in the wind.

Bachmann walked with his usual ease. His comrades had a manner of marching head-first, something like bears. He had none of that dogged submissiveness, but went easily when he was not tired, and then his shoulders, not his head, went slack with fatigue.

Now he was afraid. At the very core he was gnawed with a shame of fear. He knew the taciturn officer disliked him, and more or less saw through his braggadocio. He was afraid of the climbing. He could not bear to be at a height. It made his bowels melt, and his limbs turn to water. But there it lay before him, this afternoon, and it had to be done. He had never quite given himself away yet. He was supposed to be a reckless dare-devil. Nor was he afraid, in the water, or fencing with swords. He had accustomed himself to these things since he was a boy. But he was afraid to ride on horseback, and he was afraid of heights. And fear of these things harassed his soul like shame, in company of men. With women it did not matter.

They drew near to the walls of the town, passed down a path among trees, and came to a halt. At their feet, the grass ended in a winding canal of water, whose edge was planted with trees in little thickets. The place was silent except for the rustling of the leaves. In the distance a sentinel was seen occasionally passing through the waving shade and sunlight. Marguerite daisies and the gold of lady's slipper glimmered peacefully among the mysterious fortifications, in the deep grass. Occasionally, a puff of wind made the grass pale.

The group of soldiers stood at the end of one of the moats, in their light blue and scarlet uniforms. The officer, with his powerful body and miserable face making the young soldier's heart uneasy, was explaining tersely and brutally. The water was dead still. On the other side of it, the stone wall of a rampart rose again, a low cliff, along whose summit the grass grew and tall daisies stood, showing their form against the dark of the waving trees beyond, overhead. The soldiers felt dwarfed, down in face of the ramparts. Still and lush and mysterious the place was, gloomy with trees. And penetrating to this silence came the run of tramcars and the noise of the town, a hundred yards away.

Bachmann's heart was beating as he listened to the terse but not very intelligible instructions of the officer. Then the practice began. One man had to take the ladder along the stone ledge at the foot of the wall, over the water, and, fixing it, climb to the land above. Bachmann watched, and it seemed easy. But he felt shaky himself. He had been too long in suspense because of this climbing.

The blue-uniformed figure of the climbing soldier mounted, clambering, grasping, to the height, moved along the edge of the little precipice, and prepared to descend again. It was doing everything according to command, so that it had a blind, unintelligent look about it. Small at the height, blue and scarlet among the intense greenery, it went, apart from everything, with dull feet to the next point, crouched, and began to make ready for the descent. But it was evident from the blind groping of the feet, the tense stiffness of the legs and back, that the body was moving against its own will, almost subjugated, but yet stiff. The sight of it made a flame of rage and impotence and fear go through Bachmann. He trembled slightly. As a rule, when he obeyed, he obeyed himself, identifying his will with that of the authority. Often it cost him a bitter effort, and made his face pale with ignominy. But then, in his soul, he had acquiesced to the great fact of the Army, and so had more or less identified himself with it. Now came the supreme test— whether his will, sufficiently identifying itself with the will of the Army, could control his body. If not—. He stood waiting, the anxiety gnawing in his chest, full of the torture of fear.

His turn came. He knew by some intuitive feeling that the officer had perceived his condition. The sergeant was furious to-day. Occasionally came the long snarl of a man whose blood is disintegrated with irritation. Bachmann went in silence along the ledge at the foot of the wall. He placed his ladder at last successfully, his previous failures having made him the more chaotic and blind. Then he began to climb. The ladder was not firm. At every hitch his heart went molten hot. He hung against

the face of the wall in mid-air, in agony pawing to grip the
rungs with his toes. If one fell, one would be nicely broken
against the ledge, as one dropped into the water. His heart
began to melt. Vaguely, he was conscious of the growing space
beneath his feet. He clutched the rungs of the ladder with his
hands. Things were beginning to spin out of their places. He
was sensible to the firmness of the ledge in the space below, but
not the firmness of the ladder on which he hung. And he seemed
to be reaching to the hardness below. Already he was in mid-air
unsupported, so that there was nothing to do but fall. And so—
everything went pitching in a sickening swoop. The sergeant's
voice was thundering away underneath. That was nothing. His
heart gave another furious, circling swoop, his wrists were
melting off, his knees, his ankles going. He would fall. Then a
little, hot sensation penetrated to him as in a swoon. His water
was running down his leg. He hung on to the ladder in mid-air
like a numbed fly, neither able to fall or to mount. Quite still,
quite inert, he hung there, shame, like an anæsthetic, having for
the moment blotted him out. Perhaps his hands were growing
slacker.

The soldiers below had stirred and laughed uneasily. Now
they were silent. The officer was yellow with fury. Even he at
last was silent. They watched the inert figure, blue and pitiable,
cleaving against the wall, just below the broken grass that
bristled unconcerned. The officer, in his rage, ran to another
ladder and climbed up, giving the men instructions to come
after.

Bachmann was just coming out of his swoon of panic. Once
again he could feel his wrists and knees firm. Things were taking
their places too, as to one who wakes from a nightmare. For a
minute they had all dissolved, and there had been nothing but
space into which he had hung unsupported, with certainty of
the hard ledge far beneath, whose very blow that would break
his body would be a panting relief to his soul. Now all things
were growing fixed again. Eagerly, he was rousing. In a moment
he would be able to grasp the grasses and perform that feat
which had paralysed him in awaiting him—climb over the edge
of the wall.

But as he reached to clasp the next rungs, large hands seized his wrists, and, in a great gap of fear, he was being hauled over the edge and on to the trampled grass. He lay on his knees. Then slowly, his senses coming to him through a thick daze of disappointment and unconsciousness, he rose to his feet.

The sergeant, panting with rage, his face yellow and livid, stood glaring at him, unable to speak. Bachmann waited, still too stunned to know anything but shame, only feeling a certain flame shoot to his heart, as he was aware again of the contact of the officer's hands with his own wrists, felt the officer's strength gripping him and pulling him up. He was bewildered. Then he began to tingle with pitiable rage. He had been climbing up without the officer's interference. A flame went through his heart as he felt again those large hands suddenly grasping and hauling at his wrists, just when he was in motion to succeed of himself. Now—he was a miserable carcass hauled there. A fierce, self-destroying rage possessed him, tempered with hate and self-justification.

He became aware of the low, hissing voice of the officer, a squeezed voice that came from a big panting chest. The sound cut him through with shame. His head hung, he did not hear what was said, only he felt the low, tense flame of contempt and destructive abuse in the other man's voice. But somewhere in his heart he resisted, he would not give in. Suddenly he started back as if his heart would leap out of his body. The officer, his voice growing louder, had thrust his discoloured face forward into that of the soldier. Bachmann started away; the vision of the sergeant's face, the open mouth, the upper lip raised from the teeth, the snarling, barking look had shocked him away on the reflex. His heart was pounding, his limbs began to tremble, his nerves felt like fine, white-hot threads. There was a moment of anguished suspense. Then, the voice getting louder, the face of the officer thrust suddenly into his again, the mouth opening and gibbering with words whose noise only he heard, Bachmann starting from it in blind revulsion, was jerking up his arm to protect his face, when his elbow caught the officer's mouth and nose with a cruel blow. The elder man jumped, staggered backward, and stepped over the edge of the ramparts, while the soldiers sprang forward to stop him. There was a shout, then a loud crash of water.

Bachmann stood impotent with fear. The soldiers broke into movement.

"You'd better run, Bachmann," said one, in a voice of pleased excitement. The guilty soldier turned and walked down the tree-hidden path into the street.

There, he stood in the sunshine, watching the officers ride by, the soldiers passing, the few civilians sauntering on their errands. He went towards the town. Over the bridge the trams were running. Down below, at the water's edge, the unequal, old French houses shone gaily in sunshine. The Cathedral was fine, her myriad little pinnacles pricking into the blue sky. Everybody was easy and comfortable, this sunny afternoon. He felt for a moment quite at peace. But he was aware of a great strain in the past—and in the future. He would soon be taken. And he faltered and stood still.

But no, he would not be taken. A wave of revulsion against it all went over him. He would get away. He was himself. Rapidly, he thought of all the places in which he might hide. How heaped with purple the lilac-trees were, how clean the grass and the white walks by the river! He could not think. There was nowhere to go. It was a beautiful afternoon. He felt dark. It seemed to him curious the soldiers riding by so negligently should not notice him; that he was conspicuous like a man in a black cloak.

Perhaps it would be easier to go back to the barracks and take his punishment. He did not care what they did to him.

But then his heart hardened itself. He did care. He hated them all. They did not give him a chance to be himself. He hated the army. It had trampled him when he was willing and had made him ashamed. Why should he give in to the army any more? Why should he let it put him to prison? He was himself.

But then, how could he help himself? There was only his mother. Ah, what a shame for her! And he could not help it. He hated the army, the uniform he wore, the very movement of an officer's steed. And everybody would be against him—

everybody. Each one of the common soldiers would be there to lay hands on him. And what for?—for nothing. In a dazed heaviness he walked along. Everywhere was militarism—there was no getting away from it. France! America! suddenly he caught at the idea of another land. He wanted to be in America. To be in a foreign land would be to be himself again.

II.

There was no way out—no way out. He was walking just blindly nowhere. Yet it was only forty miles to France. He took the next bridge across the river. Soon the order would be given for his arrest. He knew it was quite hopeless to think of escape. He was too much alone.

His heart gave a sudden leap and stood still. There was Emilie. If he hid till night, then he might get away over the border. Emilie was a servant at the Baron von Freyhof's, at the big house half a mile away from his own barracks, and not more than two miles out of town. Yet it was quite in the country. He would go there. It was a chance. By taking the Scy tram, he would not have more than a mile to walk, across the fields. And soldiers were so common.

He got into the small, quick-running tramcar, all eager now to come to Scy and to Emilie. He felt he could trust her. She was proud and reserved. Once she had walked to town with him, and at evening he had talked to her in the courtyard of the Baron's house. At any rate, he would go there. He had a feeling that it was right.

He got out of the tram at the terminus and took the field path. The wind was still blowing, but not so strongly. He could hear the faint whisper of the rye, then the long swish-swish as a stronger gust came. The vines smelt sweet to him. He liked their twinings and the tender look of the young shoots. In one of the fields men and women were taking up the hay. The bullock-wagon stood on the path, and the men in their blue shirts, the women with white cloths over their heads, carried the hay in their arms to the cart. He was thinking of his own village. There the hay was being cut. It was a still, beautiful sight to see the sun on the shorn grass, and on the movement of the harvesters.

The Baron's house stood square and grey in its big garden, among the fields. Across, he could see the low swarm of the barrack's buildings. He did not hesitate, but walked as Fate led him, to the courtyard entrance of the house. The dog, Peter, seeing a soldier, only danced. The pump stood peacefully in the shadow. Everything was still.

The kitchen door was open. He hesitated, then walked in. The two women started. Emilie had just lifted the coffee-tray. She stood, questioning and superb, fronting him across the room. She was very dark, with closely-banded black hair, proud, almost cold grey eyes, and the faint shadow of hair darkening her upper lip. She wore a peasant's dress of bright blue stuff with little reddish roses scattered over it. The silver, and the white and rose of the coffee-service, shone in her hands. The outline of her firmly-covered breasts showed distinctly. She stared at the young soldier.

A look of recognition, of question devoid of feeling was in her eyes as they rested on him. He was aware of the nursery governess sitting at the table picking a dusky heap of cherries. She was a young woman of about twenty-five, pale, freckled, pretty, dark-haired. Her dark eyes were looking questioningly at him; she had a pleasant but rather hard face.

He went pale, meeting Emilie's challenging stare, and felt rather dreary. It was harder than he thought, appealing here. He was half-minded to turn and go again. But Fräulein Hesse looked kind and attentive. Bachmann seemed to feel the open courtyard behind him like an exposure.

"I had a go with Huber," he said, slowly, his tall, graceful body leaning slightly forward, his blue eyes strained and trying to smile. Emilie's inquiring look, shy eyes and haughtily defensive bearing, made it hard for him.

"How do you mean?" she asked, half-audibly.

"I knocked him down the fortifications—partly by accident—and ran." He looked at her rather vaguely. It was all so mechanical.

"You what!" cried Fräulein Hesse, rising dismayed and capable from her chair. Emilie stood unmoving. He glanced at the governess for support. But he felt the steady, hard grey eyes of Emilie watching him. And somehow, it was to this woman he belonged. Beautiful she looked, too, in the blue dress tightly covering her breasts, straight and proud in her bearing. She was still waiting for him. It was like judgment.

"I thought perhaps I might hide for a night, and then get away to France," he said. And for the first time his blue eyes met those of Emilie, and he looked back at her, straight into her. It made him suffer too. He wanted something to back him up. Slowly, she lowered her eyes.

"Yes," she said, as if she had not understood, and turned away, going through the inner door with the tray. He watched her proud, straight back, her strong loins, the thick, black plait of hair bound round her head. She was gone. He felt lost and forsaken.

"They are having coffee in the garden," said the governess, "and the children are there. What did it do to him?"

He looked at her quickly. But she was gazing direct at him, thinking, waiting.

"I don't know," he answered, rather bitterly. Seeing the cherries lying near him, he took a handful and began eating them, slowly. Fräulein Hesse regarded him, half wondering. Accustomed to the atmosphere of soldiers, she was at a loss for the moment.

"And what happened?" she said.

"He was ragging me. You've seen him push his face into yours and you mustn't move. I couldn't keep still. I put my arm up to keep him off and it caught him, and he fell down the fortifications." The young soldier had become an actor at once. He went through the scene with vigorous gestures, his blue, rather full eyes staring. Fräulein Hesse watched, fascinated. He finished, and began to stroke his reddish moustache.

"You don't know what it did to him?"

"Might have killed him—I don't know," he replied, looking at her as if calmly submissive to fate. He had rather a beautiful, abandoned pose. Nevertheless, he was gnawed with anxiety to know how much the officer had been hurt. But he kept his thoughts from the question—it was too disturbing. Fräulein Hesse stared at him, her face full of wonder and speculation. Emilie returned. She closed the door behind her, then went and closed the outer door. He continued to sniff the scent of coffee, wishing for a drink, while he ate cherries thirstily. Something was steaming on the stove. The enamel pans shone blue on the wall. He felt a little bit out of place, as if he were acting some part. The pans hung so easy and natural. And he waited for the two women to dismiss his fate.

"Where can you go?" asked Emilie, in her subdued, meaningless voice. He, helpless, looked up at her. She stared a moment at him, then at Fräulein Hesse. Her colour came, and she shrank slowly away from him, lowering her eyes, unable to speak. He looked at Fräulein Hesse. Her eyes were roused. They looked straight into his with a kind of smile. She was taking lead for him, and seemed to communicate with him privately.

"Your room would be the only safe place, Emilie," said she, bravely. Emilie flushed darkly, and did not answer. Then she raised her head and looked at him challengingly, like a woman forced into a compact and assuming a responsibility against her will.

"Come then," she said, moving to the door.

"I will see it is all right," said Fräulein Hesse.

In a moment he was following humbly and obediently. He noticed the scarlet mantle of a child on the hall-stand, the great maps on the wall, the queer engravings on the stairs. Then they went down a long corridor. Emilie, closed and withdrawn, opened the door for him, and stood, like a servant silent and inscrutable, waiting for him to enter. He passed her, and stood in the little room, his head bent. There was a good deal of humiliation. Emilie entered and silently, like a servant, closed the door behind her. She stood waiting. A little hot feeling flickered up in his heart.

It cost him an effort to raise his head to her. Then he told her, briefly what had happened. He was afraid she should see the quiver of light in his eyes. The two of them were in a kind of bondage. In her silence and dumbness, she was so close to him.

"I shall think of a plan," he said, watching her.

"Yes," she said, staring at him.

"Do you think I shall be safe here?"

"If nobody has seen you." She turned away from his eyes.

"It feels safe enough," he said, vaguely.

"Yes," she said.

And, without looking at him, a blush fading off her dark cheek, she left him.

He looked round the little room, standing in the middle, half afraid to touch anything. He knew she resented his having forced the privacy of the room. Yet there was something else, too, in her feeling, that made him rouse in his pride. The room was bare and severely tidy. He had often enough been into his mother's bedroom. Yet this gave him a curious sensation, of fear, of alertness, excitement. There was a picture of the Sacred Heart over the chest of drawers, and above a low praying-chair a crucifix, rather large, carved in wood. He stood and looked at it. He had been brought up a Protestant. He stood and looked at the symbol. His senses quickened, he perceived for the first time in his life that the carved figure on the Cross was that of a young man, thin and wasted and cramped. It was a crucifix carved by a peasant-worker in Bavaria. The Christ was lean and rather bony, with high cheek-bones and a dead face, the mouth hanging slightly open. He was a common man. Bachmann had seen many a peasant who might have been his brother. And it startled him. He was shocked to think of the cramped torture the man must have gone through. He wondered what Emilie, dark and proud and isolated, thought when she looked at the naked, dead man carved there. "It might be me," thought the soldier.

He saw her rosary beside the bed, and the strip of pictures representing the Stations of the Cross. He resented her religion, became violently Protestant. Then he looked round for water. There was none in the room. And he wondered if she would attend on him—bring him coffee perhaps. He wanted a drink.

She did not come. He sat down on the bed, feeling as if already he had crossed the sea into another land, almost into another self. Then he took off his belt and his boots, and

wondered what he should do. He felt a little bit forlorn that
she did not come at all. He would want a suit of clothes and a
bicycle, that was all. His mother would give him money. She
was well-off. There remained to cycle across the border into
France. He would start the next night. That would mean thirty
hours in this room. Better that than years in prison. The thought
of prison made him grasp the bed-post hard. And then came
the strong, curious sense of Emilie's presence in the house.

He took off his tunic and lay down, pulling the great over-
bolster across him. He felt subdued and disconsolate. There
was nothing to get hold of anywhere, and he was not a man
who could easily be much alone, or stand alone. He always
wanted to feel other lives associated with his. Now there was
nobody. Well, he would have to put up with it for the time
being. Sometimes his heart beat fast when he thought she was
coming. And then, too, he could ask her for a drink. But she
did not come.

III.

When at last she opened the door he started and sat up in bed.
His eyes, staring at her from the twilight, startled her too.

"Did you bring a drink?" he asked.

"No," she said. They were afraid of each other. She went
away, returning quickly with a jug of water. And she had to
impose a restraint on herself, to bear it, whilst he drank long
and heavily. Then he wiped his moustache on the back of his
hand. He was afraid to begin to eat before her. He sat on the
bed. She stood near the door. He looked at her strong, erect,
aloof figure. She glanced at him. He was in his shirt and trousers,
sitting bending forward on the bed.

"I thought I might. . . ." he said. And he told her quickly his
plans. She heard, almost without paying attention. She wanted
to go. A certain power, something strong and of which she was
afraid, was taking hold on her. It was growing darker. His voice
seemed to be getting slower, reaching to her, and she could not
move. At last, slowly, after a silence, he slid off the bed, and in

his silent stocking-feet, approached her. She stood like a rock.

"Emilie!" he said, afraid, and yet driven.

He put his hand on her. A shock went through her frame. Still she could not move. And in a moment his arms were round her, he was pressing her fast, holding her body hard against his own, which quivered through her in its vibrating. He had put his face on her, was kissing her throat. And there came upon her one intolerable flame, burning her breath away. She was beginning to swoon. He lifted his head.

"You'll marry me, Emilie—as soon as ever—?"

But words were a falsity, and he fell into silence. He was kissing her throat. She did not know what she was panting for, waiting for. But his mouth, with the soft moustache, was moving across her throat to her cheek, and at last their mouths met. She met him in the long, blind, final kiss that hurt them both. And then in positive pain, blind, unconscious, she clutched him to her. She did not know what it was that hurt her with sheer pain. He, shuddering slightly, was growing afraid, so unconscious and awful she seemed. With trembling fingers he unbuttoned her bodice to feel the breasts that had been in his consciousness so long, buttoned firm under her cotton dress. He found them, and she started with agony.

Then her mouth met his mouth again. And now she was sheer instinct. It was so powerful that she would have died if she had to be taken from him at this moment. It went through her limbs till she felt she was sinking loose.

IV.

Sullen, reserved, she returned home. She agreed to sleep in Fräulein Hesse's room. The governess remained excited, but kept just the same in her belief of the entire innocence of Emilie's relationship.

"He wants me to marry him when he's safe," said Emilie, in her balanced fashion, yet something gnawing in all her veins.

"Well, you will, won't you?" pleaded Fräulein Hesse. "I'm sure I would."

Emilie's face grew for a moment dull and submissive.

"Will he want anything more?" asked Fräulein Hesse, as they prepared for bed.

"No," said Emilie, before her new submissiveness could work.

She would not go near him again. And yet every second she was aware of him. Her very heart beat in painful strokes of him. She bore him some deep, unfathomed grudge. He lay safe and easy in her room. When she went upstairs, she listened. There was not a sound. He would be fast asleep. Fast asleep! Her heart set sullen as she undressed in Fräulein Hesse's room.

She could not sleep. All through the night the unsatisfaction, the slow, mean misery of half-satisfaction kept her awake. She lay suffering blindly, stubborn to what ailed her. But her heart was hot with sense of him, burning almost with hate of him. She lay and waited, waited in a slow torture, unable to sleep or to think. Something held her from going to him. It did not even occur to her. She lay almost without thought. Yet all the time she hated him that he left her so. It was for him to finish what he had begun. Every fibre of her hurt with a kind of painful sensibility of him. Why could he not set her free to be herself again? She struggled, for him, against him. Through the early, beautiful dawn she lay awake, waiting, watching, waiting for something that never came. Some inertia held her. She could not go near him of herself. Like a thing bound down, the whole woman in her was held hour after hour, all through the night.

Towards five o'clock she dozed fitfully. She awoke again at six and got up. Her heart was sullen and dull with hate. She could have trampled on him. She went downstairs. The Baron was already stirring.

Bachmann had slept uneasily, with dreams and restlessness all the night. At first, quivering with anxiety, trembling he knew not why, he had lain and listened for her, the minutes one long-drawn-out space of waiting. Then at last his heart had thudded heavily, hearing her come upstairs. She was coming. But another door closed, and there was silence—a silence that grew longer and longer and more desert. Then slowly his heart sank very deep. She would not come. Nor could he move to find her. She would not come. So there was this strain between them, bleeding away his vitality. She had left him. She did not wish to come to him.

Then the physical shame of the time when he had clung on to the ladder, the shame of being hauled up like a sack, of having failed with himself, came up strongly, under the new pressure of her not wanting him. He lay feeling without honour and without worth. And he thought of the next night's danger, and saw himself shot. Though really, he hoped for the morning, when everything would come right again. In the morning she would come. If he and she were all right, the other thing would be all right. If she had done with him, then he was afraid—there was nothing for him to grasp, to keep himself together. But his thoughts rambled on, to his escape, to his new life—and he fell fitfully asleep.

From four o'clock he lay and waited, dim, abstract, impersonal, his individuality gone, waiting dimly for her to come again. Then he might retrieve himself. He heard the doors close. She would have to come soon. And then, being pushed to the very brink of his own being, he would go to her. It was desperate for him. He seemed nothing anywhere.

He got up, looking out of the window. The bugle sounded from the barracks. Everything was fresh, steaming a faint grey vapour from off the dense greenness of the fields and the trees. There was no town anywhere. He stood looking out, feeling the world beyond him.

V.

At seven o'clock the Baron, a lieutenant from the barracks, and three soldiers came into the kitchen. Emilie stood erect and challenged them in her magnificent fashion, her grey eyes dilated. But she felt weak in herself, and foiled, feeling herself implicated.

The Baron had been working in his garden. He stood in his suit of green linen, fretted, not knowing quite what to say. He was a man of medium stature, full of life, with blue eyes, and

sudden, hot movements. As a young lieutenant his right hand
had been shattered in the Franco-Prussian war. As always, when
much agitated, he shook his wounded hand. He did not want
to question Emilie. She stood hostile to all these men. Suddenly
the Baron flashed round on her, and asked:

"Did you post a postcard to the mother of this Bachmann
last night, Emilie?"

The slim, deprecating lieutenant, the agitated, fuming Baron,
the three clumsy soldiers looked at her. She felt herself the
object of their cruel attention, and set herself back.

"Yes," she said, distinctly, mechanically. She did not feel as
if she herself had anything to do with all this.

The Baron's wounded hand fluttered with irritation.

"And what about him, then?" he asked, angrily.

The very resentment in his tone prevented her answering.
There was a pause, while everybody felt strained and falsified.
Emilie alone stood, like a slave, by herself.

"Did he come here?" asked the Baron.

He grew furious. Standing in front of her, his eyes began to
glare at her, his wounded hand, half-hidden by his side, shaking
spasmodically. She knew he wanted her to say "No." She stood
straight, stubbornly muted. It made her soul go dead in her, to
be bullied at this juncture. She did not answer. Slowly, the
Baron submitted to the effect of her silence.

"Shall we go then and see?" he said, rather bitingly, to the
lieutenant. And Emilie knew that he was hating her and
despising her.

The soldiers, heavy and bearlike, tramped with their rifles
after the two gentlemen. Emilie stood rooted, unable to move,
but her anger was deep. She listened.

Bachmann heard the heavy feet approaching the door. So
strong a tension stretched him, that he was unable to feel. He
stood watching the door. It opened, and revealed the soldiers.

"So!" exclaimed the Baron, quietly, seeing him.

Now they had got him, the common soldiers lost their up-
pricked excitement, and grew uncomfortable. As soon as the
lieutenant had given the command to finish dressing, they went
dull, and stood like clods near the door. The Baron took a pace

or two, in irritable distress. He watched the shaking hands of Bachmann fastening at the belt. Then the expressionless face of the young soldier was raised in obedience. The Baron went out of the room. The voice of the lieutenant gave the order to march. Two soldiers went first, then one soldier holding Bachmann by the arm, then the officer in his fine uniform and the Baron in his green linen.

Bachmann moved dimly, scarcely realising anything. The soldiers went lumbering down the stairs, tramped through the hall, and then down one step into the kitchen. There was a smell of coffee and of morning. The prisoner was aware of the straight form of Emilie standing apart, her fine arms, bare from the elbows, hanging at her sides. She too held her face a little averted. He did not want to look at her, but her presence was very real to him.

The Baron came to a halt in the kitchen, hesitated and looked round.

"So you share your room with a deserter, Emilie," he said to her ironically. Then he clapped his heels and shook hands very formally with the lieutenant.

"No," said Emilie, forcing her lips apart. "I was with Fräulein Hesse." Bachmann, hearing her struggling voice hating the imputation, faltered in his walk. The soldier pulled him by the sleeve, uneasily, miserable in his position. And when the prisoner started again, it was with uncertain steps, and his teeth closed on his lower lip, his eyes staring fixedly; and whichever way the soldier twitched his arm, he went obediently.

The sun was breaking through the morning. The Baron, in his old gardening-suit of green linen, stood watching the soldiers go down the drive. A cock crowed vociferously in the still new air. They were gone round the hedge. The Baron turned to Emilie. She stood more withdrawn than usual, as if waiting to defend herself. Her cheek was a little pale.

"The Baroness will be surprised," said the Baron to the stiff-standing maid. She turned her eyes to him, like a slave at bay, unable to understand his tone. He bent his head.

"Hiding one of the soldiers in your room," he continued, as if in raillery.

"He came and asked me," she said, through scarcely-moving lips.

"So! Then it's his own look-out?"

"Yes," said the maid, not understanding.

"Yes," re-echoed the Baron, and with a bitter sneer on his face, he went to the door. "In fact, you had nothing to do with it," he said, turning with a furious smile. She stared at him. Why was he so angry with her? He was gone with his head down. She continued her preparation of coffee.

THE PRUSSIAN OFFICER
[HONOUR AND ARMS]

They had marched more than thirty kilometres since dawn,
along the white, hot road, where occasional thickets of trees
threw a moment of shade, then out into the glare again. On
either hand, the valley, wide and shallow, glistered with heat;
dark green patches of rye, pale young corn, fallow and meadow
and black pine-woods spread in a dull, hot diagram under a
glistening sky. But right in front the mountains ranged across,
pale blue and very still, the snow gleaming gently out of the
deep atmosphere. And towards the mountains, on and on, the
regiment marched between the rye-fields and the meadows,
between the scraggy fruit-trees set regularly on either side the
highroad. The burnished, dark green rye threw off a suffocating
heat, the mountains drew gradually nearer and more distinct.
While the feet of the soldiers grew hotter, sweat ran through
their hair under their helmets, and their knapsacks could burn
no more in contact with their shoulders, but seemed instead to
give off a cold, prickly sensation.

He walked on and on in silence, staring at the mountains
ahead, that rose sheer out of the land, and stood fold behind
fold, half earth, half heaven, the heaven, the barrier with slits
of soft snow in the pale, bluish peaks.

He could now walk almost without pain. At the start, he had
determined not to limp. It had made him sick to take the first
steps, and during the first mile or so, he had compressed his
breath, and the cold drops of sweat had stood on his forehead.
But he had walked it off. What were they after all but bruises!
He had looked at them, as he was getting up: deep bruises on

the backs of his thighs. And since he had made his first step in the morning, he had been conscious of them, till now he had a tight, hot place in his chest, with suppressing the pain, and holding himself in. There seemed no air when he breathed. But he walked almost lightly.

The captain's hand had trembled in taking his coffee at dawn: his orderly saw it again. And he saw the fine figure of the captain wheeling on horseback at the farm-house ahead, a handsome figure in pale blue uniform with facings of scarlet, and the metal gleaming on the black helmet and the sword scabbard, and dark streaks of sweat coming on the silky bay horse. The orderly felt he was connected with that figure moving so suddenly on horseback: he followed it like a shadow, mute and inevitable and damned by it. And the officer was always aware of the tramp of the company behind, the march of his orderly among the men.

The captain was a tall man of about forty, grey at the temples. He had a handsome, finely-knit figure, and was one of the best horsemen in the West. His orderly, having to rub him down, admired the amazing riding-muscles of his loins.

For the rest, the orderly scarcely noticed the officer any more than he noticed himself. It was rarely he saw his master's face: he did not look at it. The captain had reddish-brown, stiff hair, that he wore short upon his skull. His moustache also was cut short and bristly over a full, brutal mouth. His face was rather rugged, the cheeks thin. Perhaps the man was the more handsome for the deep lines in his face, the irritable tension of his brow, which gave him the look of a man who fights with life. His fair eyebrows stood bushy over light blue eyes that were always flashing with cold fire.

He was a Prussian aristocrat, haughty and overbearing. But his mother had been a Polish Countess. Having made too many gambling debts when he was young, he had ruined his prospects in the army, and remained an infantry captain. He had never married: his position did not allow it, and no woman had ever moved him to it. His time he spent riding—occasionally he rode one of his own horses at the races—and at the officers' club. Now and then he took himself a mistress. But after such an event, he returned to duty with his brow still more tense, his eyes still more hostile and irritable. With the men, however, he was merely impersonal, though a devil when roused, so that on the whole they feared him but had no great aversion from him. They accepted him as the inevitable.

To his orderly he was at first cold and just and indifferent: he did not fuss over trifles. So that his servant knew practically nothing about him, except just what orders he would give, and how he wanted them obeyed. That was quite simple. Then the change gradually came.

The orderly was a youth of about twenty-two, of medium height, and well-built. He had strong, heavy limbs, was swarthy, with a soft, black, young moustache. There was something altogether warm and young about him. He had firmly marked eyebrows over dark, expressionless eyes, that seemed never to have thought, only to have received life direct through his senses, and acted straight from instinct.

Gradually the officer had become aware of his servant's young, vigorous, unconscious presence about him. He could not get away from the sense of the youth's person, while he was in attendance. It was like a warm flame upon the older man's tense, rigid body, that had become almost unliving, fixed. There was something so free and self-contained about him, and something in the young fellow's movement, that made the officer aware of him. And this irritated the Prussian. He did not choose to be touched into life by his servant. He might easily have changed his man, but he did not. He now very rarely looked direct at his orderly, but kept his face averted, as if to avoid seeing him. And yet as the young soldier moved unthinking about the apartment, the elder watched him, and would notice the movement of his strong young shoulders under the blue cloth, the bend of his neck. And it irritated him. To see the soldier's young, brown, shapely peasants' hands grasp the loaf or the wine-bottle sent a flash of hate or of anger through the elder man's blood. It was not that the youth was clumsy: it was rather the blind, instinctive sureness of movement of an unhampered young animal that irritated the officer to such a degree.

Once, when a bottle of wine had gone over, and the red gushed out onto the table-cloth, the officer had started up with an oath, and his eyes, bluey like fire, had held those of the confused youth for a moment. It was a shock for the young soldier. He felt something sink deeper, deeper into his soul, where nothing had ever gone before. It left him rather blank and wondering. Some of his natural completeness in himself was gone, a little uneasiness took its place. And from that time an undiscovered feeling had held between the two men.

Henceforward the orderly was afraid of really meeting his master. His subconsciousness remembered those steely blue eyes and the harsh brows, and did not intend to meet them again. So he always stared past his master, and avoided him. Also, in a little anxiety, he waited for the three months to have gone, when his time would be up. He began to feel a constraint in the captain's presence, and the soldier even more than the officer wanted to be left alone in his neutrality as servant.

He had served the captain for more than a year, and knew his duty. This he performed easily, as if it were natural to him. The officer and his commands he took for granted, as he took the sun and the rain, and he served as a matter of course. It did not implicate him personally.

But now if he were going to be forced into a personal interchange with his master, he would be like a wild thing caught, he felt he must get away.

But the influence of the young soldier's being had penetrated through the officer's stiffened discipline, and perturbed the man in him. He, however, was a gentleman, with long fine hands and cultivated movements, and was not going to allow such a thing as the stirring of his innate self. He was a man of passionate temper, who had always kept himself suppressed. Occasionally there had been a duel, an outburst before the soldiers. He knew himself to be always on the point of breaking out. But he kept himself hard to the idea of the Service. Whereas the young soldier seemed to live out his warm, full nature, to give it off in his very movements, which had a certain zest, such as wild animals have in free movement. And this irritated the officer more and more.

In spite of himself, the captain could not regain his neutrality of feeling towards his orderly. Nor could he leave the man alone. In spite of himself, he watched him, gave him sharp orders, tried to take up as much of his time as possible. Sometimes he flew into a rage with the young soldier, and bullied him. Then the orderly shut himself off, as it were out of earshot, and waited with sullen, flushed face, for the end of the noise. The words never pierced to his intelligence, he made himself, protectively, impervious to the feelings of his master.

He had a scar on his left thumb, a deep seam going across the knuckle. The officer had long suffered from it, and wanted to do something to it. Still it was there, ugly and brutal on the young, brown hand. At last the captain's reserve gave way. One day, as the orderly was smoothing out the table-cloth, the officer pinned down his thumb with a pencil, asking:

"How did you come by that?"

The young man winced and drew back at attention.

"A wood-axe, Herr Hauptmann," he answered.

The officer waited for further explanation. None came. The orderly went about his duties. The elder man was sullenly angry. His servant avoided him. And the next day he had to use all his will-power to avoid seeing the scarred thumb. He wanted to get hold of it and—. A hot flame ran in his blood.

He knew his servant would soon be free, and would be glad. As yet, the soldier had held himself off from the elder man. The captain grew madly irritable. He could not rest when the soldier was away, and when he was present, he glared at him with tormented eyes. He hated those fine black brows over the unmeaning dark eyes, he was infuriated by the free movement of the handsome limbs, which no military discipline could make stiff. And he became harsh and cruelly bullying, using contempt and satire. The young soldier only grew more mute and expressionless.

"What cattle were you bred by, that you can't keep straight eyes. Look me in the eyes when I speak to you."

And the soldier turned his dark eyes to the other's face, but there was no sight in them: he stared with the slightest possible cast, holding back his sight, perceiving the blue of his master's eyes, but receiving no look from them. And the elder man went pale, and his reddish eyebrows twitched. He gave his order, barrenly.

Once he flung a heavy military glove into the young soldier's face. Then he had the satisfaction of seeing the black eyes flare up into his own, like a blaze when straw is thrown on a fire. And he had laughed with a little tremor and a sneer.

But there were only two months more. The youth instinctively tried to keep himself intact: he tried to serve the officer as if the latter were an abstract authority, and not a man. All his instinct was to avoid personal contact, even definite hate. But in spite of himself the hate grew, responsive to the officer's passion. However, he put it in the background. When he had left the army he could dare acknowledge it. By nature he was active, and had many friends. He thought what amazing good fellows they were. But, without knowing it, he was alone. Now this solitariness was intensified. It would carry him through his term. But the officer seemed to be going irritably insane, and the youth was deeply frightened.

The soldier had a sweetheart, a girl from the mountains, independent and primitive. The two walked together, rather silently. He went with her, not to talk, but to have his arm round her, and for the physical contact. This eased him, made it easier for him to ignore the captain; for he could rest with her held fast against his chest. And she, in some unspoken fashion, was there for him. They loved each other.

The captain perceived it, and was mad with irritation. He kept the young man engaged all the evenings long, and took pleasure in the dark look that came on his face. Occasionally, the eyes of the two men met, those of the younger sullen and dark, doggedly unalterable, those of the elder sneering with restless contempt.

The officer tried hard not to admit the passion that had got hold of him. He would not know that his feeling for his orderly was anything but that of a man incensed by his stupid, *perverse* servant. So, keeping quite justified and conventional in his consciousness, he let the other thing run on. His nerves, however, were suffering. At last he slung the end of a belt in his servant's face. When he saw the youth start back, the pain-tears in his eyes and the blood on his mouth, he had felt at once a thrill of deep pleasure, and of shame.

But this, he acknowledged to himself was a thing he had never done before. The fellow was too exasperating. His own nerves must be going to pieces. He went away for some days with a woman.

It was a mockery of pleasure. He simply did not want the woman. But he stayed on for his time. At the end of it, he came back in an agony of irritation, torment, and misery. He rode all the evening, then came straight in to supper. His orderly was out. The officer sat with his long, fine hands lying on the table, perfectly still, and all his blood seemed to be corroding.

At last his servant entered. He watched the strong, easy young figure, the fine eyebrows, the thick black hair. In a week's time the youth had got back his old well-being. The hands of the officer twitched, and seemed to be full of mad flame. The young man stood at attention, unmoving, shut off.

The meal went in silence. But the orderly seemed eager. He made a clatter with the dishes.

"Are you in a hurry?" asked the officer, watching the intent, warm face of his servant. The other did not reply.

"Will you answer my question?" said the captain.

"Yes Sir," replied the orderly, standing with his pile of deep army-plates. The captain waited, looked at him, then asked again:

"Are you in a hurry?"

"Yes Sir," came the answer, that sent a flash through the listener.

"For what?"

"I was going out Sir."

"I want you this evening."

There was a moment's hesitation. The officer had a curious stiffness of countenance.

"Yes Sir," replied the servant, in his throat.

"I want you tomorrow evening also—in fact you may consider your evenings occupied, unless I give you leave."

The mouth with the young moustache set close.

"Yes Sir," answered the orderly, loosening his lips for a moment.

He again turned to the door.

"And why have you a piece of pencil in your ear?"

The orderly hesitated, then continued on his way without answering. He set the plates in a pile outside the door, took the stump of pencil from his ear, and put it in his pocket. He had been copying a verse for his sweetheart's birthday-card. He returned to finish clearing the table. The officer's eyes were dancing, he had a little, eager smile.

"Why have you a piece of pencil in your ear?" he asked.

The orderly took his hands full of dishes. His master was standing near the great green stove, a little smile on his face, his chin thrust forward. When the young soldier saw him his heart suddenly ran hot. He felt blind. Instead of answering, he turned dazedly to the door. As he was crouching to set down the dishes, he was pitched forward by a kick from behind. The pots went in a stream down the stairs, he clung to the pillar of the banisters. And as he was rising he was kicked heavily again, and again, so that he clung sickly to the post for some moments. His master had gone swiftly into the room and closed the door. The maid-servant downstairs looked up the staircase and made a mocking face at the crockery disaster.

The officer's heart was plunging. He poured himself a glass of wine, part of which he spilled on the floor, and gulped the remainder, leaning against the cool, green stove. He heard his man collecting the dishes from the stairs. Pale, as if intoxicated, he waited. The servant entered again. The captain's heart gave a pang, as of pleasure, seeing the young fellow bewildered and uncertain on his feet, with pain.

"Schöner!" he said.

The soldier was a little slower in coming to attention.

"Yes Sir!"

The youth stood before him, with pathetic young moustache, and fine eyebrows very distinct on his forehead of dark marble.

"I asked you a question."

"Yes Sir."

The officer's tone bit like acid.

"Why had you a pencil in your ear?"

Again the servant's heart ran hot, and he could not breathe. With dark, strained eyes, he looked at the officer, as if fascinated. And he stood there sturdily planted, unconscious. The dithering smile came into the captain's eyes, and he lifted his foot.

"I—I forgot it—Sir," panted the soldier, his dark eyes fixed on the other man's dancing blue ones.

"What was it doing there?"

He saw the young man's breast heaving as he made an effort for words.

"I had been writing."

"Writing what?"

Again the soldier looked him up and down. The officer could hear him panting. The smile came into the blue eyes. The soldier worked his dry throat, but could not speak. Suddenly the smile lit like a flame on the officer's face, and a kick came heavily against the orderly's thigh. The youth moved a pace sideways. His face went dead, with two black, staring eyes.

"Well?" said the officer.

The orderly's mouth had gone dry, and his tongue rubbed in it as on dry brown paper. He worked his throat. The officer raised his foot. The servant went stiff.

"Some poetry, Sir," came the crackling, unrecognisable sound of his voice.

"Poetry, what poetry?" asked the captain, with a sickly smile.

Again there was the working in the throat. The captain's heart had suddenly gone down heavily, and he stood sick and tired.

"For my girl, Sir," he heard the dry, inhuman sound.

"Oh!" he said, turning away. "Clear the table."

'Click!'—went the soldier's throat; then again, 'click!'; and then the half articulate:

"Yes Sir."

The young soldier was gone, looking old, and walking heavily. The officer, left alone, held himself rigid, to prevent himself from thinking. His instinct warned him that he must not think. Deep inside him was the intense gratification of his passion, still working powerfully. Then there was a counter-action, a horrible breaking down of something inside him, a whole agony of reaction. He stood there for an hour motionless, a chaos of sensations, but rigid with a will to keep blank his consciousness, to prevent his mind grasping. And he held himself so until the worst of the stress had passed, when he began to drink, drank himself to an intoxication, till he slept obliterated. When he woke in the morning he was shaken to the base of his nature. But he had fought off the realisation of what he had done. He had prevented his mind from taking it in, had suppressed it along with his instincts, and the conscious man had nothing to do with it. He felt only as after a bout of intoxication, weak, but the affair itself all dim and not to be recovered. Of the drunkenness of his passion he successfully refused remembrance. And when his orderly appeared with coffee, the officer assumed the same self he had had the morning before. He refused the event of the past night—denied it had ever been—and was successful in his denial. He had not done any such thing—not he himself. Whatever there might be lay at the door of a stupid, insubordinate servant.

The orderly had gone about in a stupor all the evening. He drank some beer because he was parched, but not much, the alcohol made his feeling come back, and he could not bear it. He was dulled, as if nine-tenths of the ordinary man in him were inert. He crawled about disfigured. Still, when he thought of the kicks, he went sick, and when he thought of the threats of more kicking, in the room afterwards, his heart went hot and faint, and he panted, remembering the one that had come. He had been forced to say 'For my girl'. He was much too done even to want to cry. His mouth hung slightly open, like an idiot's. He felt vacant, and wasted. So, he wandered at his work, painfully, and very slowly and clumsily, fumbling blindly with the brushes, and finding it difficult, when he sat down, to summon the energy to move again. His limbs, his jaw were slack and nerveless. But he was very tired. He got to bed at last and slept inert, relaxed, in a sleep that was rather stupor than slumber, a dead night of stupefaction shot through with gleams of anguish.

In the morning were the manœuvres. But he woke even before the bugle sounded. The painful ache in his chest, the dryness of his throat, the awful steady feeling of misery made his eyes come awake and dreary at once. He knew without thinking, what had happened. And he knew that the day had come again, when he must go on with his round. The last bit of darkness was being pushed out of the room. He would have to move his inert body and go on. He was so young, and had known so little trouble, that he was bewildered. He only wished it would stay night, so that he could lie still, covered up by the darkness. And yet nothing would prevent the day from coming, nothing would save him from having to get up, and saddle the captain's horse, and make the captain's coffee. It was there, inevitable. And then, he thought, it was impossible. Yet they would not leave him free. He must go and take the coffee to the captain. He was too stunned to understand it. He only knew it was inevitable—inevitable, however long he lay inert.

At last, after heaving at himself, for he seemed to be a mass of inertia, he got up. But he had to force every one of his movements from behind, with his will. He felt lost, and dazed, and helpless. Then he clutched hold of the bed, the pain was so keen. And looking at his thighs, he saw the darker bruises on his swarthy flesh and he knew that, if he pressed one of his fingers on one of the bruises, he should faint. But he did not want to faint—he did not want anybody to know. No one should ever know. It was between him and the captain. There were only the two people in the world now—himself and the captain.

Slowly, economically, he got dressed and forced himself to walk. Everything was obscure, except just what he had his hands on. But he managed to get through his work. The very pain revived his dulled senses. The worst remained yet. He took the tray and went up to the captain's room. The officer, pale and heavy, sat at the table. The orderly, as he saluted, felt himself put out of existence. He stood still for a moment submitting to his own nullification—then he gathered himself, seemed to regain himself, and then the captain began to grow vague, unreal, and the younger soldier's heart beat up. He clung to this sensation—that the captain did not exist, so that he himself might live. But when he saw his officer's hand tremble as he took the coffee, he felt everything falling shattered. And he went away, feeling as if he himself were coming to pieces, disintegrated. And when the captain was there on horseback, giving orders, while he himself stood, with rifle and knapsack, sick with pain, he felt as if he must shut his eyes—as if he must shut his eyes on everything. It was only the long agony of marching with a parched throat that filled him with one single, sleep-heavy intention: to save himself.

2.

He was getting used even to his parched throat. That the snowy peaks were radiant among the sky, that the whitey-green glacier river twisted through its pale shoals, in the valley below, seemed almost supernatural. But he was going mad with fever and thirst. He plodded on, uncomplaining. He did not want to speak, not to anybody. There were two gulls, like flakes of water and snow, over the river. The scent of green rye soaked in sunshine came like a sickness. And the march continued, monotonously, almost like a bad sleep.

At the next farm-house, which stood low and broad near the highroad, tubs of water had been put out. The soldiers clustered round to drink. They took off their helmets, and the steam mounted from their wet hair. The captain sat on horseback, watching. He needed to see his orderly. His helmet threw a dark shadow over his light, fierce eyes, but his moustache and mouth and chin were distinct in the sunshine. The orderly must move under the presence of the figure of the horseman. It was not that he was afraid, or cowed. It was as if he were disembowelled, made empty, like an empty shell. He felt himself as nothing, a shadow creeping under the sunshine. And, thirsty as he was, he could scarcely drink, feeling the captain near him. He would not take off his helmet to wipe his wet hair. He wanted to stay in shadow, not to be forced into consciousness. Starting, he saw the light heel of the officer prick the belly of the horse; the captain cantered away, and he himself could relapse into vacancy.

Nothing, however, could give him back his living place in the hot, bright morning. He felt like a gap among it all. Whereas the captain was prouder, overriding. A hot flash went through the young servant's body. The captain was firmer and prouder with life, he himself was empty as a shadow. Again the flash went through him, dazing him out. But his heart ran a little firmer.

The company turned up the hill, to make a loop for the return. Below, from among the trees, the farm-bell clanged. He saw the laborers mowing barefoot at the thick grass leave off their work and go downhill, their scythes hanging over their shoulders, like long, bright claws curving down behind them. They seemed like dream-people, as if they had no relation to himself. He felt as in a blackish dream: as if all the other things were there and had form, but he himself was only a consciousness, a gap that could think and perceive.

The soldiers were tramping silently up the glaring hillside. Gradually his head began to revolve slowly, rhythmically. Sometimes it was dark before his eyes, as if he saw this world through a smoked glass, frail shadows and unreal. It gave him a pain in his head to walk.

The air was too scented, it gave no breath. All the lush green-stuff seemed to be issuing its sap, till the air was deathly, sickly with the smell of greenness. There was the perfume of clover, like pure honey and bees. Then there grew a faint acrid tang—they were near the beeches; and then a queer clattering noise, and a suffocating, hideous smell: they were passing a flock of sheep, a shepherd in a black smock, holding his hook. Why should the sheep huddle together under this fierce sun? He felt that the shepherd could not see him, though he could see the shepherd.

At last there was the halt. They stacked rifles in a conical stack, put down their kit in a scattered circle around it, and dispersed a little, sitting on a small knoll high on the hillside. The chatter began. The soldiers were steaming with heat, but were lively. He sat still, seeing the blue mountains rise upon the land, twenty kilometres away. There was a blue fold in the ranges, then out of that, at the foot, the broad pale bed of the river, stretches of whitey-green water between pinkish-grey shoals among the dark pine-woods. There it was, spread out a long way off. And it seemed to come downhill, the river. There was a raft being steered, a mile away. It was a strange country. Nearer, a red-roofed, broad farm with white base and square dots of windows crouched beside the wall of beech-foliage on the wood's edge. There were long strips of rye and clover and pale green corn. And just at his feet, below the knoll, was a darkish bog, where globe flowers stood breathless still on their slim stalks. And some of the pale gold bubbles were burst, and a broken fragment hung in the air. He thought he was going to sleep.

Suddenly something moved into this coloured mirage before his eyes. The captain, a small, light blue and scarlet figure, was trotting evenly between the strips of corn, along the level brow of the hill. And the man making flag-signals was coming on.— Proud and sure moved the horseman figure, the quick, bright thing in which was concentrated all the light of this morning, which for the rest lay a fragile, shining shadow. Submissive, apathetic, the young soldier sat and stared. But as the horse slowed to a walk, coming up the last steep path, the great flash flared over the body and soul of the orderly. He sat waiting. The back of his head felt as if it were weighted with a heavy piece of fire. He did not want to eat. His hands trembled slightly as he moved them. Meanwhile the officer on horseback was approaching slowly and proudly. The tension grew in the orderly's soul. Then again, seeing the captain ease himself on the saddle, the flash blazed through him.

The captain looked at the patch of light blue and scarlet, and dark heads, scattered closely on the hillside. It pleased him. The command pleased him. And he was feeling proud. His orderly was among them in common subjection. The officer rose a little on his stirrups to look. The young soldier sat with averted, dumb face. The captain relaxed on his seat. His slim legged, beautiful horse, brown as a beech nut, walked proudly uphill.

The captain passed into the zone of the company's atmosphere: a hot smell of men, of sweat, of leather. He knew it very well. After a word with the lieutenant, he went a few paces higher, and sat there, a dominant figure, his sweat-marked horse swishing its tail, while he looked down on his men, on his orderly, a nonentity among the crowd.

The young soldier's heart was like fire in his chest, and he breathed with difficulty. The officer, looking downhill, saw three of the young soldiers, two pails of water between them, staggering across a sunny green field. A table had been set up under a tree, and there the slim lieutenant stood importantly busy. Then the captain summoned himself to an act of courage. He called his orderly.

The flame leapt into the young soldier's throat as he heard the command, and he rose blindly, stifled. He saluted, standing below the officer. He did not look up. But there was the flicker in the captain's voice.

"Go to the inn and fetch me——"—the officer gave his commands. "Quick!" he added.

At the last word, the heart of the servant leapt with a flash, and he felt the strength come over his body. But he turned in mechanical obedience, and set off at a heavy run downhill, looking almost like a bear, his trousers bagging over his military boots. And the officer watched this blind, plunging run all the way.

But it was only the outside of the orderly's body that was obeying so humbly and mechanically. Inside had gradually accumulated a core into which all the energy of that young life was compact and concentrated. He executed his commission, and plodded quickly back uphill. There was a pain in his head, as he walked, that made him twist his features unknowingly. But hard there in the centre of his chest was himself, himself, firm, and not to be plucked to pieces.

The captain had gone up into the wood.—The orderly plodded through the hot, powerfully smelling zone of the company's atmosphere. He had a curious mass of energy inside him now. The captain was less real than himself. He approached the green entrance to the wood. There, in the half-shade, he saw the horse standing, the sunshine and the flickering shadow of leaves dancing over his brown body. There was a clearing where timber had lately been felled. Here, in the gold-green shade beside the brilliant cup of sunshine, stood two figures, blue and pink, the bits of pink showing out plainly. The captain was talking to his lieutenant.

The orderly stood on the edge of the bright clearing, where great trunks of trees, stripped and glistening, lay stretched like naked, brown-skinned bodies. Chips of wood littered the trampled floor, like splashed light, and the bases of the felled trees stood here and there, with their raw, level tops. Beyond was the brilliant, sunlit green of a beech.

"Then I will ride forward," the orderly heard his captain say. The lieutenant saluted and strode away. He himself went forward. A hot flash passed through his belly, as he tramped towards his officer.

The captain watched the rather heavy figure of the young soldier stumble forward, and his veins too ran hot. This was to be man to man between them. He yielded before the solid, stumbling figure with bent head. The orderly stooped and put the food on a level-sawn tree-base. The captain watched the glistening, sun-inflamed, naked hands. He wanted to speak to the young soldier, but could not. The servant propped a bottle against his thigh, pressed open the cork, and poured out the beer into the mug. He kept his head bent. The captain accepted the mug.

"Hot!" he said, as if amiably.

The flame sprang out of the orderly's heart, nearly suffocating him.

"Yes Sir," he replied, between shut teeth.

And he heard the sound of the captain's drinking, and he clenched his fists, such a strong torment came into his wrists. Then came the faint clang of the closing of the pot-lid. He looked up. The captain was watching him. He glanced swiftly away. Then he saw the officer stoop and take a piece of bread from the tree-base. Again the flash of flame went through the young soldier, seeing the stiff body stoop beneath him, and his hands jerked. He looked away. He could feel the officer was nervous. The bread fell as it was being broken. The officer ate the other piece. The two men stood tense and still, the master laboriously chewing his bread, the servant staring with averted face, his fists clenched.

Then the young soldier started. The officer had pressed open the lid of the mug again. The orderly watched the lid of the mug, and the white hand that clenched the handle, as if he were fascinated. It was raised. The youth followed it with his eyes. And then he saw the thin, strong throat of the elder man moving up and down as he drank, the strong jaw working. And the instinct which had been jerking at the young man's wrists suddenly jerked free. He jumped, feeling as if he were rent in two by a strong flame.

The spur of the officer caught in a tree-root, he went down backwards with a crash, the middle of his back thudding sickeningly against the sharp-edged tree-base, the pot flying away. And in a second the orderly, with serious, earnest young face, and underlip between his teeth, had got his knee in the officer's chest and was pressing the chin backward over the farther edge of the tree-stump, pressing, with all his heart behind in a passion of relief, the tension of his wrists exquisite with relief. And with the base of his palms he shoved at the chin, with all his might. And it was pleasant too to have that chin, that hard jaw already slightly rough with beard, in his hands. He did not relax one hair's-breadth but, all the force of all his blood exulting in his thrust, he shoved back the head of the other man, till there was a little 'cluck' and a crunching sensation. Then he felt as if his heart went to vapour. Heavy convulsions shook the body of the officer, frightening and horrifying the young soldier. Yet it pleased him too to repress them. It pleased him to keep his hands pressing back the chin, to feel the chest of the other man yield in expiration to the weight of his strong young knee, to feel the hard twitchings of the prostrate body jerking his own whole frame, which was pressed down on it.

But it went still. He could look into the nostrils of the other man, the eyes he could scarcely see. How curiously the mouth was pushed out, exaggerating the full lips, and the moustache bristling up from them. Then, with a start, he noticed the nostrils gradually filled with blood. The red brimmed, hesitated, ran over, and went in a thin trickle down the face to the eyes.

It shocked and distressed him. Slowly, he got up. The body twitched and sprawled there inert. He stood and looked at it in silence. It was a pity *it* was broken. It represented more than the thing which had kicked and bullied him. He was afraid to look at the eyes. They were hideous now, only the whites showing, and the blood running to them. The face of the orderly was drawn with horror at the sight. Well, it was so. In his heart he was satisfied. He had hated the face of the captain. It was extinguished now. There was a heavy relief in the orderly's soul. That was as it should be. But he could not bear to see the long, military body lying broken over the tree-base, the fine fingers crisped. He wanted to hide it away.

Quickly, busily, he gathered it up and pushed it under the felled tree-trunks, which rested their beautiful smooth length either end on logs. The face was horrible with blood. He covered it with the helmet. Then he pushed the limbs straight and decent, and brushed the dead leaves off the fine cloth of the uniform. So, it lay quite still in the shadow under there. A little strip of sunshine ran along the breast, from a chink between the logs. The orderly sat by it for a few moments. Here his own life also ended.

Then, through his daze, he heard the lieutenant, in a loud voice, explaining to the men outside the wood that they were to suppose the bridge on the river below was held by the enemy. Now they were to march to the attack in such and such a manner. The lieutenant had no gift of expression. The orderly, listening from habit, got muddled. And when the lieutenant began it all again, he ceased to hear.

He knew he must go. He stood up. It surprised him that the leaves were glittering in the sun, and the chips of wood reflecting white from the ground. For him a change had come over the world. But for the rest it had not—all seemed the same. Only he had left it. And he could not go back.—It was his duty to return with the beer-pot and the bottle. He could not. He had left all that. The lieutenant was still hoarsely explaining. He must go, or they would overtake him. And he could not bear contact with anyone now.

He drew his fingers over his eyes, trying to find out where he was. Then he turned away. He saw the horse standing in the path. He went up to it and mounted. It hurt him to sit in the saddle. The pain of keeping his seat occupied him as they cantered through the wood. He would not have minded anything, but he could not get away from the sense of being divided from the others. The path led out of the trees. On the edge of the wood he pulled up and stood watching. There in the spacious sunshine of the valley soldiers were moving in a little swarm. Every now and then, a man harrowing on a strip of fallow shouted to his oxen, at the turn. The village and the white-towered church was small in the sunshine. And he no longer belonged to it—he sat there, beyond, like a man outside in the dark. He had gone out from everyday life into the unknown, and he could not, he even did not want to go back.

Turning from the sun-blazing valley, he rode deep into the wood. Tree-trunks, like people standing grey and still, took no notice as he went. A doe, herself a moving bit of sunshine and shadow, went running through the flecked shade. There were bright green rents in the foliage. Then it was all pine-wood, dark and cool. And he was sick with pain, he had an intolerable great pulse in his head, and he was sick. He had never been ill in his life. He felt lost, quite dazed with all this.

Trying to get down from the horse, he fell, astonished at the pain and his lack of balance. The horse shifted uneasily. He jerked its bridle and sent it cantering jerkily away. It was his last connection with the rest of things.

But he only wanted to lie down and not be disturbed. Stumbling through the trees, he came on a quiet place where beeches and pine trees grew on a slope. Immediately he had lain down and closed his eyes, his consciousness went racing on without him. A big pulse of sickness beat in him as if it throbbed through the whole earth. He was burning with dry heat. But he was too busy, too tearingly active in the incoherent race of delirium, to observe.

3.

He came to with a start. His mouth was dry and hard, his heart beat heavily, but he had not the energy to get up. His heart beat heavily. Where was he?—the barracks,—at home? There was something knocking. And, making an effort, he looked round—trees, and glitter of greenery, and reddish bright, still pieces of sunshine on the floor. He did not believe he was himself, he did not believe what he saw. Something was knocking. He made a struggle towards consciousness, but relapsed. Then he struggled again. And gradually his surroundings fell into relationship with himself. He knew, and a great pang of fear went through his heart. Somebody was knocking. He could see the heavy, black rags of a fir-tree overhead. Then everything went black. Yet he did not believe he had closed his eyes. He had not. Out of the blackness sight slowly emerged again. And someone was knocking. Quickly, he saw the blood-disfigured face of his captain, which he hated. And he held himself still with horror. Yet, deep inside him, he knew that it was so, the captain should be dead. But the physical delirium got hold of him. Someone was knocking. He lay perfectly still, as if dead, with fear. And he went unconscious.

When he opened his eyes again, he started, seeing something creeping swiftly up a tree-trunk. It was a little bird. And a bird was whistling overhead. Tap-tap-tap—it was the small, quick bird rapping the tree-trunk with its beak, as if its head were a little round hammer. He watched it curiously. It shifted sharply, in its creeping fashion. Then, like a mouse, it slid down the bare trunk. Its swift creeping sent a flash of revulsion through him. He raised his head. It felt a great weight. Then, the little bird ran out of the shadow across a still patch of sunshine, its little head bobbing swiftly, its white legs twinkling brightly for a moment. How neat it was in its build, so compact, with pieces of white on its wings. There were several of them. They were so pretty—but they crept like swift, erratic mice, running here and there among the beech-mast.

He lay down again exhausted, and his consciousness lapsed. He had a horror of the little creeping birds. All his blood seemed to be darting and creeping in his head. And yet he could not move.

He came to with a further ache of exhaustion. There was the pain in his head, and the horrible sickness, and his inability to move. He had never been ill in his life. He did not know where he was or what he was. Probably he had got sunstroke. Or what else?—he had silenced the captain for ever—some time ago—oh, a long time ago. There had been blood on his face, and his eyes had turned upwards. It was all right, somehow. It was peace. But now he had got beyond himself. He had never been here before. Was it life, or not-life? He was by himself. They were in a big, bright place, those others, and he was outside. The town, all the country, a big bright place of light: and he was outside, here, in the darkened open beyond, where each thing existed alone. But they would all have to come out there sometime, those others. Little, and left behind him, they all were. There had been father and mother and sweetheart. What did they all matter. This was the open land.

He sat up. Something scuffled. It was a little brown squirrel running in lovely, undulating bounds over the floor, its red tail completing the undulation of its body—and then, as it sat up, furling and unfurling. He watched it, pleased. It ran on again, friskily, enjoying itself. It flew wildly at another squirrel, and they were chasing each other, and making little scolding, chattering noises. The soldier wanted to speak to them. But only a hoarse sound came out of his throat. The squirrels burst away—they flew up the trees. And then he saw the one peeping round at him, half way up a tree-trunk. A start of fear went through him, though, in so far as he was conscious, he was amused. It still stayed, its little keen face staring at him half way up the tree-trunk, its little ears pricked up, its clawey little hands clinging to the bark, its white breast reared. He started from it in panic.

Struggling to his feet, he lurched away. He went on walking, walking, looking for something—for a drink. His brain felt hot and inflamed for want of water. He stumbled on. Then he did not know anything. He went unconscious as he walked. Yet he stumbled on, his mouth open.

When, to his dumb wonder, he opened his eyes on the world again, he no longer tried to remember what it was. There was thick, golden light behind golden-green glitterings, and tall, grey-purple shafts, and darknesses further off, surrounding him, growing deeper. He was conscious of a sense of arrival. He was amid the reality, on the real, dark bottom. But there was the thirst burning in his brain. He felt lighter, not so heavy. He supposed it was newness. The air was muttering with thunder. He thought he was walking wonderfully swiftly and was coming straight to relief—or was it to water?

Suddenly he stood still with fear. There was a tremendous flare of gold, immense—just a few dark trunks like bars between him and it. All the young level wheat was burnished, gold glaring on its silky green. A woman, full-skirted, a black cloth on her head for head dress, was passing like a block of shadow through the glistering green corn, into the full glare. There was a farm, too, pale blue in shadow, and the timber black. And there was a church spire nearly fused away in the gold. The woman moved on, away from him. He had no language with which to speak to her. She was the bright, solid unreality. She would make a noise of words that would confuse him, and her eyes would look at him without seeing him. She was crossing there to the other side. He stood against a tree.

When at last he turned, looking down the long, bare groove whose flat bed was already filling dark, he saw the mountains in a wonder-light, not far away, and radiant. Behind the soft, grey ridge of the nearest range the further mountains stood golden and pale grey, the snow all radiant like pure, soft gold. So still, gleaming in the sky, fashioned pure out of the ore of the sky, they shone in their silence. He stood and looked at them, his face illuminated. And like the golden, lustrous gleaming of the snow he felt his own thirst bright in him. He stood and gazed, leaning against a tree. And then everything slid away into space.

During the night the lightning fluttered perpetually, making the whole sky white. He must have walked again. The world hung livid around him for moments, fields a level sheen of grey-green light, trees in dark bulk, and a range of clouds black across a white sky. Then the darkness fell like a shutter, and the night was whole. A faint flutter of a half-revealed world, that could not quite leap out of the darkness!—Then there again stood a sweep of pallor for the land, dark shapes looming, a range of clouds hanging overhead. The world was a ghostly shadow, thrown for a moment upon the pure darkness, which returned ever whole and complete.

And the mere delirium of sickness and fever went on inside him—his brain opening and shutting like the night—then sometimes convulsions of terror from something with great eyes that stared round a tree—then the long agony of the march, and the sun decomposing his blood—then the pang of hate for the captain, followed by a pang of tenderness and ease. But everything was distorted, born of an ache and resolving into an ache.

In the morning he came definitely awake. Then his brain flamed with the sole horror of thirstiness. The sun was on his face, the dew was steaming from his wet clothes. Like one possessed, he got up. There, straight in front of him, blue and cool and tender, the mountains ranged across the pale edge of the morning sky. He wanted them—he wanted them alone—he wanted to leave himself and be identified with them. They did not move, they were still and soft, with white, gentle markings of snow. He stood still, mad with suffering, his hands crisping and clutching. Then he was twisting in a paroxysm on the grass.

He lay still, in a kind of dream of anguish. His thirst seemed to have separated itself from him, and to stand apart, a single demand. Then the pain he felt was another single self. Then there was the clog of his body, another separate thing. He was divided among all kinds of separate beings. There was some strange, agonised connection between them, but they were drawing further apart. Then they would all split. The sun, drilling down on him, was drilling through the bond. Then they would all fall, fall through the everlasting lapse of space.

Then again his consciousness reasserted itself. He roused onto his elbow and stared at the gleaming mountains. There they ranked, all still and wonderful between earth and heaven.

He stared till his eyes went black, and the mountains as they stood in their beauty, so clean and cool, seemed to have it, that which was lost in him.

4.

When the soldiers found him, three hours later, he was lying with his face over his arm, his black hair giving off heat under the sun. But he was still alive. Seeing the open, black mouth the young soldiers dropped him in horror.

He died in the hospital at night, without having seen again.

The doctors saw the bruises on his legs, behind, and were silent.

The bodies of the two men lay together, side by side, in the mortuary, the one white and slender, but laid rigidly at rest, the other looking as if every moment it must rouse into life again, so young and unused, from a slumber.

ENGLAND, MY ENGLAND

I.

The dream was still stronger than the reality. In the dream he was at home on a hot summer afternoon, working on the edge of the common, across the little stream at the bottom of the garden, carrying the garden path in continuation on to the common. He had cut the rough turf and the bracken, and left the grey, dryish soil bare. He was troubled because he could not get the path straight. He had set up his sticks, and taken the sights between the big pine-trees, but for some unknown reason everything was wrong. He looked again, strained and anxious, through the strong, shadowy pine-trees as through a doorway, at the green garden-path rising from the log bridge between sunlit flowers, tall purple and white columbines, to the butt-end of the old, beautiful cottage. Always, tense with anxiety, he saw the rising flowery garden and the sloping old roof of the cottage, beyond the intervening shadow, as in a mirage.

There was the sound of children's voices calling and talking: high, childish, girlish voices, plaintive, slightly didactic, and tinged with hard authoritativeness. "If you don't come soon, Nurse, I shall run out there where there are snakes."

Always this conflict of authority, echoed even in the children! His heart was hard with disillusion. He worked on in the gnawing irritation and resistance.

Set in resistance, he was all the time clinched upon himself. The sunlight blazed down upon the earth; there was a vividness of flamy vegetation and flowers, of tense seclusion amid the peace of the commons. The green garden-path went up between tall, graceful flowers of purple and white; the cottage with its great sloping roofs slept in the for-ever sunny hollow, hidden, eternal. And here he lived, in this ancient, changeless, eternal hollow of flowers and sunshine and the sloping-roofed house. It was balanced like a nest in a tree, this hollow home, always full of peace, always under heaven only. It had no context, no relation with the world; it held its cup under heaven alone, and was filled for ever with peace and sunshine and loveliness.

The shaggy, ancient heath that rose on either side, the downs that were pale against the sky in the distance, these were the extreme rims of the cup. It was held up only to heaven; the world entered in not at all.

And yet the world entered in and goaded the heart. His wife, whom he loved, who loved him—she goaded the heart of him. She was young and beautiful and strong with life like a flame in the sunshine; she moved with a slow grace of energy like a blossoming, red-flowered tree in motion. She, too, loved their hollow with all her heart. And yet she was like a weapon against him, fierce with talons of iron, to push him out of the nest-place he had made. Her soul was hard as iron against him, thrusting him away, always away. And his heart was hard as iron against her in resistance.

They never put down their weapons for a day now. For a few hours, perhaps, they ceased to be in opposition; they let the love come forth that was in them. Then the love blazed and filled the old, silent hollow where the cottage stood, with flowers and magnificence of the whole universe.

But the love passed in a few hours; only the cottage with its beauty remained like a mirage. He would abide by the mirage. The reality was the tension of the silent fight between him and his wife. He and she, as if fated, they were armed and exerting all their force to destroy each other.

There was no apparent reason for it. He was a tall, thin, fair, self-contained man of the middle class, who, never very definite or positive in his action, had now set in rigid silence of negation. He kept rigid within himself, never altering nor yielding, however much torture of repression he suffered.

Her ostensible grievance against him was that he made no

money to keep his family; that, because he had an income of a hundred and fifty a year, he made no effort to do anything at all—he merely lived from day to day. Not that she accused him of being lazy; it was not that; he was always at work in the garden; he had made the place beautiful. But was this all it amounted to? They had three children; she had said to him, savagely, she would have no more. Already her father was paying for the children's nurse, and helping the family at every turn. What would they do without her father? Could they manage on a hundred and fifty a year, with a family of three children, when they had both been brought up in plenty, and could not consider pennies? Living simply as they did, they spent two hundred and fifty a year; and now the children were tiny; what would it be when they had to go to school? Yet Evelyn would not stir to obtain any more.

Winifred, beautiful and obstinate, had all her passion driven into her conscience. Her father was of an impoverished Quaker family. He had come down from Newcastle to London when he was a young man, and there, after a hard struggle, had built up a moderate fortune again. He had ceased to be a Quaker, but the spirit persisted in him. A strong, sensual nature in himself, he had lived according to the ideas of duty inculcated upon him, though his active life had been inspired by a very worship of poetry and of poetic literature. He was a business man by tradition, but by nature he was sensual, and he was on his knees before a piece of poetry that really gratified him. Consequently, whilst he was establishing a prosperous business, a printing house and a small publishing house, at home he diffused the old Quaker righteousness with a new, æsthetic sensuousness, and his children were brought up in this sensuous heat, which was always, at the same time, kept in the iron grate of conventional ethics.

Winifred had loved her husband passionately. He came of an old south-of-England family, refined and tending towards dilettantism. He had a curious beauty of old breeding, slender and concentrated, coupled with a strange inertia, a calm, almost stoic indifference which her strong, crude, passionate, ethical nature could not understand. She could not bear it that their marriage, after all the tremendous physical passion that had convulsed them both, should resolve gradually into this nullity. Her passion gradually hardened into ethical desire. She wanted some result, some production, some new vigorous output into the world of man, not only the hot physical welter, and children.

Gradually she began to get dissatisfied with her husband. What did he stand for? She had started with a strange reverence for him. But gradually she fell away. A sense of meaninglessness came up strong in her. He was so strangely inconclusive. Her robust, undeveloped ethical nature was negated by him.

Then came the tragedy. They had three children, three fair-haired flitting creatures, all girls. The youngest was still a baby. The eldest, their love-child, was the favourite. They had wanted a boy in place of the others.

Then one day this eldest child fell on a sharp old iron in the garden and cut her knee. Because they were so remote in the country she did not have the very best attention. Blood-poisoning set in. She was driven in a motor-car to London, and she lay, in dreadful suffering, in the hospital, at the edge of death. They thought she must die. And yet in the end she pulled through.

In this dreadful time, when Winifred thought that if only they had had a better doctor at the first all this might have been averted, when she was suffering an agony every day, her husband only seemed to get more distant and more absent and exempt. He stood always in the background, like an exempt, untouched presence. It nearly drove her mad. She had to go to her father for all advice and for all comfort. Her father brought the specialist to the child; her father came to Winifred and held his arm round her, and called her his darling, his child, holding her safe, whilst all the time her husband stood aloof, silent, neutral. For this horrible neutrality, because of the horrible paralysis that seemed to come over him in these crises, when he could do nothing, she hated him. Her soul shrank from him in a revulsion. He seemed to introduce the element of horror, to make the whole thing cold and unnatural and frightful. She could not forgive him that he made the suffering so cold and rare. He seemed to her almost like a pale creature of negation, detached and cold and reserved, with his abstracted face and mouth that seemed shut in eternity.

The child recovered, but was lame. Her leg was stiff and atrophied. It was an agony to both the parents, they who lived wholly by the physical life. But to the mother it was an open, active grief; to him it was silent and incommutable, nihilistic. He would not speak of the child if he could help it, and then only in an off-hand, negligent fashion. So the distance was finally unsheathed between the parents, and it never really went away. They were separate, hostile. She hated his passivity as if it were something evil.

She taunted him that her father was having to pay the heavy bills for the child, whilst he, Evelyn, was idle, earning nothing. She asked him, did he not intend to keep his own children; did he intend her father to support them all their lives? She told him, her six brothers and sisters were not very pleased to see all the patrimony going on her children.

He asked her what could he do? She had talked all this out with her father, who could easily find a suitable post for Evelyn; Evelyn ought to work, everybody said. He was not idle; why, then, would he not do some regular work? Winifred spoke of another offer—would he accept that? He would not. But why? Because he did not think it was suitable, and he did not want it. Then Winifred was very angry. They were living in London, at double expense; the child was being massaged by an expensive doctor; her father was plainly dissatisfied; and still Evelyn would not accept the offers that were made him. He just negated everything, and went down to the cottage.

Something crystallised in Winifred's soul. She alienated herself from him. She would go on alone with her family, doing everything, not counting her negative husband.

This was the state of affairs for almost a year. The family continued chiefly in London; the child was still being massaged, in the hope of getting some use back into the leg. But she was a cripple; it was horrible to see her swing and fling herself along, a young, swift, flame-like child working her shoulders like a deformed thing. Yet the mother could bear it. The child would have other compensation. She was alive and strong; she would

have her own life. Her mind and soul should be fulfilled. That
which was lost to the body should be replaced in the soul. And
the mother watched over, endlessly and relentlessly brought up
the child when she used the side of her foot, or when she
hopped, things which the doctor had forbidden. But the father
could not bear it; he was nullified in the midst of life. The
beautiful physical life was all life to him. When he looked at his
distorted child, the crippledness seemed malignant, a triumph of
evil and of nothingness. Henceforward he was a cipher. Yet he
lived. A curious corrosive smile came on his face.

II.

It was at this point in their history that the war broke out. A
shiver went over his soul. He had been living for weeks fixed
without the slightest sentience. For weeks he had held himself
fixed, so that he was impervious. His wife was set fast against
him. She treated him with ignoring contempt; she ignored his
existence. She would not mend his clothes, so that he went
about with his shirt-shoulders slit into rags. She would not
order his meals. He went to the kitchen and got his own. There
was a state of intense hard hatred between them. The children
were tentative and uncertain, or else defiant and ugly. The
house was hard and sterile with negation. Only the mother gave
herself up in a passion of ethical submission to her duty, and
to a religion of physical self-sacrifice: which even yet she hardly
believed in.

Yet the husband and wife were in love with each other. Or,
rather, each held all the other's love dammed up.

The family was down at the cottage when war was declared.
He took the news in his indifferent, neutral way. "What difference does it make to me?" seemed to be his attitude. Yet it
soaked in to him. It absorbed the tension of his own life, this
tension of a state of war. A flicker had come into his voice, a
thin, corrosive flame, almost like a thin triumph. As he worked
in the garden he felt the seethe of the war was with him. His
consciousness had now a field of activity. The reaction in his
soul could cease from being neutral; it had a positive form to

take. There, in the absolute peace of his sloping garden, hidden deep in trees between the rolling of the heath, he was aware of the positive activity of destruction, the seethe of friction, the waves of destruction seething to meet, the armies moving forward to fight. And this carried his soul along with it.

The next time he went indoors he said to his wife, with the same thin flame in his voice:

"I'd better join, hadn't I?"

"Yes, you had," she replied; "that's just the very thing. You're just the man they want. You can ride and shoot, and you're so healthy and strong, and nothing to keep you at home."

She spoke loudly and confidently in her strong, pathetic, slightly deprecating voice, as if she knew she was doing what was right, however much it might mean to her.

The thin smile narrowed his eyes; he seemed to be smiling to himself, in a thin, corrosive manner. She had to assume all her impersonal righteousness to bear it.

"All right——" he said in his thin, jarring voice.

"We'll see what father says," she replied.

It should be left to the paternal authority to decide. The thin smile fixed on the young man's face.

The father-in-law approved heartily; an admirable thing for Evelyn to do, he thought; it was just such men as the country wanted. So it was the father-in-law who finally overcame the young man's inertia and despatched him to the war.

Evelyn Daughtry enlisted in a regiment which was stationed at Chichester, and almost at once he was drafted into the artillery. He hated very much the subordination, the being ordered about, and the having no choice over quite simple and unimportant things. He hated it strongly, the contemptible position he occupied as a private. And yet, because of a basic satisfaction he had in participating in the great destructive motion, he was a good soldier. His spirit acquiesced, however he despised the whole process of becoming a soldier.

Now his wife altered towards him and gave him a husband's dignity; she was almost afraid of him; she almost humbled herself before him. When he came home, an uncouth figure in

the rough khaki, he who was always so slender and clean-
limbed and beautiful in motion, she felt he was a stranger. She
was servant to his new arrogance and callousness as a soldier.
He was now a quantity in life; he meant something. Also he
had passed beyond her reach. She loved him; she wanted his
recognition. Perhaps she had a thrill when he came to her as
a soldier. Perhaps she too was fulfilled by him, now he had
become an agent of destruction, now he stood on the side of
the Slayer.

He received her love and homage as tribute due. And he
despised himself even for this. Yet he received her love as tribute
due, and he enjoyed it. He was her lover for twenty-four hours.
There was even a moment of the beautiful tenderness of their
first love. But it was gone again. When he was satisfied he
turned away from her again. The hardness against her was there
just the same. At the bottom of his soul he only hated her for
loving him now he was a soldier. He despised himself as a
soldier, ultimately. And she, when he had been at home longer
than a day, began to find that the soldier was a man just the
same, the same man, only become callous and outside her
ethical reach, positive now in his destructive capacity.

Still they had their days of passion and of love together when
he had leave from the army. Somewhere at the back was the
death he was going to meet. In face of it they were oblivious of
all but their own desire and passion for each other. But they
must not see each other too often, or it was too great a strain
to keep up, the closeness of love and the memory of death.

He was really a soldier. His soul had accepted the significance. He was a potential destructive force, ready to be destroyed. As a potential destructive force he now had his being.
What had he to do with love and the creative side of life? He
had a right to his own satisfaction. He was a destructive spirit
entering into destruction. Everything, then, was his to take and
enjoy, whilst it lasted; he had the right to enjoy before he
destroyed or was destroyed. It was pure logic. If a thing is only
to be thrown away, let anybody do with it what he will.

She tried to tell him he was one of the saviours of mankind.
He listened to these things; they were very gratifying to his

self-esteem. But he knew it was all cant. He was out to kill and destroy; he did not even want to be an angel of salvation. Some chaps might feel that way. He couldn't; that was all. All he could feel was that at best it was a case of kill or be killed. As for the saviour of mankind: well, a German was as much mankind as an Englishman. What are the odds? We're all out to kill, so don't let us call it anything else.

So he took leave of his family and went to France. The leave-taking irritated him, with its call upon his loving constructive self, he who was now a purely destructive principle. He knew he might not see them again, his wife and children. But what was the good of crying about it even then. He hated his wife for her little fit of passion at the last. She had wanted it, this condition of affairs; she had brought it about; why, then, was she breaking up at the last? Let her keep a straight face and carry it on as she had begun!

There followed the great disorder of the first days in France, such a misery of chaos that one just put up with it. Then he was really engaged. He hated it, and yet he was fulfilling himself. He hated it violently, and yet it gave him the only real satisfaction he could have in life now. Deeply and satisfactorily it fulfilled him, this warring on men. This work of destruction alone satisfied his deepest desire.

He had been twice slightly wounded in the two months. Now he was again in a dangerous position. There had been another retreat to be made, and he remained with three machine-guns covering the rear. The guns were stationed on a little bushy hillock just outside a village. Only occasionally—one could scarcely tell from what direction—came the sharp crackle of rifle fire, though the far-off thud of cannon hardly disturbed the unity of the winter afternoon.

Evelyn was working at the guns. Above him, in the sky, the lieutenant stood on the little iron platform at the top of the ladders, taking the sights and giving the aim, calling in a high, tense voice to the gunners below. Out of the sky came the sharp cry of the directions, then the warning numbers, then "Fire!" The shot went, the piston of the gun sprang back, there was a sharp explosion, and a very faint film of smoke in the air. Then

the other two guns were fired, and there was a lull. The officer
on the stand was uncertain of the enemy's position. Only in the
far distance the sound of heavy firing continued, so far off as
to give a sense of peace.

The gorse bushes on either hand were wintry and dark, but
there was still the flicker of a few flowers. Kissing was never out
of favour. Evelyn, waiting suspended before the guns, mused on
the abstract truth. Things were all abstract and keen. He did
not think about himself or about his wife, but the abstract fact
of kissing being always in favour interested and elated him. He
conceived of kissing as an abstraction. Isolated and suspended,
he was with the guns and the other men. There was the physical
relationship between them all, but no spiritual contact. His
reality was in his own perfect isolation and abstraction. The
comradeship, which seemed so close and real, never implicated
his individual soul. He seemed to have one physical body with
the other men; but when his mind or soul woke, it was
supremely and perfectly isolated.

Before him was the road running between the high banks of
grass and gorse. Looking down, he saw the whitish, muddy
tracks, the deep ruts and scores and hoof-marks on the wintry
road, where the English army had gone by. Now all was very
still. The sounds that came, came from the outside. They could
not touch the chill, serene, perfect isolation of the place where
he stood.

Again the sharp cry from the officer overhead, the lightning,
perfectly mechanical response from himself as he worked at the
guns. It was exhilarating, this working in pure abstraction. It
was a supreme exhilaration, the finest liberty. He was trans-
ported in the keen isolation of his own abstraction, the physical
activity at the guns keen as a consummation.

All was so intensely, intolerably peaceful that he seemed to
be immortalised. The utter suspension of the moment made it
eternal. At the corner of the high-road, where a little country
road joined on, there was a wayside crucifix knocked slanting.
So it slanted in all eternity. Looking out across the wintry fields
and dark woods, he felt that everything was thus for ever; this
was finality. There appeared a tiny group of cavalry, three

horsemen, far off, very small, on the crest of a field. They were our own men. So it is for ever. The little group disappeared. The air was always the same—a keen frost immovable for ever.

Of the Germans nothing was to be seen. The officer on the platform above waited and waited. Then suddenly came the sharp orders to train the guns, and the firing went on rapidly, the gunners grew hot at the guns.

Even so, even amid the activity, there was a new sound. A new, deep "Papp!" of a cannon seemed to fall on his palpitating tissue. Himself he was calm and unchanged and inviolable. But the deep "Papp!" of the cannon fell upon the vulnerable tissue of him. Still the unrelenting activity was kept up at his small guns.

Then, over the static inviolability of the nucleus, came a menace, the awful, faint whistling of a shell, which grew into the piercing, tearing shriek that would tear up the whole membrane of the soul. It tore all the living tissue in a blast of motion. And yet the cold, silent nerves were not affected. They were beyond, in the frozen isolation that was out of all range. The shell swung by behind, he heard the thud of its fall and the hoarseness of its explosion. He heard the cry of the soldier to the horses. And yet he did not turn round to see. He had not time. And he was cold of all interest, intact in his isolation. He saw a twig of holly with red berries fall like a gift on to the road below and remain lying there.

The Germans had got the aim with a big gun. Was it time to move? His superficial consciousness alone asked the question. The real *he* did not take any interest. He was abstract and absolute.

The faint whistling of another shell dawned, and his blood became still to receive it. It drew nearer, the full blast was upon him, his blood perished. Yet his nerves held cold and untouched, in inviolable abstraction. He saw the heavy shell swoop down to earth, crashing into the rocky bushes away to the right, and earth and stones poured up into the sky. Then these fell to the ground again; there was the same peace, the same inviolable, frozen eternality.

Would they move now? There was a space of silence, followed by the sudden explosive shouts of the officer on the platform, and the swift training of the guns, and the warning and the shout to "Fire!" In the eternal dream of this activity a shell passed unnoticed. And then, into the eternal silence and white immobility of this activity, suddenly crashed a noise and a darkness and a moment's flaring agony and horror. There was an instantaneous conflagration of life and eternity, then a profound weight of darkness.

When faintly something began to struggle in the darkness, a consciousness of pain and sick life, he was at home in the cottage troubling about something, hopelessly and sickeningly troubling, but hopelessly. And he tried to make it out, what it was. It was something inert and heavy and hopeless. Yet there was the effort to know.

There was a resounding of pain, but that was not the reality. There was a resounding of pain. Gradually his attention turned to the noise. What was it? As he listened, the noise grew to a great clanging resonance which almost dazed him. What was it, then?

He realised that he was out at the front. He remembered the retreat, the hill. He knew he was wounded. Still he did not open his eyes; his sight, at least, was not free. A very large, resounding pain in his head rang out the rest of his consciousness. It was all he could do to lie and bear it. He lay quite still to bear it. And it resounded largely. Then again there returned the consciousness of the pain. It was a little less. The resonance had subsided a little. What, then, was the pain? He took courage to think of it. It was his head. He lay still to get used to the fact. It was his head. With new energy he thought again. Perhaps he could also feel a void, a bruise, over his brow. He wanted to locate this. Perhaps he could feel the soreness. He was hit, then, on the left brow. And, lying quite still and sightless, he concentrated on the thought. He was wounded on the left brow, and his face was wet with stiffening blood. Perhaps there was the feel of hot blood flowing; he was not sure. So he lay still and waited. The tremendous sickening, resounding ache clanged again, clanged and clanged like a madness, almost bursting the membrane of his brain.

And again, as he lay still, there came the knowledge of his wife and children, somewhere in a remote, heavy despair. This was the second, and deeper, reality. But it was very remote.

How deep was the hurt to his head? He listened again. The pain rang now with a deep boom, and he was aware of a profound feeling of nausea. He felt very sick. But how deep was the wound in his head? He felt very sick, and very peaceful at the same time. He felt extraordinarily still. Soon he would have no pain, he felt so finely diffused and rare.

He opened his eyes on the day, and his consciousness seemed to grow more faint and dilute. Lying twisted, he could make out only jumbled light. He waited, and his eyes closed again. Then he waked all of a sudden, in terror lest he were able to see nothing but the jumbled light. The terror lest he should be confronted with nothing but chaos roused him to an effort of will. He made a powerful effort to see.

And vision came to him. He saw grass and earth; then he made out a piece of high-road with its tufts of wintry grass; he was lying not far from it, just above. After a while, after he had been all the while unrelaxed in his will to see, he opened his eyes again and saw the same scene. In a supreme anguish of effort he gathered his bearings and once more strove for the stable world. He was lying on his side, and the high-road ran just beneath. The bank would be above. He had more or less made his bearings. He was in the world again. He lifted his head slightly. That was the high-road, and there was the body of the lieutenant, lying on its face, with a great pool of blood coming from the small of the back and running under the body. He saw it distinctly, as in a vision. He also saw the broken crucifix lying just near. It seemed very natural.

Amid all the pain his head had become clear and light. He seemed to have a second being, very clear and rare and thin. The earth was torn. He wanted to see it all.

In his frail, clear being he raised himself a little to look, and found himself looking at his own body. He was lying with a great mass of bloody earth thrown over his thighs. He looked at it vaguely, and thought it must be heavy over him. He was anxious, with a very heavy anxiety, like a load on his life. Why was the earth on his thighs so soaked with blood? As he sat faintly looking, he saw that his leg beyond the mound was all on one side. He went sick, and his life went away from him. He remained neutral and dead. Then, relentlessly, he had to come back, to face the fact of himself. With fine, delicate fingers he pushed the earth from the sound leg, then from the wounded one. But the soil was wet with blood. The leg lay diverted. He tried to move a little. The leg did not move. There seemed a great gap in his being. He knew that part of his thigh was blown away. He could not think of the great bloody mess. It seemed to be himself, a wet, smashed, red mass. Very faintly the thin being of his consciousness hovered near. A frail, fine being seemed to be distilled out of the gaping red horror. As he sat he was detached from his wounds and his body.

Beyond his knowledge of his mutilation he remained faint and isolated in a cold, unchanging state. His being had become abstract and immutable. He sat there isolated, pure, abstract, in a state of supreme logical clarity. This he was now, a cold, clear abstraction. And as such he was going to judge. The outcome should be a pure, eternal, logical judgment: whether he should live or die. He examined his thought of his wife, and waited to see whether he should move to her. He waited still. Then his faintly beating heart died. The decision was no. He had no relation there. He fell away towards death. But still the tribunal was not closed. There were the children. He thought of them and saw them. But the thought of them did not stir the impulse back to life. He thought of them, but the thought of them left him cold and clear and abstract; they remained remote, away in life. And still he waited. Was it, then, finally decided? And out of the cold silence came the knowledge. It was decided he remained beyond, clear and untouched, in death.

In this supreme and transcendent state he remained motionless, knowing neither pain nor trouble, but only the extreme suspension of passing away.

Till the horrible sickness of dissolution came back, the overwhelming cold agony of dissolution.

As he lay in this cold, sweating anguish of dissolution, something again startled his consciousness, and, in a clear, abstract movement, he sat up. He was now no longer a man, but a disembodied, clear abstraction.

He saw two Germans who had ridden up, dismount by the body of the lieutenant.

"*Kaput?*"

"*Jawohl!*"

In a transcendent state of consciousness he lay and looked. They were turning over the body of the lieutenant. He saw the muscles of their shoulders as they moved their arms.

Clearly, in a calm, remote transcendence, he reached for his revolver. A man had ridden past him up the bank. He knew, but he was as if isolated from everything in this distinct, fine will of his own. He lay and took careful, supreme, almost absolute aim. One of the Germans started up, but the body of the other, who was bending over the dead lieutenant, pitched forward and collapsed, writhing. It was inevitable. A fine, transcendent spirituality was on the face of the Englishman, a white gleam. The other German, with a curious, almost ludicrous bustling movement had got out his revolver and was running forwards, when he saw the wounded, subtle Englishman luminous with an abstract smile on his face. At the same instant two bullets entered his body, one in the breast, and one in the belly. The body stumbled forward with a rattling, choking, coughing noise, the revolver went off in the air, the body fell on to its knees. The Englishman, still luminous and clear, fired at the dropped head. The bullet broke the neck.

Another German had ridden up, and was reining his horse in terror. The Englishman aimed at the red, sweating face. The body started with horror and began slipping out of the saddle, a bullet through its brain.

At the same moment the Englishman felt a sharp blow, and knew he was hit. But it was immaterial. The man above was firing at him. He turned round with difficulty as he lay. But he was struck again, and a sort of paralysis came over him. He saw the red face of a German with blue, staring eyes coming upon him, and he knew a knife was striking him. For one moment he felt the searing of steel, another final agony of suffocating darkness.

The German cut and mutilated the face of the dead man as if he must obliterate it. He slashed it across, as if it must not be a face any more; it must be removed. For he could not bear the clear, abstract look of the other's face, its almost ghoulish, slight smile, faint but so terrible in its suggestion, that the German was mad, and ran up the road when he found himself alone.

THE HORSE-DEALER'S DAUGHTER

"Well, Mabel, and what are you going to do with yourself?" asked Joe, with foolish flippancy. He felt quite safe himself. Without listening for an answer, he turned aside, worked a grain of tobacco to the tip of his tongue, and spat it out. He did not care about anything, since he felt safe himself.

The three brothers and the sister sat round the desolate breakfast-table, attempting some sort of desultory consultation. The morning's post had given the final tap to the family fortunes, and all was over. The dreary dining-room itself, with its heavy mahogany furniture, looked as if it were waiting to be done away with.

But the consultation amounted to nothing. There was a strange air of ineffectuality about the three men, as they sprawled at table, smoking and reflecting vaguely on their own condition. The girl was alone, a rather short, sullen-looking young woman of twenty-seven. She did not share the same life as her brothers. She would have been good-looking, save for the impassive fixity of her face, "bull-dog," as her brothers called it.

There was a confused tramping of horses' feet outside. The three men all sprawled round in their chairs, to watch. Beyond the dark holly-bushes that separated the strip of lawn from the high road, they could see a cavalcade of shire horses swinging out of their own yard, being taken for exercise. This was the last time. These were the last horses that would go through their hands. The young men watched with critical, callous look. They were all frightened at the collapse of their lives, and the sense of disaster in which they were involved left them no inner freedom.

Yet they were three fine, well-set fellows enough. Joe, the eldest, was a man of thirty-three, broad and handsome in a hot, flushed way. His face was red, he twisted his black moustache over a thick finger, his eyes were shallow and restless. He had a sensual way of uncovering his teeth when he laughed, and his bearing was stupid. Now he watched the horses with a glazed look of helplessness in his eyes, a certain stupor of downfall.

The great draught-horses swung past. They were tied head to tail, four of them, and they heaved along to where a lane branched off from the high road, planting their great hoofs floutingly in the fine black mud, swinging their great rounded haunches sumptuously, and trotting a few sudden steps as they were led into the lane, round the corner. Every movement showed a massive, slumbrous strength, and a stupidity which held them in subjection. The groom at the head looked back, jerking the leading rope. And the cavalcade moved out of sight up the lane, the tail of the last horse, bobbed up tight and stiff, held out taut from the swinging great haunches as they rocked behind the hedges in a motion like sleep.

Joe watched with glazed, hopeless eyes. The horses were almost like his own body to him. He felt he was done for now. Luckily he was engaged to a woman as old as himself, and therefore her father, who was steward of a neighbouring estate, would provide him with a job. He would marry and go into harness. His life was over, he would be a subject animal now.

He turned uneasily aside, the retreating steps of the horses echoing in his ears. Then, with foolish restlessness, he reached for the scraps of bacon-rind from the plates, and, making a faint whistling sound, flung them to the terrier that lay against the fender. He watched the dog swallow them, and waited till the creature looked into his eyes. Then a faint grin came on his face, and in a high, foolish voice he said:

"You won't get much more bacon, shall you, you little b——?"

The dog faintly and dismally wagged its tail, then lowered its haunches, circled round, and lay down again.

There was another helpless silence at the table. Joe sprawled uneasily in his seat, not willing to go till the family conclave was dissolved. Fred Henry, the second brother, was erect, clean-limbed, alert. He had watched the passing of the horses with more *sang-froid*. If he was an animal, like Joe, he was an animal which controls, not one which is controlled. He was master of any horse, and he carried himself with a well-tempered air of mastery. But he was not master of the situations of life. He pushed his coarse brown moustache upwards, off his lip, and glanced irritably at his sister, who sat impassive and inscrutable.

"You'll go and stop with Lucy for a bit, shan't you?" he asked. The girl did not answer.

"I don't see what else you can do," persisted Fred Henry.

"Go as a skivvy," Joe interpolated laconically.

The girl did not move a muscle.

"If I was her, I should go in for training for a nurse," said Malcolm, the youngest of them all. He was the baby of the family, a young man of twenty-two, with a fresh, jaunty *museau*.

But Mabel did not take any notice of him. They had talked at her and round her for so many years, that she hardly heard them at all.

The marble clock on the mantelpiece softly chimed the half-hour, the dog rose uneasily from the hearthrug and looked at the party at the breakfast-table. But still they sat on in ineffectual conclave.

"Oh all right," said Joe suddenly, *à propos* of nothing. "I'll get a move on."

He pushed back his chair, straddled his knees with a downward jerk, to get them free, in horsey fashion, and went to the fire. Still he did not go out of the room, he was curious to know what the others would do or say. He began to charge his pipe, looking down at the dog and saying, in a high, affected voice:

"Going wi' me? Going wi' me are ter? Tha'rt goin' further than tha counts on just now, dost hear?"

The dog faintly wagged its tail, the man stuck out his jaw and covered his pipe with his hands, and puffed intently, losing himself in the tobacco, looking down all the while at the dog, with an absent brown eye. The dog looked up at him in mournful distrust. Joe stood with his knees stuck out, in real horsey fashion.

"Have you had a letter from Lucy?" Fred Henry asked of his sister.

"Last week," came the neutral reply.

"And what does she say?"

There was no answer.

"Does she *ask* you to go and stop there?" persisted Fred Henry.

"She says I can if I like."

"Well, then, you'd better. Tell her you'll come on Monday."

This was received in silence.

"That's what you'll do then, is it?" said Fred Henry, in some exasperation.

But she made no answer. There was a silence of futility and irritation in the room. Malcolm grinned fatuously.

"You'll have to make up your mind between now and next Wednesday," said Joe loudly, "or else find yourself lodgings on the kerbstone."

The face of the young woman darkened, but she sat on immutable.

"Here's Jack Fergusson!" exclaimed Malcolm, who was looking aimlessly out of the window.

"Where?" exclaimed Joe loudly.

"Just gone past."

"Coming in?"

Malcolm craned his neck to see the gate.

"Yes," he said.

There was a silence. Mabel sat on like one condemned, at the head of the table. Then a whistle was heard from the kitchen. The dog got up and barked sharply. Joe opened the door and shouted:

"Come on."

After a moment, a young man entered. He was muffled up in overcoat and a purple woollen scarf, and his tweed cap, which he did not remove, was pulled down on his head. He was of medium height, his face was rather long and pale, his eyes looked tired.

"Hallo, Jack! Well, Jack!" exclaimed Malcolm and Joe. Fred Henry merely said "Jack!"

"What's doing?" asked the newcomer, evidently addressing Fred Henry.

"Same. We've got to be out by Wednesday.—Got a cold?"

"I have—got it bad, too."

"Why don't you stop in?"

"*Me* stop in? When I can't stand on my legs, perhaps I shall have a chance." The young man spoke huskily. He had a slight Scotch accent.

"It's a knock-out, isn't it," said Joe boisterously, "if a doctor goes round croaking with a cold. Looks bad for the patients, doesn't it?"

The young doctor looked at him slowly.

"Anything the matter with *you*, then?" he asked sarcastically.

"Not as I know of. Damn your eyes, I hope not. Why?"

"I thought you were very concerned about the patients, wondered if you might be one yourself."

"Damn it, no, I've never been patient to no flaming doctor, and hope I never shall be," returned Joe.

At this point Mabel rose from the table, and they all seemed to become aware of her existence. She began putting the dishes together. The young doctor looked at her, but did not address her. He had not greeted her. She went out of the room with the tray, her face impassive and unchanged.

"When are you off then, all of you?" asked the doctor.

"I'm catching the eleven-forty," replied Malcolm. "Are you goin' down wi' th' trap, Joe?"

"Yes, you young b——, I've told you I'm going down wi' th' trap, haven't I?"

"We'd better be getting her in then.—So long, Jack, if I don't see you before I go," said Malcolm, shaking hands.

He went out, followed by Joe, who seemed to have his tail between his legs.

"Well, this is the devil's own," exclaimed the doctor when

he was left alone with Fred Henry. "Going before Wednesday, are you?"

"That's the orders," replied the other.

"Where, to Northampton?"

"That's it."

"The devil!" exclaimed Fergusson with quiet chagrin.

And there was silence between the two.

"All settled up, are you?" asked Fergusson.

"About."

There was another pause.

"Well, I shall miss yer, Freddy boy," said the young doctor.

"And I shall miss thee, Jack," returned the other.

"Miss you like Hell," mused the doctor.

Fred Henry turned aside. There was nothing to say. Mabel came in again, to finish clearing the table.

"What are *you* going to do then, Miss Pervin?" asked Fergusson. "Going to your sister's, are you?"

Mabel looked at him with her steady, dangerous eyes, that always made him uncomfortable, unsettling his superficial ease.

"No," she said.

"Well, what in the name of fortune *are* you going to do? Say what you *mean* to do," cried Fred Henry with futile intensity.

But she only averted her head and continued her work. She folded the white tablecloth, and put on the chenille cloth.

"The sulkiest bitch that ever trod!" muttered her brother.

But she finished her task with perfectly impassive face, the young doctor watching her interestedly all the while. Then she went out.

Fred Henry stared after her, clenching his lips, his blue eyes fixing in sharp antagonism, as he made a grimace of sour exasperation.

"You could bray her into bits, and that's all you'd get out of her," he said in a small, narrowed tone.

The doctor smiled faintly.

"What's she *going* to do then?" he asked.

"Strike me if *I* know!" returned the other.

There was a pause. Then the doctor stirred.

"I'll be seeing you to-night, shall I?" he said to his friend.

"Ay—where's it to be? Are we going over to Jessdale?"

"I don't know. I've got such a cold on me. I'll come round to the Moon and Stars, anyway."

"Let Lizzie and May miss their night for once, eh?"

"That's it—if I feel as I do now."

"All's one——"

The two young men went through the passage and down to the back door together. The house was large, but it was servantless now, and desolate. At the back was a small bricked house-yard, and beyond that a big square, gravelled fine and red, and having stables on two sides. Sloping, dank, winter-dark fields stretched away on the open sides.

But the stables were empty. Joseph Pervin, the father of the family, had been a man of no education, who had become a fairly large horse-dealer. The stables had been full of horses, there was a great turmoil and come-and-go of horses and of dealers and grooms. Then the kitchen was full of servants. But of late things had declined. The old man had married a second time, to retrieve his fortunes. Now he was dead and everything was gone to the dogs, there was nothing but debt and threatening.

For months Mabel had been servantless in the big house, keeping the home together in penury for her ineffectual brothers. She had kept house for ten years. But previously it was with unstinted means. Then, however brutal and coarse everything was, the sense of money had kept her proud, confident. The men might be foul-mouthed, the women in the kitchen might have bad reputations, her brothers might have illegitimate children. But so long as there was money, the girl felt herself established, and brutally proud, reserved.

No company came to the house, save dealers and coarse men. Mabel had no associates of her own sex, after her sister went away. But she did not mind. She went regularly to church, she attended to her father. And she lived in the memory of her mother, who had died when she was fourteen, and whom she had loved. She had loved her father too, in a different way, depending upon him, and feeling secure in him, until at the age of fifty-four he married again. And then she had set hard against him. Now he had died and left them all hopelessly in debt.

She had suffered badly during the period of poverty. Nothing, however, could shake the curious sullen, animal pride that dominated each member of the family. Now, for Mabel, the end had come. Still she would not cast about her. She would follow her own way just the same. She would always hold the keys of her own situation. Mindless and persistent, she endured from day to day. Why should she think? Why should she answer anybody? It was enough that this was the end, and there was no way out. She need not pass any more darkly along the main street of the small town, avoiding every eye. She need not demean herself any more, going into the shops and buying the cheapest food. This was at an end. She thought of nobody, not even of herself. Mindless and persistent, she seemed in a sort of ecstasy to be coming nearer to her fulfilment, her own glorification, approaching her dead mother, who was glorified.

In the afternoon she took a little bag, with shears and sponge and a small scrubbing brush, and went out. It was a grey, wintry day, with saddened, dark-green fields and an atmosphere blackened by the smoke of foundries not far off. She went quickly, darkly along the causeway, heeding nobody, through the town to the churchyard.

There she always felt secure, as if no one could see her, although as a matter of fact she was exposed to the stare of everyone who passed along under the churchyard wall. Nevertheless, once under the shadow of the great looming church, among the graves, she felt immune from the world, reserved within the thick churchyard wall as in another country.

Carefully she clipped the grass from the grave, and arranged the pinky-white, small chrysanthemums in the tin cross. When this was done, she took an empty jar from a neighbouring grave, brought water, and carefully, most scrupulously sponged the marble headstone and the coping-stone.

It gave her sincere satisfaction to do this. She felt in immediate contact with the world of her mother. She took minute pains, went through the work in a state bordering on pure happiness, as if in performing this task she came into a subtle, intimate connection with her mother. For the life she followed here in the world was far less real than the world of death she inherited from her mother.

The doctor's house was just by the church. Fergusson, being a mere hired assistant, was slave to the countryside. As he hurried now to attend to the out-patients in the surgery, glancing across the graveyard with his quick eye he saw the girl at her task at the grave. She seemed so intent and remote, it was like looking into another world. Some mystical element was touched in him. He slowed down as he walked, watching her as if spellbound.

She lifted her eyes, feeling him looking. Their eyes met. And each looked away again at once, each feeling in some way found out by the other. He lifted his cap and passed on down the road. There remained distinct in his consciousness, like a vision, the memory of her face, lifted from the tombstone in the churchyard, and looking at him with slow, large, portentous eyes. It *was* portentous, her face. It seemed to mesmerise him. There was a heavy power in her eyes which laid hold of his whole being, as if he had drunk some powerful drug. He had been feeling weak and done before. Now the life came back into him, he felt delivered from his own fretted, daily self.

He finished his duties at the surgery as quickly as might be, hastily filling up the bottles of the waiting people with cheap drugs. Then, in perpetual haste, he set off again to visit several cases in another part of his round before tea-time. At all times he preferred to walk, if he could, but particularly when he was not well. He fancied the motion restored him.

The afternoon was falling. It was grey, deadened, and wintry, with a slow, moist, heavy coldness sinking in and deadening all the faculties. But why should he think or notice? He hastily climbed the hill and turned across the dark-green fields, following the black cinder-track. In the distance, across a shallow dip in the country, the small town was clustered like smouldering ash, a tower, a spire, a heap of low, raw, extinct houses. And on the nearest fringe of the town, sloping into the dip, was Oldmeadow, the Pervins' house. He could see the stables and the outbuildings distinctly, as they lay towards him on the slope.

Well, he would not go there many more times! Another resource would be lost to him, another place gone: the only company he cared for in the alien, ugly little town, he was losing. Nothing but work, drudgery, constant hastening from dwelling to dwelling among the colliers and the iron-workers. It wore him out, but at the same time he had a craving for it. It was a stimulant to him to be in the homes of the working people, moving, as it were, through the innermost body of their life. His nerves were excited and gratified. He could come so near, into the very lives of the rough, inarticulate, powerfully emotional men and women. He grumbled, he said he hated the hellish hole. But as a matter of fact it excited him, the contact with the rough, strongly-feeling people was a stimulant applied direct to his nerves.

Below Oldmeadow, in the green, shallow, soddened hollows of fields, lay a square deep pond. Roving across the landscape, the doctor's quick eye detected a figure in black passing through the gates of the field, down towards the pond. He looked again. It would be Mabel Pervin. His mind suddenly became alive and attentive.

Why was she going down there? He pulled up on the path on the slope above, and stood staring. He could just make sure of the small black figure moving in the hollow of the failing day. He seemed to see her in the midst of such obscurity, that he was like a clairvoyant, seeing rather with the mind's eye than with ordinary sight. Yet he could see her positively enough, whilst he kept his eye attentive. He felt, if he looked away from her, in the thick, ugly, falling dusk, he would lose her altogether.

He followed her minutely as she moved, direct and intent, like something transmitted rather than stirring in voluntary activity, straight down the field towards the pond. There she stood on the bank for a moment. She never raised her head. Then she waded slowly into the water.

He stood motionless as the small black figure walked slowly and deliberately towards the centre of the pond, very slowly, gradually moving deeper into the motionless water, and still moving forward as the water got up to her breast. Then he could see her no more in the dusk of the dead afternoon.

"There!" he exclaimed. "Would you believe it?"

And he hastened straight down, running over the wet, soddened fields, pushing through the hedges, down into the depression of callous wintry obscurity. It took him several minutes to come to the pond. He stood on the bank, breathing heavily. He could see nothing. His eyes seemed to penetrate the dead water. Yes, perhaps that was the dark shadow of her black clothing beneath the surface of the water.

He slowly ventured into the pond. The bottom was deep, soft clay; he sank in, and the water clasped dead cold round his legs. As he stirred he could smell the cold, rotten clay that fouled up into the water. It was objectionable in his lungs. Still, repelled and yet not heeding, he moved deeper into the pond. The cold water rose over his thighs, over his loins, upon his abdomen. The lower part of his body was all sunk in the hideous cold element. And the bottom was so deeply soft and uncertain, he was afraid of pitching with his mouth underneath. He could not swim, and was afraid.

He crouched a little, spreading his hands under the water and moving them round, trying to feel for her. The dead cold pond swayed upon his chest. He moved again, a little deeper, and again, with his hands underneath, he felt all around under the water. And he touched her clothing. But it evaded his fingers. He made a desperate effort to grasp it.

And so doing he lost his balance and went under, horribly, suffocating in the foul, earthy water, struggling madly for a few moments. At last, after what seemed an eternity, he got his footing, rose again into the air and looked around. He gasped, and knew he was in the world. Then he looked at the water. She had risen near him. He grasped her clothing, and, drawing her nearer, turned to take his way to land again.

He went very slowly, carefully, absorbed in the slow progress. He rose higher, climbing out of the pond. The water was now only about his legs; he was thankful, full of relief to be out of the clutches of the pond. He lifted her and staggered on to the bank, out of the horror of wet grey clay.

He laid her down on the bank. She was quite unconscious and running with water. He made the water come from her mouth, he worked to restore her. He did not have to work very long before he could feel the breathing begin again in her, she was breathing naturally. He worked a little longer. He could feel her live beneath his hands, she was coming back. He wiped her face, wrapped her in his overcoat, looked round into the dim, dark-grey world, then lifted her and staggered down the bank and across the fields.

It seemed an unthinkably long way, and his burden so heavy he felt he would never get to the house. But at last he was in the stable-yard, and then in the house-yard. He opened the door and went into the house. In the kitchen he laid her down on the hearthrug, and called. The house was empty. But the fire was burning in the grate.

Then again he kneeled to attend to her. She was breathing regularly, her eyes were wide open and as if conscious, but there seemed something missing in her look. She was conscious in herself, but unconscious of her surroundings.

He ran upstairs, took blankets from a bed, and put them before the fire to warm. Then he removed her saturated, earthy-smelling clothing, rubbed her dry with a towel, and wrapped her naked in the blankets. Then he went into the dining-room to look for spirits. There was a little whisky. He drank a gulp himself, and put some into her mouth.

The effect was instantaneous. She looked full into his face, as if she had been seeing him for some time, and yet had only just become conscious of him.

"Dr. Fergusson?" she said.

"What?" he answered.

He was divesting himself of his coat, intending to find some dry clothing upstairs. He could not bear the smell of the dead, clayey water, and he was mortally afraid for his own health.

"What did I do?" she asked.

"Walked into the pond," he replied. He had begun to shudder like one sick, and could hardly attend to her. Her eyes remained full on him; he seemed to be going dark in his mind, looking back at her helplessly. The shuddering became quieter in him, his life came back in him, dark and unknowing, but strong again.

"Was I out of my mind?" she asked, while her eyes were fixed on him all the time.

"Maybe, for the moment," he replied. He felt quiet, because his strength had come back. The strange fretful strain had left him.

"Am I out of my mind now?" she asked.

"Are you?" he reflected a moment. "No," he answered truthfully, "I don't see that you are." He turned his face aside. He was afraid, now, because he felt dazed, and felt dimly that her power was stronger than his, in this issue. And she continued to look at him fixedly all the time. "Can you tell me where I shall find some dry things to put on?" he asked.

"Did you dive into the pond for me?" she asked.

"No," he answered. "I walked in. But I went in overhead as well."

There was silence for a moment. He hesitated. He very much wanted to go upstairs to get into dry clothing. But there was another desire in him. And she seemed to hold him. His will seemed to have gone to sleep, and left him, standing there slack before her. But he felt warm inside himself. He did not shudder at all, though his clothes were sodden on him.

"Why did you?" she asked.

"Because I didn't want you to do such a foolish thing," he said.

"It wasn't foolish," she said, still gazing at him as she lay on the floor, with a sofa cushion under her head. "It was the right thing to do. *I* knew best, then."

"I'll go and shift these wet things," he said. But still he had not the power to move out of her presence, until she sent him. It was as if she had the life of his body in her hands, and he could not extricate himself. Or perhaps he did not want to.

Suddenly she sat up. Then she became aware of her own immediate condition. She felt the blankets about her, she knew her own limbs. For a moment it seemed as if her reason were going. She looked round, with wild eye, as if seeking something. He stood still with fear. She saw her clothing lying scattered.

"Who undressed me?" she asked, her eyes resting full and inevitable on his face.

"I did," he replied, "to bring you round."

For some moments she sat and gazed at him awfully, her lips parted.

"Do you love me then?" she asked.

He only stood and stared at her fascinated. His soul seemed to melt.

She shuffled forward on her knees, and put her arms round him, round his legs, as he stood there, pressing her breasts against his knees and thighs, clutching him with strange, convulsive certainty, pressing his thighs against her, drawing him to her face, her throat, as she looked up at him with flaring, humble eyes of transfiguration, triumphant in first possession.

"You love me," she murmured, in strange transport, yearning and triumphant and confident. "You love me. I know you love me, I know."

And she was passionately kissing his knees through the wet clothing, passionately and indiscriminately kissing his knees, his legs, as if unaware of everything.

He looked down at the tangled wet hair, the wild, bare, animal shoulders. He was amazed, bewildered, and afraid. He had never thought of loving her. He had never wanted to love her. When he rescued her and restored her, he was a doctor and she was a patient. He had had no single personal thought of her. Nay, this introduction of the personal element was very distasteful to him, a violation of his professional honour. It was horrible to have her there embracing his knees. It was horrible. He revolted from it violently. And yet—and yet—he had not the power to break away.

She looked at him again, with the same supplication of powerful love, and that same transcendent, frightening light of triumph. In view of the delicate flame which seemed to come from her face like a light, he was powerless. And yet he had never intended to love her. He had never intended. And something stubborn in him could not give way.

"You love me," she repeated, in a murmur of deep, rhapsodic assurance. "You love me."

Her hands were drawing him, drawing him down to her. He was afraid, even a little horrified. For he had really no intention of loving her. Yet her hands were drawing him towards her. He put out his hand quickly to steady himself, and grasped her bare shoulder. A flame seemed to burn the hand that grasped her soft shoulder. He had no intention of loving her: his whole will was against his yielding. It was horrible—— And yet wonderful was the touch of her shoulder, beautiful the shining of her face. Was she perhaps mad? He had a horror of yielding to her. Yet something in him ached also.

He had been staring away at the door, away from her. But his hand remained on her shoulder. She had gone suddenly very still. He looked down at her. Her eyes were now wide with fear, with doubt, the light was dying from her face, a shadow of terrible greyness was returning. He could not bear the touch of her eyes' question upon him, and the look of death behind the question.

With an inward groan he gave way, and let his heart yield towards her. A sudden gentle smile came on his face. And her eyes, which never left his face, slowly, slowly filled with tears. He watched the strange water rise in her eyes, like some slow fountain coming up. And his heart seemed to burn and melt in his breast.

He could not bear to look at her any more. He dropped on his knees and caught her head with his arm and pressed her face against his throat. She was very still. His heart, which seemed to have broken, was burning with a kind of agony in his breast. And he felt her slow, hot tears wetting his throat. But he could not move.

He felt the hot tears wet his neck and the hollows of his neck, and he remained motionless, suspended through one of man's eternities. Only now it had become indispensable to him to have her face pressed close to him, he could never let her go again. He could never let her head go away from the close clutch of his arm. He wanted to remain like that for ever, with his heart hurting him in a pain that was also life to him. Without knowing, he was looking down on her damp, soft brown hair.

Then, as it were suddenly, he smelt the horrid stagnant smell of that water. And at the same moment she drew away from him and looked at him. Her eyes were wistful and unfathomable. He was afraid of them, and he fell to kissing her, not knowing what he was doing. He wanted her eyes not to have that terrible wistful, unfathomable look.

When she turned her face to him again, a faint delicate flush was glowing, and there was again dawning that terrible shining of joy in her eyes, which really terrified him, and yet which he now wanted to see, because he feared the look of doubt still more.

"You love me?" she said, rather faltering.

"Yes." The word cost him a painful effort. Not because it wasn't true. But because it was too newly true, the *saying* seemed to tear open again his newly-torn heart. And he hardly wanted it to be true, even now.

She lifted her face to him, and he bent forward and kissed her on the mouth, gently, with the one kiss that is an eternal pledge. And as he kissed her his heart strained again in his breast. He never intended to love her. But now it was over. He had crossed over the gulf to her, and all that he had left behind had shrivelled and become void.

After the kiss, her eyes again slowly filled with tears. She sat still, away from him, with her face dropped aside, and her hands folded in her lap. The tears fell very slowly. There was complete silence. He too sat there motionless and silent on the hearthrug. The strange pain of his heart that was broken seemed to consume him. That he should love her! That this was love! That he should be ripped open in this way!—him, a doctor!— How they would all jeer if they knew!—It was agony to him to think they might know.

In the curious naked pain of the thought he looked again to her. She was sitting there drooped into a muse. He saw a tear fall, and his heart flared hot. He saw for the first time that one of her shoulders was quite uncovered, one arm bare, he could see one of her small breasts; dimly, because it had become almost dark in the room.

"Why are you crying?" he asked in an altered voice.

She looked up at him, and behind her tears the consciousness of her situation for the first time brought a dark look of shame to her eyes.

"I'm not crying, really," she said, watching him half frightened.

He reached his hand, and softly closed it on her bare arm.

"I love you! I love you!" he said in a soft, low, vibrating voice, unlike himself.

She shrank, and dropped her head. The soft, penetrating grip of his hand on her arm distressed her. She looked up at him.

"I want to go," she said, "I want to go and get you some dry things."

"Why?" he said. "I'm all right."

"But I want to go," she said. "And I want you to change your things."

He released her arm, and she wrapped herself in the blanket, looking at him rather frightened. And still she did not rise.

"Kiss me," she said wistfully.

He kissed her, but briefly, half in anger.

Then, after a second, she rose nervously, all mixed up in the blanket. He watched her in her confusion, as she tried to extricate herself and wrap herself up so that she could walk. He watched her relentlessly, as she knew. And as she went, the blanket trailing, and as he saw a glimpse of her feet and her white leg, he tried to remember her as she was when he had wrapped her in the blanket. But he didn't want to remember, because she had been nothing to him then, and his nature revolted from remembering what she was when she was nothing to him.

A tumbling, muffled noise from within the dark house startled him. Then he heard her voice:—"There are clothes." He rose and went to the foot of the stairs, and gathered up the garments she had thrown down. Then he came back to the fire, to rub himself down and dress. He grinned at his own appearance when he had finished.

The fire was sinking, so he put on coal. The house was now quite dark, save for the light of a street-lamp that shone in faintly from beyond the holly trees. He lit the gas with matches he found on the mantelpiece. Then he emptied the pockets of his own clothes, and threw all his wet things in a heap into the scullery. After which he gathered up her sodden clothes, gently, and put them in a separate heap on the copper-top in the scullery.

It was six o'clock on the clock. His own watch had stopped. He ought to go back to the surgery. He waited, and still she did not come down. So he went to the foot of the stairs and called:

"I shall have to go."

Almost immediately he heard her coming down. She had on her best dress of black voile, and her hair was tidy, but still damp. She looked at him—and, in spite of herself, smiled.

"I don't like you in those clothes," she said.

"Do I look a sight?" he answered.

They were shy of one another.

"I'll make you some tea," she said.

"No, I must go."

"Must you?" And she looked at him again with the wide, strained, doubtful eyes. And again, from the pain of his breast, he knew how he loved her. He went and bent to kiss her, gently, passionately, with his heart's painful kiss.

"And my hair smells so horrible," she murmured in distraction. "And I'm so awful, I'm so awful! Oh, no, I'm too awful," and she broke into bitter, heart-broken sobbing. "You can't want to love me, I'm horrible."

"Don't be silly, don't be silly," he said, trying to comfort her, kissing her, holding her in his arms. "I want you, I want to marry you; we're going to be married, quickly, quickly—to-morrow if I can."

But she only sobbed terribly, and cried:

"I feel awful. I feel awful. I feel I'm horrible to you."

"No, I want you, I want you," was all he answered, blindly, with that terrible intonation which frightened her almost more than her horror lest he should *not* want her.

THE BLIND MAN

Isabel Pervin was listening for two sounds—for the sound of wheels on the drive outside and for the noise of her husband's footsteps in the hall. Her dearest and oldest friend, a man who seemed almost indispensable to her living, would drive up in the rainy dusk of the closing November day. The trap had gone to fetch him from the station. And her husband, who had been blinded in Flanders, and who had a disfiguring mark on his brow, would be coming in from the out-houses.

He had been home for a year now. He was totally blind. Yet they had been very happy. The Grange was Maurice's own place. The back was a farmstead, and the Wernhams, who occupied the rear premises, acted as farmers. Isabel lived with her husband in the handsome rooms in front. She and he had been almost entirely alone together since he was wounded. They talked and sang and read together in a wonderful and unspeakable intimacy. Then she reviewed books for a Scottish newspaper, carrying on her old interest, and he occupied himself a good deal with the farm. Sightless, he could still discuss everything with Wernham, and he could also do a good deal of work about the place, menial work, it is true, but it gave him satisfaction. He milked the cows, carried in the pails, turned the separator, attended to the pigs and horses. Life was still very full and strangely serene for the blind man, peaceful with the almost incomprehensible peace of immediate contact in darkness. With his wife he had a whole world, rich and real and invisible.

They were newly and remotely happy. He did not even regret

the loss of his sight in these times of dark, palpable joy. A certain exultance swelled his soul.

But as time wore on, sometimes the rich glamour would leave them. Sometimes, after months of this intensity, a sense of burden overcame Isabel, a weariness, a terrible *ennui*, in that silent house approached between a colonnade of tall-shafted pines. Then she felt she would go mad, for she could not bear it. And sometimes he had devastating fits of depression, which seemed to lay waste his whole being. It was worse than depression—a black misery, when his own life was a torture to him, and when his presence was unbearable to his wife. The dread went down to the roots of her soul as these black days recurred. In a kind of panic she tried to wrap herself up still further in her husband. She forced the old spontaneous cheerfulness and joy to continue. But the effort it cost her was almost too much. She knew she could not keep it up. She felt she would scream with the strain, and would give anything, anything, to escape. She longed to possess her husband utterly; it gave her inordinate joy to have him entirely to herself. And yet, when again he was gone in a black and massive misery, she could not bear him, she could not bear herself; she wished she could be snatched away off the earth altogether, anything rather than live at this cost.

Dazed, she schemed for a way out. She invited friends, she tried to give him some further connection with the outer world. But it was no good. After all their joy and suffering, after their dark, great year of blindness and solitude and unspeakable nearness, other people seemed to them both shallow, prattling, rather impertinent. Shallow prattle seemed presumptuous. He became impatient and irritated, she was wearied. And so they lapsed into their solitude again. For they preferred it.

But now, in a few weeks' time, her second baby would be born. The first had died, an infant, when her husband first went out to France. She looked with joy and relief to the coming of the second. It would be her salvation. But also she felt some anxiety. She was thirty years old, her husband was a year younger. They both wanted the child very much. Yet she could not help feeling afraid. She had her husband on her hands, a terrible joy to her, and a terrifying burden. The child would occupy her love and attention. And then, what of Maurice? What would he do? If only she could feel that he, too, would be at peace and happy when the child came! She did so want to luxuriate in a rich, physical satisfaction of maternity. But the man, what would he do? How could she provide for him, how avert those shattering black moods of his, which destroyed them both?

She sighed with fear. But at this time Bertie Reid wrote to Isabel. He was her old friend, a second or third cousin, a Scotchman, as she was a Scotchwoman. They had been brought up near to one another, and all her life he had been her friend, like a brother, but better than her own brothers. She loved him—though not in the marrying sense. There was a sort of kinship between them, an affinity. They understood one another instinctively. But Isabel would never have thought of marrying Bertie. It would have seemed like marrying in her own family.

Bertie was a barrister and a man of letters, a Scotchman of the intellectual type, quick, ironical, sentimental, and on his knees before the woman he adored but did not want to marry. Maurice Pervin was different. He came of a good old country family—the Grange was not a very great distance from Oxford. He was passionate, sensitive, perhaps over-sensitive, wincing— a big fellow with heavy limbs and a forehead that flushed painfully. For his mind was slow, as if drugged by the strong provincial blood that beat in his veins. He was very sensitive to his own mental slowness, his feelings being quick and acute. So that he was just the opposite to Bertie, whose mind was much quicker than his emotions, which were not so very fine.

From the first the two men did not like each other. Isabel felt that they *ought* to get on together. But they did not. She felt that if only each could have the clue to the other there would be such a rare understanding between them. It did not come off, however. Bertie adopted a slightly ironical attitude, very offensive to Maurice, who returned the Scotch irony with English resentment, a resentment which deepened sometimes into stupid hatred.

This was a little puzzling to Isabel. However, she accepted it in the course of things. Men were made freakish and unreasonable. Therefore, when Maurice was going out to France for the second time, she felt that, for her husband's sake, she must discontinue her friendship with Bertie. She wrote to the barrister to this effect. Bertram Reid simply replied that in this, as in all other matters, he must obey her wishes, if these were indeed her wishes.

For nearly two years nothing had passed between the two friends. Isabel rather gloried in the fact: she had no compunction. She had one great article of faith, which was, that husband and wife should be so important to one another, that the rest of the world simply did not count. She and Maurice were husband and wife. They loved one another. They would have children. Then let everybody and everything else fade into insignificance outside this connubial felicity. She professed herself quite happy and ready to receive Maurice's friends. She was happy and ready: the happy wife, the ready woman in possession. Without knowing why, the friends retired abashed, and came no more. Maurice, of course, took as much satisfaction in this connubial absorption as Isabel did.

He shared in Isabel's literary activities, she cultivated a real interest in agriculture and cattle-raising. For she, being at heart perhaps an emotional enthusiast, always cultivated the practical side of life, and prided herself on her mastery of practical affairs. Thus the husband and wife had spent the five years of their married life. The last had been one of blindness and unspeakable intimacy. And now Isabel felt a great indifference coming over her, a sort of lethargy. She wanted to be allowed to bear her child in peace, to nod by the fire and drift vaguely, physically, from day to day. Maurice was like an ominous thundercloud. She had to keep waking up to remember him.

When a little note came from Bertie, asking if he were to put up a tombstone to their dead friendship, and speaking of the real pain he felt on account of her husband's loss of sight, she felt a pang, a fluttering agitation of re-awakening. And she read the letter to Maurice.

"Ask him to come down," he said.

"Ask Bertie to come here!" she re-echoed.

"Yes—if he wants to."

Isabel paused for a few moments.

"I know he wants to—he'd only be too glad," she replied. "But what about you, Maurice? How would you like it?"

"I should like it."

"Well—in that case—— But I thought you didn't care for him——"

"Oh, I don't know. I might think different of him now," the blind man replied. It was rather abstruse to Isabel.

"Well, dear," she said, "if you're quite sure——"

"I'm sure enough. Let him come," said Maurice.

So Bertie was coming, coming this evening, in the November rain and darkness. Isabel was agitated, racked with her old restlessness and indecision. She had always suffered from this pain of doubt, just an agonising sense of uncertainty. It had begun to pass off, in the lethargy of maternity. Now it returned, and she resented it. She struggled as usual to maintain her calm, composed, friendly bearing, a sort of mask she wore over all her body.

A woman had lighted a tall lamp beside the table, and spread the cloth. The long dining-room was dim, with its elegant but rather severe pieces of old furniture. Only the round table glowed softly under the light. It had a rich, beautiful effect. The white cloth glistened and dropped its heavy, pointed lace corners almost to the carpet, the china was old and handsome, creamy-yellow, with a blotched pattern of harsh red and deep blue, the cups large and bell-shaped, the teapot gallant. Isabel looked at it with superficial appreciation.

Her nerves were hurting her. She looked automatically again at the high, uncurtained windows. In the last dusk she could just perceive outside a huge fir-tree swaying its boughs: it was as if she thought it rather than saw it. The rain came flying on the window panes. Ah, why had she no peace? These two men, why did they tear at her? Why did they not come—why was there this suspense?

She sat in a lassitude that was really suspense and irritation. Maurice, at least, might come in—there was nothing to keep him out. She rose to her feet. Catching sight of her reflection in a mirror, she glanced at herself with a slight smile of recognition, as if she were an old friend to herself. Her face was oval and calm, her nose a little arched. Her neck made a beautiful line down to her shoulder. With hair knotted loosely behind, she had something of a warm, maternal look. Thinking this of herself, she arched her eyebrows and her rather heavy eye-lids, with a little flicker of a smile, and for a moment her grey eyes looked amused and wicked, a little sardonic, out of her transfigured Madonna face.

Then, resuming her air of womanly patience—she was really fatally self-determined—she went with a little jerk towards the door. Her eyes were slightly reddened.

She passed down the wide hall, and through a door at the end. Then she was in the farm premises. The scent of dairy, and of farm-kitchen, and of farm-yard and of leather almost overcame her: but particularly the scent of dairy. They had been scalding out the pans. The flagged passage in front of her was dark, puddled and wet. Light came out from the open kitchen door. She went forward and stood in the doorway. The farm-people were at tea, seated at a little distance from her, round a long, narrow table, in the centre of which stood a white lamp. Ruddy faces, ruddy hands holding food, red mouths working, heads bent over the tea-cups: men, land-girls, boys: it was tea-time, feeding-time. Some faces caught sight of her. Mrs. Wernham, going round behind the chairs with a large black tea-pot, halting slightly in her walk, was not aware of her for a moment. Then she turned suddenly.

"Oh, is it Madam!" she exclaimed. "Come in, then, come in! We're at tea." And she dragged forward a chair.

"No, I won't come in," said Isabel. "I'm afraid I interrupt your meal."

"No—no—not likely, Madam, not likely."

"Hasn't Mr. Pervin come in, do you know?"

"I'm sure I couldn't say! Missed him, have you, Madam?"

"No, I only wanted him to come in," laughed Isabel, as if shyly.

"Wanted him, did ye? Get up, boy—get up, now——"

Mrs. Wernham knocked one of the boys on the shoulder. He began to scrape to his feet, chewing largely.

"I believe he's in top stable," said another face from the table.

"Ah! No, don't get up. I'm going myself," said Isabel.

"Don't you go out of a dirty night like this. Let the lad go. Get along wi' ye, boy," said Mrs. Wernham.

"No, no," said Isabel, with a decision that was always obeyed. "Go on with your tea, Tom. I'd like to go across to the stable, Mrs. Wernham."

"Did ever you hear tell!" exclaimed the woman.

"Isn't the trap late?" asked Isabel.

"Why, no," said Mrs. Wernham, peering into the distance at the tall, dim clock. "No, Madam—we can give it another quarter or twenty minutes yet, good—yes, every bit of a quarter."

"Ah! It seems late when darkness falls so early," said Isabel.

"It do, that it do. Bother the days, that they draw in so," answered Mrs. Wernham. "Proper miserable!"

"They are," said Isabel, withdrawing.

She pulled on her overshoes, wrapped a large Tartan shawl around her, put on a man's felt hat, and ventured out along the causeways of the first yard. It was very dark. The wind was roaring in the great elms behind the outhouses. When she came to the second yard the darkness seemed deeper. She was unsure of her footing. She wished she had brought a lantern. Rain blew against her. Half she liked it, half she felt unwilling to battle.

She reached at last the just visible door of the stable. There was no sign of a light anywhere. Opening the upper half, she looked in: into a simple well of darkness. The smell of horses, and ammonia, and of warmth was startling to her, in that full night. She listened with all her ears, but could hear nothing save the night, and the stirring of a horse.

"Maurice!" she called, softly and musically, though she was afraid. "Maurice—are you there?"

Nothing came from the darkness. She knew the rain and wind blew in upon the horses, the hot animal life. Feeling it wrong, she entered the stable, and drew the lower half of the door shut, holding the upper part close. She did not stir, because she was aware of the presence of the dark hind-quarters of the horses, though she could not see them, and she was afraid. Something wild stirred in her heart.

She listened intensely. Then she heard a small noise in the distance—far away, it seemed—the chink of a pan, and a man's voice speaking a brief word. It would be Maurice, in the other part of the stable. She stood motionless, waiting for him to come through the partition door. The horses were so terrifyingly near to her, in the invisible.

The loud jarring of the inner door-latch made her start; the door was opened. She could hear and feel her husband entering and invisibly passing among the horses near to her, in darkness as they were, actively intermingled. The rather low sound of his voice as he spoke to the horses came velvety to her nerves. How near he was, and how invisible! The darkness seemed to be in a strange swirl of violent life, just upon her. She turned giddy.

Her presence of mind made her call, quietly and musically: "Maurice! Maurice—dea-ar!"

"Yes," he answered. "Isabel?"

She saw nothing, and the sound of his voice seemed to touch her.

"Hello!" she answered cheerfully, straining her eyes to see him. He was still busy, attending to the horses near her, but she saw only darkness. It made her almost desperate.

"Won't you come in, dear?" she said.

"Yes, I'm coming. Just half a minute. *Stand over—now!* Trap's not come, has it?"

"Not yet," said Isabel.

His voice was pleasant and ordinary, but it had a slight suggestion of the stable to her. She wished he would come away. Whilst he was so utterly invisible, she was afraid of him.

"How's the time?" he asked.

"Not yet six," she replied. She disliked to answer into the dark. Presently he came very near to her, and she retreated out of doors.

"The weather blows in here," he said, coming steadily forward, feeling for the doors. She shrank away. At last she could dimly see him.

"Bertie won't have much of a drive," he said, as he closed the doors.

"He won't indeed!" said Isabel calmly, watching the dark shape at the door.

"Give me your arm, dear," she said.

She pressed his arm close to her, as she went. But she longed to see him, to look at him. She was nervous. He walked erect, with face rather lifted, but with a curious tentative movement of his powerful, muscular legs. She could feel the clever, careful, strong contact of his feet with the earth, as she balanced against him. For a moment he was a tower of darkness to her, as if he rose out of the earth.

In the house-passage he wavered, and went cautiously, with a curious look of silence about him as he felt for the bench. Then he sat down heavily. He was a man with rather sloping shoulders, but with heavy limbs, powerful legs that seemed to know the earth. His head was small, usually carried high and light. As he bent down to unfasten his gaiters and boots, he did not look blind. His hair was brown and crisp, his hands were large, reddish, intelligent, the veins stood out in the wrists; and his thighs and knees seemed massive. When he stood up his face and neck were surcharged with blood, the veins stood out on his temples. She did not look at his blindness.

Isabel was always glad when they had passed through the dividing door into their own regions of repose and beauty. She was a little afraid of him, out there in the animal grossness of the back. His bearing also changed, as he smelt the familiar indefinable odour that pervaded his wife's surroundings, a delicate, refined scent, very faintly spicy. Perhaps it came from the pot-pourri bowls.

He stood at the foot of the stairs, arrested, listening. She watched him, and her heart sickened. He seemed to be listening to fate.

"He's not here yet," he said. "I'll go up and change."

"Maurice," she said, "you're not wishing he wouldn't come, are you?"

"I couldn't quite say," he answered. "I feel myself rather on the *qui vive*."

"I can see you are," she answered. And she reached up and kissed his cheek. She saw his mouth relax into a slow smile.

"What are you laughing at?" she said, roguishly.

"You consoling me," he answered.

"Nay," she answered. "Why should I console you? You know we love each other—you know *how* married we are! What does anything else matter?"

"Nothing at all, my dear."

He felt for her face, and touched it, smiling.

"*You're* all right, aren't you?" he asked, anxiously.

"I'm wonderfully all right, love," she answered. "It's you I am a little troubled about, at times."

"Why me?" he said, touching her cheeks delicately with the tips of his fingers. The touch had an almost hypnotising effect on her.

He went away upstairs. She saw him mount into the darkness, unseeing and unchanging. He did not know that the lamps on the upper corridor were unlighted. He went on into the darkness with unchanging step. She heard him in the bath-room.

Pervin moved about almost unconsciously in his familiar surroundings, dark though everything was. He seemed to know the presence of objects before he touched them. It was a pleasure to him to rock thus through a world of things, carried on the flood in a sort of blood-prescience. He did not think much or trouble much. So long as he kept this sheer immediacy of blood-contact with the substantial world he was happy, he wanted no intervention of visual consciousness. In this state there was a certain rich positivity, bordering sometimes on rapture. Life seemed to move in him like a tide lapping, lapping, and advancing, enveloping all things darkly. It was a pleasure to stretch forth the hand and meet the unseen object, clasp it, and possess it in pure contact. He did not try to remember, to visualise. He did not want to. The new way of consciousness substituted itself in him.

The rich suffusion of this state generally kept him happy, reaching its culmination in the consuming passion for his wife.

But at times the flow would seem to be checked and thrown back. Then it would beat inside him like a tangled sea, and he was tortured in the shattered chaos of his own blood. He grew to dread this arrest, this throw-back, this chaos inside himself, when he seemed merely at the mercy of his own powerful and conflicting elements. How to get some measure of control or surety, this was the question. And when the question rose maddening in him, he would clench his fists as if he would *compel* the whole universe to submit to him. But it was in vain. He could not even compel himself.

To-night, however, he was still serene, though little tremors of unreasonable exasperation ran through him. He had to handle the razor very carefully, as he shaved, for it was not at one with him, he was afraid of it. His hearing also was too much sharpened. He heard the woman lighting the lamps on the corridor, and attending to the fire in the visitors' room. And then, as he went to his room, he heard the trap arrive. Then came Isabel's voice, lifted and calling, like a bell ringing:

"Is it you, Bertie? Have you come?"

And a man's voice answered out of the wind:

"Hello, Isabel! There you are."

"Have you had a miserable drive? I'm so sorry we couldn't send a closed carriage. I can't see you at all, you know."

"I'm coming. No, I liked the drive—it was like Perthshire. Well, how are you? You're looking fit as ever, as far as I can see."

"Oh, yes," said Isabel. "I'm wonderfully well. How are you? Rather thin, I think——"

"Worked to death—everybody's old cry. But I'm all right, Ciss. How's Pervin?—isn't he here?"

"Oh, yes, he's upstairs changing. Yes, he's awfully well. Take off your wet things; I'll send them to be dried."

"And how are you both, in spirits? He doesn't fret?"

"No—no, not at all. No, on the contrary, really. We've been wonderfully happy, incredibly. It's more than I can understand—so wonderful: the nearness, and the peace——"

"Ah! Well, that's awfully good news——"

They moved away. Pervin heard no more. But a childish sense

of desolation had come over him, as he heard their brisk voices. He seemed shut out—like a child that is left out. He was aimless and excluded, he did not know what to do with himself. The helpless desolation came over him. He fumbled nervously as he dressed himself, in a state almost of childishness. He disliked the Scotch accent in Bertie's speech, and the slight response it found on Isabel's tongue. He disliked the slight purr of complacency in the Scottish speech. He disliked intensely the glib way in which Isabel spoke of their happiness and nearness. It made him recoil. He was fretful and beside himself like a child, he had almost a childish nostalgia to be included in the life circle. And at the same time he was a man, dark and powerful and infuriated by his own weakness. By some fatal flaw, he could not be by himself, he had to depend on the support of another. And this very dependence enraged him. He hated Bertie Reid, and at the same time he knew the hatred was nonsense, he knew it was the outcome of his own weakness.

He went downstairs. Isabel was alone in the dining-room. She watched him enter, head erect, his feet tentative. He looked so strong-blooded and healthy, and, at the same time, cancelled. Cancelled—that was the word that flew across her mind. Perhaps it was his scar suggested it.

"You heard Bertie come, Maurice?" she said.

"Yes—isn't he here?"

"He's in his room. He looks very thin and worn."

"I suppose he works himself to death."

A woman came in with a tray—and after a few minutes Bertie came down. He was a little dark man, with a very big forehead, thin, wispy hair, and sad, large eyes. His expression was inordinately sad—almost funny. He had odd, short legs.

Isabel watched him hesitate under the door, and glance nervously at her husband. Pervin heard him and turned.

"Here you are, now," said Isabel. "Come, let us eat."

Bertie went across to Maurice.

"How are you, Pervin?" he said, as he advanced.

The blind man stuck his hand out into space, and Bertie took it.

"Very fit. Glad you've come," said Maurice.

Isabel glanced at them, and glanced away, as if she could not bear to see them.

"Come," she said. "Come to table. Aren't you both awfully hungry? I am, tremendously."

"I'm afraid you waited for me," said Bertie, as they sat down.

Maurice had a curious monolithic way of sitting in a chair, erect and distant. Isabel's heart always beat when she caught sight of him thus.

"No," she replied to Bertie. "We're very little later than usual. We're having a sort of high tea, not dinner. Do you mind? It gives us such a nice long evening, uninterrupted."

"I like it," said Bertie.

Maurice was feeling, with curious little movements, almost like a cat kneading her bed, for his plate, his knife and fork, his napkin. He was getting the whole geography of his cover into his consciousness. He sat erect and inscrutable, remote-seeming. Bertie watched the static figure of the blind man, the delicate tactile discernment of the large, ruddy hands, and the curious mindless silence of the brow, above the scar. With difficulty he looked away, and without knowing what he did, picked up a little crystal bowl of violets from the table, and held them to his nose.

"They are sweet-scented," he said. "Where do they come from?"

"From the garden—under the windows," said Isabel.

"So late in the year—and so fragrant! Do you remember the violets under Aunt Bell's south wall?"

The two friends looked at each other and exchanged a smile, Isabel's eyes lighting up.

"Don't I?" she replied. "*Wasn't* she queer!"

"A curious old girl," laughed Bertie. "There's a streak of freakishness in the family, Isabel."

"Ah—but not in you and me, Bertie," said Isabel. "Give them to Maurice, will you?" she added, as Bertie was putting down the flowers. "Have you smelled the violets, dear? Do!—they are so scented."

Maurice held out his hand, and Bertie placed the tiny bowl against his large, warm-looking fingers. Maurice's hand closed over the thin white fingers of the barrister. Bertie carefully extricated himself. Then the two watched the blind man smelling the violets. He bent his head and seemed to be thinking. Isabel waited.

"Aren't they sweet, Maurice?" she said at last, anxiously.

"Very," he said. And he held out the bowl. Bertie took it. Both he and Isabel were a little afraid, and deeply disturbed.

The meal continued. Isabel and Bertie chatted spasmodically. The blind man was silent. He touched his food repeatedly, with quick, delicate touches of his knife-point, then cut irregular bits. He could not bear to be helped. Both Isabel and Bertie suffered: Isabel wondered why. She did not suffer when she was alone with Maurice. Bertie made her conscious of a strangeness.

After the meal the three drew their chairs to the fire, and sat down to talk. The decanters were put on a table near at hand. Isabel knocked the logs on the fire, and clouds of brilliant sparks went up the chimney. Bertie noticed a slight weariness in her bearing.

"You will be glad when your child comes now, Isabel?" he said.

She looked up to him with a quick, wan smile.

"Yes, I shall be glad," she answered. "It begins to seem long. Yes, I shall be very glad. So will you, Maurice, won't you?" she added.

"Yes, I shall," replied her husband.

"We are both looking forward so much to having it," she said.

"Yes, of course," said Bertie.

He was a bachelor, three or four years older than Isabel. He lived in beautiful rooms overlooking the river, guarded by a faithful Scottish man-servant. And he had his friends among the fair sex—not lovers, friends. So long as he could avoid any danger of courtship or marriage, he adored a few good women with constant and unfailing homage, and he was chivalrously fond of quite a number. But if they seemed to encroach on him, he withdrew and detested them.

Isabel knew him very well, knew his beautiful constancy, and kindness, also his incurable weakness, which made him unable ever to enter into close contact of any sort. He was ashamed of himself, because he could not marry, could not approach women physically. He wanted to do so. But he could not. At the centre of him he was afraid, helplessly and even brutally afraid. He had given up hope, had ceased to expect any more that he could escape his own weakness. Hence he was a brilliant and successful barrister, also a *littérateur* of high repute, a rich man, and a great social success. At the centre he felt himself neuter, nothing.

Isabel knew him well. She despised him even while she admired him. She looked at his sad face, his little short legs, and felt contempt of him. She looked at his dark grey eyes, with their uncanny, almost childlike intuition, and she loved him. He understood amazingly—but she had no fear of his understanding. As a man she patronised him.

And she turned to the impassive, silent figure of her husband. He sat leaning back, with folded arms, and face a little uptilted. His knees were straight and massive. She sighed, picked up the poker, and again began to prod the fire, to rouse the clouds of soft brilliant sparks.

"Isabel tells me," Bertie began suddenly, "that you have not suffered unbearably from the loss of sight."

Maurice straightened himself to attend, but kept his arms folded.

"No," he said, "not unbearably. Now and again one struggles against it, you know. But there are compensations."

"They say it is much worse to be stone deaf," said Isabel.

"I believe it is," said Bertie. "Are there compensations?" he added, to Maurice.

"Yes. You cease to bother about a great many things." Again Maurice stretched his figure, stretched the strong muscles of his back, and leaned backwards, with uplifted face.

"And that is a relief," said Bertie. "But what is there in place of the bothering? What replaces the activity?"

There was a pause. At length the blind man replied, as out of a negligent, unattentive thinking:

"Oh, I don't know. There's a good deal when you're not active."

"Is there?" said Bertie. "What, exactly? It always seems to me
that when there is no thought and no action, there is nothing."

Again Maurice was slow in replying.

"There is something," he replied. "I couldn't tell you what
it is."

And the talk lapsed once more, Isabel and Bertie chatting
gossip and reminiscence, the blind man silent.

At length Maurice rose restlessly, a big, obtrusive figure. He
felt tight and hampered. He wanted to go away.

"Do you mind," he said, "if I go and speak to Wernham?"

"No—go along, dear," said Isabel.

And he went out. A silence came over the two friends. At
length Bertie said:

"Nevertheless, it is a great deprivation, Cissie."

"It is, Bertie. I know it is."

"Something lacking all the time," said Bertie.

"Yes, I know. And yet—and yet—Maurice is right. There is
something else, something *there*, which you never knew was
there, and which you can't express."

"What is there?" asked Bertie.

"I don't know—it's awfully hard to define it—but something
strong and immediate. There's something strange in Maurice's
presence—indefinable—but I couldn't do without it. I agree
that it seems to put one's mind to sleep. But when we're alone
I miss nothing; it seems awfully rich, almost splendid, you
know."

"I'm afraid I don't follow," said Bertie.

They talked desultorily. The wind blew loudly outside, rain
chattered on the window-panes, making a sharp drum-sound,
because of the closed, mellow-golden shutters inside. The logs
burned slowly, with hot, almost invisible small flames. Bertie
seemed uneasy, there were dark circles round his eyes. Isabel,
rich with her approaching maternity, leaned looking into the
fire. Her hair curled in odd, loose strands, very pleasing to the
man. But she had a curious feeling of old woe in her heart, old,
timeless night-woe.

"I suppose we're all deficient somewhere," said Bertie.

"I suppose so," said Isabel wearily.

"Damned, sooner or later."

"I don't know," she said, rousing herself. "I feel quite all right, you know. The child coming seems to make me indifferent to everything, just placid. I can't feel that there's anything to trouble about, you know."

"A good thing, I should say," he replied slowly.

"Well, there it is. I suppose it's just Nature. If only I felt I needn't trouble about Maurice, I should be perfectly content——"

"But you feel you must trouble about him?"

"Well—I don't know——" She even resented this much effort.

The night passed slowly. Isabel looked at the clock.

"I say," she said. "It's nearly ten o'clock. Where can Maurice be? I'm sure they're all in bed at the back. Excuse me a moment."

She went out, returning almost immediately.

"It's all shut up and in darkness," she said. "I wonder where he is. He must have gone out to the farm——"

Bertie looked at her.

"I suppose he'll come in," he said.

"I suppose so," she said. "But it's unusual for him to be out now."

"Would you like me to go out and see?"

"Well—if you wouldn't mind. I'd go, but——" She did not want to make the physical effort.

Bertie put on an old overcoat and took a lantern. He went out from the side door. He shrank from the wet and roaring night. Such weather had a nervous effect on him: too much moisture everywhere made him feel almost imbecile. Unwilling, he went through it all. A dog barked violently at him. He peered in all the buildings. At last, as he opened the upper door of a sort of intermediate barn, he heard a grinding noise, and looking in, holding up his lantern, saw Maurice, in his shirt-sleeves, standing listening, holding the handle of a turnip-pulper. He had been pulping sweet roots, a pile of which lay dimly heaped in a corner behind him.

"That you, Wernham?" said Maurice, listening.

"No, it's me," said Bertie.

A large, half-wild grey cat was rubbing at Maurice's leg. The blind man stooped to rub its sides. Bertie watched the scene, then unconsciously entered and shut the door behind him. He was in a high sort of barn-place, from which, right and left, ran off the corridors in front of the stalled cattle. He watched the slow, stooping motion of the other man, as he caressed the great cat.

Maurice straightened himself.

"You came to look for me?" he said.

"Isabel was a little uneasy," said Bertie.

"I'll come in. I like messing about doing these jobs."

The cat had reared her sinister, feline length against his leg, clawing at his thigh affectionately. He lifted her claws out of his flesh.

"I hope I'm not in your way at all at the Grange here," said Bertie, rather shy and stiff.

"My way? No, not a bit. I'm glad Isabel has somebody to talk to. I'm afraid it's I who am in the way. I know I'm not very lively company. Isabel's all right, don't you think? She's not unhappy, is she?"

"I don't think so."

"What does she say?"

"She says she's very content—only a little troubled about you."

"Why me?"

"Perhaps afraid that you might brood," said Bertie, cautiously.

"She needn't be afraid of that." He continued to caress the flattened grey head of the cat with his fingers. "What I am a bit afraid of," he resumed, "is that she'll find me a dead weight, always alone with me down here."

"I don't think you need think that," said Bertie, though this was what he feared himself.

"I don't know," said Maurice. "Sometimes I feel it isn't fair that she's saddled with me." Then he dropped his voice curiously. "I say," he asked, secretly struggling, "is my face much disfigured? Do you mind telling me?"

"There is the scar," said Bertie, wondering. "Yes, it is a disfigurement. But more pitiable than shocking."

"A pretty bad scar, though," said Maurice.

"Oh, yes."

There was a pause.

"Sometimes I feel I am horrible," said Maurice, in a low voice, talking as if to himself. And Bertie actually felt a quiver of horror.

"That's nonsense," he said.

Maurice again straightened himself, leaving the cat.

"There's no telling," he said. Then again, in an odd tone, he added: "I don't really know you, do I?"

"Probably not," said Bertie.

"Do you mind if I touch you?"

The lawyer shrank away instinctively. And yet, out of very philanthropy, he said, in a small voice: "Not at all."

But he suffered as the blind man stretched out a strong, naked hand to him. Maurice accidentally knocked off Bertie's hat.

"I thought you were taller," he said, starting. Then he laid his hand on Bertie Reid's head, closing the dome of the skull in a soft, firm grasp, gathering it, as it were; then, shifting his grasp and softly closing again, with a fine, close pressure, till he had covered the skull and the face of the smaller man, tracing the brows, and touching the full, closed eyes, touching the small nose and the nostrils, the rough, short moustache, the mouth, the rather strong chin. The hand of the blind man grasped the shoulder, the arm, the hand of the other man. He seemed to take him, in the soft, travelling grasp.

"You seem young," he said quietly, at last.

The lawyer stood almost annihilated, unable to answer.

"Your head seems tender, as if you were young," Maurice repeated. "So do your hands. Touch my eyes, will you?—touch my scar."

Now Bertie quivered with revulsion. Yet he was under the power of the blind man, as if hypnotised. He lifted his hand, and laid the fingers on the scar, on the scarred eyes. Maurice suddenly covered them with his own hand, pressed the fingers of the other man upon his disfigured eye-sockets, trembling in every fibre, and rocking slightly, slowly, from side to side. He remained thus for a minute or more, whilst Bertie stood as if in a swoon, unconscious, imprisoned.

Then suddenly Maurice removed the hand of the other man from his brow, and stood holding it in his own.

"Oh, my God," he said, "we shall know each other now, shan't we? We shall know each other now."

Bertie could not answer. He gazed mute and terror-struck, overcome by his own weakness. He knew he could not answer. He had an unreasonable fear, lest the other man should suddenly destroy him. Whereas Maurice was actually filled with hot, poignant love, the passion of friendship. Perhaps it was this very passion of friendship which Bertie shrank from most.

"We're all right together now, aren't we?" said Maurice. "It's all right now, as long as we live, so far as we're concerned?"

"Yes," said Bertie, trying by any means to escape.

Maurice stood with head lifted, as if listening. The new delicate fulfilment of mortal friendship had come as a revelation and surprise to him, something exquisite and unhoped-for. He seemed to be listening to hear if it were real.

Then he turned for his coat.

"Come," he said, "we'll go to Isabel."

Bertie took the lantern and opened the door. The cat disappeared. The two men went in silence along the causeways. Isabel, as they came, thought their footsteps sounded strange. She looked up pathetically and anxiously for their entrance. There seemed a curious elation about Maurice. Bertie was haggard, with sunken eyes.

"What is it?" she asked.

"We've become friends," said Maurice, standing with his feet apart, like a strange colossus.

"Friends!" re-echoed Isabel. And she looked again at Bertie. He met her eyes with a furtive, haggard look; his eyes were as if glazed with misery.

"I'm so glad," she said, in sheer perplexity.

"Yes," said Maurice.

He was indeed so glad. Isabel took his hand with both hers, and held it fast.

"You'll be happier now, dear," she said.

But she was watching Bertie. She knew that he had one desire—to escape from this intimacy, this friendship, which had been thrust upon him. He could not bear it that he had been touched by the blind man, his insane reserve broken in. He was like a mollusc whose shell is broken.

ADOLF

When we were children our father often worked on the night-shift. Once it was spring-time, and he used to arrive home, black and tired, just as we were downstairs in our nightdresses. Then night met morning face to face, and the contact was not always happy. Perhaps it was painful to my father to see us gaily entering upon the day into which he dragged himself soiled and weary. He didn't like going to bed in the spring morning sunshine.

But sometimes he was happy, because of his long walk through the dewy fields in the first daybreak. He loved the open morning, the crystal and the space, after a night down pit. He watched every bird, every stir in the trembling grass, answered the whinneying of the pee-wits and tweeted to the wrens. If he could he also would have whinnied and tweeted and whistled in a native language that was not human. He liked non-human things best.

One sunny morning we were all sitting at table when we heard his heavy slurring walk up the entry. We became uneasy. His was always a disturbing presence, trammelling. He passed the window darkly, and we heard him go into the scullery and put down his tin bottle. But directly he came into the kitchen. We felt at once that he had something to communicate. No one spoke. We watched his black face for a second.

"Give me a drink," he said.

My mother hastily poured out his tea. He went to pour it out into his saucer. But instead of drinking he suddenly put something on the table among the teacups. A tiny brown rabbit!

A small rabbit, a mere morsel, sitting against the bread as still as if it were a made thing.

"A rabbit! A young one! Who gave it you, father?"

But he laughed enigmatically, with a sliding motion of his yellow-grey eyes, and went to take off his coat. We pounced on the rabbit.

"Is it alive? Can you feel its heart beat?"

My father came back and sat down heavily in his armchair. He dragged his saucer to him, and blew his tea, pushing out his red lips under his black moustache.

"Where did you get it, father?"

"I picked it up," he said, wiping his naked forearm over his mouth and beard.

"Where?"

"Is it a wild one?" came my mother's quick voice.

"Yes, it is."

"Then why did you bring it?" cried my mother.

"Oh, we wanted it," came our cry.

"Yes, I've no doubt you did——" retorted my mother. But she was drowned in our clamour of questions.

On the field path my father had found a dead mother rabbit and three dead little ones—this one alive, but unmoving.

"But what had killed them, daddy?"

"I couldn't say, my child. I s'd think she'd aten something."

"Why did you bring it!" again my mother's voice of condemnation. "You know what it will be."

My father made no answer, but we were loud in protest.

"He must bring it. It's not big enough to live by itself. It would die," we shouted.

"Yes, and it will die now. And then there'll be *another* outcry."

My mother set her face against the tragedy of dead pets. Our hearts sank.

"It won't die, father, will it? Why will it? It won't."

"I s'd think not," said my father.

"You know well enough it will. Haven't we had it all before—!" said my mother.

"They dunna always pine," replied my father testily.

But my mother reminded him of other little wild animals he had brought, which had sulked and refused to live, and brought storms of tears and trouble in our house of lunatics.

Trouble fell on us. The little rabbit sat on our lap, unmoving, its eye wide and dark. We brought it milk, warm milk, and held it to its nose. It sat as still as if it were far away, retreated down some deep burrow, hidden, oblivious. We wetted its mouth and whiskers with drops of milk. It gave no sign, did not even shake off the wet white drops. Somebody began to shed a few secret tears.

"What did I say?" cried my mother. "Take it and put it down in the field."

Her command was in vain. We were driven to get dressed for school. There sat the rabbit. It was like a tiny obscure cloud. Watching it, the emotions died out of our breast. Useless to love it, to yearn over it. Its little feelings were all ambushed. They must be circumvented. Love and affection were a trespass upon it. A little wild thing, it became more mute and asphyxiated still in its own arrest, when we approached with love. We must not love it. We must circumvent it, for its own existence.

So I passed the order to my sister and my mother. The rabbit was not to be spoken to, nor even looked at. Wrapping it in a piece of flannel I put it in an obscure corner of the cold parlour, and put a saucer of milk before its nose. My mother was forbidden to enter the parlour whilst we were at school.

"As if I should take any notice of your nonsense," she cried, affronted. Yet I doubt if she ventured into that parlour.

At midday, after school, creeping into the front room, there we saw the rabbit still and unmoving in the piece of flannel. Strange grey-brown neutralisation of life, still living! It was a sore problem to us.

"Why won't it drink its milk, mother?" we whispered. Our father was asleep.

"It prefers to sulk its life away, silly little thing." A profound problem. Prefers to sulk its life away! We put young dandelion leaves to its nose. The sphinx was not more oblivious. Yet its eye was bright.

At tea-time, however, it had hopped a few inches, out of its flannel, and there it sat down again, uncovered, a little solid cloud of muteness, brown, with unmoving whiskers. Only its side palpitated slightly with life.

Darkness came; my father set off to work. The rabbit was still unmoving. Dumb despair was coming over the sisters, a threat of tears before bedtime. Clouds of my mother's anger gathered as she muttered against my father's wantonness.

Once more the rabbit was wrapped in the old pit-singlet. But now it was carried into the scullery and put under the copper fireplace, that it might imagine itself inside a burrow. The saucers were placed about, four or five, here and there on the floor, so that if the little creature *should* chance to hop abroad, it could not fail to come across some food. After this my mother was allowed to take from the scullery what she wanted and then she was forbidden to open the door.

When morning came and it was light, I went downstairs. Opening the scullery door, I heard a slight scuffle. Then I saw dabbles of milk all over the floor and tiny rabbit-droppings in the saucers. And there the miscreant, the tips of his ears showing behind a pair of boots. I peeped at him. He sat bright-eyed and askance, twitching his nose and looking at me while not looking at me.

He was alive—very much alive. But still we were afraid to trespass much on his confidence.

"Father!" My father was arrested at the door. "Father, the rabbit's alive."

"Back your life it is," said my father.

"Mind how you go in."

By evening, however, the little creature was tame, quite tame. He was christened Adolf. We were enchanted by him. We couldn't really love him, because he was wild and loveless to the end. But he was an unmixed delight.

We decided he was too small to live in a hutch—he must live at large in the house. My mother protested, but in vain. He was so tiny. So we had him upstairs, and he dropped his tiny pills on the bed and we were enchanted.

Adolf made himself instantly at home. He had the run of the

house, and was perfectly happy, with his tunnels and his holes behind the furniture.

We loved him to take meals with us. He would sit on the table humping his back, sipping his milk, shaking his whiskers and his tender ears, hopping off and hobbling back to his saucer, with an air of supreme unconcern. Suddenly he was alert. He hobbled a few tiny paces, and reared himself up inquisitively at the sugar-basin. He fluttered his tiny fore-paws, and then reached and laid them on the edge of the basin, whilst he craned his thin neck and peeped in. He trembled his whiskers at the sugar, then did his best to lift down a lump.

"*Do* you think I will have it! Animals in the sugar pot!" cried my mother, with a rap of her hand on the table.

Which so delighted the electric Adolf that he flung his hind-quarters and knocked over a cup.

"It's your own fault, mother. If you had left him alone——"

He continued to take tea with us. He rather liked warm tea. And he loved sugar. Having nibbled a lump, he would turn to the butter. There he was shooed off by our parent. He soon learned to treat her shooing with indifference. Still, she hated him to put his nose in the food. And he loved to do it. And so one day between them they overturned the cream-jug. Adolf deluged his little chest, bounced back in terror, was seized by his little ears by my mother and bounced down on the hearth-rug. There he shivered in momentary discomfort, and suddenly set off in a wild flight to the parlour.

This last was his happy hunting ground. He had cultivated the bad habit of pensively nibbling certain bits of cloth in the hearth-rug. When chased from this pasture he would retreat under the sofa. There he would twinkle in Buddhist meditation until suddenly, no one knew why, he would go off like an alarm clock. With a sudden bumping scuffle he would whirl out of the room, going through the doorway with his little ears flying. Then we would hear his thunderbolt hurtling in the parlour, but before we could follow, the wild streak of Adolf would flash past us, on an electric wind that swept him round the scullery and carried him back, a little mad thing, flying possessed like a ball round the parlour. After which ebullition he would sit in a corner composed and distant, twitching his whiskers in abstract meditation. And it was in vain we questioned him about his outbursts. He just went off like a gun, and was as calm after it as a gun that smokes placidly.

Alas, he grew up rapidly. It was almost impossible to keep him from the outer door.

One day, as we were playing by the stile, I saw his brown shadow loiter across the road and pass into the field that faced the houses. Instantly a cry of "Adolf!" a cry he knew full well. And instantly a wind swept him away down the sloping meadow, his tail twinkling and zig-zagging through the grass. After him we pelted. It was a strange sight to see him, ears back, his little loins so powerful, flinging the world behind him. We ran ourselves out of breath, but could not catch him. Then somebody headed him off, and he sat with sudden unconcern, twitching his nose under a bunch of nettles.

His wanderings cost him a shock. One Sunday morning my father had just been quarrelling with a pedlar, and we were hearing the aftermath indoors, when there came a sudden unearthly scream from the yard. We flew out. There sat Adolf cowering under a bench, whilst a great black and white cat glowered intently at him, a few yards away. Sight not to be forgotten. Adolf rolling back his eyes and parting his strange muzzle in another scream, the cat stretching forward in a slow elongation.

Ha, how we hated that cat! How we pursued him over the chapel wall and across the neighbours' gardens.

Adolf was still only half grown.

"Cats!" said my mother. "Hideous detestable animals, why do people harbour them?"

But Adolf was becoming too much for her. He dropped too many pills. And suddenly to hear him clumping downstairs when she was alone in the house was startling. And to keep him from the door was impossible. Cats prowled outside. It was worse than having a child to look after.

Yet we would not have him shut up. He became more lusty, more callous than ever. He was a strong kicker, and many a scratch on face and arms did we owe him. But he brought his own doom on himself. The lace curtains in the parlour—my mother was rather proud of them—fell on to the floor very full. One of Adolf's joys was to scuffle wildly through them as though through some foamy undergrowth. He had already torn rents in them.

One day he entangled himself altogether. He kicked, he whirled round in a mad nebulous inferno. He screamed—and brought down the curtain-rod with a smash, right on the best beloved pelargonium, just as my mother rushed in. She extricated him, but she never forgave him. And he never forgave either. A heartless wildness had come over him.

Even we understood that he must go. It was decided, after a long deliberation, that my father should carry him back to the wild-woods. Once again he was stowed into the great pocket of the pit-jacket.

"Best pop him i' th' pot," said my father, who enjoyed raising the wind of indignation.

And so, next day, our father said that Adolf, set down on the edge of the coppice, had hopped away with utmost indifference, neither elated nor moved. We heard it and believed. But many, many were the heartsearchings. How would the other rabbits receive him? Would they smell his tameness, his humanised degradation, and rend him? My mother pooh-poohed the extravagant idea.

However, he was gone, and we were rather relieved. My father kept an eye open for him. He declared that several times passing the coppice in the early morning, he had seen Adolf peeping through the nettlestalks. He had called him, in an odd, high-voiced, cajoling fashion. But Adolf had not responded. Wildness gains so soon upon its creatures. And they become so contemptuous then of our tame presence. So it seemed to me. I myself would go to the edge of the coppice, and call softly. I myself would imagine bright eyes between the nettlestalks, flash of a white, scornful tail, past the bracken. That insolent white tail, as Adolf turned his flank on us! It reminded me always of a certain rude gesture, and a certain unprintable phrase, which may not even be suggested.

But when naturalists discuss the meaning of the white rabbit's tail, that rude gesture and still ruder phrase always come to my mind. Naturalists say that the rabbit shows his white tail in order to guide his young safely after him, as a nursemaid's flying strings are the signal to her toddling charges to follow on. How nice and naïve! I only know that my Adolf wasn't naïve. He used to whisk his flank at me, push his white feather in my eye, and say *Merde*! It's a rude word—but one which Adolf was always semaphoring at me, flag-wagging it with all the derision of his narrow haunches.

That's a rabbit all over—insolence, and the white flag of spiteful derision. Yes, and he keeps his flag flying to the bitter end, sporting, insolent little devil that he is. See him running for his life. Oh, how his soul is fanned to an ecstasy of fright, a fugitive whirlwind of panic. Gone mad, he throws the world behind him, with astonishing hind legs. He puts back his head and lays his ears on his sides and rolls the white of his eyes in sheer ecstatic agony of speed. He knows the awful approach behind him; bullet or stoat. He knows! He knows, his eyes are turned back almost into his head. It is agony. But it is also ecstasy. Ecstasy! See the insolent white flag bobbing. He whirls on the magic wind of terror. All his pent-up soul rushes into agonised electric emotion of fear. He flings himself on, like a falling star swooping into extinction. White heat of the agony of fear. And at the same time, bob! bob! bob! goes the white tail, *merde*! *merde*! *merde*! it says to the pursuer. The rabbit can't help it. In his utmost extremity he still flings the insult at the pursuer. He is the inconquerable fugitive, the indomitable meek. No wonder the stoat becomes vindictive.

And if he escapes, this precious rabbit! Don't you see him sitting there, in his earthly nook, a little ball of silence and rabbit-triumph? Don't you see the glint on his black eye? Don't you see, in his very immobility, how the whole world is *merde* to him? No conceit like the conceit of the meek. And if the avenging angel in the shape of the ghostly ferret steals down on him, there comes a shriek of terror out of that little hump of self-satisfaction sitting motionless in a corner. Falls the fugitive. But even fallen, his white feather floats. Even in death it seems to say: "I am the meek, I am the righteous, I am the rabbit. All you rest, you are evil doers, and you shall be *bien emmerdés*!"

THE LAST STRAW
[FANNY AND ANNIE]

Flame-lurid his face as he turned among the throng of flame-lit and dark faces upon the platform. In the light of the furnace she caught sight of his drifting countenance, like a piece of floating fire. And the nostalgia, the doom of home-coming went through her veins like a drug. His eternal face, flame-lit now! The pulse and darkness of red fire from the furnace towers in the sky, lighting the desultory, industrial crowd on the wayside station, lit him and went out.

Of course, he did not see her. Flame-lit and unseeing! Always the same, with his meeting eyebrows, his common cap, and his red-and-black scarf knotted round his throat. Not even a collar to meet her! The flames had sunk, there was shadow.

She opened the door of her grimy, branch-line carriage and began to get down her bags. The porter was nowhere, of course, but there was Harry, obscure, on the outer edge of the little crowd, missing her, of course.

"Here! Harry!" she called, waving her umbrella in the twilight. He hurried forward.

"Tha's come, has ter?" he said, in a sort of cheerful welcome. She got down, rather flustered, and gave him a peck of a kiss.

"Two suit-cases!" she said.

Her soul groaned within her, as he clambered into the carriage after her bags. Up shot the fire in the twilight sky, from the great furnace behind the station. She felt the red flame go across her face. She had come back, she had come back for good. And her spirit groaned dismally. She doubted if she could bear it.

There, on the sordid little station under the furnaces she

stood, tall and distinguished, in her well-made coat and skirt and her broad, grey velour hat. She held her umbrella, her bead chatelaine, and a little leather case in her grey-gloved hands, while Harry staggered out of the ugly little train with her bags.

"There's a trunk at the back," she said, in her bright voice. But she was not feeling bright. The twin black cones of the iron foundry blasted their sky-high fires into the night. The whole scene was lurid. The train waited cheerfully. It would wait another ten minutes. She knew it. It was all so deadly familiar.

Let us confess it at once. She was a lady's maid, thirty years old, come back to marry her first love, a foundry worker, after having kept him dangling, off and on, for a dozen years. Why had she come back—did she love him? No! She didn't pretend to. She had loved her brilliant and ambitious cousin, who had jilted her, and who had died. She had had other affairs which had come to nothing. So here she was, come back suddenly to marry her first-love, who had waited—or remained single—all these years.

"Won't a porter carry those?" she said, as Harry strode with his workman's stride down the platform towards the guard's van.

"I can manage," he said.

And with her umbrella, her chatelaine, and her little leather case, she followed him.

The trunk was there.

"We'll get Heather's greengrocer's cart to fetch it up," he said.

"Isn't there a cab?" said Fanny, knowing dismally enough that there wasn't.

"I'll just put it aside o' the penny-in-the-slot, and Heather's greengrocer's 'll fetch it about half past eight," he said.

He seized the box by its two handles and staggered with it across the level-crossing, bumping his legs against it as he waddled. Then he dropped it by the red sweetmeats machine.

"Will it be safe there?" she said.

"Ay—safe as houses," he answered. He returned for the two bags. Thus laden, they started to plod up the hill, under the great long black building of the foundry. She walked beside him—workman of workmen, he was, trudging with that luggage. The red lights flared over the deepening darkness. From the foundry came the horrible, slow clang, clang, clang, of iron, a great noise, with an interval just long enough to make it unendurable.

Compare this with the arrival at Gloucester; the carriage for her mistress, the dog-cart for herself with the luggage; the drive out past the river, the pleasant trees of the carriage approach; and herself sitting beside Arthur, everybody so polite to her.

She had come home—for good! Her heart nearly stopped beating as she trudged up that hideous and interminable hill, beside the laden figure. What a come-down! What a come-down! She could not take it with her usual bright cheerfulness. She knew it all too well. It is easy to bear up against the unusual, but the deadly familiarity of an old stale past!

He dumped the bags down under a lamp-post, for a rest. There they stood, the two of them, in the lamp-light. Passers-by stared at her, and gave good-night to Harry. Her they hardly knew, she had become a stranger.

"They're too heavy for you, let me carry one," she said.

"They begin to weigh a bit by the time you've gone a mile," he answered.

"Let me carry the little one," she insisted.

"Tha can ha'e it for a minute, if ter's a mind," he said, handing over the valise.

And thus they arrived in the street of shops of the little ugly town on top of the hill. How everybody stared at her; my word! how they stared! And the cinema was just going in, and the queues were tailing down the road to the corner. And everybody took full stock of her. "'Night, Harry!" shouted the fellows, in an interested voice.

However, they arrived at her aunt's—a little sweet-shop in a side street. They "pinged" the door-bell, and her aunt came running forward out of the kitchen.

"There you are, child! Dying for a cup of tea, I'm sure. How are you?"

Fanny's aunt kissed her, and it was all Fanny could do to refrain from bursting into tears, she felt so low. Perhaps it was her tea she wanted.

"You've had a drag with that luggage," said Fanny's aunt to Harry.

"Ay, I'm not sorry to put it down," he said, looking at his hand which was crushed and cramped by the bag handle.

Then he departed to see about Heather's greengrocery cart.

When Fanny sat at tea, her aunt, a grey-haired, fair-faced little woman, looked at her with an admiring heart, feeling bitterly sore for her. For Fanny was beautiful: tall, erect, finely coloured, with her delicately arched nose, her rich brown hair, her large lustrous grey eyes. A passionate woman—a woman to be afraid of. So proud, so inwardly violent. She came of a violent race.

It needed a woman to sympathise with her. Men had not the courage. Poor Fanny! She was such a lady, and so straight and magnificent. And yet everything seemed to do her down. Every time she seemed to be doomed to humiliation and disappointment, this handsome, brilliantly sensitive woman, with her nervous over-wrought laugh.

"So you've really come back, child?" said her aunt.

"I really have, Aunt," said Fanny.

"Poor Harry! I'm not sure, you know, Fanny, that you're not taking a bit of an advantage of him."

"Oh, Aunt, he's waited so long, he may as well have what he's waited for." Fanny laughed grimly.

"Yes, child, he's waited so long, that I'm not sure it isn't a bit hard on him. You know, I *like* him, Fanny—though, as you know quite well, I don't think he's good enough for you. And I think he thinks so himself, poor fellow."

"Don't you be so sure of that, Aunt. Harry is common, but he's not humble. He wouldn't think the Queen was any too good for him, if he'd a mind to her."

"Well, it's as well if he has a proper opinion of himself."

"It depends what you call proper," said Fanny. "But he's got his good points——"

"Oh, he's a nice fellow, and I like him. I do like him. Only, as I tell you, he's not good enough for you."

"I've made up my mind, Aunt," said Fanny grimly.

"Yes," mused the aunt; "they say all things come to him who waits——"

"More than he's bargained for, eh, Aunt?" laughed Fanny, rather bitterly.

The poor aunt, this bitterness grieved her for her niece.

They were interrupted by the ping of the shop-bell, and Harry's call of "Right?" But as he did not come in at once, Fanny, feeling solicitous for him presumably at the moment, rose and went into the shop. She saw a cart outside, and went to the door.

And the moment she stood in the doorway she heard a woman's common vituperative voice crying from the darkness of the opposite side of the road:

"Tha'rt theer, are ter! I'll shame thee, Mester! I'll shame thee, see if I dunna."

Startled, Fanny stared across the darkness, and saw a woman in a black bonnet go under one of the lamps up the side street.

Harry and Bill Heather had dragged the trunk off the little dray and she retreated before them as they came up the shop step with it.

"Wheer shalt ha'e it?" asked Harry.

"Best take it upstairs," said Fanny.

She went up first to light the gas.

When Heather had gone, and Harry was sitting down having tea and pork pie, Fanny asked:

"Who was that woman shouting?"

"Nay, I canna tell thee. To somebody, I s'd think," replied Harry. Fanny looked at him, but asked no more.

He was a fair-haired fellow of thirty-two, with a fair moustache. He was broad in his speech and looked like a foundry-hand, which he was. But women always liked him. There was something of a mother's lad about him—something warm and playful and really sensitive.

He had his attractions, even for Fanny. What she rebelled against so bitterly was that he had no sort of ambition. He was a moulder, but of very commonplace skill. He was thirty-two years old, and hadn't saved twenty pounds. She would have to provide the money for the home. He didn't care. He just didn't

care. He had no initiative at all. He had no vices—no obvious
ones. But he was just indifferent, spending as he went, and not
caring. Yet he did not look happy. She remembered his face in
the fire-glow: something haunted, abstracted about it. As he sat
there eating his pork pie, bulging his cheek out, she felt he was
like a doom to her. And she raged against the doom of him. It
wasn't that he was gross. His *way* was common, almost on
purpose. But he himself wasn't really common. For instance,
his food was not particularly important to him, he was not
greedy. He had a charm, too, particularly for women, with his
blondness and his sensitiveness and his way of making a woman
feel that she was a higher being. But Fanny knew him, knew
the peculiar obstinate limitedness of him, that would nearly
send her mad.

He stayed till about half-past nine. She went to the door with
him.

"When are you coming up?" he said jerking his head in the
direction, presumably, of his own home.

"I'll come to-morrow afternoon," she said brightly. Between
Fanny and Mrs Goodall, his mother, there was naturally no
love lost.

Again she gave him an awkward little kiss, and said good-
night.

"You can't wonder, you know, child, if he doesn't seem so
very keen," said her aunt. "It's your own fault."

"Oh, Aunt, I couldn't stand him when he was keen. I can do
with him a lot better as he is."

The two women sat and talked far into the night. They
understood each other. The aunt, too, had married as Fanny
was marrying, a man who was no companion to her—a violent
man, brother of Fanny's father. He was dead; Fanny's father
was dead.

Poor Aunt Lizzie, she cried woefully over her bright niece,
when she had gone to bed.

Fanny paid the promised visit to his people the next afternoon. Mrs Goodall was a large woman with smooth-parted
hair, a common, obstinate woman who had spoiled her four
lads and her one vixen of a married daughter. She was one of

those old-fashioned powerful natures that couldn't do with looks or education or any form of showing off. She fairly hated the sound of correct English. She *thee'd* and *tha'd* her prospective daughter-in-law, and said:

"I'm none as ormin' as I look, seest ta."

Fanny did not think her prospective mother-in-law looked at all orming, so the speech was unnecessary.

"I towd him mysen," said Mrs Goodall—"'Er's held back all this long, let 'er stop as 'er is. 'E'd none ha' had thee for *my* tellin', tha hears. No, 'e's a fool, an' I know it. I says to him, 'Tha looks a man, doesn't ter, at thy age, goin' an' openin' to her when ter hears her scrat' at th' gate, after she's done gallivantin' round wherever she'd a mind. Tha looks rare an' soft.' But it's no use o' any talking; he answered that letter o' thine, and made his own bad bargain."

But in spite of the old woman's anger, she was also flattered at Fanny's coming back to Harry. For Mrs Goodall was impressed by Fanny—a woman of her own match. And more than this, everybody knew that Fanny's Aunt Kate had left her two hundred pounds, this apart from the girl's savings.

So there was high tea in Princes Street, when Harry came home black from work, and a rather acrid odour of cordiality, the vixen Jinny darting in to say vulgar things. Of course, Jinny lived in a house whose garden end joined the paternal garden. They were a clan who stuck together, these Goodalls.

It was arranged that Fanny should come to tea again on the Sunday, and the wedding was discussed. It should take place in a fortnight's time at Morley Chapel. Morley was a hamlet on the edge of the real country, and in its little Congregational Chapel Fanny and Harry had first met.

What a creature of habit he was! He was still in the choir of Morley Chapel—not very regular. He belonged just because he had a tenor voice and enjoyed singing. Indeed, his solos were only spoilt to local fame because, when he sang, he handled his aitches so hopelessly.

> "And I saw 'eaven hopened
> And be'old, a wite 'orse——"

This was one of Harry's classics, only surpassed by the fine outburst of his heaving:

"Hangels—hever bright an' fair——"

It was a pity, but it was unalterable. He had a good voice, and he sang with a certain lacerating fire, but his pronunciation made it all funny. And *nothing* could alter him.

So he was never heard save at cheap concerts, and in the little, poorer chapels. The others scoffed.

Now the month was September, and Sunday was Harvest Festival at Morley Chapel, and Harry was singing solos. So that Fanny was to go to afternoon service, and come home to a grand spread of Sunday tea with him. Poor Fanny! One of the most wonderful afternoons had been a Sunday afternoon service, with her cousin Luther at her side, Harvest Festival at Morley Chapel. Harry had sung solos then—ten years ago. She remembered his pale blue tie, and the purple asters and the great vegetable marrows in which he was framed, and her cousin Luther at her side, young, clever, come down from London, where he was getting on well, learning his Latin and his French and German so brilliantly.

However, once again it was Harvest Festival at Morley Chapel, and once again, as ten years before, a soft, exquisite September day, with the last roses pink in the cottage gardens, the last dahlias crimson, the last sunflowers yellow. And again the little old chapel was a bower, with its famous sheaves of corn and corn-plaited pillars, its great bunches of grapes, dangling like tassels from the pulpit corners, its marrows and potatoes and pears and apples and damsons, its purple asters and yellow Japanese sunflowers. Just as before, the red dahlias round the pillars were dropping, weak-headed, among the oats. The place was crowded and hot, the plates of tomatoes seemed balanced perilously on the gallery front, the Rev. Enderby was weirder than ever to look at, so long and emaciated and hairless.

The Rev. Enderby, probably forewarned, came and shook hands with her and welcomed her, in his broad northern, melancholy sing-song before he mounted the pulpit. Fanny was hand-

some in a gauzy dress and a beautiful lace hat. Being a little
late, she sat in a chair in the side-aisle wedged in, right in the
front of the chapel. Harry was in the gallery above, and she
could only see him from the eyes upwards. She noticed again
how his eyebrows met, blond and not very marked, over his
nose. He was attractive too: physically lovable, very. If only—
if only her *pride* had not suffered! She felt he dragged her down.

> "*Come, ye thankful people, come,*
> *Raise the song of harvest-home.*
> *All is safely gathered in*
> *Ere the winter storms begin*——"

Even the hymn was a falsehood, as the season had been wet,
and half the crops were still out, and in a poor way.

Poor Fanny! She sang little, and looked beautiful through
that inappropriate hymn. Above her stood Harry—mercifully
in a dark suit and a dark tie—looking almost handsome. And
his lacerating, pure tenor sounded well, when the words were
drowned in the general commotion. Brilliant she looked, and
brilliant she felt, for she was hot and angrily miserable and
inflamed with a sort of fatal despair. Because there was about
him a physical attraction which she really hated, but which she
could not escape from. He was the first man who had ever
kissed her. And his kisses, even while she rebelled from them,
had lived in her blood and sent roots down into her soul. After
all this time she had come back to them. And her soul groaned,
for she felt dragged down, dragged down to earth, as a bird
which some dog has got down in the dust. She knew her life
would be unhappy. She knew that what she was doing was
fatal. Yet it was her doom. She had to come back to him.

He had to sing two solos this afternoon: one before the
"address" from the pulpit, and one after. Fanny looked up at
him, and wondered he was not too shy to stand up there in
front of all the people. But no, he was not shy. He had even a
kind of assurance on his face as he looked down from the choir
gallery at her: the assurance of a common man deliberately
entrenched in his commonness. Oh, such a rage went through

her veins as she saw the air of triumph, laconic, indifferent triumph which sat so obstinately and recklessly on his eyelids as he looked down at her. Ah, she despised him! But there he stood up in that choir gallery like Balaam's ass in front of her, and she could not get beyond him. A certain winsomeness also about him. A certain physical winsomeness, and as if his flesh were new and lovely to touch. The thorn of desire rankled bitterly in her heart.

He, it goes without saying, sang like a canary this particular afternoon, with a certain defiant passion which pleasantly crisped the blood of the congregation. Fanny felt the crisp flames go through her veins as she listened. Even the curious loud-mouthed vernacular had a certain fascination. But oh, also, it was so repugnant. He would triumph over her, obstinately he would drag her right back into the common people: a doom, a vulgar doom.

The second performance was an anthem, in which Harry sang the solo parts. It was clumsy, but beautiful, with lovely words:

> "They that sow in tears shall reap in joy;
> He that goeth forth and weepeth, bearing precious seed,
> Shall doubtless come again with rejoicing, bringing his sheaves
>   with him."

"Shall doubtless come, shall doubtless come," softly intoned the altos, "Bringing his she-e-eaves with him," the trebles flourished brightly, and then again began the half-wistful solo:

> "They that sow in tears shall reap in joy."

Yes, it was effective and moving.

But at the moment when Harry's voice sank carelessly down to his close, and the choir, standing behind him, were opening their mouths for the final triumphant outburst, a shouting female voice rose up from the body of the congregation. The organ gave one startled trump, and went silent; the choir stood transfixed.

"You look well standing there, singing in God's holy house," came the loud, angry female shout. Everybody turned electrified. A stoutish, red-faced woman in a black bonnet was standing up denouncing the soloist. Almost fainting with shock, the congregation realised it. "You look well, don't you, standing there singing solos in God's holy house—you, Goodall. But I said I'd shame you. You look well, bringing your young woman here with you, don't you? I'll let her know who she's dealing with. A scamp as won't take the consequences of what he's done." The hard-faced, frenzied woman turned in the direction of Fanny. "*That's* what Harry Goodall is, if you want to know."

And she sat down again in her seat. Fanny, startled like all the rest, had turned to look. She had gone white, and then a burning red, under the attack. She knew the woman: a Mrs Nixon, a devil of a woman, who beat her pathetic, drunken, red-nosed second husband, Bob, and her two lanky daughters, grown-up as they were. A notorious character. Fanny turned round again, and sat motionless as eternity in her seat.

There was a minute of perfect silence and suspense. The audience was open-mouthed and dumb; the choir stood like Lot's wife; and Harry, with his music-sheet uplifted, stood there, looking down with a dumb sort of indifference on Mrs Nixon, his face naïve and faintly mocking. Mrs Nixon sat defiant in her seat, braving them all.

Then a rustle, like a wood when the wind suddenly catches the leaves. And then the tall, weird minister got to his feet, and in his strong, bell-like beautiful voice—the only beautiful thing about him—he said with infinite mournful pathos:

"Let us unite in singing the last hymn on the hymn-sheet; the last hymn on the hymn-sheet, number eleven.

> *'Fair waved the golden corn*
> *In Canaan's pleasant land.'"*

The organ tuned up promptly. During the hymn the offertory was taken. And after the hymn, the prayer.

Mr Enderby came from Northumberland. Like Harry, he had never been able to conquer his accent, which was very broad. He was a little simple, one of God's fools, perhaps, an odd bachelor soul, emotional, ugly, but very gentle.

"And if, Oh our dear Lord, beloved Jesus, there should fall a shadow of sin upon our harvest, we leave it to Thee to judge, for Thou art Judge. We lift our spirits and our sorrow, Jesus, to Thee, and our mouths are dumb. Oh Lord, keep us from forward speech, restrain us from foolish words and thoughts, we pray Thee, Lord Jesus, who knowest all and judgest all."

Thus the minister said, in his sad, resonant voice, washing his hands before the Lord. Fanny bent forward open-eyed during the prayer. She could see the roundish head of Harry, also bent forward. His face was inscrutable and expressionless. The shock left her bewildered. Anger perhaps was her dominating emotion.

The audience began to rustle to its feet, to ooze slowly and excitedly out of the chapel, looking with wildly-interested eyes at Fanny, at Mrs Nixon and at Harry. Mrs Nixon, shortish, stood defiant in her pew, facing the aisle, as if announcing that, without rolling her sleeves up, she was ready for anybody. Fanny sat quite still. Luckily the people did not have to pass her. And Harry, with red ears, was making his way sheepishly out of the gallery. The loud noise of the organ covered all the downstairs commotion of exit.

The minister sat silent and inscrutable in his pulpit, rather like a death's-head, while the congregation filed out. When the last lingerers had unwillingly departed, craning their necks to stare at the still seated Fanny, he rose, stalked in his hooked fashion down the little country chapel, and fastened the door. Then he returned and sat down by the silent young woman.

"This is most unfortunate, most unfortunate," he moaned. "I am so sorry, I am so sorry, indeed, indeed, ah! indeed!" he sighed himself to a close.

"It's a sudden surprise, that's one thing," said Fanny brightly.

"Yes—yes—indeed. Yes, a surprise, yes. I don't know the woman, I don't know her."

"I know her," said Fanny. "She's a bad one."

"Well, well!" said the minister. "I don't know her. I don't

understand. I don't understand at all. But it is to be regretted, it is very much to be regretted. I am very sorry."

Fanny was watching the vestry door. The gallery stairs communicated with the vestry, not with the body of the chapel. She knew the choir members had been peeping for information.

At last Harry came—rather sheepishly, with his hat in his hand.

"Well!" said Fanny, rising to her feet.

"We've had a bit of an extra," said Harry.

"I should think so," said Fanny.

"A most unfortunate circumstance—a most *unfortunate* circumstance. Do you understand it, Harry? I don't understand it at all."

"Ay, I understand it. The daughter's goin' to have a childt, an' 'er lays it on to me."

"And has she no occasion to?" asked Fanny, rather censorious.

"It's no more mine than it is some other chap's," said Harry, looking aside.

There was a moment of pause.

"Which girl is it?" asked Fanny.

"Annie, the young one——"

There followed another silence.

"I don't think I know them, do I?" asked the minister.

"I shouldn't think so. Their name's Nixon, mother married old Bob for her second husband. She's a tanger—'s driven the gel to what she is. They live in Manners Road."

"Why, what's amiss with the girl?" asked Fanny sharply. "She was all right when I knew her."

"Ay, she's all right. But she's always in an' out o' th' pubs, wi' th' fellows," said Harry.

"A nice thing!" said Fanny.

Harry glanced towards the door. He wanted to get out.

"Most distressing indeed!" The minister slowly shook his head.

"What about to-night, Mr Enderby?" asked Harry, in rather a small voice. "Shall you want me?"

Mr Enderby looked up painedly, and put his hand to his brow. He studied Harry for some time, vacantly. There was the faintest sort of a resemblance between the two men.

"Yes," he said. "Yes, I think. I think we must take no notice, and cause as little remark as possible."

Fanny hesitated. Then she said to Harry:

"But *will* you come?"

He looked at her.

"Ay, I s'll come," he said.

Then he turned to Mr Enderby.

"Well, good afternoon, Mr Enderby," he said.

"Good afternoon, Harry, good afternoon!" replied the mournful minister. Fanny followed Harry to the door, and for some time they walked in silence through the late afternoon.

"And it's yours as much as anybody else's?" she said.

"Ay," he answered, shortly.

And they went, without another word, for the long mile or so, till they came to the corner of the street where Harry lived. Fanny hesitated. Should she go on to her aunt's? Should she? It would mean leaving all this for ever! Harry stood silent.

Some obstinacy made her turn with him along the road to his own home. When they entered the house-place, the whole family was there, mother and father and Jinny, with Jinny's husband and children and Harry's two brothers.

"You've been having your ears warmed, th' tell me," said Mrs Goodall grimly.

"Who told thee?" asked Harry, shortly.

"Maggie and Luke's both been in."

"You look well, don't you!" said interfering Jinny.

Harry went and hung his hat up, without replying.

"Come upstairs and take your hat off," said Mrs Goodall to Fanny, almost kindly. It would have annoyed her very much if Fanny had dropped her son at this moment.

"What's 'er say, then?" asked the father secretly, of Harry, jerking his head in the direction of the stairs whence Fanny had disappeared.

"Nowt yet," said Harry.

"Serve you right if she chucks you now," said Jinny. "I'll bet it's right about Annie Nixon an' you."

"Tha bets so much," said Harry.

"Yi, but you can't deny it," said Jinny.

"I can if I've a mind."

His father looked at him enquiringly.

"It's no more mine than it is Bill Bowers' or Ted Slaney's, or six or seven on 'em," said Harry to his father.

And the father nodded silently.

"That'll not get you out of it, in court," said Jinny.

Upstairs Fanny evaded all the thrusts made by his mother, and did not declare her hand. She tidied her hair, washed her hands, and put the tiniest bit of powder on her face, for coolness, there in front of Mrs Goodall's indignant gaze. It was like a declaration of independence. But the old woman said nothing.

They came down to Sunday tea, with sardines and tinned salmon and tinned peaches, besides tarts and cakes. The chatter was general. It concerned the Nixon family and the scandal.

"Oh, she's a foul-mouthed woman," said Jinny of Mrs Nixon. "She may well talk about God's holy house, *she* had. It's first time she's set foot in it, ever since she dropped off from being converted. She's a devil and she always was one. Can't you remember how she treated Bob's children, mother, when we lived down in the Buildings? I can remember when I was a little girl, she used to bathe them in the yard, in the cold, so that they shouldn't splash the house. She'd half kill them if they made a mark on the floor—and the language she'd use. And one Saturday I can remember Garry, that was Bob's own girl, she ran off when her stepmother was going to bathe her—ran off without a rag of clothes on—can you remember, mother? And she hid in Smedley's close—it was the time of mowing grass—and nobody could find her. She hid out there all night, didn't she, mother? Nobody could find her. My word, there was a talk. They found her on Sunday morning——"

"Fred Coutts threatened to break every bone in the woman's body if she touched the children again," put in the father.

"Anyhow, they frightened her," said Jinny. "But she was

nearly as bad with her own two. And anybody can see that she's driven old Bob till he's gone soft."

"Ah, soft as mush," said Jack Goodall. "'E'd never addle a week's wage, nor yet a day's if th' chaps didn't make it up to him."

"My word, if he didn't bring her a week's wage, she'd pull his head off," said Jinny.

"But a clean woman and respectable, except for her foul mouth," said Mrs Goodall. "Keeps to herself like a bull-dog. Never lets anybody come near the house, and neighbours with nobody."

"Wanted it thrashing out of her," said Mr Goodall, a silent, evasive sort of man.

"Where Bob gets the money for his drink from is a mystery," said Jinny.

"Chaps treat him," said Harry.

"Well, he's got the pair of frightenedest rabbit-eyes you'd wish to see," said Jinny.

"Ay, with a drunken man's murder in them, *I* think," said Mrs Goodall.

So the talk went on after tea, till it was practically time to start off to chapel again.

"You'll have to be getting ready, Fanny," said Mrs Goodall.

"I'm not going to-night," said Fanny abruptly. And there was a sudden halt in the family. "I'll stop with *you* to-night, Mother," she added.

"Best you had, my gel," said Mrs Goodall, flattered and assured.

SUN

"Take her away, into the sun," the doctors said. She herself was sceptical of the sun, but she permitted herself to be carried away, with her child, and a nurse, and her mother, over the sea.

The ship sailed at midnight. And for two hours her husband stayed with her, while the child was put to bed, and the passengers came on board. It was a black night, the Hudson swayed with heaving blackness, shaken over with spilled dribbles of light. She leaned on the rail, and looking down thought: This is the sea! It is deeper than one imagines, and fuller of memories.—At that moment, the sea seemed to heave like the serpent of chaos, that has lived for ever.

"These partings are no good, you know," her husband was saying, at her side. "They're no good. I don't like them."

His tone was full of apprehension, misgiving, and there was a certain clinging to the last straw of hope.

"No, neither do I," she responded in a flat voice.

She remembered how bitterly they wanted to get away from one another, he and she. The emotion of parting gave a slight tug at her emotions, but only caused the iron that had gone into her soul to gore deeper.

So, they looked at their sleeping son, and the father's eyes were wet. But it is not the wetting of eyes which counts, it is the deep iron rhythm of habit, the year-long, life-long habits: the deep-set stroke of power.

And in their two lives, the stroke of power was hostile, his and hers. Like two engines running at variance, they shattered one another.

"All ashore! All ashore!"

"Maurice, you must go."

And she thought to herself: For him, it is: *All ashore*! For me it is: *Out to sea!*

Well, he waved his hanky on the midnight dreariness of the pier, as the boat inched away; one among a crowd. One among a crowd! *C'est ça*!

The ferry-boats, like great dishes piled with rows of lights, were still slanting across the Hudson. That black mouth must be the Lackawanna station.

The ship ebbed on between the lights, the Hudson seemed interminable. But at last they were round the bend, and there was the poor harvest of lights at the Battery. Liberty flung up her torch in a tantrum: There was the wash of the sea.

And though the Atlantic was grey as lava, they did come at last into the sun. Even she had a house above the bluest of seas, with a vast garden, or vineyard, all vines and olives, dropping steeply in terrace after terrace, to the strip of coast plain: and the garden full of secret places, deep groves of lemon far down in the cleft of earth, and hidden, pure green reservoirs of water; then a spring issuing out of a little cavern, where the old Sicules had drunk before the Greeks came; and a grey goat bleating, stabled in an ancient tomb, with the niches empty. There was the scent of mimosa, and beyond, the snow of the volcano.

She saw it all, and in a measure it was soothing. But it was all external. She didn't really care about it. She was herself just the same, with all her anger and frustration inside her, and her incapacity to feel anything real. The child irritated her, and preyed on her peace of mind. She felt so horridly, ghastly responsible for him: as if she must be responsible for every breath he drew. And that was torture to her, to the child, and to everybody else concerned.

"You know, Juliet, the doctor told you to lie in the sun, without your clothes. Why don't you?" said her mother.

"When I am fit to do so, I will. Do you want to kill me?" Juliet flew at her.

"To kill you, no! Only to do you good."

"For God's sake, leave off wanting to do me good."

The mother at last was so hurt and incensed, she departed.

The sea went white,—and then invisible. Pouring rain fell. It was cold, in the house built for the sun.

Again a morning when the sun lifted himself molten and sparkling, naked over the sea's rim. The house faced south-east, Juliet lay in her bed and watched him rise. It was as if she had never seen the sun rise before. She had never seen the naked sun stand up pure upon the sea-line, shaking the night off himself, like wetness. And he was full and naked. And she wanted to come to him.

So the desire sprang secretly in her, to be naked to the sun. She cherished her desire like a secret. She wanted to come together with the sun.

But she would have to go away from the house—away from people. And it is not easy, in a country where every olive tree has eyes, and every slope is seen from afar, to go hidden, and have intercourse with the sun.

But she found a place: a rocky bluff shoved out to the sea and sun, and overgrown with the large cactus called prickly pear. Out of this thicket of cactus rose one cypress tree, with a pallid, thick trunk, and a tip that leaned over, flexible, in the blue. It stood like a guardian looking to sea; or a candle whose huge flame was darkness against light; the long tongue of darkness licking up at the sky.

Juliet sat down by the cypress tree, and took off her clothes. The contorted cactus made a forest, hideous yet fascinating, about her. She sat and offered her bosom to the sun, sighing, even now, with a certain hard pain, against the cruelty of having to give herself: but exulting that at last it was no human lover.

But the sun marched in blue heaven, and sent down his rays as he went. She felt the soft air of the sea on her breasts, that seemed as if they would never ripen. But she hardly felt the sun. Fruits that would wither and not mature, her breasts.

Soon, however, she felt the sun inside them, warmer than ever love had been, warmer than milk or the hands of her baby.

At last, at last her breasts were like long white grapes in the hot sun.

She slid off all her clothes, and lay naked in the sun. And as she lay, she looked up through her fingers at the central sun, his blue pulsing roundness, whose outer edges streamed brilliance. Pulsing with marvellous blue, and alive, and streaming white fire from his edges, the sun! He faced down to her, with blue body of fire, and enveloped her breasts and her face, her throat, her tired belly, her knees, her thighs and her feet.

She lay with shut eyes, the colour of rosy flame through her lids. It was too much. She reached and put leaves over her eyes. Then she lay again, like a long gourd in the sun, green that must ripen to gold.

She could feel the sun penetrating into her bones: nay, further, even into her emotions and thoughts. The dark tensions of her emotion began to give way, the cold dark clots of her thoughts began to dissolve. She was beginning to be warm right through. Turning over, she let her shoulders lie in the sun, her loins, the backs of her thighs, even her heels. And she lay half stunned with the strangeness of the thing that was happening to her. Her weary, chilled heart was melting, and in melting, evaporating. Only her womb remained tense and resistant, the eternal resistance. It would resist even the sun.

When she was dressed again, she lay once more and looked up at the cypress tree, whose crest, a filament, fell this way and that, in the breeze. Meanwhile, she was conscious of the great sun roaming in heaven, and of her own resistance.

So, dazed, she went home, only half-seeing, sun-blinded and sun-dazed. And her blindness was like a richness to her, and her dim, warm, heavy half-consciousness was like wealth.

"Mummy! Mummy!" her child came running towards her, calling in that peculiar bird-like little anguish of want, always wanting her. She was surprised that her drowsed heart for once felt none of the anxious love-tension in return. She caught the child up in her arms, but she thought: He should not be such a lump! If he had any sun in him, he would spring up.—And she felt again the unyielding resistance of her womb, against him and everything.

She resented, rather, his little hands clutching at her, especially her neck. She pulled her throat away. She did not want him getting hold of it. She put the child down.

"Run!" she said. "Run in the sun!"

And there and then she took off his clothes, and set him naked on the warm terrace.

"Play in the sun!" she said.

He was frightened, and wanted to cry. But she, in the warm indolence of her body, and the complete indifference of her heart, and the resistance of her womb, rolled him an orange across the red tiles, and with his soft, unformed little body he toddled after it. Then, immediately he had it, he dropped it because it felt strange against his flesh. And he looked back at her, wrinkling his face to cry, frightened because he was stark.

"Bring me the orange," she said, amazed at her own deep indifference to his trepidation. "Bring Mummy the orange."

"He shall not grow up like his father," she said to herself. "Like a worm that the sun has never seen."

II

She had had the child so much on her mind, in a torment of responsibility, as if, having borne him, she had to answer for his whole existence. Even if his nose were running, it had been repulsive and a goad in her vitals, as if she must say to herself: Look at the thing you brought forth!

Now a change took place. She was no longer vitally consumed about the child, she took the strain of her anxiety and her will from off him. And he thrived all the more for it.

She was thinking inside herself, of the sun in his splendour, and his entering into her. Her life was now a secret ritual. She always lay awake, before dawn, watching for the grey to colour to pale gold, to know if clouds lay on the sea's edge. Her joy was when he rose all molten in his nakedness, and threw off blue-white fire, into the tender heaven.

But sometimes he came ruddy, like a big, shy creature. And sometimes slow and crimson red, with a look of anger, slowly pushing and shouldering. Sometimes again she could not see him, only the level cloud threw down gold and scarlet from above, as he moved behind the wall.

She was fortunate. Weeks went by, and though the dawn was sometimes clouded, and afternoon was sometimes grey, never a day passed sunless, and most days, winter though it was, streamed radiant. The thin little wild crocuses came up mauve and striped, the wild narcissus hung their winter stars.

Every day she went down to the cypress tree, among the cactus grove on the knoll with yellowish cliffs at the foot. She was wiser and subtler now, wearing only a dove-grey wrapper, and sandals. So that in an instant, in any hidden niche, she was naked to the sun. And the moment she was covered again she was grey and invisible.

Every day, in the morning towards noon, she lay at the foot of the powerful, silver-pawed cypress tree, while the sun strode jovial in heaven. By now, she knew the sun in every thread of her body. Her heart of anxiety, that anxious, straining heart, had disappeared altogether, like a flower that falls in the Sun, and leaves only a little ripening fruit. And her tense womb, though still closed, was slowly unfolding, slowly, slowly, like a lily bud under water, as the sun mysteriously touched it. Like a lily bud under water it was slowly rising to the sun, to expand at last, to the sun, only to the sun.

She knew the sun in all her body, the blue-molten with his white fire edges, throwing off fire. And though he shone on all the world, when she lay unclothed he focussed on her. It was one of the wonders of the sun, he could shine on a million people, and still be the radiant, splendid, unique sun, focussed on her alone.

With her knowledge of the sun, and her conviction that the sun was gradually penetrating her to *know* her, in the cosmic carnal sense of the word, came over her a feeling of detachment from people, and a certain contemptuous tolerance for human beings altogether. They were so un-elemental, so un-sunned. They were so like graveyard worms.

Even the peasants passing up the rocky, ancient little road with their donkeys, sun-blackened as they were, were not sunned right through. There was a little soft white core of fear, like a snail in a shell, where the soul of the man cowered in fear of death, and still more in fear of the natural blaze of life. He dared not quite see the sun: always innerly cowed. All men were like that.—Why admit men!

With her indifference to people, to men, she was not now so cautious about being seen. She had told Marinina, who went shopping for her in the village, that the doctor had ordered sun-baths. Let that suffice.

Marinin' was a woman of sixty or more, tall, thin, erect, with curling dark-grey hair, and dark-grey eyes that had the shrewdness of thousands of years in them, with the laugh, half mockery, that underlies all long experience. Tragedy is lack of experience.

"It must be beautiful to go naked in the sun," said Marinin', with a shrewd laugh in her eyes, as she looked keenly at the other woman. Juliet's fair, bobbed hair curled in a little cloud at her temples. Marinin' was a woman of Magna Graecia, and had far memories. She looked again at Juliet. "But when a woman is beautiful, she can show herself to the sun! eh? isn't it true?"—she added, with that queer, breathless little laugh of the women of the past.

"Who knows if I am beautiful!" said Juliet.

But beautiful or not, she felt that by the sun, she was appreciated. Which is the same.

When, out of the sun at noon, sometimes she stole down over the rocks and past the cliff-edge, down to the deep gully where the lemons hung in cool eternal shadow; and in the silence slipped off her wrapper to wash herself quickly at one of the deep, clear-green basins, she would notice, in the bare, green twilight under the lemon-leaves, that all her body was rosy, rosy and turning to gold. She was like another person. She *was* another person.

So she remembered that the Greeks had said, a white, unsunned body was unhealthy, and fishy.

And she would rub a little olive oil into her skin, and wander a moment in the dark underworld of the lemons, balancing a lemon-flower in her navel, laughing to herself. There was just a chance some peasant might see her. But if he did, he would

be more afraid of her, than she of him. She knew the white core
of fear in the clothed bodies of men.

She knew it even in her little son. How he mistrusted her,
now that she laughed at him, with the sun in her face! She
insisted on his toddling naked in the sunshine, every day. And
now his little body was pink too, his blond hair was pushed
thick from his brow, his cheeks had a pomegranate scarlet, in
the delicate gold of the sunny skin. He was bonny and healthy,
and the servants, loving his gold and red and blue, called him
an angel from heaven.

But he mistrusted his mother: she laughed at him. And she
saw, in his wide blue eyes, under the little frown, that centre of
fear, misgiving, which she believed was at the centre of all male
eyes, now. She called it fear of the sun. And her womb stayed
shut against all men, sun-fearers.

"He fears the sun," she would say to herself, looking down
into the eyes of the child.

And as she watched him toddling, swaying, tumbling in the
sunshine, making his little bird-like noises, she saw that he held
himself tight and hidden from the sun, inside himself, and his
balance was clumsy, his movements a little gross. His spirit was
like a snail in a shell, in a damp, cold crevice inside himself. It
made her think of his father. And she wished she could make
him come forth, break out in a gesture of recklessness, a salu-
tation to the sun.

She determined to take him with her, down to the cypress
tree among the cactus. She would have to watch him, because
of the thorns. But surely in that place he would come forth
from the little shell, deep inside him. That little civilised tension
would disappear off his brow.

She spread a rug for him, and sat him down. Then she slid
off her wrapper and lay down herself, watching a hawk high in
the blue, and the tip of the cypress hanging over.

The boy played with stones on the rug. When he got up to
toddle away, she got up too. He turned and looked at her.
Almost, from his blue eyes, it was the challenging, warm look
of the true male. And he was handsome, with the scarlet in the

golden blond of his skin. He was not really white. His skin was gold-dusky.

"Mind the thorns, darling," she said.

"Thorns!" re-echoed the child, in a birdy chirp, still looking at her over his shoulder, like some naked *putto* in a picture, doubtful.

"Nasty prickly thorns."

"'Ickly thorns!"

He staggered in his little sandals over the stones, pulling at the dry mint. She was quick as a serpent, leaping to him, when he was going to fall against the prickles. It surprised even herself.—"What a wild cat I am, really!" she said to herself.

She brought him every day, when the sun shone, to the cypress tree.

"Come!" she said. "Let us go to the cypress tree."

And if there was a cloudy day, with the tramontana blowing, so that she could not go down, the child would chirp incessantly: "Cypress tree! Cypress tree!"

He missed it as much as she did.

It was not just taking sun-baths. It was much more than that. Something deep inside her unfolded and relaxed, and she was given to a cosmic influence. By some mysterious will inside her, deeper than her known consciousness and her known will, she was put into connection with the sun, and the stream of the sun flowed through her, round her womb. She herself, her conscious self, was secondary, a secondary person, almost an onlooker. The true Juliet lived in the dark flow of the sun within her deep body, like a river of dark rays circling, circling dark and violet round the sweet, shut bud of her womb.

She had always been mistress of herself, aware of what she was doing, and held tense in her own command. Now she felt inside her quite another sort of power, something greater than herself, darker and more savage, the element flowing upon her. Now she was vague, in the spell of a power beyond herself.

III

The end of February was suddenly very hot. Almond blossom was falling like pink snow, in the touch of the smallest breeze. The mauve, silky little anemones were out, the asphodels tall in bud, and the sea was cornflower blue.

Juliet had ceased to care about anything. Now, most of the day, she and the child were naked in the sun, and it was all she wanted. Sometimes she went down to the sea to bathe: often she wandered in the gullies where the sun shone in, and she was out of sight. Sometimes she saw a peasant with an ass, and he saw her. But she went so simply and quietly with her child; and the fame of the sun's healing power, for the soul as well as for the body, had already spread among the people; so that there was no excitement.

The child and she were now both tanned with a rosy-golden tan, all over.—"I am another being," she said to herself, as she looked at her red-gold breasts and thighs.

The child, too, was another creature, with a peculiar quiet, sun-darkened absorption. Now he played by himself in silence, and she need hardly notice him. He seemed no longer to notice when he was alone.

There was not a breeze, and the sea was ultramarine. She sat by the great silver paw of the cypress tree, drowsed in the sun, but her breasts alert, full of sap. She was becoming aware of an activity rousing in her, an activity which would bring another self awake in her. Still she did not want to be aware. The new rousing would mean a new contact, and this she did not want. She knew well enough the vast cold apparatus of civilisation, and what contact with it meant; and how difficult it was to evade.

The child had gone a few yards down the rocky path, round the great sprawling of a cactus. She had seen him, a real gold-brown infant of the winds, with burnt gold hair and red cheeks, collecting the speckled pitcher-flowers and laying them in rows. He could balance now, and was quick for his own emergencies, like an absorbed young animal playing.

Suddenly she heard him speaking: *Look, Mummy! Mummy*

look! A note in his bird-like voice made her lean forward sharply.

Her heart stood still. He was looking over his naked little shoulder at her, and pointing with a loose little hand at a snake which had reared itself up a yard away from him, and was opening its mouth so that its forked, soft tongue flickered black like a shadow, uttering a short hiss.

"Look! Mummy!"

"Yes darling, it's a snake!" came the slow, deep voice.

He looked at her, his wide blue eyes uncertain whether to be afraid or not. Some stillness of the sun in her reassured him.

"Snake!" he chirped.

"Yes darling! Don't touch it, it can bite."

The snake had sunk down, and was reaching away from the coils in which it had been basking asleep, and slowly was easing its long, gold-brown body into the rocks, with slow curves. The boy turned and watched it, in silence. Then he said:

"Snake going!"

"Yes! Let it go. It likes to be alone."

He still watched the slow, easing length as the creature drew itself apathetic out of sight.

"Snake gone back," he said.

"Yes, it's gone back.—Come to Mummy a moment."

He came and sat with his plump, naked little body on her naked lap, and she smoothed his burnt, bright hair. She said nothing, feeling that everything was past. The curious careless power of the sun filled her, filled the whole place like a charm, and the snake was part of the place, along with her and the child.

Another day, in the dry stone wall of one of the olive terraces, she saw a black snake horizontally creeping.

"Marinin'," she said, "I saw a black snake. Are they harmful?"

"Ah, the black snakes, no! But the yellow ones, yes! If the yellow one bites you, you die. But they frighten me, they frighten me, even the black ones, when I see one."

Juliet still went to the cypress tree with the child. But she always looked carefully round, before she sat down, examining everywhere where the child might go. Then she would lie and turn to the sun again, her tanned, pear shaped breasts pointing up. She would take no thought for the morrow. She refused to think outside her garden, and she could not write letters. She would tell the nurse to write. So she lay in the sun, but not for long, for it was getting strong, fierce. And in spite of herself, the bud that had been tight and deep immersed in the innermost gloom of her, was rearing, rearing and straightening its curved stem, to open its dark tips and show a gleam of rose. Her womb was coming open, in spite of herself. In spite of herself, it would open wide with rosy ecstasy, like a lotus flower.

IV.

Spring was becoming summer, in the south of the sun, and the rays were very powerful. In the hot hours she would lie in the shade of trees, or she would even go down to the depths of the cool lemon grove. Or sometimes she went in the shadowy deeps of the gullies, at the bottom of the little ravine, towards home. The child fluttered around in silence, like a young animal absorbed in life.

Going slowly home in her nakedness down among the bushes of the dark ravine, one noon, she came round a rock suddenly upon the peasant of the next podere, who was stooping binding up a bundle of brush-wood he had cut, his ass standing near. He was wearing summer cotton trousers, and stooping his buttocks towards her. It was utterly still and private down in the dark bed of the little ravine. A weakness came over her, for a moment she could not move.

The man lifted the bundle of wood with powerful shoulders, and turned to the ass. He started and stood transfixed as he saw her, as if it were a vision. Then his eyes met hers, and she felt the blue fire running through her limbs to her womb, which was spreading in the helpless ecstasy. Still they looked into each other's eyes, and the fire flowed between them, like the blue, streaming fire from the heart of the sun. And she saw the

phallus rise under his clothing, and knew he would come towards her.

"Mummy, a man! Mummy!"—The child had put a hand
against her thigh. "Mummy, a man!"

She heard the note of fear, and swung round.

"It's all right, boy!" she said, and taking him by the hand,
she led him back round the rock again, while the peasant
watched her naked, retreating buttocks lift and fall.

She put on her wrap, and taking the boy in her arms, began
to stagger up a steep goat-track through the yellow-flowering
tangle of shrubs, up to the level of day, and the olive trees
below the house. There she sat down under a tree, to collect
herself.

The sea was blue, very blue and soft and still-looking and
her womb inside her was wide open, wide open like a lotus
flower, or a cactus flower, in a radiant sort of eagerness. She
could feel it, and it dominated her consciousness. And a biting
chagrin burned in her breast, against the child, against the
complication of frustration.

She knew the peasant by sight: a man something over thirty,
broad and very powerfully set. She had many times watched
him from the terrace of her house: watched him come with his
ass, watched him trimming the olive trees, working alone,
always alone and physically powerful, with a broad red face
and a quiet self-possession. She had spoken to him once or
twice, and met his big blue eyes, dark and Southern hot. And
she knew his sudden gestures, a little violent and over-generous.
But she had never thought of him. Save she had noticed he was
always very clean and well-cared for; and then she had seen his
wife one day, when the latter had brought the man's meal, and
they sat in the shade of a carob tree, on either side the spread
white cloth. And then Juliet had seen that the man's wife was
older than he, a dark, proud, gloomy woman. And then a young
woman had come with a child, and the man had danced with
the child, so young and passionate. But it was not his own child:
he had no children. It was when he danced with the child, in
such a queer sprightly way, as if full of suppressed passion, that
Juliet had first really noticed him. But even then, she had never

thought of him. Such a broad red face, such a great chest, and rather short legs. Too much a crude beast for her to think of, a peasant.

But now the strange challenge of his eyes had held her, blue and overwhelming like the blue sun's heart. And she had seen the fierce stirring of the phallus under his thin trousers: for her. And with his red face, and with his broad body, he was like the sun to her, the sun in its broad heat.

She felt him so powerfully, that she could not go further from him. She continued to sit there under the tree. Then she heard nurse tinkling a bell at the house, and calling. And the child called back. She had to rise and go home.

In the afternoon she sat on the terrace of her house, that looked over the olive slopes to the sea. The man came and went, came and went to the little hut on his podere, on the edge of the cactus grove. And he glanced again at her house, at her sitting on the terrace. And her womb was open to him.

Yet she had not the courage to go down to him. She was paralysed. She had tea, and still sat there on the terrace. And the man came and went, and glanced, and glanced again. Till the evening bell had jangled from the capuchin church at the village gate, and the darkness came on. And still she sat on the terrace. Till at last in the moonlight she saw him load his ass and drive it sadly along the path to the little road. She heard him pass on the stones of the road behind her house. He was gone—gone home to the village, to sleep, to sleep with his wife, who would want to know why he was so late. He was gone in dejection.

Juliet sat late on into the night, watching the moon on the sea. The sun had opened her womb, and she was no longer free. The trouble of the open lotus blossom had come upon her, and now it was she who had not the courage to take the steps across the gully.

But at last she slept. And in the morning she felt better. Her womb seemed to have closed again: the lotus flower seemed back in bud again. She wanted so much that it should be so. Only the immersed bud, and the sun! She would never think of that man.

She bathed in one of the great tanks away down in the lemon-grove, down in the far ravine, far as possible from the other wild gully, and cool. Below, under the lemons, the child was wading among the yellow oxalis flowers of the shadow, gathering fallen lemons, passing with his tanned little body into flecks of light, moving all dappled. She sat in the sun on the steep bank down in the gully, feeling almost free again, the flower drooping in shadowy bud, safe inside her.

Suddenly high over the land's edge, against the full-lit pale blue sky, Marinin' appeared, a black cloth tied round her head, calling quietly: *Signora! Signora Giulietta!*

Juliet faced round, standing up. Marinin' paused a moment, seeing the naked woman standing alert, her sun-faded fair hair in a little cloud. Then the swift old woman came on down the slant of the steep, sun-blazed track.

She stood a few steps, erect, in front of the sun-coloured woman, and eyed her shrewdly.

"But how beautiful you are, you!" she said coolly, almost cynically. "Your husband has come."

"What husband?" cried Juliet.

The old woman gave a shrewd bark of a little laugh, the mockery of the women of the past.

"Haven't you got one, a husband, you?" she said, taunting.

"How? Where? In America," said Juliet.

The old woman glanced over her shoulder, with another noiseless laugh.

"No America at all. He was following me here. He will have missed the path." And she threw back her head in the noiseless laugh of women.

The paths were all grown high with grass and flowers and nepitella, till they were like bird-tracks in an eternally wild place. Strange, the vivid wildness of the old classic places, that have known men so long.

Juliet looked at the Sicilian woman with meditating eyes.

"Oh very well," she said at last. "Let him come."

And a little flame leaped in her. It was the opening flower. At least he was a man.

"Bring him here? Now?" asked Marinin', her mocking,

smoke-grey eyes looking with laughter into Juliet's eyes. Then
she gave a little jerk of her shoulders.

"All right! As you wish! But for him it is a rare one!"

She opened her mouth with a noiseless laugh of amusement.
Then she pointed down to the child, who was heaping lemons
against his little chest. "Look how beautiful the child is! An
angel from heaven! That, certainly, will please him, poor
thing.—Then I shall bring him?"

"Bring him," said Juliet.

The old woman scrambled rapidly up the track again, and
found Maurice at a loss among the vine terraces, standing
there in his grey felt hat and dark-grey city suit. He looked
pathetically out of place, in that resplendent sunshine and the
grace of the old Greek world; like a blot of ink on the pale,
sun-glowing slope.

"Come!" said Marinin' to him. "She is down here."

And swiftly she led the way, striding with a long stride,
making her way through the grasses. Suddenly she stopped on
the brow of the slope. The tops of the lemon trees were dark,
away below.

"You, you go down here," she said to him, and he thanked
her, glancing up at her swiftly.

He was a man of forty, clean-shaven, grey-faced, very quiet
and really shy. He managed his own business carefully, without
startling success, but efficiently. And he confided in nobody.
The old woman of Magna Graecia saw him at a glance: he is
good, she said to herself, but not a man, poor thing.

"Down there is the Signora," said Marinin', pointing like
one of the Fates.

And again he said: Thank you! Thank you! without a twinkle,
and stepped carefully into the track. Marinin' lifted her chin
with a joyful wickedness. Then she strode off towards the
house.

Maurice was watching his step, through the tangle of Mediterranean herbage, so he did not catch sight of his wife till he
came round a little bend, quite near her. She was standing erect
and nude by the jutting rock, glistening with the sun and with
warm life. Her breasts seemed to be lifting up, alert, to listen,

her thighs looked brown and fleet. Inside her, the lotus of her womb was wide open, spread almost gaping in the violet rays of the sun, like a great lotus flower. And she thrilled helplessly: a man was coming. Her glance on him, as he came gingerly, like ink on blotting-paper, was swift and nervous.

Maurice, poor fellow, hesitated and glanced away from her, turning his face aside.

"Hello Julie!" he said, with a little nervous cough. "Splendid! Splendid!"

He advanced with his face averted, shooting further glances at her, furtively, as she stood with the peculiar satiny gleam of the sun on her tanned skin. Somehow, she did not seem so terribly naked. It was the golden-rose tan of the sun that clothed her.

"Hello Maurice!" she said, hanging back from him, and a cold shadow falling on the open flower of her womb. "I wasn't expecting you so soon."

"No!" he said. "No! I managed to slip away a little earlier."

And again he coughed unawares. Furtively, purposely he had taken her by surprise. They stood several yards away from one another, and there was silence.—But this was a new Julie to him, with the sun-tanned, wind-stroked thighs: not that nervous New York woman.

"Well!" he said. "Er—this is splendid—splendid! You are—er splendid!—Where is the boy?"

He felt, in his far-off depths, the desire stirring in him for the limbs and sunwrapped flesh of the woman: the woman of flesh. It was a new desire in his life, and it hurt him. He wanted to side-track.

"There he is!" she said, pointing down to where a naked urchin in the deep shade was piling fallen lemons together.

The father gave an odd little laugh, almost neighing.

"Ah yes! There he is! So there's the little man! Fine!" His nervous, suppressed soul was thrilling with violent thrills, he clung to the straw of his upper consciousness. "Hello Johnny!" he called, and it sounded rather feeble. "Hello Johnny!"

The child looked up, spilling lemons from his chubby arms, but did not respond.

"I guess we'll go down to him," said Juliet, as she turned and went striding down the path. In spite of herself, the cold shadow was lifting off the open flower of her womb, and every petal was thrilling again. Her husband followed, watching the rosy, fleet-looking lifting and sinking of her quick hips, as she swayed a little in the socket of her waist. He was dazed with admiration, but also, at a deadly loss. He was used to her as a person. And this was no longer a person, but a fleet sun-strong body, soulless and alluring as a nymph, twinkling its haunches. What should he do with himself? He was utterly out of the picture, in his dark-grey suit and pale grey hat, and his grey, monastic face of a shy business man, and his grey mercantile mentality. Strange thrills shot through his loins and his legs. He was terrified, and he felt he might give a wild whoop of triumph, and jump towards that woman of tanned flesh.

"He looks alright, doesn't he?" said Juliet, as they came through the deep sea of yellow-flowering oxalis, under the lemon-trees.

"Ah!—yes! yes! Splendid! Splendid!—Hello Johnny! Do you know Daddy? Do you know Daddy, Johnny?"

He squatted down, forgetting his trouser-crease, and held out his hands.

"Lemons!" said the child, birdily chirping. "Two lemons!"

"Two lemons!" replied the father. "Lots of lemons!"

The infant came and put a lemon in each of his father's open hands. Then he stood back to look.

"Two lemons!" repeated the father. "Come, Johnny! Come and say Hello! to Daddy."

"Daddy going back?" said the child.

"Going back? Well—well—not today."

And he took his son in his arms.

"Take a coat off! Daddy take a coat off!" said the boy, squirming debonair away from the cloth.

"All right, son! Daddy take a coat off."

He took off his coat and laid it carefully aside, then looked at the creases in his trousers, hitched them a little, and crouched down and took his son in his arms. The child's warm, naked body against him made him feel faint. The naked woman looked down at the rosy infant, in the arms of the man in his shirt-sleeves. The boy had pulled off his father's hat, and Juliet looked at the sleek, black-and-grey hair of her husband, not a hair out of place. And utterly, utterly sunless! The cold shadow was over the flower of her womb again. She was silent for a long time, while the father talked to the child, who had been fond of his Daddy.

"What are you going to do about it, Maurice?" she said suddenly.

He looked at her swiftly, sideways, hearing her abrupt American voice. He had forgotten her.

"Er—about what, Julie?"

"Oh, everything! About this! I can't go back into East Forty-Seventh."

"Er—," he hesitated, "no. I suppose not—Not just now, at least."

"Never!" she said abruptly, and there was a silence.

"Well—er—I don't know," he said.

"Do you think you can come out here?" she said savagely.

"Yes!—I can stay for a month. I think I can manage a month," he hesitated. Then he ventured a complicated, shy peep at her, and turned away his face again.

She looked down at him, her alert breasts lifted with a sigh, as if she would impatiently shake the cold shadow of sunlessness off her.

"I can't go back," she said slowly. "I can't go back on this sun. If you can't come here—"

She ended on an open note. But the voice of the abrupt, personal American woman had died out, and he heard the voice of the woman of flesh, the sun-ripe body. He glanced at her again and again, with growing desire and lessening fear.

"No!" he said. "This kind of thing suits you. You are splendid!—No, I don't think you can go back."

And at the caressive sound of his voice, in spite of her, her womb-flower began to open and thrill its petals.

He was thinking visionarily of her in the New York flat, pale, silent, oppressing him terribly. He was the soul of gentle timidity in his human relations, and her silent, awful hostility after the baby was born had frightened him deeply. Because, he had realised that she could not help it. Women were like that. Their feelings took a reverse direction, even against their own selves, and it was awful—devastating. Awful, awful, to live in the house with a woman like that, whose feelings were reversed even against herself. He had felt himself borne down under the stream of her heavy hostility. She had ground even herself down to the quick, and the child as well. No, anything rather than that. Thank God, that menacing ghost woman seemed to be sunned out of her now.

"But what about *you*—?" she asked.

"I? Oh, I!—I can carry on in the business, and—er—come over here for long holidays—so long as you like to stay here. You stay as long as you wish—" He looked down a long time at the earth. He was so frightened of rousing that menacing avenging spirit of womanhood in her, he did so hope she might stay as he had seen her now, like a naked, ripening strawberry, a female like a fruit. He glanced up at her, with a touch of supplication in his uneasy eyes.

"Even for ever?" she said.

"Well—er—yes, if you like. Forever is a long time.—One can't set a date."

"And can I do anything I like?"—She looked him straight in the eyes, challenging. And he was powerless against her rosy, wind-hardened nakedness, in his fear of arousing that other woman in her, the personal American woman, spectral and vengeful.

"Er—yes!—I suppose so! So long as you don't make yourself unhappy—or the boy."

Again he looked up at her with a complicated, uneasy appeal—thinking of the child, but hoping for himself.

"I won't," she said quickly.

"No!" he said. "No! I don't think you will."

There was a pause. The bells of the village were hastily clanging mid-day. That meant lunch.

She slipped into her grey crêpe kimono, and fastened a broad green sash round her waist. Then she slipped a little blue shirt over the boy's head, and they went up to the house.

At table she watched her husband, his grey city face, his
glued, grey-black hair, his very precise table manners, and his
extreme moderation in eating and drinking. Sometimes he
glanced at her furtively, from under his black lashes. He had
the uneasy, gold-grey eyes of a creature that has been caught
young, and reared entirely in captivity, strange and cold, knowing no warm hopes. Only his black eye-brows and eye-lashes
were nice. She did not take him in. She did not realise him.
Being so sunned, she could not *see* him, his sunlessness was like
nonentity.

They went on to the balcony for coffee, under the rosy mass
of the bougainvillea. Below, beyond, on the next podere, the
peasant and his wife were sitting under the carob tree, near the
tall green wheat, sitting facing one another across a little white
cloth spread on the ground. There was still a huge piece of
bread—but they had finished eating, and sat with dark wine in
their glasses.

The peasant looked up at the terrace, as soon as the American
emerged. Juliet put her husband with his back to the scene.
Then she sat down, and looked back at the peasant. Until she
saw his dark-visaged wife turn to look too.

V

The man was hopelessly in love with her. She saw his broad,
rather short red face gazing up at her fixedly: till his wife turned
too to look, then he picked up his glass and tossed the wine
down his throat. The wife stared long at the figures on the
balcony. She was handsome and rather gloomy, and surely
older than he, with that great difference that lies between a
rather overbearing, superior woman over forty, and her more
irresponsible husband of thirty-five or so. It seemed like the
difference of a whole generation. "He is my generation,"
thought Juliet, "and she is Maurice's generation."—Juliet was
not yet thirty.

The peasant, in his white cotton trousers and pale pink shirt,
and battered old straw hat, was attractive, so clean, and full of
the cleanliness of health. He was stout and broad, and seemed

shortish, but his flesh was full of vitality, as if he were always about to spring up into movement, to work, even, as she had seen him with the child, to play. He was the type of Italian peasant that wants to make an offering of himself, passionately wants to make an offering of himself, of his powerful flesh and thudding blood-stroke. But he was also completely a peasant, in that he would wait for the woman to make the move. He would hang round in a long, consuming passivity of desire, hoping, hoping for the woman to come for him. But he would never try to advance to her: never. She would have to make the advance. Only he would hang round, within reach.

Feeling her look at him, he flung off his old straw hat, showing his round, close-cropped brown head, and reached out with a large, brown-red hand for the great loaf, from which he broke a piece and started chewing with bulging cheek. He knew she was looking at him. And she had such power over him, the hot, inarticulate animal, with such a hot, massive blood-stream down his great veins! He was hot through with countless suns, and mindless as noon. And shy with a violent, farouche shyness, that would wait for her with consuming wanting, but would never, never move towards her.

With him, it would be like bathing in another kind of sunshine, heavy and big and perspiring: and afterwards one would forget. Personally, he would not exist. It would be just a bath of warm, powerful life—then separating and forgetting. Then again, the procreative bath, like sun.

But would that not be good! She was so tired of personal contacts, and having to talk with the man afterwards. With that healthy creature, one would just go satisfied away, afterwards. As she sat there, she felt the life streaming from him to her, and her to him. She knew by his movements he felt her even more than she felt him. It was almost a definite pain of consciousness in the body of each of them, and each sat as if distracted, watched by a keen-eyed spouse, possessor.

And Juliet thought: Why shouldn't I go to him! Why shouldn't I bear his child? It would be like bearing a child to the unconscious sun and the unconscious earth, a child like a fruit.—And the flower of her womb radiated. It did not care about sentiment or possession. It wanted man-dew only, utterly improvident. But her heart was clouded with fear. She dare not! She dare not! If only the man would find some way! But he would not. He would only hover and wait, hover in endless desire, waiting for her to cross the gully. And she dare not, she dare not. And he would hang round.

"You are not afraid of people seeing you when you take your sun-baths?" said her husband, turning round and looking across at the peasants. The saturnine wife over the gully turned also to face the villa. It was a kind of battle.

"No! One needn't be seen.—Will you do it too? Will you take sun-baths?" said Juliet to him.

"Why—er—yes! I think I should like to, while I am here."

There was a gleam in his eyes, a desperate kind of courage of desire to taste this new fruit, this woman with rosy, sun-ripening breasts tilting within her wrapper. And she thought of him with his blanched, etiolated little city figure, walking in the sun in the desperation of a husband's rights. And her mind swooned again. The strange, branded little fellow, the good citizen, branded like a criminal in the naked eye of the sun. How he would hate exposing himself!

And the flower of her womb went dizzy, dizzy. She knew she would take him. She knew she would bear his child. She knew it was for him, the branded little city man, that her womb was open radiating like a lotus, like the purple spread of a daisy anemone, dark at the core. She knew she would not go across to the peasant: she had not enough courage, she was not free enough. And she knew the peasant would never come for her, he had the dogged passivity of the earth, and would wait, wait, only putting himself in her sight, again and again, lingering across her vision, with the persistency of animal yearning.

She had seen the flushed blood in the peasant's burnt face, and felt the jetting, sudden blue heat pouring over her from his kindled eyes, and the rousing of his big penis against his body— for her, surging for her. Yet she would never come to him— she daren't, she daren't, so much was against her. And the little etiolated body of her husband, city-branded, would possess her, and his little, frantic penis would beget another child in her. She could not help it. She was bound to the vast, fixed wheel of circumstance, and there was no Perseus in the universe, to cut the bonds.

THE ROCKING-HORSE WINNER

There was a woman who was beautiful, who started with all the advantages, yet she had no luck. She married for love, and the love turned to dust. She had bonny children, yet she felt they had been thrust upon her, and she could not love them. They looked at her coldly, as if they were finding fault with her. And hurriedly, she felt she must cover up some fault in herself. Yet what it was that she must cover up, she never knew. Nevertheless, when her children were present, she always felt the centre of her heart go hard. This troubled her, and in her manner she was all the more gentle and anxious for her children, as if she loved them very much. Only she herself knew that at the centre of her heart was a hard little place that could not feel love, no, not for anybody. Everybody else said of her: "She is such a good mother. She adores her children." Only she herself, and her children themselves, knew it was not so. They read it in each other's eyes.

There was a boy and two little girls. They lived in a pleasant house, with a garden, and they had discreet servants, and felt themselves superior to anyone in the neighbourhood.

Although they lived in style, they felt always an anxiety in the house. There was never enough money. The mother had a small income, and the father had a small income, but not nearly enough for the social position which they had to keep up. The father went in to town to some office. But though he had good prospects, these prospects never materialised. There was always the grinding sense of the shortage of money, though the style was always kept up.

At last the mother said: "I will see if *I* can't make something."

But she did not know where to begin. She racked her brains, and tried this thing and the other, but could not find anything successful. The failure made deep lines come into her face. Her children were growing up, they would have to go to school. There must be more money, there must be more money. The father, who was always very handsome and expensive in his tastes, seemed as if he never *would* be able to do anything worth doing. And the mother, who had a great belief in herself, did not succeed any better, and her tastes were just as expensive.

And so the house came to be haunted by the unspoken phrase: *There must be more money*! *There must be more money*! The children could hear it all the time, though nobody ever said it aloud. They heard it at Christmas, when the expensive and splendid toys filled the nursery. Behind the shining modern rocking-horse, behind the smart doll's house, a voice would start whispering: There *must* be more money! There *must* be more money! And the children would stop playing, to listen for a moment. They would look into each other's eyes, to see if they had all heard. And each one saw in the eyes of the other two, that they too had heard. "There *must* be more money! There *must* be more money."

It came whispering from the springs of the still-swaying rocking-horse, and even the horse, bending his wooden, champing head, heard it. The big doll, sitting so pink and smirking in her new pram, could hear it quite plainly, and seemed to be smirking all the more self-consciously because of it. The foolish puppy, too, that took the place of the teddy bear, he was looking so extraordinarily foolish for no other reason but that he heard the secret whisper all over the house: "There must be more money."

Yet nobody ever said it aloud. The whisper was everywhere, and therefore no-one spoke it. Just as no-one ever says: "We are breathing!", in spite of the fact that breath is coming and going all the time.

"Mother!" said the boy Paul one day. "Why don't we keep a car of our own? Why do we always use uncle's, or else a taxi?"

"Because we're the poor members of the family," said the mother.

"But why *are* we, Mother?"

"Well—I suppose—" she said slowly and bitterly—"it's because your father has no luck."

The boy was silent for some time.

"Is luck money, Mother?" he asked, rather timidly.

"No, Paul! Not quite. It's what causes you to have money."

"Oh!" said Paul vaguely. "I thought when Uncle Oscar said *filthy lucker* it meant money."

"*Filthy lucre* does mean money," said the mother. "But it's lucre, not luck."

"Oh!" said the boy. "Then what *is* luck, Mother?"

"It's what causes you to have money. If you're lucky you have money. That's why it's better to be born lucky than rich. If you're rich, you may lose your money. But if you're lucky, you will always get more money."

"Oh! Will you! And is father not lucky?"

"Very unlucky, I should say," she said bitterly.

The boy watched her with unsure eyes.

"Why?" he asked.

"I don't know. Nobody ever knows why one person is lucky and another unlucky."

"Don't they? Nobody at all? Does *nobody* know?"

"Perhaps God! But he never tells."

"He ought to then.—And aren't you lucky either, Mother?"

"I can't be, if I married an unlucky husband."

"But by yourself, aren't you?"

"I used to think I was, before I married. Now I think I am very unlucky indeed."

"Why?"

"Well—never mind! Perhaps I'm not really," she said.

The child looked at her, to see if she meant it. But he saw, by the lines at her mouth, that she was only trying to hide something from him.

"Well anyhow," he said stoutly, "I'm a lucky person."

"Why?" said his mother, with a sudden laugh.

He stared at her. He didn't even know why he had said it.

"God told me," he asserted, brazening it out.

"I hope he did, Dear!" she said, again with a laugh, but rather bitter.

"He did, Mother!"

"Excellent!" said the mother, using one of her husband's exclamations.

The boy saw she did not believe him: or rather, that she paid no attention to his assertion. This angered him somewhere, and made him want to compel her attention.

He went off by himself, vaguely, in a childish way, seeking for the clue to "luck." Absorbed, taking no heed of other people, he went about with a sort of stealth, seeking inwardly for luck. He wanted luck, he wanted it, he wanted it. When the two girls were playing dolls, in the nursery, he would sit on his big rocking horse, charging madly into space, with a frenzy that made the little girls peer at him uneasily. Wildly the horse careered, the waving dark hair of the boy tossed, his eyes had a strange glare in them. The little girls dared not speak to him.

When he had ridden to the end of his mad little journey, he climbed down and stood in front of his rocking-horse, staring fixedly into its lowered face. Its red mouth was slightly open, its big eye was wide and glassy bright.

"Now!" he would silently command the snorting steed. "Now take me to where there is luck! Now take me!"

And he would slash the horse on the neck with the little whip he had asked Uncle Oscar for. He *knew* the horse could take him to where there was luck, if only he forced it. So he would mount again, and start on his furious ride, hoping at last to get there. He knew he could get there.

"You'll break your horse, Paul!" said the nurse.

"He's always riding like that! I wish he'd leave off!" said his elder sister Joan.

But he only glared down on them in silence. Nurse gave him up. She could make nothing of him. Anyhow he was growing beyond her.

One day his mother and his Uncle Oscar came in when he was on one of his furious rides. He did not speak to them.

"Hello! you young jockey! Riding a winner?" said his Uncle.

"Aren't you growing too big for a rocking horse? You're not a very little boy any longer, you know," said his mother.

But Paul only gave a blue glare from his big, rather close-set eyes. He would speak to nobody when he was in full tilt. His mother watched him with a curious expression on her face.

At last he suddenly stopped forcing his horse into the mechanical gallop, and slid down.

"Well I got there!" he announced fiercely, his blue eyes still flaring, and his sturdy long legs straddling apart.

"Where did you get to?" asked his mother.

"Where I wanted to go to," he flared back at her.

"That's right, Son!" said Uncle Oscar. "Don't you stop till you get there.—What's the horse's name?"

"He doesn't have a name," said the boy.

"Gets on without all right?" asked the Uncle.

"Well, he has different names. He was called Sansovino last week."

"Sansovino, eh? Won the Ascot. How did you know his name?"

"He always talks about horse-races with Bassett," said Joan.

The uncle was delighted to find that his small nephew was posted with all the racing news. Bassett, the young gardener who had been wounded in the left foot in the war, and had got his present job through Oscar Cresswell, whose batman he had been, was a perfect blade of the "turf." He lived in the racing events. And the small boy lived with him.

Oscar Cresswell got it all from Bassett.

"Master Paul comes and asks me, so I can't do more than tell him, Sir," said Bassett, his face terribly serious, as if he were speaking of religious matters.

"And does he ever put anything on a horse he fancies?"

"Well—I don't want to give him away—he's a young sport, a fine sport, Sir. Would you mind asking him himself? He sort of takes a pleasure in it, and perhaps he'd feel I was giving him away, Sir, if you don't mind."

Bassett was serious as a church.

The uncle went back to his nephew, and took him off for a ride in the car.

"Say, Paul, old man, do you ever put anything on a horse?" the uncle asked.

The boy watched the handsome man closely.

"Why, do you think I oughtn't to?" he parried.

"Not a bit of it! I thought perhaps you might give me a tip for the Lincoln."

The car sped on into the country, going down to Uncle Oscar's place in Hampshire.

"Honour bright?" said the nephew.

"Honour bright, Son!" said the Uncle.

"Well then, Daffodil."

"Daffodil! I doubt it, Sonny. What about Mirza?"

"I only know the winner," said the boy. "That's Daffodil!"

"Daffodil, eh?"

There was a pause. Daffodil was an obscure horse, comparatively.

"Uncle!"

"Yes Son!"

"You won't let it go any further, will you? I promised Bassett."

"Bassett be damned, old man! What's he got to do with it?"

"We're partners! We've been partners from the first! Uncle, he lent me my first five shillings which I lost. I promised him, honour bright, it was only between me and him: only you gave me that ten shilling note I started winning with, so I thought you were lucky. You won't let it go any further, will you?"

The boy gazed at his uncle from those big, hot blue eyes, set rather close together. The uncle stirred and laughed uneasily.

"Right you are, Son! I'll keep your tip private. Daffodil, eh?—How much are you putting on him?"

"All except twenty pounds," said the boy. "I keep that in reserve."

The uncle thought it a good joke.

"You keep twenty pounds in reserve, do you, you young romancer? What are you betting, then?"

"I'm betting three hundred," said the boy gravely. "But it's between you and me, Uncle Oscar! Honour bright?"

The uncle burst into a roar of laughter.

"It's between you and me all right, you young Nat Gould," he said, laughing. "But where's your three hundred?"

"Bassett keeps it for me. We're partners."

"You are, are you! And what is Bassett putting on Daffodil?"

"He won't go quite as high as I do, I expect. Perhaps he'll go a hundred and fifty."

"What, pennies?" laughed the Uncle.

"Pounds," said the child, with a surprised look at his uncle. "Bassett keeps a bigger reserve than I do."

Between wonder and amusement, Uncle Oscar was silent. He pursued the matter no further, but he determined to take his nephew with him to the Lincoln races.

"Now Son," he said, "I'm putting twenty on Mirza, and I'll put five for you on any horse you fancy. What's your pick?"

"Daffodil, Uncle!"

"No, not the fiver on Daffodil!"

"I should if it was my own fiver," said the child.

"Good! Good! Right you are! A fiver for me and a fiver for you, on Daffodil."

The child had never been to a race-meeting before, and his eyes were blue fire. He pursed his mouth tight, and watched. A Frenchman just in front had put his money on Lancelot. Wild with excitement, he flayed his arms up and down, yelling *Lancelot! Lancelot!*—in his French accent.

Daffodil came in first, Lancelot second, Mirza third. The child, flushed and with eyes blazing, was curiously serene. His uncle brought him five five-pound notes: four to one.

"What am I to do with these?" he cried, waving them before the boy's eyes.

"I suppose we'll talk to Bassett," said the boy. "I expect I have fifteen hundred now: and twenty in reserve: and this twenty."

His uncle studied him for some moments.

"Look here, Son!" he said. "You're not serious about Bassett and that fifteen hundred, are you?"

"Yes, I am. But it's between you and me, Uncle! Honour bright!"

"Honour bright all right, Son! But I must talk to Bassett."

"If you'd like to be a partner, Uncle, with Bassett and me, we could all be partners. Only you'd have to promise, Honour bright, Uncle, not to let it go beyond us three. Bassett and I are lucky, and you must be lucky, because it was your ten shillings I started winning with——"

Uncle Oscar took both Bassett and Paul into Richmond Park for an afternoon, and there they talked.

"It's like this, you see, Sir," Bassett said. "Master Paul would get me talking about racing events, spinning yarns you know, Sir. And he was always keen on knowing if I'd made or if I'd lost. It's about a year since, now, that I put five shillings on Blush of Dawn for him: and we lost. Then the luck turned, with that ten shillings he had from you, that we put on Singhalese. And since that time, it's been pretty steady, all things considering. What do you say, Master Paul?"

"We're all right when we're *sure*," said Paul. "It's when we're not quite sure that we go down."

"Oh, but we're careful then," said Bassett.

"But when are you *sure*?" smiled Uncle Oscar.

"It's Master Paul, Sir!" said Bassett, in a secret, religious voice. "It's as if he had it from heaven. Like Daffodil, now, for the Lincoln. That was as sure as eggs."

"Did you put anything on Daffodil?" asked Oscar Cresswell.

"Yes Sir! I made my bit."

"And my nephew?"

Bassett was obstinately silent, looking at Paul.

"I made twelve hundred, didn't I, Bassett? I told Uncle I was putting three hundred on Daffodil."

"That's right!" said Bassett, nodding.

"But where's the money?" asked the uncle.

"I keep it safe locked up, Sir. Master Paul, he can have it any minute he likes to ask for it."

"What, fifteen hundred pounds?"

"And twenty! And *forty*, that is, with the twenty he made on the course."

"It's amazing!" said the uncle.

"If Master Paul offers you to be partners, Sir, I would if I were you: if you'll excuse me," said Bassett.

Oscar Cresswell thought about it.

"I'll see the money," he said.

They drove home again, and sure enough, Bassett came round to the garden house with fifteen hundred pounds in notes. The twenty pounds reserve was left with Joe Glee, in the Turf Commission deposit.

"You see it's all right, Uncle, when I'm *sure*! Then we go strong, for all we're worth. Don't we, Bassett?"

"We do that, Master Paul."

"And when are you sure?" said the Uncle, laughing.

"Oh well, sometimes I'm *absolutely* sure, like about Daffodil," said the boy. "And sometimes I have an idea; and sometimes I haven't even an idea, do I Bassett? Then we're careful, because we mostly go down."

"You do, do you! And when you're sure, like about Daffodil, what makes you sure, Sonny?"

"Oh well, I don't know," said the boy uneasily. "I'm sure, you know, Uncle, that's all."

"It's as if he had it from heaven, Sir!" Bassett reiterated.

"I should say so!" said the uncle.

But he became a partner. And when the Leger was coming on, Paul was "sure" about Lively Spark, which was a quite inconsiderable horse. The boy insisted on putting a thousand on the horse, Bassett went for five hundred, and Oscar Cresswell two hundred. Lively Spark came in first, and the betting had been ten to one against him. Paul had made ten thousand.

"You see," he said, "I was absolutely sure of him."

Even Oscar Cresswell had cleared two thousand.

"Look here, Son," he said. "This sort of thing makes me nervous."

"It needn't, Uncle! Perhaps I shan't be sure again for a long time."

"But what are you going to do with your money?" asked the uncle.

"Of course," said the boy, "I started it for mother. She said she had no luck, because father is unlucky, so I thought if *I* was lucky, it might stop whispering."

"What might stop whispering?"

"Our house! I *hate* our house for whispering."

"What does it whisper?"

"Why? Why?"—the boy fidgetted—"Why, I don't know! But it's always short of money, you know, Uncle."

"I know it, Son, I know it."

"You know people send mother Writs, don't you, Uncle?"

"I'm afraid I do," said the uncle.

"And then the house whispers like people laughing at you behind your back. It's awful, that is! I thought if I was lucky————"

"You might stop it—" added the uncle.

The boy watched him with big blue eyes, that had an uncanny cold fire in them, and he said never a word.

"Well then!" said the uncle. "What are we doing?"

"I shouldn't like mother to know I was lucky," said the boy.

"Why not, Son?"

"She'd stop me."

"I don't think she would."

"Oh!"—and the boy writhed in an odd way. "I *don't* want her to know, Uncle."

"All right, Son! We'll manage it without her knowing."

They managed it very easily. Paul, at the other's suggestion, handed over five thousand pounds to his uncle, who deposited it with the family lawyer, who was then to inform Paul's mother that a relative had put five thousand pounds into his hands, which sum was to be paid out a thousand pounds at a time, on the mother's birthday, for the next five years.

"So she'll have a birthday present of a thousand pounds for five successive years," said Uncle Oscar. "I hope it won't make it all the harder for her later."

Paul's mother had her birthday in November. The house had

been "whispering" worse than ever, lately, and even in spite of
his luck, Paul could not bear up against it. He was very anxious
to see the effect of the birthday letter, telling his mother about
the thousand pounds.

When there were no visitors, Paul now took his meals with
his parents, as he was beyond the nursery control. His mother
went in to town nearly every day. She had discovered that she
had an odd knack of sketching furs and dress materials, so she
worked secretly in the studio of a friend who was the chief
"artist" for the leading drapers. She drew the figures of ladies
in furs and ladies in silk and sequins, for the newspaper advertisements. This young woman artist earned several thousand
pounds a year, but Paul's mother only made several hundreds,
and she was again dissatisfied. She so wanted to be first in
something, and she did not succeed, even in making sketches
for drapery advertisements.

She was down to breakfast on the morning of her birthday.
Paul watched her face as she read her letters. He knew the
lawyer's letter. As his mother read it, her face hardened and
became more expressionless. Then a cold, determined look
came on her mouth. She hid the letter under the pile of others,
and said not a word about it.

"Didn't you have anything nice in the post, for your birthday,
Mother?" said Paul.

"Quite moderately nice," she said, her voice cold and absent.

She went away to town without saying more.

But in the afternoon Uncle Oscar appeared. He said Paul's
mother had had a long interview with the lawyer, asking if the
whole five thousand could not be advanced at once, as she was
in debt.

"What do you think, Uncle?" said the boy.

"I leave it to you, Son."

"Oh, let her have it, then! We can get some more with the
other," said the boy.

"A bird in the hand is worth two in the bush, Laddie!" said
Uncle Oscar.

"But I'm sure to *know* for the Grand National: or the

Lincoln: or else the Derby. I'm sure to know for *one* of them,"
said Paul.

So Uncle Oscar signed the agreement, and Paul's mother
touched the whole five thousand. Then something very curious
happened. The voices in the house suddenly went mad, like a
chorus of frogs on a spring evening. There were certain new
furnishings, and Paul had a tutor. He was *really* going to Eton,
his father's school, in the following autumn. There were flowers
in the winter, and a blossoming of the luxury Paul's mother
had been used to. And yet the voices in the house, behind the
sprays of mimosa and almond blossom, and from under the
piles of iridescent cushions, simply trilled and screamed in a
sort of ecstasy: "There *must* be more money! Oh-h-h! There
must be more money! Oh now, now-w! now-w-w!—there *must*
be more money!"—More than ever! More than ever!

It frightened Paul terribly. He studied away at his Latin and
Greek, with his tutor. But his intense hours were spent with
Bassett. The Grand National had gone by: he had not "known,"
and had lost a hundred pounds. Summer was at hand. He was
in agony, for the Lincoln. But even for the Lincoln, he didn't
"know," and he lost fifty pounds. He became wild-eyed and
strange, as if something were going to explode in him.

"Let it alone, Son! Don't you bother about it!" urged Uncle
Oscar. But it was as if the boy couldn't really hear what his
Uncle was saying.

"I've got to know for the Derby! I've *got* to know for the
Derby!" the child re-iterated, his big blue eyes blazing with a
sort of madness.

His mother noticed how overwrought he was.

"You'd better go to the sea-side! Wouldn't you like to go
now to the seaside, instead of waiting? I think you'd better!"
she said, looking down at him anxiously, her heart curiously
heavy because of him.

But the child lifted his uncanny blue eyes.

"I couldn't possibly go before the Derby, Mother!" he said.
"I couldn't possibly!"

"Why not?" she said, her voice becoming heavy when she
was opposed. "Why not? You can still go from the seaside to

see the Derby, with your Uncle Oscar, if that's what you wish. No need for you to wait here.—Besides, I think you care too much about these races. It's a bad sign. My family has been a gambling family, and you won't know till you grow up how much damage it has done. But it has done damage. I shall have to send Bassett away, and ask Uncle Oscar not to talk racing to you, unless you promise to be reasonable about it: go away to the seaside and forget it. You're all nerves!"

"I'll do what you like, Mother, so long as you don't send me away till after the Derby," the boy said.

"Send you away from where? just from this house?"

"Yes!" he said, gazing at her.

"Why, you curious child, what makes you care about this house so much, suddenly? I never knew you loved it!"

He gazed at her without speaking. He had a secret within a secret, something he had not divulged, even to Bassett or to his Uncle Oscar.

But his mother, after standing undecided and a little bit sullen for some moments, said:

"Very well, then! Don't go to the seaside till after the Derby, if you don't wish it. But promise me you won't let your nerves go to pieces! Promise you won't think so much about horse-racing and *events*, as you call them!"

"Oh no!" said the boy, casually. "I won't think much about them, Mother. You needn't worry. I wouldn't worry, Mother, if I were you."

"If you were me and I were you," said his mother, "I wonder what we *should* do!"

"But you know you needn't worry, Mother, don't you?" the boy repeated.

"I should be awfully glad to know it," she said wearily.

"Oh well, you *can*, you know. I mean you *ought* to know you needn't worry!" he insisted.

"Ought I? Then I'll see about it," she said.

Paul's secret of secrets was his wooden horse, that which had no name. Since he was emancipated from a nurse and a nursery governess, he had had his rocking-horse removed to his own bedroom at the top of the house.

"Surely you're too big for a rocking horse!" his mother had remonstrated.

"Well, you see, Mother, till I can have a *real* horse, I like to have *some* sort of animal about," had been his quaint answer.

"Do you feel he keeps you company?" she laughed.

"Oh yes! He's very good, he always keeps me company, when I'm there," said Paul.

So the horse, rather shabby, stood in an arrested prance in the boy's bedroom.

The Derby was drawing near, and the boy grew more and more tense. He hardly heard what was spoken to him, he was very frail, and his eyes were really uncanny. His mother had sudden strange seizures of uneasiness about him. Sometimes, for half an hour, she would feel a sudden anxiety about him, that was almost anguish. She wanted to rush to him at once, and know he was safe.

Two nights before the Derby, she was at a big party in town, when one of her rushes of anxiety about her boy, her first-born, gripped her heart till she could hardly speak. She fought with the feeling, might and main, for she believed in common-sense. But it was too strong. She had to leave the dance and go downstairs to telephone to the country. The children's nursery governess was terribly surprised and startled at being rung up in the night.

"Are the children all right, Miss Wilmot?"

"Oh yes, they are quite all right."

"Master Paul? Is he all right?"

"He went to bed as right as a trivet. Shall I run up and look at him?"

"No!" said Paul's mother reluctantly. "No! Don't trouble. It's all right. Don't sit up. We shall be home fairly soon." She did not want her son's privacy intruded upon.

"Very good!" said the governess.

It was about one o'clock when Paul's mother and father drove up to their house. All was still. Paul's mother went to her room and slipped off her white fur cloak. She had told her maid not to wait up for her. She heard her husband downstairs, mixing a whiskey and soda.

And then, because of the strange anxiety at her heart, she stole upstairs to her son's room. Noiselessly she went along the upper corridor. Was there a faint noise? What was it?

She stood with arrested muscles outside his door, listening. There was a strange, heavy and yet not loud noise. Her heart stood still. It was a soundless noise, yet rushing and powerful. Something huge, in violent, hushed motion. What was it? What in God's name was it? She ought to know. She felt that she *knew* the noise. She knew what it was.

Yet she could not place it. She couldn't say what it was. And on and on it went, like a madness.

Softly, frozen with anxiety and fear, she turned the door-handle.

The room was dark. Yet in the space near the window, she heard and saw something plunging to and fro. She gazed in fear and amazement.

Then suddenly she switched on the light, and saw her son, in his green pyjamas, madly surging on his rocking-horse. The blaze of light suddenly lit him up, as he urged the wooden horse, and lit her up, as she stood, blonde, in her dress of pale green and crystal, in the doorway.

"Paul!" she cried. "Whatever are you doing?"

"It's Malabar!" he screamed, in a powerful strange voice. "It's Malabar!"

His eyes blazed at her for one strange and senseless second, as he ceased urging his wooden horse. Then he fell with a crash to the ground, and she, all her tormented motherhood flooding upon her, rushed to gather him up.

But he was unconscious, and unconscious he remained, with some brain fever. He talked and tossed, and his mother sat stonily by his side.

"Malabar! It's Malabar! Bassett, Bassett, I *know*: it's Malabar!"

So the child cried, trying to get up and urge the rocking-horse that gave him his inspiration.

"What does he mean by Malabar?" asked the heart-frozen mother.

"I don't know," said the father, stonily.

"What does he mean by Malabar?" she asked her brother Oscar.

"It's one of the horses running for the Derby," was the answer.

And in spite of himself, Oscar Cresswell spoke to Bassett, and himself put a thousand on Malabar: at fourteen to one.

The third day of the illness was critical: they were watching for a change. The boy, with his rather long, curly hair, was tossing ceaselessly on the pillow. He neither slept nor regained consciousness, and his eyes were like blue stones. His mother sat, feeling her heart had gone, turned actually into a stone.

In the evening, Oscar Cresswell did not come, but Bassett sent a message, saying could he come up for one moment, just one moment. Paul's mother was angry at the intrusion, but on second thoughts she agreed. The boy was the same. Perhaps Bassett might bring him to consciousness.

The gardener, a shortish fellow with a little brown moustache and sharp little brown eyes, tiptoed into the room, touched his imaginary cap to Paul's mother, and stole to the bedside, staring with glittering, smallish eyes at the tossing, dying child.

"Master Paul!" he whispered. "Master Paul! Malabar came in first all right, a clean win. I did as you told me. You've made over seventy thousand pounds, you have, you've got over eighty thousand. Malabar came in all right, Master Paul."

"Malabar! Malabar! Did I say Malabar, Mother? Did I say Malabar? Do you think I'm lucky, Mother? I knew Malabar, didn't I? Over eighty thousand pounds! I call that lucky, don't you, Mother? Over eighty thousand pounds! I knew, didn't I know I knew? Malabar came in all right! If I ride my horse till I'm sure, then I tell you, Bassett, you can go as high as you like. Did you go for all you were worth, Bassett?"

"I went a thousand on it, Master Paul."

"I never told you, Mother, that if I can ride my horse, and *get there*, then I'm absolutely sure—Oh absolutely! Mother, did I ever tell you? I *am* lucky!"

"No, you never did," said the mother.

But the boy died in the night.

And even as he lay dead, his mother heard her brother's voice saying to her: "My God, Hester, you're eighty-odd thousand to the good, and a poor devil of a son to the bad. But poor devil, poor devil, he's best gone out of a life where he rides his rocking-horse to find a winner."

THE MAN WHO LOVED ISLANDS

First Island

There was a man who loved islands. He was born on one, but it didn't suit him, as there were too many other people on it, besides himself. He wanted an island all of his own: not necessarily to be alone on it, but to make it a world of his own.

An island, if it is big enough, is no better than a continent. It has to be really quite small, before it *feels like* an island; and this story will show how tiny it has to be, before you can presume to fill it with your own personality.

Now circumstances so worked out, that this lover of islands, by the time he was thirty-five, actually acquired an island of his own. He didn't own it as freehold property, but he had a ninety-nine years lease of it, which, as far as a man and an island are concerned, is as good as everlasting. Since, if you are like Abraham, and want your offspring to be numberless as the sands of the sea-shore, you don't choose an island to start breeding on. Too soon there would be overpopulation, over-crowding, and slum conditions. Which is a horrid thought, for one who loves an island for its insulation. No, an island is a nest which holds one egg, and one only. This egg is the islander himself.

The island acquired by our potential islander was not in the remote oceans. It was quite near at home, no palm trees nor boom of surf on the reef, nor any of that kind of thing; but a good solid dwelling-house, rather gloomy, above the landing-place, and beyond, a small farm-house with sheds, and a few outlying fields. Down on the little landing bay were three cottages in a row, like coastguards' cottages, all neat and white-washed.

What could be more cosy and home-like? It was four miles if you walked all round your island, through the gorse and the blackthorn bushes, above the steep rocks of the sea and down in the little glades where the primroses grew. If you walked straight over the two humps of hills, the length of it, through the rocky fields where the cows lay chewing, and through the rather sparse oats, on into the gorse again, and so to the low cliffs' edge, it took you only twenty minutes. And when you came to the edge, you could see another, bigger island lying beyond. But the sea was between you and it. And as you returned over the turf where the short, downland cowslips nodded, you saw to the east still another island, a tiny one this time, like the calf of the cow. This tiny island also belonged to the islander.

Thus it seems that even islands like to keep each other company.

Our islander loved his island very much. In early spring, the little ways and glades were a snow of blackthorn, a vivid white among the celtic stillness of close green and grey rock, black-birds calling out in the whiteness their first long, triumphing calls. After the blackthorn and the nestling primroses came the blue apparition of hyacinths, like elfin lakes and slipping sheets of blue, among the bushes and under the glade of trees. And many birds with nests you could peep into, on the island all your own. Wonderful what a great world it was!

Followed summer, and the cowslips gone, the wild roses faintly fragrant through the haze. There was a field of hay, the fox-gloves stood looking down. In a little cove, the sun was on the pale granite where you bathed, and the shadow was in the rocks. Before the mist came stealing, and you went home through the ripening oats, the glare of the sea fading from the high air as the fog-horn started to moo from the other island. And then the sea-fog went, it was autumn, the oat-sheaves lying prone; the great moon, another island, rose golden out of the sea, and, rising higher, the world of the sea was white.

So autumn ended with rain, and winter came, dark skies and dampness and rain, but rarely frost. The island, your island, cowered dark, holding away from you. You could feel, down in the wet, sombre hollows, the resentful spirit coiled upon itself, like a wet dog coiled in gloom, or a snake that is neither asleep nor awake. Then in the night, when the wind left off blowing in great gusts and volleys, as at sea, you felt that your island was a universe, infinite and old as the darkness; not an island at all, but an infinite dark world where all the souls from all the other bygone nights lived on, and the infinite distance was near.

Strangely, from your little island in space, you were gone forth into the dark, great realms of time, where all the souls that never die veer and swoop on their vast, strange errands. The little earthly island has dwindled, like a jumping-off place, into nothingness, for you have jumped off, you know not how, into the dark wide mystery of time, where the past is vastly alive, and the future is not separated off.

This is the danger of becoming an islander. When, in the city, you wear your white spats and dodge the traffic with the fear of death down your spine, then you are quite safe from the terrors of infinite time. The moment is your little islet in time, it is the spatial universe that careers round you.

But once isolate yourself on a little island in the sea of space, and the moment begins to heave and expand in great circles, the solid earth is gone, and your slippery, naked dark soul finds herself out in the timeless world, where the chariots of the so-called dead dash down the old streets of centuries, and souls crowd on the footways that we, in the moment, call bygone years. The souls of all the dead are alive again, and pulsating actively around you. You are out in the other infinity.

Something of this happened to our islander. Mysterious "feelings" came upon him, that he wasn't used to; strange awarenesses of old, far-gone men, and other influences; men of Gaul, with big moustaches, who had been on his island, and had vanished from the face of it, but not out of the air of night. They were there still, hurtling their big, violent, unseen bodies through the night. And there were priests, with golden knives and mistletoe; then other priests with a crucifix; then pirates with murder on the sea.

Our islander was uneasy. He didn't believe, in the daytime, in any of this nonsense. But at night it just was so. He had reduced himself to a single point in space, and a point being that which has neither length nor breadth, he had to step off it into somewhere else. Just as you must step into the sea, if the waters wash your foothold away, so he had, at night, to step off into the otherworld of undying time.

He was uncannily aware, as he lay in the dark, that the blackthorn grove that seemed a bit uncanny even in the realm of space and day, at night was crying with old men of an invisible race, around the altar stone. What was a ruin under the hornbeam trees by day, was a moaning of bloodstained priests with crucifixes, on the ineffable night. What was a cave and a hidden beach between coarse rocks, became in the invisible dark the purple-lipped imprecation of pirates.

To escape any more of this sort of awareness, our islander daily concentrated upon his material island. Why should it not be the Happy Isle at last? Why not the last small isle of the Hesperides, the perfect place, all filled with his own gracious, blossom-like spirit? A minute world of pure perfection, made by man, himself.

He began, as we begin all our attempts to regain Paradise, by spending money. The old, semi-feudal dwelling house he restored, let in more light, put clear lovely carpets on the floor, clear, flower-petal curtains at the sullen windows, and wines in the cellars of rock. He brought over a buxom housekeeper from the world, and a soft-spoken, much-experienced butler. These too were to be islanders.

In the farm-house he put a bailiff, with two farm-hands. There were Jersey cows, tinkling a slow bell, among the gorse. There was a call to meals at midday, and the peaceful smoking of chimneys at evening, when rest descended.

A jaunty sailing-boat with a motor accessory rode in the shelter in the bay, just below the row of three white cottages. There was also a little yawl, and two row-boats drawn up on the sand. A fishing net was drying on its supports, a boat-load of new white planks stood criss-cross, a woman was going to the well with a bucket.

In the end cottage lived the skipper of the yacht, and his wife and son. He was a man from the other, large island, at home on this sea. Every fine day he went out fishing, with his son, every fine day there was fresh fish on the island.

In the middle cottage lived an old man and wife, a very faithful couple. The old man was a carpenter, and man of many jobs. He was always working, always the sound of his plane or his saw: lost in his work, he was another kind of islander.

In the third cottage was the mason, a widower with a son and two daughters. With the help of his boys, this man dug ditches and built fences, raised buttresses and erected a new outbuilding, and hewed stone from the little quarry. His daughter worked at the big house.

It was a quiet, busy little world. When the islander brought you over as his guest, you met first the dark-bearded, thin, smiling skipper, Arnold, then his boy Charles. At the house, the smooth-lipped butler who had lived all over the world valeted you, and created that curious creamy-smooth, disarming sense of luxury around you which only a perfect and rather untrustworthy servant can create. He disarmed you and had you at his mercy. The buxom housekeeper smiled and treated you with the subtly respectful familiarity, that is only dealt out to the true gentry. And the rosy maid threw a glance at you, as if you were very wonderful, coming from the great outer world. Then you met the smiling but watchful bailiff, who came from Cornwall, and the shy farm-hand from Berkshire, with his clean wife and two little children, then the rather sulky farm-hand from Suffolk. The mason, a Kent man, would talk to you by the yard, if you let him. Only the old carpenter was gruff and elsewhere absorbed.

Well then, it was a little world to itself, and everybody feeling very safe, and being very nice to you, as if you were really something special. But it was the islander's world, not yours. He was the master. The special smile, the special attention was to the Master. They all knew how well off they were. So the islander was no longer Mr. So-and-so. To everyone on the island, even to you yourself, he was "the Master."

Well, it was ideal. The Master was no tyrant. Ah no! He was a delicate, sensitive, handsome Master, who wanted everything perfect and everybody happy. Himself, of course, to be the fount of this happiness and perfection.

But in his way, he was a poet. He treated his guests royally, his servants liberally. Yet he was shrewd, and very wise. He never came the boss over his people. Yet he kept his eye on everything, like a shrewd, blue-eyed young Hermes. And it was amazing what a lot of knowledge he had at hand. Amazing what he knew about Jersey cows, and cheese-making, ditching and fencing, flowers and gardening, ships and the sailing of ships. He was a fount of knowledge about everything, and this knowledge he imparted to his people in an odd, half-ironical, half-portentous fashion, as if he really belonged to the quaint, half-real world of the gods.

They listened to him with their hats in their hands. He loved white clothes; or creamy white; and cloaks, and broad hats. So, in fine weather, the bailiff would see the elegant tall figure in creamy-white serge coming like some bird over the fallow, to look at the weeding of the turnips. Then there would be a doffing of hats, and a few minutes of whimsical, shrewd, wise talk, to which the bailiff answered admiringly, and the farm-hands listened in silent wonder, leaning on their hoes. The bailiff was almost tender, to the Master.

Or, on a windy morning, he would stand with his cloak blowing in the sticky sea-wind, on the edge of the ditch that was being dug to drain a little swamp, talking in the teeth of the wind to the man below, who looked up at him with steady and inscrutable eyes.

Or at evening in the rain he would be seen hurrying across the yard, the broad hat turned against the rain. And the farm-wife would hurriedly exclaim: "The Master! Get up John, and clear him a place on the sofa." And then the door opened, and it was a cry of: "Why of all things, if it isn't the Master! Why, have ye turned out then of a night like this, to come across to the like of we?" And the bailiff took his cloak, and the farm-wife his hat, the two farm-hands drew their chairs to the back, he sat on the sofa and took a child up near him. He was wonderful with children, talked to them simply wonderful, made you think of Our Saviour Himself, said the woman.

Always he was greeted with smiles, and the same peculiar deference, as if he were a higher, but also frailer being. They handled him almost tenderly, and almost with adulation. But when he left, or when they spoke of him, they had often a subtle, mocking smile on their faces. There was no need to be afraid of "the Master." Just let him have his own way. Only the old carpenter was sometimes sincerely rude to him; so he didn't care for the old man.

It is doubtful whether any of them really liked him, man to man, or even woman to man. But then it is doubtful if he really liked any of them, as man to man, or man to woman. He wanted them to be happy, and the little world to be perfect. But any one who wants the world to be perfect, must be careful not to have real likes and dislikes. A general good-will is all you can afford.

The sad fact is, alas, that general good-will is always felt as something of an insult, by the mere object of it; and so it breeds a quite special brand of malice. Surely general good-will is a form of egoism, that it should have such a result!

Our islander, however, had his own resources. He spent long hours in his library, for he was compiling a book of reference to all the flowers mentioned in the Greek and Latin authors. He was not a great classical scholar: the usual public-school equipment. But there are such excellent translations nowadays. And it was so lovely, tracing flower after flower as it blossomed in the ancient world.

So the first year on the island passed by. A great deal had been done. Now the bills flooded in, and the Master, conscientious in all things, began to study them. The study left him pale and breathless. He was not a rich man. He knew he had been making a hole in his capital, to get the island into running order. When he came to look, however, there was hardly anything left but hole. Thousands and thousands of pounds had the island swallowed into nothingness.

But surely the bulk of the spending was over! Surely the island would now begin to be self-supporting, even if it made no profit! Surely he was safe. He paid a good many of the bills, and took a little heart. But he had had a shock, and the next year, the coming year, there must be economy, frugality. He told his people so, in simple and touching language. And they said: "Why surely! Surely!"

So, while the wind blew and the rain lashed outside, he would sit in his library with the bailiff over a pipe and a pot of beer, discussing farm projects. He lifted his narrow handsome face, and his blue eye became dreamy. "*What* a wind!" It blew like cannon shots. He thought of his island, lashed with foam, and inaccessible, and he exulted . . . No, he must not lose it. He turned back to the farm projects with the zest of genius, and his hands flicked white emphasis, while the bailiff intoned: "Yes, Sir! Yes, Sir! You're right, Master!"

But the man was hardly listening. He was looking at the Master's blue lawn shirt and curious pink tie with the fiery red stone, at the enamel sleevelinks, and at the ring with the peculiar scarab. The brown searching eyes of the man of the soil glanced repeatedly over the fine, immaculate figure of the Master, with a sort of slow, calculating wonder. But if he happened to catch the Master's bright, exalted glance, his own eye lit up with a careful cordiality and deference, as he bowed his head slightly.

Thus between them they decided what crops should be sown, what fertilisers should be used in different places, which breed of pigs should be imported, and which line of turkeys. That is to say, the bailiff, by continually cautiously agreeing with the Master, kept out of it, and let the young man have his own way.

The Master knew what he was talking about. He was brilliant at grasping the gist of a book, and knowing how to apply his knowledge. On the whole, his ideas were sound. The bailiff even knew it. But in the man of the soil there was no answering enthusiasm. The brown eyes smiled their cordial deference, but the thin lips never changed. The Master pursed his own flexible mouth in a boyish versatility, as he cleverly sketched in his ideas to the other man, and the bailiff made eyes of admiration, but in his heart he was not attending, he was only watching the Master as he would have watched a queer, alien animal, quite without sympathy, not implicated.

So, it was settled, and the Master rang for Elvery, the butler, to bring a sandwich. He, the Master, was pleased. The butler saw it, and came back with anchovy and ham sandwiches, and a newly opened bottle of vermouth. There was always a newly opened bottle of something.

It was the same with the mason. The Master and he discussed the drainage of a bit of land, and more pipes were ordered, more special bricks, more this, more that.

Fine weather came at last, there was a little lull in the hard work on the island. The Master went for a short cruise in his yacht. It was not really a yacht, just a neat little bit of a yawl. They sailed along the coast of the mainland, and put in at the ports. At every port some friend turned up, the butler made elegant little meals in the cabin. Then the Master was invited to villas and hotels, his people disembarked him as if he were a prince.

And oh! how expensive it turned out! He had to telegraph to the bank for money. And he went home again, to economise.

The marsh-marigolds were blazing in the little swamp where the ditches were being dug for drainage. He almost regretted, now, the work in hand. The yellow beauties would not blaze again.

Harvest came, and a bumper crop. There must be a harvest-home supper. The long barn was now completely restored and added to. The carpenter had made long tables. Lanterns hung from the beams of the high-pitched roof. All the people of the island were assembled. The bailiff presided. It was a gay scene.

Towards the end of the supper the Master, in a velvet jacket, appeared with his guests. Then the bailiff rose and proposed: "The Master! Long life and health to the Master!"—All the people drank the health with great enthusiasm and cheering. The Master replied with a little speech: They were on an island in a little world of their own. It depended on them all to make this world a world of true happiness and content. Each must do his part. He hoped he himself did what he could, for his heart was in his island, and with the people of his island.

The butler responded: As long as the island had such a Master, it could not help but be a little heaven for all the people on it.—This was seconded with virile warmth by the bailiff and the mason, the skipper was beside himself. Then there was dancing, the old carpenter was fiddler.

But under all this, things were not well. The very next morning came the farm-boy to say that a cow had fallen over the cliff. The master went to look. He peered over the not very high declivity, and saw her lying dead, on a green ledge under a bit of late-flowering broom. A beautiful, expensive creature, already looking swollen. But what a fool, to fall so unnecessarily!

It was a question of getting several men to haul her up the bank: and then of skinning and burying her. No-one would eat the meat. How repulsive it all was!

This was symbolic of the island. As sure as the spirits rose in the human breast, with a movement of joy, an invisible hand struck malevolently out of the silence. There must not be any joy, nor even any quiet peace. A man broke a leg, another was crippled with rheumatic fever. The pigs had some strange disease. A storm drove the yacht on a rock. The mason hated the butler, and refused to let his daughter serve at the house.

Out of the very air came a stony, heavy malevolence. The island itself seemed malicious. It would go on being hurtful and evil for weeks at a time. Then suddenly again one morning it would be fair, lovely as a morning in Paradise, everything beautiful and flowing. And everybody would begin to feel a great relief, and a hope for happiness.

Then as soon as the Master was opened out in spirit like an open flower, some ugly blow would fall. Somebody would send him an anonymous note, accusing some other person on the island. Somebody else would come hinting things against one of his servants.

"Some folks thinks they've got an easy job out here, with all

296 SELECTED STORIES

the pickings they make!" the mason's daughter screamed at the
suave butler, in the Master's hearing. He pretended not to hear.

"My man says this island is surely one of the lean kine of
Egypt, it would swallow a sight of money, and you'd never get
anything back out of it," confided the farm-hand's wife to one
of the Master's visitors.

The people were not contented. They were not islanders.
"We feel we're not doing right by the children," said those who
had children. "We feel we're not doing right by ourselves," said
those who had no children. And the various families fairly came
to hate one another.

Yet the island was so lovely. When there was a scent of
honeysuckle, and the moon brightly flickering down on the sea,
then even the grumblers felt a strange nostalgia for it. It set you
yearning, with a wild yearning; perhaps for the past, to be far
back in the mysterious past of the island, when the blood had
a different throb. Strange floods of passion came over you,
strange violent lusts and imaginations of cruelty. The blood
and the passion and the lust which the island had known.
Uncanny dreams, half-dreams, half-evoked yearnings.

The Master himself began to be a little afraid of his island.
He felt here strange violent feelings he had never felt before,
and lustful desires that he had been quite free from. He knew
quite well now that his people didn't love him at all. He knew
that their spirits were secretly against him, malicious, jeering,
envious, and lurking to down him. He became just as wary and
secretive with regard to them.

But it was too much. At the end of the second year, several
departures took place. The housekeeper went. The Master
always blamed self-important women most. The mason said he
wasn't going to be monkeyed about any more, so he took his
departure, with his family. The rheumatic farm-hand left.

And then the year's bills came in, the Master made up his
accounts. In spite of good crops, the assets were ridiculous,
against the spending. The island had again lost, not hundreds
but thousands of pounds. It was incredible. But you simply
couldn't believe it! Where had it all gone?

The Master spent gloomy nights and days, going through

accounts in the library. He was thorough. It became evident, now the housekeeper had gone, that she had swindled him. Probably everybody was swindling him. But he hated to think it, so he put the thought away.

He emerged, however, pale and hollow-eyed from his balancing of unbalanceable accounts, looking as if something had kicked him in the stomach. It was pitiable. But the money had gone, and there was an end of it. Another great hole in his capital. How could people be so heartless?

It couldn't go on, that was evident. He would soon be bankrupt. He had to give regretful notice to his butler. He was afraid to find out how much his butler had swindled him. Because the man was such a wonderful butler, after all. And the farm-bailiff had to go. The Master had no regrets in that quarter. The losses on the farm had almost embittered him.

The third year was spent in rigid cutting down of expenses. The island was still mysterious and fascinating. But it was also treacherous and cruel, secretly, fathomlessly malevolent. In spite of all its fair show of white blossom and bluebells, and the lovely dignity of foxgloves bending their rose-red bells, it was your implacable enemy.

With reduced staff, reduced wages, reduced splendour, the third year went by. But it was fighting against hope. The farm still lost a good deal. And once more, there was a hole in that remnant of capital. Another hole, in that which was already a mere remnant round the old holes. The island was mysterious in this also: it seemed to pick the very money out of your pocket, as if it were an octopus with invisible arms stealing from you in every direction.

Yet the Master still loved it. But with a touch of rancour now.

He spent, however, the second half of the fourth year intensely working on the mainland, to be rid of it. And it was amazing how difficult he found it, to dispose of an island. He had thought that everybody was pining for such an island as his; but not at all. Nobody would pay any price for it. And he wanted now to get rid of it, as a man who wants a divorce at any cost.

It was not till the middle of the fifth year that he transferred it, at a considerable loss to himself, to an hotel company who were willing to speculate in it. They were to turn it into a handy honeymoon-and-golf island.

There, take that, island which didn't know when it was well off! Now be a honeymoon-and-golf island!

Second Island

The islander had to move. But he was not going to the mainland. Oh no! He moved to the smaller island, which still belonged to him. And he took with him the faithful old carpenter and wife, the couple he never really cared for; also a widow and daughter, who had kept house for him the last year; also an orphan lad, to help the old man.

The small island was very small; but being a hump of rock in the sea, it was bigger than it looked. There was a little track among rocks and bushes, winding and scrambling up and down around the islet, so that it took you twenty minutes to do the circuit. It was more than you would have expected.

Still, it was an island. The islander moved himself, with all his books, into the common-place six-roomed house up to which you had to scramble from the rocky landing-place. There were also two joined-together cottages. The old carpenter lived in one, with his wife and the lad, the widow and daughter lived in the other.

At last all was in order. The Master's books filled two rooms. It was already autumn, Orion lifting out of the sea. And in the dark nights, the Master could see the lights on his late island, where the hotel company were entertaining guests who would advertise the new resort for honeymoon-golfers.

On his hump of rock, however, the Master was still master. He explored the crannies, the odd handbreadths of grassy level, the steep little cliffs where the last harebells hung, and the seeds of summer were brown above the sea, lonely and untouched. He peered down the old well. He examined the stone pen where the pig had been kept. Himself, he had a goat.

Yes, it was an island. Always, always, underneath among the

rocks the celtic sea sucked and washed and smote its feathery
greyness. How many different noises of the sea! deep ex-
plosions, rumblings, strange long sighs and whistling noises;
then voices, real voices of people clamouring as if they were in
a market, under the waters: and again, the far-off ringing of a
bell, surely an actual bell! then a tremulous trilling noise, very
long and alarming, and an undertone of hoarse gasping.

On this island there were no human ghosts, no ghosts of any
ancient race. The sea, and the spume and the wind and the
weather, had washed them all out, washed them out, so there
was only the sound of the sea itself, its own ghost, myriad-
voiced, communing and plotting and shouting all winter long.
And only the smell of the sea, with a few bristly bushes of gorse
and coarse tufts of heather, among the grey, pellucid rocks, in
the grey, more-pellucid air. The coldness, the greyness, even the
soft, creeping fog of the sea! and the islet of rock humped up
in it all, like the last point in space.

Green star Sirius stood over the sea's rim. The island was a
shadow. Out at sea a ship showed small lights. Below, in the
rocky cove, the row-boat and the motor-boat were safe. A light
shone in the carpenter's kitchen. That was all.

Save, of course, that the lamp was lit in the house, where
the widow was preparing supper, her daughter helping. The
islander went in to his meal. Here he was no longer the Master,
he was an islander again and he had peace. The old carpenter,
the widow and daughter were all faithfulness itself. The old
man worked while ever there was light to see, because he had
a passion for work. The widow and her quiet, rather delicate
daughter of thirty-three worked for the Master, because they
loved looking after him, and they were infinitely grateful for
the haven he provided them. But they didn't call him "the
Master." They gave him his name: "Mr Cathcart, Sir!" softly,
and reverently. And he spoke back to them also softly, gently,
like people far from the world, afraid to make a noise.

The island was no longer a "world." It was a sort of refuge.
The islander no longer struggled for anything. He had no need.
It was as if he and his few dependants were a small flock of
sea-birds alighted on this rock, as they travelled through space,

and keeping together without a word. The silent mystery of travelling birds.

He spent most of his day in his study. His book was coming along. The widow's daughter could type out his manuscript for him, she was not uneducated. It was the one strange sound on the island, the typewriter. But soon even its spattering fitted in with the sea's noises, and the wind's.

The months went by. The islander worked away in his study, the people of the island went quietly about their concerns. The goat had a little black kid with yellow eyes. There were mackerel in the sea. The old man went fishing in the row-boat, with the lad. When the weather was calm enough, they went off in the motor-boat to the biggest island, for the post. And they brought supplies, never a penny wasted. And the days went by, and the nights, without desire, without ennui.

The strange stillness from all desire was a kind of wonder to the islander. He didn't want anything. His soul at last was still in him, his spirit was like a dim-lit cave under water, where strange sea-foliage expands upon the watery atmosphere, and scarcely sways, and a mute fish shadowily slips in and slips away again. All still and soft and uncrying, yet alive as rooted sea-weed is alive.

The islander said to himself: "Is this happiness?" He said to himself: "I am turned into a dream. I feel nothing, or I don't know what I feel. Yet it seems to me I am happy."

Only he had to have something upon which his mental activity could work. So he spent long, silent hours in his study, working not very fast, nor very importantly, letting the writing spin softly from him as if it were drowsy gossamer. He no longer fretted whether it were good or not, what he produced. He slowly, softly spun it like gossamer, and if it were to melt away as gossamer in autumn melts, he would not mind. It was only the soft evanescence of gossamy things which now seemed to him permanent. The very mist of eternity was in them. Whereas stone buildings, cathedrals for example, seemed to him to howl with temporary resistance, knowing they must fall at last; the tension of their long endurance seemed to howl forth from them all the time.

Sometimes he went to the mainland and to the city. Then he went elegantly, dressed in the latest style, to his club. He sat in a stall at the theatre, he shopped in Bond Street. He discussed terms for publishing his book. But over his face was that gossamy look of having dropped out of the race of progress, which made the vulgar city people feel they had won it over him, and made him glad to go back to his island.

He didn't mind if he never published his book. The years were blending into a soft mist, from which nothing obtruded. Spring came. There was never a primrose on his island, but he found a winter-aconite. There were two little sprayed bushes of blackthorn, and some wind-flowers. He began to make a list of the flowers of his islet, and that was absorbing. He noted a wild currant bush, and watched for the elder flowers on a stunted little tree, then for the first yellow rags of the broom, and wild roses. Bladder campion, orchids, stitchwort, celandine, he was prouder of them than if they had been people on his island. When he came across the golden saxifrage, so inconspicuous in a damp corner, he crouched over it in a trance, he knew not for how long, looking at it. Yet it was nothing to look at. As the widow's daughter found, when he showed it her.

He had said to her, in real triumph:

"I found the golden saxifrage this morning."

The name sounded splendid. She looked at him with fascinated brown eyes, in which was a hollow ache that frightened him a little.

"Did you, Sir? Is it a nice flower?"

He pursed his lips and tilted his brows.

"Well—not showy exactly. I'll show it you if you like."

"I should like to see it."

She was so quiet, so wistful. But he sensed in her a persistency which made him uneasy. She said she was so happy: really happy. She followed him quietly, like a shadow, on the rocky track where there was never room for two people to walk side by side. He went first, and could feel her there, immediately behind him, following so submissively, gloating on him from behind.

It was a kind of pity for her which made him become her lover: though he never realised the extent of the power she had gained over him, and how *she* willed it. But the moment he had fallen, a jangling feeling came upon him, that it was all wrong. He felt a nervous dislike of her. He had not wanted it. And it seemed to him, as far as her physical self went, she had not wanted it either. It was just her will. He went away, and climbed at the risk of his neck down to a ledge near the sea. There he sat for hours, gazing all jangled at the sea, and saying miserably to himself: "We didn't want it. We didn't really want it."

It was the automatism of sex that had caught him again. Not that he hated sex. He deemed it, as the Chinese do, one of the great life-mysteries. But it had become mechanical, automatic, and he wanted to escape that. Automatic sex shattered him, and filled him with a sort of death. He thought he had come through, to a new stillness of desirelessness. Perhaps beyond that, there was a new fresh delicacy of desire, an unentered frail communion of two people meeting on untrodden ground.

But be that as it might, this was not it. This was nothing new or fresh. It was automatic, and driven from the will. Even she, in her true self, hadn't wanted it. It was automatic in her.

When he came home, very late, and saw her face white with fear and apprehension of his feeling against her, he pitied her, and spoke to her delicately, reassuringly. But he kept himself remote from her.

She gave no sign. She served him with the same silence, the same hidden hunger to serve him, to be near where he was. He felt her love following him with strange, awful persistency. She claimed nothing. Yet now, when he met her bright, brown, curiously vacant eyes, he saw in them the mute question. The question came direct at him, with a force and a power of will he never realised.

So he succumbed, and asked her again.

"Not," she said, "if it will make you hate me."

"Why should it?" he replied, nettled. "Of course not."

"You know I would do anything on earth for you."

It was only afterwards, in his exasperation, he remembered what she had said, and was more exasperated. Why should she pretend to do this *for him*? Why not for herself? But in his exasperation, he drove himself deeper in. In order to achieve some sort of satisfaction, which he never did achieve, he abandoned himself to her. Everybody on the island knew. But he did not care.

Then even what desire he had, left him, and he felt only shattered. He felt that only with her will had she wanted him. Now he was shattered and full of self-contempt. His island was smirched and spoiled. He had lost his place in the rare, desireless levels of Time to which he had at last arrived, and he had fallen right back. If only it had been true, delicate desire between them, and a delicate meeting on the third rare place where a man might meet a woman, when they were both true to the frail, sensitive, crocus flame of desire in them. But it had been no such thing: automatic, an act of will, not of true desire, it left him feeling humiliated.

He went away from the islet, in spite of her mute reproach. And he wandered about the continent, vainly seeking a place where he could stay. He was out of key; he did not fit in the world any more.

There came a letter from Flora—her name was Flora—to say she was afraid she was going to have a child. He sat down as if he were shot, and he remained sitting. But he replied to her: "Why be afraid? If it is so, it is so, and we should rather be pleased than afraid."

At this very moment, it happened there was an auction of islands. He got the maps, and studied them. And at the auction he bought, for very little money, another island. It was just a few acres of rock away in the north, on the outer fringe of the isles. It was low, it rose low out of the great ocean. There was not a building, not even a tree on it. Only northern sea-turf, a pool of rain-water, a bit of sedge, rock, and sea-birds. Nothing else. Under the weeping wet western sky.

He made a trip to visit his new possession. For several days, owing to the seas, he could not approach it. Then, in a light sea-mist, he landed, and saw it hazy, low, stretching apparently a long way. But it was illusion. He walked over the wet, springy turf, and dark-grey sheep tossed away from him, spectral, bleating hoarsely. And he came to the dark pool, with the sedge. Then on in the dampness, to the grey sea sucking angrily among the rocks.

This was indeed an island.

So he went home to Flora. She looked at him with guilty fear, but also with a triumphant brightness in her uncanny eyes. And again he was gentle, he reassured her, even he wanted her again, with that curious desire that was almost like toothache. So he took her to the mainland, and they were married, since she was going to have his child.

They returned to the island. She still brought in his meals, her own along with them. She sat and ate with him. He would have it so. The widowed mother preferred to stay in the kitchen. And Flora slept in the guest-room of his house, mistress of his house.

His desire, whatever it was, died in him with nauseous finality. The child would still be months coming. His island was hateful to him, vulgar, a suburb. He himself had lost all his finer distinction. The weeks passed in a sort of prison, in humiliation. Yet he stuck it out, till the child was born. But he was meditating escape. Flora did not even know.

A nurse appeared, and ate at table with them. The doctor came sometimes, and if the sea were rough, he too had to stay. He was cheery over his whiskey.

They might have been a young couple in Golders Green.

The daughter was born at last. The father looked at the baby, and felt depressed, almost more than he could bear. The millstone was tied round his neck. But he tried not to show what he felt. And Flora did not know. She still smiled with a kind of half-witted triumph in her joy, as she got well again. Then she began again to look at him with those aching, suggestive, somehow impudent eyes. She adored him so.

This he could not stand. He told her that he had to go away for a time. She wept, but she thought she had got him. He told her he had settled the best part of his property on her, and wrote down for her what income it would produce. She hardly listened, only looked at him with those heavy, adoring, impudent eyes. He gave her a cheque-book, with the amount of her credit duly entered. This did arouse her interest. And he told her, if she got tired of the island, she could choose her home wherever she wished.

She followed him with those aching, persistent brown eyes, when he left, and he never even saw her weep.

He went straight north, to prepare his third island.

The Third Island

The third island was soon made habitable. With cement and the big pebbles from the shingle beach, two men built him a hut, and roofed it with corrugated iron. A boat brought over a bed and table, and three chairs, with a good cupboard, and a few books. He laid in a supply of coal and paraffin and food—he wanted so little.

The house stood near the flat shingle bay where he landed, and where he pulled up his light boat. On a sunny day in August the men sailed away and left him. The sea was still and pale blue. On the horizon he saw the small mail-steamer slowly passing northwards, as if she were walking. She served the outer isles twice a week. He could row out to her if need be, in calm weather, and he could signal her from a flagstaff behind his cottage.

Half-a-dozen sheep still remained on the island, as company; and he had a cat to rub against his legs. While the sweet, sunny days of the northern autumn lasted, he would walk among the rocks, and over the springy turf of his small domain, always coming to the ceaseless, restless sea. He looked at every leaf, that might be different from another, and he watched the endless expansion and contraction of the water-tossed sea-weed. He had never a tree, not even a bit of heather to guard. Only the turf, and tiny turf-plants, and the sedge by the pool, the sea-weed in the ocean. He was glad. He didn't want trees or bushes. They stood up like people, too assertive. His bare, low-pitched island in the pale blue sea was all he wanted.

He no longer worked at his book. The interest had gone. He liked to sit on the low elevation of his island, and see the sea; nothing but the pale, quiet sea. And to feel his mind turn soft and hazy, like the hazy ocean. Sometimes, like a mirage, he would see the shadow of land rise hovering to northwards. It was a big island beyond. But quite without substance.

He was soon almost startled when he perceived the steamer on the near horizon, and his heart contracted with fear, lest it were going to pause and molest him. Anxiously he watched it go, and not till it was out of sight did he feel truly relieved, himself again. The tension of waiting for human approach was cruel. He did not want to be approached. He did not want to hear voices. He was shocked by the sound of his own voice, if he inadvertently spoke to his cat. He rebuked himself for having broken the great silence. And he was irritated when his cat would look up at him and mew faintly, plaintively. He frowned at her. And she knew. She was becoming wild, lurking in the rocks, perhaps fishing.

But what he disliked most was when one of the lumps of sheep opened its mouth and baa-ed its hoarse, raucous baa. He watched it, and it looked to him hideous and gross. He came to dislike the sheep very much.

He wanted only to hear the whispering sound of the sea, and the sharp cries of the gulls, cries that came out of another world to him. And best of all, the great silence.

He decided to get rid of the sheep, when the boat came. They were accustomed to him now, and stood and stared at him with yellow or colourless eyes, in an insolence that was almost cold ridicule. There was a suggestion of cold indecency about them. He disliked them very much. And when they jumped with staccato jumps off the rocks, and their hoofs made the dry, sharp hit, and the fleece flopped on their square backs,—he found them repulsive, degrading.

The fine weather passed, and it rained all day. He lay a great deal on his bed, listening to the water trickling from his roof into the zinc water-butt, looking through the open door at the rain, the dark rocks, the hidden sea. Many gulls were on the island now: many sea-birds of all sorts. It was another world of life. Many of the birds he had never seen before. His old impulse came over him, to send for a book, to know their names. In a flicker of the old passion, to know the name of

everything he saw, he even decided to row out to the steamer.
The names of these birds! he must know their names, otherwise
he had not got them, they were not quite alive to him.

But the desire left him, and he merely watched the birds as
they wheeled or walked around him, watched them vaguely,
without discrimination. All interest had left him. Only there
was one gull, a big handsome fellow, who would walk back
and forth, back and forth in front of the open door of the cabin,
as if he had some mission there. He was big, and pearl-grey,
and his roundnesses were as smooth and lovely as a pearl. Only
the folded wings had shut black pinions, and on the closed
black feathers were three very distinct white dots, making a
pattern. The islander wondered very much, why this bit of
trimming on the bird out of the far, cold seas. And as the gull
walked back and forth, back and forth in front of the cabin,
strutting on pale-dusky gold feet, holding up his pale yellow
beak, that was curved at the tip, with curious alien importance,
the man wondered over him. He was portentous, he had a
meaning.

Then the bird came no more. The island, which had been full
of sea-birds, the flash of wings, the sound and cut of wings and
sharp eerie cries in the air, began to be deserted again. No
longer they sat like living eggs on the rocks and turf, moving
their heads, but scarcely rising into flight round his feet. No
longer they ran across the turf among the sheep, and lifted
themselves upon low wings. The host had gone. But some
remained, always.

The days shortened, and the world grew eerie. One day the
boat came: as if suddenly, swooping down. The islander found
it a violation. It was torture to talk to those two men, in their
homely clumsy clothes. The air of familiarity around them was
very repugnant to him. Himself, he was neatly dressed, his
cabin was neat and tidy. He resented any intrusion, the clumsy
homeliness, the heavy-footedness of the two fishermen was
really repulsive to him.

The letters they had brought, he left lying unopened in a little
box. In one of them was his money. But he could not bear to
open even that one. Any kind of contact was repulsive to

him. Even to read his name on an envelope. He hid the letters away.

And the hustle and horror of getting the sheep caught and tied and put in the ship made him loathe with profound repulsion the whole of the animal creation. What repulsive god invented animals, and evil-smelling men? To his nostrils, the fishermen and the sheep alike smelled foul; an uncleanness on the fresh earth.

He was still nerve-racked and tortured when the ship at last lifted sail and was drawing away, over the still sea. And sometimes days after, he would start with repulsion, thinking he heard the munching of sheep.

The dark days of winter drew on. Sometimes there was no real day at all. He felt ill, as if he were dissolving, as if dissolution had already set in inside him. Everything was twilight, outside, and in his mind and soul. Once, when he went to the door, he saw black heads of men swimming in his bay. For some moments he swooned unconscious. It was the shock, the horror of unexpected human approach. The horror in the twilight! And not till the shock had undermined him and left him disembodied, did he realise that the black heads were the heads of seals swimming in. A sick relief came over him. But he was barely conscious, after the shock. Later on, he sat and wept with gratitude, because they were not men. But he never realised that he wept. He was too dim. Like some strange, ethereal animal, he no longer realised what he was doing.

Only he still derived his single satisfaction from being alone, absolutely alone, with the space soaking into him. The grey sea alone, and the footing of his sea-washed island. No other contact. Nothing human to bring its horror into contact with him. Only space, damp, twilit, sea-washed space! This was the bread of his soul.

For this reason, he was most glad when there was a storm, or when the sea was high. Then nothing could get at him. Nothing could come through to him from the outer world. True, the terrific violence of the wind made him suffer badly. At the same time, it swept the world utterly out of existence for him. He always liked the sea to be heavily rolling and tearing.

Then no boat could get at him. It was like eternal ramparts round his island.

He kept no track of time, and no longer thought of opening a book. The print, the printed letters, so like the depravity of speech, looked obscene. He tore the brass label from his paraffin stove. He obliterated any bit of lettering in his cabin.

His cat had disappeared. He was rather glad. He shivered at her thin, obtrusive call. She had lived in the coal shed. And each morning he had put her a dish of porridge, the same as he ate. He washed her saucer with repulsion. He did not like her writhing about. But he fed her scrupulously. Then one day she did not come for her porridge: she always mewed for it. She did not come again.

He prowled about his island in the rain, in a big oil-skin coat, not knowing what he was looking at, nor what he went out to see. Time had ceased to pass. He stood for long spaces, gazing from a white, sharp face, with those keen, far-off blue eyes of his, gazing fiercely and almost cruelly at the dark sea under the dark sky. And if he saw the labouring sail of a fishing boat away on the cold waters, a strange malevolent anger passed over his features.

Sometimes he was ill. He knew he was ill, because he staggered as he walked, and easily fell down. Then he paused to think what it was. And he went to his stores and took out dried milk and malt, and ate that. Then he forgot again. He ceased to register his own feelings.

The days were beginning to lengthen. All winter the weather had been comparatively mild, but with much rain, much rain. He had forgotten the sun. Suddenly, however, the air was very cold, and he began to shiver. A fear came over him. The sky was level and grey, and never a star appeared at night. It was very cold. More birds began to arrive. The island was freezing. With trembling hands he made a fire in his grate. The cold frightened him.

And now it continued, day after day, a dull, deathly cold. Occasional crumblings of snow were in the air. The days were greyly longer, but no change in the cold. Frozen grey daylight. The birds passed away, flying away. Some he saw lying frozen.

It was as if all life were drawing away, contracting away from the north, contracting southwards. "Soon," he said to himself, "it will all be gone, and in all these regions nothing will be alive." He felt a cruel satisfaction in the thought.

Then one night there seemed to be a relief: he slept better, did not tremble half awake, and writhe so much, half-conscious. He had become so used to the quaking and writhing of his body, he hardly noticed it. But when for once it slept deep, he noticed that.

He woke in the morning to a curious whiteness. His window was muffled. It had snowed. He got up and opened his door, and shuddered. Ugh! how cold! All white, with a dark leaden sea, and black rocks curiously speckled with white. The foam was no longer pure. It seemed dirty. And the sea ate at the whiteness of the corpse-like land. Crumbles of snow were silting down the dead air.

On the ground the snow was a foot deep, white and smooth and soft, windless. He took a shovel to clear round his house and shed. The pallor of morning darkened. There was a strange rumbling of far-off thunder, in the frozen air, and through the newly-falling snow, a dim flash of lightning. Snow now fell steadily down, in the motionless obscurity.

He went out for a few minutes. But it was difficult. He stumbled and fell in the snow, which burned his face. Weak, faint, he toiled home. And when he recovered, he took the trouble to make hot milk.

It snowed all the time. In the afternoon again there was a muffled rumbling of thunder, and flashes of lightning blinking reddish through the falling snow. Uneasy, he went to bed and lay staring fixedly at nothingness.

Morning seemed never to come. An eternity long he lay and waited for one alleviating pallor on the night. And at last it seemed the air was paler. His house was a cell faintly illuminated with white light. He realised the snow was walled outside his window. He got up, in the dead cold. When he opened his door, the motionless snow stopped him in a wall as high as his breast. Looking over the top of it, he felt the dead wind slowly driving, saw the snow-powder lift and travel like a funeral train. The blackish sea churned and champed, seeming to bite at the snow, impotent. The sky was grey, but luminous.

He began to work in a frenzy, to get at his boat. If he was to be shut in, it must be by his own choice, not by the mechanical power of the elements. He must get to the sea. He must be able to get at his boat.

But he was weak, and at times the snow overcame him. It fell on him, and he lay buried and lifeless. Yet every time, he struggled alive before it was too late, and fell upon the snow with the energy of fever. Exhausted, he would not give in. He crept indoors and made coffee and bacon. Long since he had cooked so much. Then he went at the snow once more. He must conquer the snow, this new, white brute force which had accumulated against him.

He worked in the awful, dead wind, pushing the snow aside, pressing it with his shovel. It was cold, freezing hard in the wind, even when the sun came out for a while, and showed him his white, lifeless surroundings, the black sea rolling sullen, flecked with dull spume, away to the horizons. Yet the sun had power on his face. It was March.

He reached the boat. He pushed the snow away, then sat down under the lee of the boat, looking at the sea, which nearly swirled to his feet, in the high tide. Curiously natural the pebbles looked, in a world gone all uncanny. The sun shone no more. Snow was falling in hard crumbs, that vanished as if by miracle as they touched the hard blackness of the sea. Hoarse waves rang in the shingle, rushing up at the snow. The wet rocks were brutally black. And all the time the myriad swooping crumbs of snow, demonish, touched the dark sea and disappeared.

During the night there was a great storm. It seemed to him he could hear the vast mass of the snow striking all the world with a ceaseless thud; and over it all, the wind roared in strange hollow volleys, in between which came a jump of blindfold lightning, then the low roll of thunder heavier than the wind. When at last the dawn faintly discoloured the dark, the storm had more or less subsided, but a steady wind drove on. The snow was up to the top of his door.

Sullenly, he worked to dig himself out. And he managed,

through sheer persistency, to get out. He was in the tail of a great drift, many feet high. When he got through, the frozen snow was not more than two feet deep. But his island was gone. Its shape was all changed, great heaping white hills rose where no hills had been, inaccessible, and they fumed like volcanoes, but with snow powder. He was sickened and overcome.

His boat was in another, smaller drift. But he had not the strength to clear it. He looked at it helplessly. The shovel slipped from his hands, and he sank in the snow, to forget. In the snow itself, the sea resounded.

Something brought him to. He crept to his house. He was almost without feeling. Yet he managed to warm himself, just that part of him which leaned in snow-sleep over the coal fire. Then again, he made hot milk. After which, carefully, he built up the fire.

The wind dropped. Was it night again? In the silence, it seemed he could hear the panther-like dropping of infinite snow. Thunder rumbled nearer, crackled quick after the bleared reddened lightning. He lay in bed in a kind of stupor. The elements! The elements! His mind repeated the word dumbly. You can't win against the elements.

How long it went on, he never knew. Once, like a wraith, he got out, and climbed to the top of a white hill on his unrecognisable island. The sun was hot. "It is summer," he said to himself, "and the time of leaves." He looked stupidly over the whiteness of his foreign island, over the waste of the lifeless sea. He pretended to imagine he saw the wink of a sail. Because he knew too well there would never again be a sail on that stark sea.

As he looked, the sky mysteriously darkened and chilled. From far off came the mutter of the unsatisfied thunder, and he knew it was the signal of the snow rolling over the sea. He turned, and felt its breath on him.

THINGS

They were true idealists, from New England. But that is some time ago: before the war. Several years before the war, they met and married; he, a tall, keen-eyed young man from Connecticut, she, a smallish, demure, Puritan-looking young woman from Massachusetts. They both had a little money. Not much, however. Even added together, it didn't make three thousand dollars a year. Still—they were free. Free!

Ah!—freedom! To be free to live one's own life! To be twenty-five and twenty-seven, a pair of true idealists with a mutual love of beauty, and an inclination towards "Indian thought"—meaning, alas, Mrs Besant—and an income of little under three thousand dollars a year! But what is money! All one wishes to do, is to live a full and beautiful life. In Europe, of course, right at the fountain-head of tradition. It might possibly be done in America: in New England, for example. But at a forfeiture of a certain amount of "beauty." True beauty takes a long time to mature. The baroque is only half beautiful; only half-matured. No, the real silver bloom, the real golden sweet bouquet of beauty has its roots in the Renaissance, not in any later, or shallower period.

Therefore the two idealists, who were married in New Haven, sailed at once to Paris: Paris of the old days. They had a studio apartment on the Boulevard Montparnasse, and they became real Parisians, in the old, delightful sense, not in the modern, vulgar. It was the shimmer of the pure impressionists, Monet and his followers, the world seen in terms of pure light, light broken and unbroken. How lovely! How lovely the nights, the river, the mornings in the old streets and by the flower stalls and the book-stalls, the afternoons up on Montmartre or in the Tuileries, the evenings on the boulevards!

They both painted, but not desperately. Art had not taken them by the throat, and they did not take art by the throat. They painted: that's all. They knew people—nice people, if possible, though one had to take them mixed. And they were happy.

Yet it seems as if human beings must set their claws in *something*. To be "free," to be "living a full and beautiful life," you must, alas, be attached to something. A "full and beautiful life" means a tight attachment to *something*—at least, it is so for all idealists—or else a certain boredom supervenes, there is a certain waving of loose ends upon the air, like the waving, yearning tendrils of the vine that spread and rotate seeking something to clutch, something up which to climb, up towards the necessary sun. Finding nothing, the vine can only trail half-fulfilled, upon the ground. Such is freedom!—a clutching of the right pole. And human beings are all vines. But especially the idealist. He is a vine, and he needs to clutch and climb. And he despises the man who is a mere *potato*, or turnip, or lump of wood.

Our idealists were frightfully happy, but they were all the time reaching out for something to cotton on to. At first, Paris was enough. They explored Paris *thoroughly*. And they learned French till they almost felt like French people, they could speak quite glibly.

Still, you know, you never talk French with your *soul*. It can't be done. And though it's very thrilling, at first, talking in French to clever Frenchmen—they seem *so* much cleverer than one-self—still, in the long run, it is not satisfying. The endlessly clever *materialism* of the French leaves you cold, in the end, gives a sense of barrenness and incompatibility with true New England depth. So our two idealists felt.

They turned away from France—but ever so gently. France had disappointed them. "We've loved it, and we've got a great deal out of it. But after a while, after a considerable while, several years, in fact, Paris leaves one feeling disappointed. It hasn't quite got what one wants."

"But this isn't France."

"No, perhaps not. France is quite different from Paris. And France is lovely—quite lovely. But *to us*, though we love it, it doesn't say a great deal."

So, when the war came, the idealists moved to Italy. And they loved Italy. They found it beautiful, and more poignant than France. It seemed much nearer to the New England conception of beauty: something pure, and full of sympathy, without the *materialism* and the *cynicism* of the French. The two idealists seemed to breathe their own true air in Italy.

And in Italy, much more than in Paris, they felt they could thrill to the teachings of the Buddha. They entered the swelling stream of modern Buddhistic emotion, and they read the books, and they practised meditation, and they deliberately set themselves to eliminate from their own souls greed, pain, and sorrow. They did not realise—yet—that Buddha's very eagerness to free himself from pain and sorrow is in itself a sort of greed. No, they dreamed of a perfect world, from which all greed, and nearly all pain, and a great deal of sorrow, were eliminated.

But America entered the war, so the two idealists had to help. They did hospital work. And though their experience made them realise more than ever that greed, pain, and sorrow *should* be eliminated from the world, nevertheless, the Buddhism, or the theosophy, didn't emerge very triumphant from the long crisis. Somehow, somewhere, in some part of themselves, they felt that greed, pain and sorrow would never be eliminated, because most people don't care about eliminating them, and never will care. Our idealists were far too western to think of abandoning all the world to damnation, while they saved their two selves. They were far too unselfish to sit tight under a bho tree and reach Nirvana, in a mere couple.

It was more than that, though. They simply hadn't enough *Sitzfleisch* to squat under a bho-tree and get to Nirvana by contemplating anything, least of all their own navel.

If the whole wide world was not going to be saved, they, personally, were not so very keen on being saved just by themselves. No, it would be so lonesome. They were New Englanders, so it must be all or nothing. Greed, pain and sorrow must either be eliminated from *all the world*, or else, what was the use of eliminating them from oneself! No use at all! One was just a victim.

And so, although they still *loved* "Indian thought," and felt very tender about it: well, to go back to our metaphor, the pole up which the green and anxious vines had clambered so far now proved dry-rotten. It snapped and the vines came slowly subsiding to earth again. There was no crack and crash. The vines held themselves up by their own foliage, for a while. But they subsided. The bean-stalk of "Indian thought" had given way, before Jack and Jill had climbed off the tip of it to a further world.

They subsided with a slow rustle back to earth again. But they made no outcry. They were again "disappointed." But they never admitted it. "Indian thought" had let them down. But they never complained. Even to one another, they never said a word. But they were disappointed, faintly but deeply disillusioned, and they both knew it. But the knowledge was tacit.

And they still had so much in their lives. They still had Italy— dear Italy. And they still had freedom, the priceless treasure. And they still had so much "beauty." About the fulness of their lives they were not quite so sure. They had one little boy, whom they loved as parents love their children, but whom they wisely refrained from fastening upon, to build their lives on him. No no, they must live their own lives! They still had strength of mind to know that.

But they were now no longer so very young. Twenty-five and twenty-seven had become thirty-five and thirty-seven. And though they had had a very wonderful time in Europe, and though they still loved Italy—dear Italy!—yet: they were disappointed. They had got a lot out of it: oh, a very great deal indeed! Still, it hadn't given them quite, not *quite* what they had expected. Europe was lovely, but it was dead. Living in Europe, you were living on the past. And Europeans, with all their superficial charm, were not *really* charming. They were materialistic, they had no *real* soul. They just did not understand the inner urge of the spirit, because the inner urge was dead in them, they were all survivals. There, that was the truth about Europeans: they were survivals, with no more getting ahead in them.

It was another bean-pole, another vine-support crumbled under the green life of the vine. And very bitter it was, this time. For up the old tree-trunk of Europe the green vine had been clambering silently for more than ten years, ten hugely important years, the years of real living. The two idealists had *lived* in Europe, lived on Europe and on European life and European things, as vines in an everlasting vineyard.

They had made their home here: a home such as you could never make in America. Their watchword had been "beauty." They had rented, the last four years, the second floor of an old Palazzo on the Arno, and here they had all their "things." And they derived profound, profound satisfaction from their apartment: the lofty, silent, ancient rooms with windows on the river, with glistening, dark-red floors, and the beautiful furniture that the idealists had "picked up."

Yes, unknown to themselves, the lives of the idealists had been running with a fierce swiftness horizontally, all the time. They had become tense, fierce hunters of "things" for their home. While their Soul was climbing up to the sun of old European culture or old Indian thought, their passions were running horizontally, clutching at "things." Of course they did not buy the things for the things' sakes, but for the sake of "beauty." They looked upon their home as a place entirely furnished by loveliness, not by "things" at all. Valerie had some very lovely curtains at the windows of the long salotta, looking on the river: curtains of queer ancient material that looked like finely knitted silk, most beautifully faded down from vermilion and orange and gold and black, down to a sheer soft glow. Valerie hardly ever came in to the salotta without mentally falling on her knees before the curtains.—"Chartres!" she said. "To me they are Chartres!" And Melville never turned and looked at his sixteenth-century Venetian book-case, with its two or three dozen of choice books, without feeling his marrow stir in his bones. The holy of holies!

The child silently, almost sinisterly avoided any rude contact

with these ancient monuments of furniture, as if they had been
nests of sleeping cobras, or that "thing" most perilous to the
touch, the Ark of the Covenant. His childish awe was silent,
and cold, but final.

Still, a couple of New England idealists cannot live merely
on the bygone glory of their furniture. At least, our couple
could not. They got used to the marvellous Bologna cupboard,
they got used to the wonderful Venetian book-case, and the
books, and the Siena curtains and bronzes, and the lovely sofas
and side-tables and chairs they had "picked up" in Paris. Oh,
they had been picking things up since the first day they landed
in Europe. And they were still at it. It is the last interest Europe
can offer to an outsider: or to an insider either.

When people came, and were thrilled by the Melville interior,
then Valerie and Erasmus felt they had not lived in vain: that
they still were living. But in the long mornings, when Erasmus
was desultorily working at Renaissance Florentine literature,
and Valerie was attending to the apartment: and in the long
hours after lunch; and in the long, usually very cold and oppres-
sive evenings in the ancient palazzo: then the halo died from
around the furniture, and the things became things, lumps of
matter that just stood there or hung there, ad infinitum, and
said nothing; and Valerie and Erasmus almost hated them. The
glow of beauty, like every other glow, dies down unless it is
fed. The idealists still dearly loved their things. But they had
got them. And the sad fact is, things that glow vividly while
you're getting them, go almost quite cold after a year or two.
Unless, of course, people envy you them very much, and the
museums are pining for them. And the Melvilles' "things,"
though very good, were not quite as good as that.

So, the glow gradually went out of everything, out of Europe,
out of Italy, "the Italians are dears," even out of that marvellous
apartment on the Arno. "Why if I had this apartment, I'd
never, never even want to go out of doors! It's too lovely and
perfect."—That was something, of course, to hear that.

And yet Valerie and Erasmus went out of doors: they even
went out to get away from its ancient, cold-floored, stone-heavy

silence and dead dignity. "We're living on the past, you know, Dick!" said Valerie to her husband. She called him Dick.

They were grimly hanging on. They did not like to give in. They did not like to own up that they were through. For twelve years, now, they had been "free" people, living a "full and beautiful life." And America for twelve years had been their anathema, the Sodom and Gomorrah of industrial materialism.

It wasn't easy to own that you were "through." They hated to admit that they wanted to go back. But at last, reluctantly, they decided to go, "for the boy's sake."—'We can't *bear* to leave Europe. But Peter is an American, so had better look at America while he's young."—The Melvilles had an entirely English accent and manner; almost; a little Italian and French here and there.

They left Europe behind, but they took as much of it along with them as possible. Several van-loads, as a matter of fact. All those adorable and irreplaceable "things." And all arrived in New York, idealists, child, and the huge bulk of Europe they had lugged along.

Valerie had dreamed of a pleasant apartment, perhaps on Riverside drive, where it was not so expensive as east of Fifth Avenue, and where all their wonderful things would look marvellous. She and Erasmus house-hunted. But alas! their income was quite under three thousand dollars a year. They found— well, everybody knows what they found. Two small rooms and a kitchenette, and don't let us unpack a *thing*.

The chunk of Europe which they had bitten off went into a warehouse, at fifty dollars a month. And they sat in two small rooms and a kitchenette, and wondered why they'd done it.

Erasmus, of course, ought to get a job. This was what was written on the wall, and what they both pretended not to see. But it had been the strange, vague threat that the Statue of Liberty had always held over them. "Thou shalt get a job!" Erasmus had the tickets, as they say. A scholastic career was still possible for him. He had taken his exams brilliantly at Yale, and had kept up his "researches," all the time he had been in Europe.

But both he and Valerie shuddered. A scholastic career! The scholastic world! The *American* scholastic world!—Shudder upon shudder! Give up their freedom, their full and beautiful life? Never! Never! Erasmus would be forty next birthday.

The "things" remained in warehouse. Valerie went to look at them. It cost her a dollar an hour, and horrid pangs. The "things," poor things, looked a bit shabby and wretched, in that warehouse.

However, New York was not all America. There was the great clean west. So the Melvilles went west, with Peter, but without the things. They tried living the simple life, in the mountains. But doing their own chores became almost a nightmare. "Things" are all very well to look at, but it's awful handling them, even when they're beautiful. To be the slave of hideous things, to keep a stove going, cook meals, wash dishes, carry water and clean floors: pure horror of sordid anti-life!

In the cabin on the mountains, Valerie dreamed of Florence, the lost apartment, and her Bologna cupboard and Louis Quinze chairs, above all, her "Chartres" curtains, stored in New York—and costing fifty dollars a month.

A millionaire friend came to the rescue, offering them a cottage on the Californian coast.—California! Where the new soul is to be born in man. With joy the idealists moved a little further west, catching at new vine-props of hope.

And finding them straws!—The millionaire cottage was perfectly equipped. It was perhaps as labour-savingly perfect as is possible: electric heating and cooking, a white-and-pearl enamelled kitchen, nothing to make dirt except the human being himself. In an hour or so the idealists had got through their chores. They were "free"—free to hear the great Pacific pounding the coast, and to feel a new soul filling their bodies.

Alas! the Pacific pounded the coast with hideous brutality, brute force itself! And the new soul, instead of sweetly stealing into their bodies, seemed only meanly to gnaw the old soul out of their bodies. To feel you are under the fist of the most blind and crunching brute force: to feel that your cherished idealist's soul is being gnawed out of you, and only irritation left in place of it: well, it isn't good enough.

After about nine months, the idealists departed from the Californian west. It had been a great experience, they were glad to have had it. But, in the long run, the west was not the place for them, and they knew it. No, the people who wanted new souls had better get them. They, Valerie and Erasmus Melville, would like to develop the old soul a little further. Anyway, they had not felt any influx of new soul, on the Californian coast. On the contrary.

So, with a slight hole in their material capital, they returned to Massachusetts, and paid a visit to Valerie's parents, taking the boy along. The grand-parents welcomed the child—poor expatriated boy—and were rather cold to Valerie, but really cold to Erasmus. Valerie's mother definitely said to Valerie, one day, that Erasmus ought to take a job, so that Valerie could live decently. Valerie haughtily reminded her mother of the beautiful apartment on the Arno, and the "wonderful" things in store in New York, and of the "marvellous and satisfying life" she and Erasmus had led. Valerie's mother said that she didn't think her daughter's life looked so very marvellous at present: homeless, with a husband idle at the age of forty, a child to educate, and a dwindling capital: looked the reverse of marvellous, to *her*. Let Erasmus take some post in one of the universities—

"What post? what university?" interrupted Valerie.

"That could be found, considering your father's connections and Erasmus' qualifications," replied Valerie's mother. "And you could get all your valuable things out of store, and have a really lovely home, which everybody in America would be proud to visit. As it is, your furniture is eating up your income, and you are living like rats in a hole, with nowhere to go to."

This was very true. Valerie was beginning to pine for a home, with her "things." Of course she could have sold her furniture for a substantial sum. But nothing would have induced her. Whatever else passed away, religions, cultures, continents, and hopes, Valerie would *never* part from the "things" which she and Erasmus had collected with such passion. To these she was nailed.

But she and Erasmus still would not give up that freedom,

that full and beautiful life they had so believed in. Erasmus cursed America. He did not *want* to earn a living. He panted for Europe.

Leaving the boy in charge of Valerie's parents, the two idealists once more set off for Europe. In New York, they paid two dollars and looked for a brief, bitter hour at their "things." They sailed "student class"—that is, third. Their income now was less than two thousand dollars, instead of three. And they made straight for Paris—cheap Paris.

They found Europe, this time, a complete failure. "We have returned like dogs to our vomit," said Erasmus; "but the vomit has staled in the meantime." He found he couldn't stand Europe. It irritated every nerve in his body. He hated America too. But America at least was a darn sight better than this miserable dirt-eating continent; which was by no means cheap any more either.

Valerie, with her heart on her things—she had really burned to get them out of that warehouse, where they had stood now for three years, eating up two thousand dollars—wrote to her mother she thought Erasmus would come back if he could get some suitable work in America. Erasmus, in a state of frustration bordering on rage and insanity, just went round Italy in a poverty-stricken fashion, his coat-cuffs frayed, hating everything with intensity. And when a post was found for him in Cleveland university, to teach French, Italian and Spanish literature, his eyes grew more beady, and his long, queer face grew sharper and more rat-like, with utter baffled fury. He was forty, and the job was upon him.

"I think you'd better accept, dear. You don't care for Europe any longer. As you say, it's dead and finished. They offer us a house on the college lot, and mother says there's room in it for all our things. I think we'd better cable 'accept.'" He glowered at her like a cornered rat. One almost expected to see rat's whiskers twitching at the sides of the sharp nose.

"Shall I send the cablegram?" she asked.

"Send it!" he blurted.

And she went out and sent it.

He was a changed man, quieter, much less irritable. A load was off him. He was inside the cage.

But when he looked at the furnaces of Cleveland, vast and like the greatest of black forests, with red and white-hot cascades of gushing metal, and tiny gnomes of men, and terrific noises, gigantic, he said to Valerie:

"Say what you like, Valerie, this is the biggest thing the modern world has to show."

And when they were in their up-to-date little house on the college lot of Cleveland University, and that woebegone débris of Europe, Bologna cupboard, Venice book-shelves, Ravenna bishop's chair, Louis Quinze side-tables, "Chartres" curtains, Siena bronze lamps, all were arrayed, and all looked perfectly out of keeping, and therefore very impressive; and when the idealists had had a bunch of gaping people in, and Erasmus had showed off his best European manner, but still quite cordial and American; and Valerie had been most ladylike, but for all that, "we prefer America;" then Erasmus said, looking at her with queer sharp eyes of a rat:

"Europe's the mayonnaise all right, but America supplies the good old lobster—what?"

"Every time!" she said, with satisfaction.

And he peered at her. He was in the cage: but it was safe inside. And she, evidently, was her real self at last. She had got the goods.—Yet round his nose was a queer, evil scholastic look, of pure scepticism. But he liked lobster.

Explanatory Notes

The Note on the Texts gives details concerning the composition, revision and publication history of each story. Unusual, foreign, slang and dialect words and phrases are explained in the Glossary. Bible quotations are from the King James Authorised Version.

List of Abbreviations

Letters, i. *The Letters of D. H. Lawrence 1901–13*, vol. i, ed. James T. Boulton (Cambridge University Press, 1979).

Letters, ii. *The Letters of D. H. Lawrence 1913–16*, vol. ii, ed. George J. Zytaruk and James T. Boulton (Cambridge University Press, 1981).

Letters, iii. *The Letters of D. H. Lawrence 1916–21*, vol. iii, ed. James T. Boulton and Andrew Robertson (Cambridge University Press, 1984).

Letters, vi. *The Letters of D. H. Lawrence 1927–8*, vol. vi, ed. James T. Boulton and Margaret H. Boulton with Gerald M. Lacy (Cambridge University Press, 1991).

Letters, vii. *The Letters of D. H. Lawrence 1928–30*, vol. vii, ed. Keith Sagar and James T. Boulton (Cambridge University Press, 1993).

LOVE AMONG THE HAYSTACKS

3:1–2 **LOVE AMONG THE HAYSTACKS** In July 1908, Lawrence wrote that 'All last week, and all this, I have been in the hay' (*Letters*, i. 64). As described in the story, he had helped the Chambers family (a daughter of whom was Jessie (1887–1944), one of his closest friends during his youth) with their harvest at 'two great fields at Greasley, running to the top of a sharp, irregular hillside, with . . . the Vicar's garden on one side, and low, wild rushy fields on the other' (*Letters*, i. 67).

5:17–18 **"Ich bin klein . . . Christ allein."** Traditional German children's prayer: 'I am small, my heart is pure / There is no one in it except Christ alone.'

11:22 **Bill** Presumably the name of the labourer mentioned at 10:29 and 11:14.

16:28 *Nation* The *Nation* published poems by Lawrence in November 1911 and his story 'The Miner at Home' in March 1912. He told his sister Ada, 'I am pleased to get a footing in the *Nation*. It is a sixpenny weekly, of very good standing' (*Letters*, i. 324).

23:31–4 **For a moment . . . the wonder in himself before** Compare Lawrence's admiration of his own body following his days of haymaking with the Chambers family: 'as I was rubbing myself down in the late twilight . . . and as I passed my hands over my sides where the muscles lie suave and secret, I did love myself' (*Letters*, i. 65).

27:16 **We fast up here** Trapped, probably from the German word 'fest', with an identical meaning, that Paula would naturally use as a German speaker.

31:34 **glossy** Glossy skin was often considered a symptom of ill health.

35:12 **phosphorescent glare** The matches are tipped with phosphorous, luminous when ignited but also poisonous; prohibited in Britain after 1908.

36:24–5 **bruise the lips of the scornful** Biblical phraseology but not an exact quotation; at Genesis iii.15, mankind will 'bruise [the serpent's] head, and [it] shalt bruise his heel', whereas Psalm i.1 reads, 'Blessed is the man that walketh not in the counsel of the ungodly . . . nor sitteth in the seat of the scornful.'

41:32–3 **take the stack-cloth up** Lift the cloth from the haystack and take it down to the ground.

42:8 **German girl** Paula Jablonowsky is German-speaking and from Hanover, but with a Polish name and perhaps ancestry; Lawrence had identified her as 'a Pole' (13:33).

THE MINER AT HOME

43:15–16 **sitting there in his pit-dirt** The grime from coal mining had to be washed off at home; collieries provided no washing facilities.

45:5–6 **blue seam . . . in the pit** The wound has healed over coal dust, leaving a blue mark beneath the skin.

45:17–18 **fourteen days from above date** The Miners' Federation of Great Britain issued such tickets for signatures on 12–14 February 1912, threatening national strike action if mine owners rejected its proposed new schedule of wages. In the Midlands, strikes did indeed begin on 26 February at Alfreton in Derbyshire and 28 February at the Eastwood pits in Nottinghamshire. A subsequent ballot in April rejected a settlement, but by too narrow a margin for strike action to be maintained and miners returned to work between 9 and 11 April 1912. Lawrence's father balloted for a return to work, but those men who balloted against angered many Eastwood women, who, according to Lawrence, 'would murder any man at any minute if he refused to be a good servant to the family' (*Letters*, i. 379).

46:2 **last two strikes** The collieries owned by Barber Walker & Co. in Eastwood closed from January to March 1908 and again from June to November 1910.

46:7 **Yorkshire an' Welsh colliers** Miners in both areas had a reputation for greater militancy than their counterparts in the Midlands; this disparity could cause acute problems when national ballots took place.

46:19–20 **Who wants . . . Butties doesn't** The 1912 strike was partly motivated by a demand from the Miners' Federation for a minimum wage of seven shillings and sixpence (37½ pence today) for piece workers at the coal face. 'Butties' (see Glossary) would be obliged to pay this minimum wage to their day workers.

THE WHITE STOCKING

49:19–20 **Rise up . . . and shine forth** A biblical version of 'rise and shine'; see Mark xiv.42, Matthew xiii.43 and Isaiah lx.1: 'Arise, shine; for thy light is come, and the glory of the Lord is risen upon thee.'

51:25–6 **"Pearls may be fair . . . the wearer."** No source has been identified; Lawrence probably invented the verse.

52:14–15 **"E for Elsie, / Nice little gelsie,"** An invented verse.

52:22 **comic** Valentine, the 'long, hideous, cartoon' mentioned at 50:34–5. In the earlier version of the story published in the *Smart Set*, the picture is of 'a man glancing lugubriously over his shoulder at the ghost face of a young lady smiling and showing her teeth. It was entitled: "Her Bright Smile Haunts Me Still."'

53:7-9 **"Doctor Wyer . . . puff!"** Probably derived from the nursery rhyme, 'Jeremiah, blow the fire, / Puff, puff, puff! / First you blow it gently, / Then you blow it rough.' This verse was also part of a popular nineteenth-century music-hall song; the identity and significance of 'Doctor Wyer' is unclear.

55:9 **Royal** Royal Café and Restaurant at 32 Market Street, Nottingham.

56:7-8 **like chickens . . . to roost** Proverbially, 'Curses, like chickens, come home to roost.' A curse will rebound on the person who makes it.

56:14 **Adams' lace factory** Samuel Adams & Sons, Lace Manufacturers, were based at 2 Commerce Square, Nottingham.

57:1 **"True, true till death——"** Taken from the popular song 'Just Like the Ivy' (1902) by A. J. Mills and Harry Castling: 'Just watch the ivy on that old garden wall / Clinging so tightly what e'er may befall; / As you grow older I'll be constantly true, / And just like the ivy, I'll cling to you.'

57:18-20 **Castle Rock . . . the boulevard** Nottingham Castle is built on a high sandstone ridge known as Castle Rock; the tree-lined Castle Boulevard runs below.

58:1-2 **her card . . . the dances** Adams selects Elsie as his dancing partner by writing his initials on her printed card listing each dance.

61:33-5 **She ate her custard . . . her employer** This sentence reads oddly; proofs for *The Prussian Officer and Other Stories* (1914) read: 'She ate her custard, all the while sustained and contained within the fusion with her employer.' Syntactical sense is satisfied if the revised second clause is understood to mean that 'an incomplete fusion all the while sustained and contained within [her] the being of her employer.'

ODOUR OF CHRYSANTHEMUMS

74:5 **Selston** Selston Colliery, located near Underwood, Nottinghamshire. The Eastwood-based mine owners Barber Walker & Co. used small locomotives to transport coal to the main railway line at Langley Mill.

74:21-3 **pit-bank . . . its ashy sides** The pit-bank would be made up of earth and small fragments of coal; the carboniferous elements of this waste material would tend to oxidise and catch fire, leaving ash as a residue.

74:25 **Brinsley Colliery** The mine where Lawrence's father and at least two paternal uncles worked; one, James Lawrence (1851–80), was killed by a fall of coal in Brinsley Colliery in 1880. His wife and children lived in the cottage next to the railway line as described in the story; their third child was also born after the father's death.

75:1–2 **squat a low cottage** This construction is a result of cuts Lawrence made to the 1910 *English Review* proofs of the story. The sentence originally read: 'The train slowed down as it drew near a small cottage squat beside the great bay of railway-lines.'

77:5 **'Lord Nelson'** Real-life public house. The Prince of Wales and Yew Tree mentioned later were also local pubs popular with miners.

88:14–15 **it fell ... shut 'im in** Walter had been cutting into the bottom of a coal seam to create a space into which the overhanging coal could later be broken. He worked himself 'under th' face' but was trapped by a rock fall behind him.

94:7 **not dead** The *English Review* proofs, as revised by Lawrence, read 'dead'. The reading changed when he made final revisions for *The Prussian Officer and Other Stories*.

95:10 **fear and shame** The *English Review* proofs continued: 'For in death she would have no life, for she had never loved. She had life on earth with her children, that was all.'

NEW EVE AND OLD ADAM

96:1 **NEW EVE AND OLD ADAM** Images favoured by Lawrence, pairing in conflict modern woman and unregenerate man. This title was used by Rudolf Golm (1870–1931) for the novel *Der alte Adam und die neue Eva* (1895), translated in 1898, a work that Lawrence certainly knew by 1910. He later applied the terms to his own fraught relationship with his wife Frieda von Richthofen Weekley (1879–1956) (see, for example, *Letters*, ii. 662); several other biographical echoes in the story are noted below.

96:11 **Parisian Nights' Entertainments** Variation on *The Arabian Nights' Entertainments*, a collection of folk tales in Arabic dating from the tenth century.

96:16 **married a year** In May 1913, at the time this story was written, Lawrence wrote that 'I have been married for this last year' (*Letters*, i. 553), after going to Germany with Frieda on 3 May 1912. They were legally married on 13 July 1914, following her divorce from Ernest Weekley (1865–1954).

97:4 **Gretchen** Virtuous and innocent character in *Faust* (1808) by
Johann Wolfgang von Goethe (1749–1832). She is seduced by
Faust and bears his child.

97:24 **flat** Used in its original sense of 'storey' or 'floor' (and at
111:28).

99:30 **Pietro** Italianate nickname; the protagonists are subsequently
identified as 'Peter' and 'Paula Moest'. Lawrence knew the German sculptor Josef Moest (1873–1914) by 1913 and probably
took the name from him.

100:9 **Marble Arch** Monument, or the underground railway station
of the same name, at the west end of Oxford Street in London.

104:14–15 **his brother-in-law's** Identified as 'Edmund' below; perhaps a re-creation of Lawrence's future brother-in-law Edgar Jaffe
(1866–1921).

106:2 **Madge, her friend** Also the name of a close Nottingham friend
of Frieda; Madge Bradley and her sister Gladys had encouraged
the relationship between Frieda and Lawrence. Frieda stayed
with Gladys Bradley at the end of April 1912 while Lawrence
waited to hear her intentions about her relationship with him
(see *Letters*, i. 388–9).

109:23–4 **twenty lire for a sovereign** A sovereign was a gold coin
nominally worth one pound sterling; during 1912–13, the
exchange rate for a sovereign would be at least 24 Italian lire
(the plural form of lira, the monetary currency of Italy until
2002).

109:24 **Strand** Prestigious central London shopping street, running
from Charing Cross to Fleet Street.

112:11 **Hampstead** Fashionable middle- and upper-class suburb in
north London.

112:37–8 **most famous ... poet and 'Meister'** The most famous
contemporary 'Meister' ('Master') of German poetry was probably Stefan George (1868–1933).

117:15 **'The Black Sheep'** Four plays with this title have been identified, but Lawrence may instead be playing with the title of *The
Blue Bird* by Maurice Maeterlinck (1862–1949), famous in its
time and first performed in London in 1909. The reasons why
Maeterlinck could be considered a 'black sheep', his family's
disapproval of his literary ambitions and his long relationship
with a married woman, may have been especially pertinent to
Lawrence at the time of writing this story.

119:10–13 **"On my breasts ... perfumed sheets—"** From 'A Preach-
ing from a Spanish Ballad' (1887), ll. 33–6 by George Meredith

(1828–1909): 'At my breasts I cool thy footsoles; / Wine I pour, I dress thy meats; / Humbly, when my lord it pleaseth, / Lie with him on perfumed sheets'.

120:1 **his hair ... like an Apollo's** Curled and bunched hair, like that of the statue of the Apollo Belvedere in the Vatican Museum in Rome.

120:14 **Flesh of my flesh** From Genesis ii.23 as Eve is created from Adam's rib: 'And Adam said, This is now bone of my bones, and flesh of my flesh: she shall be called Woman, because she was taken out of Man.'

121:15–16 **You *wouldn't* love *me* ... except generally** Moest's resentment of Paula's attempts at undiscriminating goodwill recalls Gilbert Noon's complaint to Johanna (also fictional re-creations of Lawrence and Frieda), in Lawrence's uncompleted novel *Mr Noon*: 'If there is *physical* love, it is exclusive. It *is* exclusive. It's only spiritual love that is all-embracing. And I'm off spiritual love. I *don't want* it' (ed. Lindeth Vasey (Cambridge University Press, 1984), p. 166).

VIN ORDINAIRE

122:1 **VIN ORDINAIRE** Lawrence gave the story this title 'because I thought it *was* vin ordinaire' (*Letters*, ii. 199); see Glossary. By July 1914, he had rewritten it with the title 'The Thorn in the Flesh' and it was this revised version that appeared in *The Prussian Officer and Other Stories*.

122:11–12 **climbing ambitiously up** The vigour of the plants in climbing over the walls of the barracks contrasts with the difficulties of Bachmann's ascent of the fortifications.

122:16 **Bachmann** Literally, 'Brookman' (German).

123:7 **fortifications** The story is set in Metz, now a French city in the north-east of the country and capital of the Lorraine region. Following the Franco-Prussian War (1870–71), however, Metz had been formally ceded to Germany. By 1905, some 25,000 German troops were stationed there and the city was increasingly fortified. Lawrence travelled to Metz in May 1912, following Frieda, whose father Baron Friedrich von Richthofen (1844–1915) held a post as an administrative officer with the German army. Lawrence was obliged to leave the city under suspicion of spying: 'they were going to arrest me for staring at their idiotic fortifications' (*Letters*, i. 397). He dismissed Metz as 'a ghastly medley ... new town, old town, barracks, barracks, barracks, cathedral, Montigny' (*Letters*, i. 393). See also note to 129:15–17.

123:10 **Heidelberg** City in south-west Germany on the Neckar river, between Stuttgart and Frankfurt.

128:12–13 **Cathedral . . . blue sky** Cathédrale Saint-Etienne in Metz, built in the Gothic style between 1220 and 1520.

129:9 **forty miles to France** In fact, the nearest point of the French border was just over seven miles from Metz.

129:15–17 **Baron von Freyhof's . . . two miles out of town** The equivalent 'big house' of Baron von Richthofen was located in Montigny, a small village about three and a half miles from Metz.

129:18 **Scy** Now known as Scy-Chazelles, a village on the slopes of Mont St Quentin with a view over Metz.

138:1–2 **his right hand . . . Franco-Prussian war** Baron von Richthofen had a damaged finger on his right hand caused by a war injury.

138:11 **"Yes," . . . mechanically** No mention is made in the story of Emilie posting Bachmann's postcard to his mother, although the report of her returning home at the beginning of section IV could be after such a trip. It is likely that this detail was lost when cuts were made to 'Vin Ordinaire' by the editors of the *English Review*.

THE PRUSSIAN OFFICER

141:1–2 **THE PRUSSIAN OFFICER [HONOUR AND ARMS]** Edward Garnett (1868–1937), reader for the publisher Duckworth, altered Lawrence's title 'Honour and Arms' to 'The Prussian Officer', a change that was carried over into the title of Duckworth's collection. Lawrence did not approve: 'Garnett was a devil to call my book of stories *The Prussian Officer* – what Prussian Officer?' (*Letters*, ii. 241). Despite Lawrence's comment that 'I have written the best story I have ever done – about a German officer in the army and his orderly' (*Letters*, ii. 21), the officer is indeed Prussian by birth. He is, however, serving in the Bavarian army, which maintained its independence from Prussian forces until the outbreak of the First World War in 1914.

'Honour and Arms' is taken from Newburgh Hamilton's libretto for the dramatic oratorio *Samson* (1743) by George Frideric Handel (1685–1759), as adapted from *Samson Agonistes* (1671) by John Milton (1608–74). Harapha, the giant of Gath, taunts the blind Samson in an aria from scene 4: 'Honour and Arms scorn such a Foe, / Tho' I cou'd end thee at a Blow; / Poor Victory, / To conquer thee, / Or glory in thy Overthrow: / Vanquish a Slave that is half slain! / So mean a Triumph I disdain.'

142:9–11 **pale blue uniform . . . sword scabbard** Field uniform of an officer in the Bavarian Infantry Regiments. Lawrence would have seen these units in Bavaria during two visits in May–August 1912 and April–June 1913.

149:5 **dithering** An unusual but correct usage: the captain's smile unnerves and confuses the orderly, rather than being hesitant itself; 'dithering' is the manuscript reading, but all later texts have 'withering'.

154:7 **strange country** The landscapes Lawrence describes are those of the Isar valley and Loisach river. His impressions of Bavaria are also recorded in *Letters*, i. 411–16 and 540–54.

ENGLAND, MY ENGLAND

165:1 **ENGLAND, MY ENGLAND** Taken from the refrain to W. E. Henley's (1849–1903) poem 'England' (1900), which begins 'What have I done for you, / England, my England? / What is there I would not do, / England, my own?' Henley advocates service to and sacrifice for country, sentiments revived at the outbreak of the First World War but subject to irony here.

Lawrence wrote the story while living in Greatham, Sussex, at a cottage on 'the Meynell settlement' (*Letters*, ii. 255) lent by Viola Meynell (1885–1956), the daughter of author and editor Wilfred Meynell (1852–1948) and poet Alice Meynell (1847–1922). His characters Winifred and Evelyn were modelled on Viola's sister Madeline (1884–1975) and her husband Perceval Lucas (1879–1916). Madeline did have six siblings (169:16), and the eldest of the Lucases' three daughters, Sylvia, injured her leg in the summer of 1913 by falling on a sickle left lying in long grass. Lucas was drafted into the infantry during the First World War, having previously been stationed in Epsom and Nottinghamshire (see 171:27–9). He died of wounds in France in July 1916, after which Lawrence briefly wished this prophetic story 'at the bottom of the sea' (*Letters*, ii. 635). This version of the story was written and published in 1915, prior to Lucas's death (see also the Note on the Texts).

167:17–21 **Her father . . . persisted in him** This description matches the background of Wilfred Meynell, whose Quaker family came from Newcastle upon Tyne; he later converted to Roman Catholicism.

167:34 **old south-of-England family** Re-creation of the Sussex origins of the family of Perceval Lucas.

168:20–21 **she pulled through** The local doctor was similarly unable to treat the complications that followed the injury to Sylvia Lucas; her life was also saved by hospital treatment in London.

THE HORSE-DEALER'S DAUGHTER

181:1–2 **THE HORSE-DEALER'S DAUGHTER** Originally entitled 'The Miracle'; Lawrence changed the title when he revised the story in 1921.

187:2 **Jessdale** Perhaps Lawrence's re-creation of the small town of Jacksdale in Nottinghamshire.

187:4 **Moon and Stars** Lawrence's re-creation (also used in his novel *Sons and Lovers*) of the Three Tuns public house in Eastwood.

188:21 **smoke of foundries** Bennerley Iron Works (see note to 229:4) would be one local source of this black smoke.

THE BLIND MAN

199:2 **Isabel Pervin** Based on Catherine Carswell (1879–1946), Scottish novelist, journalist and friend of Lawrence; she also reviewed books for the *Glasgow Herald* (199:17–18). Her first husband Herbert Jackson, a veteran of the Boer War, was admitted into a mental institution just months after their marriage where he remained for the rest of his life. She married Donald Carswell (1882–1940), an old acquaintance from the *Glasgow Herald*, in 1915.

199:8 **blinded in Flanders** The Flanders region of north-east France and Belgium was the scene of hundreds of thousands of deaths and injuries during extended trench warfare in the First World War.

199:11 **The Grange** Based on the Carswells' borrowed holiday home known as The Vicarage in Upper Lydbrook, Ross-on-Wye. Lawrence visited them there 26–31 August 1918, judging them 'very nice but depressed' (*Letters*, iii. 277).

201:9 **Bertie Reid** Partly based on the philosopher and mathematician Bertrand Russell (1872–1970), with whom Lawrence had planned a series of lectures on ethics and immortality in 1915. Lawrence's enthusiasm for Russell's thinking foundered when their metaphysical and political positions proved irreconcilable.

By 1916, he put Russell among 'that old "advanced" crowd' who 'are our disease, not our hope' (*Letters*, iii. 49), and urged Russell to 'have the courage to be a creature' rather than exist merely as an 'ego' (*Letters*, ii. 547), a criticism applicable to Bertie Reid here.

ADOLF

220:10–11 **his long walk . . . first daybreak** When Lawrence's family lived at 3 Walker Street in Eastwood, his father walked about a mile to his work at Brinsley Colliery across similar countryside. His return from the nightshift would be between six and seven o'clock in the morning.

220:26–7 **pour it out into his saucer** Drinking tea from the saucer rather than the cup was considered a working-class habit and, invariably, coarse behaviour.

224:30 **Buddhist meditation** Contemplative Asian religion or philosophy that teaches that the elimination of selfish desires is the highest goal (see also note to 315:12).

227:4–5 **nursemaid's flying strings** Long white ties used to fasten a nursemaid's apron behind her back.

227:7 **white feather** Symbol of cowardice, especially during the First World War when campaigners sought to give white feathers to men who did not respond to the voluntary army recruitment drive in autumn 1914 and later to those apparently not serving in the conscripted army.

227:34 **conceit of the meek** According to Matthew v.5, 'Blessed are the meek: for they shall inherit the earth', a reason for their apparently paradoxical 'conceit'.

THE LAST STRAW

229:1–2 **THE LAST STRAW [FANNY AND ANNIE]** Lawrence wrote to his English publisher Martin Secker (1882–1978) on 29 December 1921 saying, 'I should like the title "Fanny and Annie" changed to "The Last Straw". Please note it' (*The Letters of D. H. Lawrence 1921–4*, vol. iv, ed. Warren Roberts, James T. Boulton and Elizabeth Mansfield (Cambridge University Press, 1987), p. 152). There is no record of Lawrence making the same request to his American publisher, Thomas Seltzer (1875–1943), who published the story under its original title in the collection *England My England and Other Stories* (1922).

229:4 **light of the furnace** Bennerley Iron Works (otherwise known as Bennerley Furnaces) near Ilkeston, Derbyshire could be the local inspiration for the 'furnace towers in the sky' and the flame-lit effect described here. In a letter to the writer Katherine Mansfield (1888–1923) on 5 December 1918, Lawrence recalled a similar scene on a railway station platform in Ripley, Derbyshire: 'the train runs just above the surface of Butterley reservoir, and the iron-works on the bank were flaming, a massive roar of flame and burnt smoke in the black sky ... On Butterley platform – where I got out – everything was lit up red' (*Letters*, iii. 302).

235:21 **Princes Street** In Eastwood, Princes Street adjoins Victoria Street where Lawrence was born.

235:28 **Morley Chapel** A name perhaps taken from the village of Morley, west of Ilkeston in Derbyshire.

235:36–7 *"And I saw ... a wite 'orse——"* No hymn containing this solo part has been identified, but the words are taken from Revelation xix.11. Lawrence may have chosen this verse for the opportunities it gives Harry to drop and add aitches.

236:3 *"Hangels—hever bright an' fair——"* Part of an aria from Handel's dramatic oratorio *Theodora* (premiered in 1750) about Christian martyrs in ancient Rome.

237:8–11 *"Come, ye ... storms begin——"* Hymn written for harvest festivals by Henry Alford (1810–71).

238:4 **Balaam's ass** Wiser than her master, the ass refused to pass the angel of the Lord standing in her way as Balaam tried to join the Princes of Moab to drive the children of Israel from Moab, Jordan and Jericho (Numbers xxii.1–41).

238:20–23 *"They that sow ... sheaves with him."* Psalm cxxvi.5–6.

239:21 **Lot's wife** Lot and his family were taken out of Sodom and forbidden to look back as it and Gomorrah, cities notorious for their wickedness and corruption, were destroyed by fire and brimstone; his wife disobeyed and was turned into a pillar of salt (Genesis xix.26).

239:31–2 *'Fair waved ... pleasant land.'* Hymn by John Hampden Gurney (1802–62).

240:9–10 **washing his hands before the Lord** Reference to Pontius Pilate's gesture before the crowd, denying responsibility for Christ's death: 'When Pilate saw that he could prevail nothing, but that rather a tumult was made, he took water, and washed his hands before the multitude, saying, I am innocent of the blood of this just person' (Matthew xxvii.24).

SUN

245:9   Hudson The ship leaves New York Harbor via the Hudson river, passing the Statue of Liberty and sailing out into the Atlantic Ocean. Lawrence and Frieda made the crossing from New York to Southampton on the SS *Resolute* 21–30 September 1925.

245:14   serpent of chaos Possibly an image of Satan (expanding Revelation xx.1–3). However, in Egyptian mythology the serpent god Apep (otherwise Apepi or Apophis) of the celestial Nile was also known as the 'serpent of chaos' for attempting to swallow the sun.

246:12   Lackawanna station Waterfront terminal of the Delaware, Lackawanna and Western Railway at Hoboken, New Jersey, one of many that lined the shores of the Hudson river in the 1920s.

246:15–16   Battery. Liberty flung up her torch The Battery is a park created by landfill on the southern tip of Manhattan Island at the upper end of New York Bay, in which the Statue of Liberty (1886), designed by Frédéric Auguste Bartholdi (1834–1904), a gift from France to the United States, is situated. From its base to the top of the upheld torch, the statue measures over 46 metres.

246:18–26   house above the bluest of seas . . . snow of the volcano Lawrence sent an early draft of 'Sun' to a friend Millicent Beveridge (1871–1955) on 11 September 1926 'to see if you recognise the garden at Fontana Vecchia, and where you used to sit and sketch, above the Lemon grove' (*The Letters of D. H. Lawrence 1924–7*, vol. v, ed. James T. Boulton and Lindeth Vasey (Cambridge University Press, 1989), p. 533). The house is a re-creation of the Villa Fontana Vecchia ('Old Fountain') and its garden at Taormina in Sicily where the Lawrences lived from March 1920 to February 1922.

251:17   Magna Graecia Greek seaport colonies of Sicily and southern Italy established from the eighth to fourth century BC, prior to Roman occupation.

251:33–4   Greeks had said . . . unhealthy, and fishy In ancient Greece, athletic training for young men was an integral part of their education; such training was typically undertaken naked and so a tan also became linked with physical fitness.

255:35   black snakes . . . yellow ones The western whip snake found in Sicily is a shiny black colour and potentially aggressive but not poisonous; the dangerous yellow snake is probably an Asp

Viper, the poison of which can be fatal. However, the subspecies of Asp Viper more common in Sicily has red-orange rather than yellow markings and so the identification is not certain.

256:4 **take no thought for the morrow** From Matthew vi.34: 'Take therefore no thought for the morrow: for the morrow shall take thought for the things of itself. Sufficient unto the day is the evil thereof.'

258:21 **capuchin church** Church founded by an order of Franciscan monks, the Capuchin Friars Minor, an organisation dating back to 1525 in Italy. There was a capuchin church close to the town gates in Taormina.

260:29 **Fates** In Greek mythology, the three Fates controlled human destinies: Clotho spins the thread of life, Lachesis determines its length and Atropos cuts it off.

263:13-14 **East Forty-Seventh** Fashionable address in Manhattan.

268:3-4 **Perseus ... cut the bonds** Son of Zeus in Greek mythology; Zeus appeared to Perseus' imprisoned mother Danaë in the form of a sun-like stream of gold. Perseus later rescued Andromeda, the daughter of the king and queen of Ethiopia, who was bound to a rock by the sea as a sacrifice to Poseidon, god of the sea.

THE ROCKING-HORSE WINNER

269:3-4 **There was a woman ... no luck** Hester and her family are partly a re-creation of Lady Cynthia (1887-1960) and Herbert Asquith (1881-1947), whose eldest son John was autistic. Herbert, a barrister (see 269:26), was the son of the Liberal politician H. H. Asquith (1852-1928), who served as British Prime Minister 1908-16. Lady Cynthia was a novelist, diarist and editor of several volumes of ghost stories (one of which included this story); Herbert Asquith was also a part-time novelist and poet. Their financial difficulties were well known to Lawrence.

273:18-20 **Sansovino ... Won the Ascot** The racehorse Sansovino, owned by the 17th Earl of Derby, was a strong colt with staying power. He was foaled in 1921 and won six races in his career, including, as Oscar correctly notes, the Prince of Wales's Stakes at Royal Ascot in 1924.

274:9 **Lincoln** Lincolnshire Handicap, an important early meeting in the flat racing season, now run at Doncaster, Yorkshire.

274:14-15 **Daffodil ... Mirza** Oscar is right to doubt the tip. The real Daffodil, foaled in 1922, ran six races in the season 1924-5 and was unplaced in all; Mirza, foaled in 1915, won three races in 1919. However, a race with both horses in the field is fictional.

275:3 **betting three hundred** An extraordinary amount of money for a boy to bet in 1926 when this story was written. Today's equivalent would be over £11,000. When Paul wins 'ten thousand' (277:32) on Lively Spark, the modern equivalent would be £375,700; his final total winnings of 'over eighty thousand' (284:23–4) would be worth approximately £3 million today.

275:6 **Nat Gould** Sports reporter (1857–1919) for newspapers and magazines in Australia, where he had emigrated in 1884. Returning to England in 1895, he became a prolific popular novelist, producing more than 150 titles, mostly about horse racing.

275:28 **Lancelot** A fictional racehorse; nor have any contemporary registration records been found for 'Blush of Dawn', 'Singhalese' or 'Lively Spark'.

276:12 **Richmond Park** Royal park in Surrey, on the outskirts of south-west London, with an area of almost 2,500 acres.

277:11–12 **Joe Glee ... Turf Commission deposit** The 'Turf Commission' is a regulatory body for betting, while 'Joe Glee' is an apt business name for a 'turf commission agent' or bookmaker. Gamblers could deposit some of their winnings as a reserve to be used for future bets.

277:27 **Leger** The St Leger takes place annually at Town Moor, Doncaster.

279:37–280:1 **Grand National ... Derby** The first is the premier event over fences in the calendar of British horse racing, now run annually at Aintree racecourse near Liverpool. The Derby Stakes is a prestigious race over the flat held each year at Epsom Downs Racecourse, Surrey.

283:23 **Malabar** Bay gelding racehorse, foaled in 1920, who enjoyed some success but was never a Derby winner. In the racing seasons 1924–6, just prior to and when Lawrence was writing this story, Malabar ran twenty-six races, winning three times and gaining six second places.

THE MAN WHO LOVED ISLANDS

286:4 **man who loved islands** Six years before composing this story, Lawrence had teased the novelist Compton Mackenzie (1883–1972) about his successful application for a sixty-year lease on the Channel Islands of Herm and Jethou (at £900 and £100 per annum). Mackenzie was 'Lord of the Isles', Lawrence declared;

furthermore, 'I shall write a skit on you one day' (*Letters*, iii. 594). When this story was published in a periodical in 1927, Lawrence assured Martin Secker that Mackenzie 'only *suggests* the idea – it's no portrait' (*Letters*, vi. 69). Mackenzie, however, did object strongly to 'the lunatic story', for 'if Lawrence used my background of a Channel Island and an island in the Hebrides [the likely location of Cathcart's third island] for one of his preposterous Lawrentian figures the public would suppose that it was a portrait' (*My Life and Times: Octave Six 1923–1930* (Chatto and Windus, 1967), p. 131). Should the story be reissued in book form, he informed Lawrence and his publisher that he 'would certainly take proceedings for libel' (*Letters*, vii. 391). Mackenzie was also published by Secker and had investments in the company; Secker subsequently refused to include the story in *The Woman Who Rode Away and Other Stories*, although Lawrence ensured that the story did appear in the American edition published by Alfred A. Knopf (1892–1984) in May 1928. Far from admitting a libel on Mackenzie's character, Lawrence came to esteem his fictional creation much more highly than his initial model: 'The Man Who Loved Islands is a much purer and finer character than the vain, shallow, theatrical, and somewhat ridiculous Mackenzie. If people identify him with my story, they will inevitably have a deeper respect for him ... What was his whole island scheme but showing off? The Man who loved islands has a philosophy behind him, and a real significance' (*Letters*, vi. 218).

286:17–18 **Abraham ... sands of the sea-shore** Abraham is told that he 'shalt be a father of many nations' and 'exceeding fruitful' (Genesis xvii.4–6), but it is his grandson Jacob to whom these particular words are addressed: 'I will surely do thee good, and make thy seed as the sand of the sea, which cannot be numbered for multitude' (Genesis xxxii.12).

287:11–12 **bigger island lying beyond** Herm is three miles off the east coast of Guernsey, the closest of the larger Channel Islands. The 'tiny' 44-acre island Jethou (287:14) is immediately south of Herm.

288:34 **Gaul** Ancient region of western Europe that included modern France, northern Italy, Belgium and parts of Germany and the Netherlands.

288:38–289:1 **priests, with golden knives ... priests with a crucifix** From the evidence of its stone circles and Neolithic chamber tombs, Herm was inhabited in prehistoric times. From the sixth century BC, its isolation attracted monks, from the Celtic monk Tugal to the Benedictine monks of Mont-Saint-Michel in the eleventh century. Herm has been a place of both pagan and Christian rituals.

289:1 **pirates** By repute, Herm and Sark were the lair of pirates in the early sixteenth century; pirates were also known to have used Jethou as a temporary base until it was inhabited in 1717.

289:20–21 **isle of the Hesperides** In Greek mythology, the Hesperides were nymphs who tended an orchard where golden apples grew that could bestow immortality when eaten. The name can also refer to a set of islands, alternatively known as the Fortunate Islands or Isles of the Blest, where mortals were received into a state of paradise.

291:10 **Hermes** In Greek mythology, the son of Zeus and Maia who delivered messages from the gods and conducted souls to Hades; he was also god of travellers, eloquence, commerce, cunning, invention, good luck and young men, as well as a patron of cheats and thieves.

292:3–5 **wonderful with children ... Our Saviour Himself** Displeased at the way his disciples prevented people bringing their children to him, Jesus 'said unto them, Suffer the little children to come unto me, and forbid them not ... And he took them up in his arms, put his hands upon them, and blessed them' (Mark x.14–16).

294:24 **economise** A gibe likely to anger Compton Mackenzie further. His financial difficulties in running the farm on Herm were a source of amusement to Lawrence who wrote in 1921 that Mackenzie 'is in Herm, in kilts, finding his island full of atmosphere and ghosts, and very expensive' (*Letters*, iii. 664–5).

296:3–5 **lean kine of Egypt ... back out of it** As Joseph interprets Pharaoh's dream, seven fat cows foretell seven years of plenty in Egypt but the 'seven thin and ill favoured' cows seven years of famine; just as the fat cows disappeared, in the period of famine 'all the plenty shall be forgotten' (Genesis xli.25–31).

298:4 **honeymoon-and-golf island** Mackenzie experienced just such difficulties in selling the lease for Herm after the financial losses of its farm. Sir Percival Perry, a chairman of the Ford Motor Company, took over the lease in 1923 and did indeed build a golf course to attract tourists.

298:26 **Orion** Constellation of stars located on the celestial equator, but bright and conspicuous in the winter sky in the northern hemisphere. Orion is named after a favoured hunting companion of Artemis (Diana, the goddess of hunting in Roman mythology), who, after being tricked into slaying him by Apollo, immortalised him in the heavens as a constellation.

299:18 **Green star Sirius** Brightest star in the sky, also known as the Dog Star. Sirius appears to be bluish white so Lawrence's identification of it as green is mysterious; however, the first line of his poem 'Winter Dawn' also refers to 'Green star Sirius' (*The Complete Poems of D. H. Lawrence*, ed. Vivian de Sola Pinto and Warren Roberts (Penguin Books, 1977), p. 250).

301:3 **Bond Street** Fashionable shopping street in Mayfair, central London.

303:28–30 **a few acres of rock . . . outer fringe of the isles** In 1925, Mackenzie paid £500 for the Shiant Isles, consisting of two small islands, several islets and other outlying rocks in the North Minch off the east coast of Lewis in the Outer Hebrides, Scotland.

304:25 **Golders Green** Suburb of north-west London.

THINGS

313:1 **THINGS** In a letter of 13 September 1928, Lawrence wrote to his friend Earl Henry Brewster (1878–1957): 'Have a most amusing story of mine in Amer. *Bookman* – called "Things" – you'll think it's you, but it isn't' (*Letters*, vi. 562). Despite the disclaimer, Lawrence used significant details from the lives of Earl and his wife Achsah Barlow Brewster (1878–1945), expatriate Americans living near Florence in Italy. The Brewsters were committed Buddhists (see note to 315:12), in doctrine and meditative practices, provoking Lawrence to complain that 'I seriously think Buddha and deep breathing are rather a bane, both of them' (*Letters*, vii.316). He could also be exasperated by the Brewsters' priorities for expenditure: 'They say they have no money, so the first thing they do is to hire a grand piano' (*Letters*, vii. 577). However, when his neighbours at the Villa Mirenda near Florence in 1928, Arthur Gair Wilkinson (1882–1957) and family, came to move from their Villa Poggi, Lawrence described them too as 'mere wraiths, having packed up every old rag, pot, pan and whisker with the sanctity of pure idealists cherishing their goods' (*Letters*, vi. 343). Nevertheless, it is doubtful whether either family ever secured the financial means to gather such European treasures as the Melvilles accumulate. Another possible influence is the wealthy American patron of the arts Mabel Dodge Luhan (1879–1962), whom Lawrence had known when he lived in New Mexico and who had acquired significant quantities of furniture and other artefacts on her visits to Europe.

313:2 **New England** Region in the north-east of the United States, with a reputation for refined taste, manners and culture, comprising the states of Maine, New Hampshire, Vermont, Massachusetts, Connecticut and Rhode Island.

313:11–12 **"Indian thought" ... Mrs Besant** Annie Besant (1847–1933) embraced theosophy (see note to 315:24) in 1889 and, as the protégée of its founder Helena Petrovna Blavatsky (1831–91), became President of the Theosophical Society in New York by 1907. Theosophy borrows many doctrines and much of its vocabulary from Hindu and Buddhist teaching, hence Lawrence's association of her with 'Indian thought'. Mrs Besant was also involved in Indian nationalist politics, founding the Indian Home Rule League in 1916 and becoming president of the Indian National Congress in 1917.

313:24 **Boulevard Montparnasse** Situated on the Left Bank of the Seine and renowned as a bohemian centre for painters, composers and writers. The favourable exchange rate during much of the 1920s ensured that expatriates in particular could live here cheaply. The name 'Montparnasse' derives from Mount Parnassus which, in Greek mythology, was the home of the Muses.

313:26–7 **pure impressionists, Monet and his followers** Impressionism was a movement in painting originating in France during the 1870s which sought to capture immediate visual impressions as determined by the effect of changing light and atmosphere. Claude Monet (1840–1926) was an initiator of the Impressionist style; his painting *Impression, Sunrise* (1872) gave the movement its name.

314:1–2 **Montmartre ... Tuileries** Montmartre is the Right Bank counterpart to the district of Montparnasse and similarly renowned as a bohemian area. The Tuileries are formal gardens next to the Louvre.

315:12 **Buddha** The 'Awakened' or 'Enlightened' one and founder of Buddhism. Known at birth as Siddhartha Gautama (c. 563–c. 483 BC), he abandoned a life of luxury to devote himself first to asceticism and then meditation. The fundamental insight of Buddhism is that the causes of suffering are attachment and desire; wisdom and virtue teach that liberation from such impulses is the key to the blissful state of Nirvana (see Glossary).

315:24 **theosophy** Literally 'divine wisdom', theosophy understands the universe as a spiritual rather than material formation.

God is the source of all being and all good, while the existence of evil can be ascribed to human desire for material benefits; like Buddhism, theosophy teaches that such desires may be overcome by absorption in the spiritual realm. For Lawrence's estimation of Madame Blavatsky's theosophy, see *Letters*, iii. 150, 298–9.

316:10–12 **bean-stalk . . . a further world** Lawrence combines a fairy-tale and a nursery rhyme. In the fairytale 'Jack and the Beanstalk', Jack acquires magic beans from which a beanstalk grows up into the clouds, leading him to the castle of a giant and a goose that lays golden eggs. The nursery rhyme 'Jack and Jill' begins: 'Jack and Jill went up the hill / To fetch a pail of water; / Jack fell down and broke his crown / And Jill came tumbling after.'

317:14 **Arno** River flowing through Florence and Pisa.

317:34 **To me they are Chartres** City south-west of Paris, famous for its thirteenth-century cathedral, often considered the world's finest Gothic building. The colours of Valerie's curtains recall for her the effect of the stained-glass windows in this cathedral.

317:35 **sixteenth-century Venetian book-case** Venetian furniture of the sixteenth century was typically highly decorated and often used designs based on architectural features such as columns, arches and pediments.

317:37 **holy of holies** Figuratively, sacred and awe-inspiring. In the instructions issued to Moses about 'the pattern of the tabernacle' (Exodus xxv.9) that is to be built within a future Temple of Jerusalem, a veil is to divide 'the holy place' from the 'most holy' (Exodus xxvi.33) where the spirit of God will dwell. The latter is the 'holy of holies'.

318:2–3 **perilous . . . Ark of the Covenant** The Ark of the Covenant was an ornate gold-plated chest containing the stone tablets given by God to Moses on Mount Sinai, on which the Ten Commandments were inscribed. Its last resting place was in the 'most holy' area in the Temple of Jerusalem (see note above). The holiness of the Ark made contact with it highly perilous (see Leviticus xvi.1–13).

318:7–9 **Bologna . . . Siena** Bologna is at the foot of the Apennines mountains, north of Florence; Siena is south of Florence.

319:7 **Sodom and Gomorrah** See note to 239:21.

319:21–2 **Fifth Avenue** Major thoroughfare in Manhattan, running along the eastern side of Central Park, with elegant mansions that justified the name Millionaires' Row even in the 1920s.

319:32–3 **Statue of Liberty** See note to 246:15–16.

322:11 **returned like dogs to our vomit** Proverbs xxvi.11: 'As a dog returneth to his vomit, so a fool returneth to his folly.'

322:25 **Cleveland university** Earl Brewster studied at the Cleveland School of Art (established 1882); this may have motivated Lawrence to inaugurate a Cleveland University to employ his fictional character. (Cleveland State University did not come into formal existence until 1964.)

323:3 **furnaces of Cleveland** On the southern shore of Lake Erie and therefore positioned to take advantage of the coal and oil fields of Pennsylvania and the Minnesota iron-ore mines, Cleveland, Ohio, grew rapidly into a major steel and industrial centre during the late nineteenth and early twentieth centuries, and was the fifth largest city in the United States by 1920.

323:11–12 **Ravenna bishop's chair** The Melvilles' bishop's chair recalls the famous ivory throne of Archbishop Maximian of Ravenna (d. 556) with carved panels depicting biblical scenes.

Glossary

Page and line references are given only for the first occurrence of entries where context is crucial to the meaning of the term. All foreign words are French unless otherwise stated.

a, 'a Have.
a' All.
à propos **of nothing** Unconnected with what went before, incidentally.
ad infinitum To infinity, having no end (Latin).
addle Acquire as one's own, earn.
a'ef A half.
Ah I.
American cloth Oilcloth, commonly used as a waterproof tablecloth that can be easily wiped clean.
amourette Cupid.
'am-pat In North Country dialect, 'ham-sam' means confused; the combination ''am-pat' implies a muddled 'pat' answer.
'appen, happen Perhaps.
Aquila Nera Black Eagle (Italian).
arena Aren't.
Art Are.
'As Has.
aside Beside.
asphodels Flowers of the lily family; in classical mythology, immortal flowers growing in the paradise of Elysium.
aten Eaten.
axed Asked.

bacca Tobacco.
backfire Burn by placing at the back of a fireplace.
bailiff Overseer of an estate or a steward.

bantle Batch.

batman Orderly assigned to serve a military officer.

bead chatelaine Crocheted handbag or purse, often suspended from a belt, with a pattern of beads worked into the stitching.

beech-mast Small rough-skinned fruit of a beech tree, especially when accumulated on the ground.

behint Behind.

Benedictine Brandy liqueur.

bho tree Large fig tree native to Asia, also known as a 'bo-tree' or 'bodhi-tree' ('tree of wisdom'); Buddha attained Enlightenment while resting beneath such a tree.

bien emmerdés Plagued by troubles, or, more profanely, 'deeply in the shit'.

blade of the "turf" Dashing young man with knowledge of horse racing.

bobbed hair Hair cut to ear level; in Lawrence's time, a conspicuously short and modern hairstyle for a woman.

bout (77:3) Period of drunkenness.

bray . . . into bits Pound or crush into powder by a pestle in a mortar.

brush-wood Twigs, sticks or branches cut from the undergrowth.

bug (46:8) Conceited, proud.

Butties, butty Subcontractor for individual work 'stalls' at a coal face; small employer and workmate.

ca', ca's Call, calls.

câline Soft and caressable.

Can (5:21) Probably a local pronounciation of the dialect word 'ken', to know.

carob tree Mediterranean evergreen shrub or tree; its seed pods can be used as an ingredient for a confection similar to chocolate.

carte blanche Full discretionary power; literally 'blank paper'.

cast (101:24) Squint.

celandine In Europe, a plant with bright yellow flowers.

C'est ça That's it.

chenille Tufty and velvety yarn used as a trim on cloth or furniture.

chiffonier Low cupboard with a sideboard top.

childer Children.

chunterin' Muttering complaints, grumbling.

clinched Locked together *or* concluded, confirmed.

clinched upon himself Locked within himself, isolated and self-absorbed.

commin', com'n Coming.

Congregational Chapel Nonconformist ecclesiastical organization where individual chapels are largely self-governing.

Coop (24:27) Come up.

copper fireplace Fireplace under a 'copper', a boiler made from copper (or, more often in Lawrence's time, iron) used for washing clothes.

copper-top Lid of a 'copper' (*see* copper fireplace).

crêpe kimono Loose robe made of a light gauze-like fabric.

crisped (158:14) Stiffened and curled ('crisping' often refers to curling hair) *or* (238:11) enliven, add zest.

crozzled up Shrivelled or dried up.

day man Miner who is employed and paid by the day, typically by a 'butty'.

death's-head Skull, an emblem of human mortality.

dog-cart Open two-wheeled horse-drawn cart with back-to-back seats.

done me one Got one over on me, gained an advantage.

dost Do you.

draught-horses Shire-horses used for pulling heavy cart loads or ploughing.

drawing in (9:7) Narrowing a haystack as it grows upwards to prevent loose hay falling down the sides.

Dutch ovens Cast iron or earthenware cooking pots with tightly fitting lids to keep steam inside; used for slow cooking or stew making.

'e He.

ennui Mental weariness, boredom.

entry (84:35) Passage between two terraced houses leading to the back door.

'er Her *or* she.

fallow Land left unsown to recover nutrients.

farouche Can mean 'fierce' or 'wild'; at 266:19, it also denotes a 'sullen' shyness.

fast (25:34) Tightly.

feyther Father.

fillet Headband for holding back or binding hair.

filthy lucre Money; in the Bible, the phrase refers to the dishonest rewards of those 'Whose mouths must be stopped, who subvert whole houses, teaching things which they ought not, for filthy lucre's sake' (Titus i.11).

fire back Back wall of a fireplace.

flig Eager, enthusiastic.

float Low, flat cart.
Fräulein Literally 'little woman', a courtesy title for girls and unmarried women (German).

gel, gelsie Girl.
gi'e, gie Give.
Gi'e ower Stop it.
gives over Stops.
glass afore . . . bed Nightcap, typically either alcoholic or milky.
Gormin' Vacantly staring and so appearing stupid.
grind (21:1) Fuck.

ha', ha'e Have.
han Have *or* hand.
hang my rags An oath perhaps derived from Capel Lofft's (1806–73) meditation on misplaced pride in the poem 'Ernest: The Rule of Right' (1868): ' 'Twas pride – one word – / That brought me to this haunt of poverty: / I would not hang my rags on that same staff' (II.455–7).
harrowing Dragging a heavy frame with metal teeth over ploughed land to break up clods and strip out weeds.
hay close Hayfield.
Herr Hauptmann Captain (German).
hollin' Hauling or throwing.
horse-raking Using a horse-drawn implement to rake cut hay into rows for drying and collection.

i' In.
I'n I'm, I am *or* I've, I have.
innerest Innermost (obsolete).

Jawohl Yes, indeed (German).

Kaput Correctly spelt 'kaputt': broken, exhausted or finished (German).

lamp cabin Pit-head storage room for miners' safety lamps.
landed Blamed.
lief Willingly.
line (86:24) Railway track.
littérateur Literary person.

lodgings on the kerbstone Out on the street, homeless.

loose 'a 'Loose all': the end of an afternoon shift at a colliery, signalled at 4 p.m. by a hooter or whistle.

lotus flower Water lily growing up through water from the beds of ponds, streams or swamps; its flowers sink and close at nightfall, rising and opening again at dawn. A symbol of the sun, creation and rebirth, particularly in Egyptian mythology.

Louis Quinze chairs Furniture with elaborate ornamentation, made during the reign of Louis XV, king of France (1715–74).

mash Brew tea.

mean crawl Variant of 'crawler', one who behaves obsequiously in hope of advantage.

mending Attention to keep a household fire burning well.

Merde Shit.

mester Manager or owner of a colliery *or* husband *or* local pronunciation of 'Master', a courtesy title for a boy.

moiled Weary, hot and sweaty through 'moil': hard work, drudgery.

morbid Unwholesome, unhealthy.

moulder Sometimes called a coremaker, a moulder produces the hollow moulds into which molten metal is poured to make castings in a foundry.

mun Must.

museau Literally 'muzzle', but at 183:19 referring to the whole face.

'n On *or* of.

-na Suffix to negate a preceding verb, as in ''Asna': hasn't, 'dunna': don't, 'shanna': shan't, 'wouldna': wouldn't.

nepitella Plant of the mint family, with aromatic foliage and clusters of pink, lilac or white flowers.

nettled Stung by nettles.

nine o'clock deputy Manager in charge of safety measures during the nightshift at a mine.

Nirvana In Buddhism, a state of liberation and bliss achieved upon the cessation of all desires.

nog Block.

non, none Not; also acts to negate a following word, as in 'non want': don't want, 'non knowed': didn't know, 'none as ormin'': not so awkward.

nowt Nothing.

o', on Of.

offertory Collection of money typically taken at the end of a religious service.

ormin' Awkward, clumsy.

ostler Stableman in charge of pit ponies.

over-bolster Lawrence's usual word for a continental quilt.

ower Over.

owt Anything.

oxalis flowers Wood sorrel, with trifoliate leaves and white, pink or yellow flowers.

Palazzo In Italian has a wider application than its literal English translation, 'palace'; the imposing buildings to which it refers can include, for instance, blocks of flats.

Panacea Universal remedy; the term is often used pejoratively to imply that such a remedy is merely illusory. Panacea was the daughter of Asclepius, the god of medicine and healing in Greek mythology.

panchion Typically, a large and heavy earthenware bowl.

paper spill Length of paper used to transfer a flame.

pee-wits Lapwings, birds with black and white plumage and a shrill cry.

pelargonium More commonly known as a geranium, an indoor plant with red, pink or white flowers and often fragrant leaves.

penny-in-the-slot Vending machine.

pent-house More usually called a 'lean-to': outhouse with a sloping roof, joined on to the main house and often used as a pantry.

pet (40:6) State of resentment, sulking.

pick (15:26) Gather cut hay.

pitcher-flowers Carnivorous plants have 'pitcher-flowers' to trap insects and reopen invitingly when the insect is digested; can also mean low-growing leaves easily accessible for pollination by ants or beetles.

podere Small agricultural holding, typically a family farm (Italian).

praying-chair Chair with a low, cushioned kneeling piece, a high back and sometimes a shelf on which a book can be placed; used for devotional reading or by a person at prayer.

pulping sweet roots Shedding and crushing raw root vegetables for use as cattle fodder.

putto Representation of a naked boy, typically a cupid or cherub, in Renaissance or Baroque art (Italian).

qui vive Alert, waiting for something to happen.

repellant Nineteenth-century spelling of 'repellent'.

right as a trivet In a perfectly good state, healthy. A trivet is a very stable three-legged tripod.

ripping (78:37) Cutting into the roof of a coal stall, or the underground route to it, to increase its height.

road (34:30) Way.

rosary In Roman Catholicism, a series of fifteen meditations on 'mysteries' in the lives of Jesus and Mary, during which the Lord's Prayer is said once, 'Hail Mary' ten times and 'Glory Be to the Father' once; rosary beads are slipped through the fingers to keep count during this series of recitations.

roué Debauchee or rake, typically elderly.

'rt Art, are.

's As *or* has.

Sacred Heart In Roman Catholicism, the heart of Christ as an object of devotion.

salotta Correctly spelt 'salotto': living room or drawing room (Italian).

sang-froid Composure under difficult or dangerous circumstances.

scalding out the pans Cleaning milk containers with boiling water.

scarab Refers both to the scarabaeid beetle, a large dung-beetle, held sacred by the ancient Egyptians and to the talismans representing this beetle, often cut gems.

Schöner Literally, 'more handsome' (German).

scotches Wedges or blocks placed under wheels to stop them rolling.

scrat' Scratch.

screets Cries.

scroddy Rotten.

s'd Should.

separator Machine in a dairy for separating cream from milk.

settler Conclusive argument.

seven and sixpenny house House with a weekly rent of seven shillings and sixpence (37½ pence now).

sheered, sheering To swerve, change course.

sheering down Falling quickly.

Sicules Original inhabitants of Sicily from whom the island takes its name.

Signora Courtesy title for a married woman, equivalent to 'Mrs' (Italian).

sin, sin' Since.

Sithee See thou, look.

Sitzfleisch Literally, 'flesh for sitting' (German), hence patience and perseverance.

skivvy Derogatory and colloquial term for a woman doing menial or poorly paid work.

sleepers Series of beams laid at right angles to a railway track to support and level it from below.

s'll Shall.

snipe Contemptible person or cheat.

Sorry (5:25) Corruption of 'sirrah', the archaic form of 'sir'.

sphinx Mythical creature with the body of a lion, eagle's wings and the head and breasts of a woman, reputed to strangle all those who could not answer her riddles; a symbol of inscrutability.

squab Cushion on a sofa or ottoman.

stall Area of coal face allotted for a 'butty' to work.

stalled cattle Cattle in individual stalls or compartments inside a shed.

Stations of the Cross Scenes commemorating the fourteen stages of Christ's Passion.

stitchwort Plant with small white star-shaped flowers, so named because of its reputation for relieving 'stitch' pains in the side.

stop (4:15) Stay, reside.

strap (44:15) Belt.

strike tickets Letters for workers' signature issued by their union to warn of impending strike action.

sumb'dy Somebody.

summat Something.

sure as eggs 'Sure as eggs is eggs', that is, absolutely certain.

sward Area of short grass; where, for example, grass has been cut for hay.

sweetmeats machine Vending machine dispensing sweets.

syrens In classical mythology, female monsters, part-woman and part-bird, who lured sailors on to the rocks and to their deaths through enchanting songs.

ta You *or* thank you.

tanger Person with a sharp tongue, a maker of stinging remarks.

teem Unload.

ter To *or* thou, you.

th' the *or* they.

tha Thou, you.

Thaïgh Thee, you.

thowt Thought.

thysen Thyself, yourself.

tines Prongs or points of a fork.

to-do Fuss, trouble.

toque Small hat.

towd Told.

trammelling Acting as an impediment or hindrance.

tramontana North wind that brings cold air into the Mediterranean.

trap (185:30) Open two-wheeled horse-drawn carriage.

trolley Trollop, disreputable woman; also a prostitute.

'ud Would *or* had.

unabateable Lawrence's coinage; that which cannot be abated or diminished.

've Have.

Vin Ordinaire 'Ordinary' or everyday wine; simple, unpretentious and inexpensive.

waflin Moving aimlessly.

wanting (13:30) Unintelligent, slow-witted.

What the Hanover's got you? 'What's got into you?' Derived from 'Go to Hanover', an oath coined upon the unpopularity of the Hanoverian kings. ('Hanover' here is a euphemism for hell.)

whimsey Source of water, usually a pond, used to supply the steam engines driving the winding gear at a pit-head.

whoam Home.

wi' With.

wik Week.

winder Unpleasant surprise, like a blow that 'winds' one.

wind-flowers Early spring-flowering plant, also known as wood anemones; can be poisonous.

winrows Rows into which cut hay is raked for drying and to simplify its collection.

winter-aconite Yellow flower from the buttercup family that can appear as early as February; can be poisonous.

winter-crack trees Plum trees producing small, late-ripening fruit.

wor Was *or* were.

writing sachet From 'un sachet de papier', a packet of paper.

Yi Yes.

yis'day Yesterday.

PENGUIN CLASSICS

THE WOMAN WHO RODE AWAY/ST. MAWR/THE PRINCESS
D. H. LAWRENCE

These three works, all written in 1924, explore the profound effects on protagonists who embark on psychological voyages of liberation. In *St. Mawr*, Lou Witt buys a beautiful, untamable bay stallion and discovers an intense emotional affinity with the horse that she cannot feel with her husband. This superb novella displays Lawrence's mastery of satirical comedy in a scathing depiction of London's fashionable high society. In 'The Woman Who Rode Away' a woman's religious quest in Mexico brings great danger – and astonishing self-discovery, while 'The Princess' portrays the intimacy between an aloof woman and her male guide as she ventures into the wilderness of New Mexico in search of new experiences.

In his introduction, James Lasdun discusses the theme of liberation and the ways in which it is conveyed in these works. Using the restored texts of the Cambridge edition, this volume includes a new chronology by Paul Poplawski.

'Lawrence urged men and women to live ... to glory in the exhilarating terror of this brief life' Frederic Raphael, *Sunday Times*

Edited by Brian Finney, Christa Jansohn and Dieter Mehl
with notes by Paul Poplawski and an introduction by James Lasdun

PENGUIN CLASSICS

SONS AND LOVERS D. H. LAWRENCE

The marriage of Gertrude and Walter Morel has become a battleground. Repelled by her uneducated and sometimes violent husband, fastidious Gertrude devotes her life to her children, especially to her sons, William and Paul – determined they will not follow their father into working down the coal mines. But conflict is inevitable when Paul seeks to escape his mother's suffocating grasp by entering into relationships with other women. Set in Lawrence's native Nottinghamshire, *Sons and Lovers* (1913) is a highly autobiographical and compelling portrayal of childhood, adolescence and the clash of generations.

In his introduction, Blake Morrison discusses the novel's place in Lawrence's life and his depiction of the mother-son relationship, sex and politics. Using the complete and restored text of the Cambridge edition, this volume includes a new chronology and further reading by Paul Poplawski.

'Lawrence's masterpiece … a revelation' Anthony Burgess

'Momentous – a great book' Blake Morrison

Edited by Helen Baron and Carl Baron
With an introduction by Blake Morrison

PENGUIN CLASSICS

LADY CHATTERLEY'S LOVER D. H. LAWRENCE

Constance Chatterley feels trapped in her sexless marriage to the invalid Sir Clifford. Unable to fulfil his wife emotionally or physically, Clifford encourages her to have a liaison with a man of their own class. But Connie is attracted instead to Mellors, her husband's gamekeeper, with whom she embarks on a passionate affair that brings new life to her stifled existence. Can she find true equality with Mellors, despite the vast gulf between their positions in society? One of the most controversial novels in English literature, *Lady Chatterley's Lover* is an erotically charged and psychologically powerful depiction of adult relationships.

In her introduction, Doris Lessing discusses the influence of Lawrence's sexual politics, his relationship with his wife Frieda and his attitude towards the First World War. Using the complete and restored text of the Cambridge edition, this volume includes a new chronology and further reading by Paul Poplawski.

'No one ever wrote better about the power struggles of sex and love'
Doris Lessing

'A masterpiece' *Guardian*

Edited by Michael Squires
With an introduction by Doris Lessing

PENGUIN CLASSICS

THE FOX/THE CAPTAIN'S DOLL/THE LADYBIRD
D. H. LAWRENCE

These three novellas show D. H. Lawrence's brilliant and insightful evocation of human relationships – both tender and cruel – and the devastating results of war. In 'The Fox', two young women living on a small farm during the First World War find their solitary life interrupted. As a fox preys on their poultry, a human predator has the women in his sights. 'The Captain's Doll' explores the complex relationship between a German countess and a married Scottish soldier in occupied Germany, while in 'The Ladybird', a wounded prisoner of war has a disturbing influence on the Englishwoman who visits him in hospital.

In her introduction, Helen Dunmore discusses the profound effect the First World War had on Lawrence's writing. Using the restored texts of the Cambridge edition, this volume includes a new chronology and further reading by Paul Poplawski.

'As wonderful to read as they are disturbing … Lawrence's prose is breath-taking'
Helen Dunmore

'A marvellous writer … bold and witty' Claire Tomalin

Edited by Dieter Mehl
With an introduction by Helen Dunmore

PENGUIN CLASSICS

THE DIARY OF A NOBODY
GEORGE AND WEEDON GROSSMITH

'I fail to see – because I do not happen to be a "Somebody" – why my diary should not be interesting'

Mr Pooter is a man of modest ambitions, content with his ordinary life. Yet he always seems to be troubled by disagreeable tradesmen, impertinent young office clerks and wayward friends, not to mention his devil-may-care son Lupin's unsuitable choice of bride. Try as he might, he cannot avoid life's embarrassing mishaps. In the bumbling, absurd yet ultimately endearing figure of Pooter, the Grossmiths created an immortal comic character and a superb satire on the snobberies of middle-class suburbia – one which also sends up late Victorian crazes for Aestheticism, spiritualism and bicycling, as well as the fashion for publishing diaries by anybody and everybody.

This edition contains the original illustrations by Weedon Grossmith, further reading and an introduction by Ed Glinert discussing the novel's initial serialization in *Punch*, reactions to Pooter, the growth of suburbs and the figure of Mrs Pooter.

'The jewel at the heart of English comic literature' William Trevor

'The funniest book in the world' Evelyn Waugh

Edited with an introduction and notes by Ed Glinert

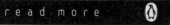
PENGUIN CLASSICS

FAR FROM THE MADDING CROWD
THOMAS HARDY

'I *hate* to be thought men's property in that way'

Independent and spirited Bathsheba Everdene has come to Weatherbury
to take up her position as a farmer on the largest estate in the area. Her
bold presence draws three very different suitors: the gentleman-farmer
Boldwood, soldier-seducer Sergeant Troy and the devoted shepherd
Gabriel Oak. Each, in contrasting ways, unsettles her decisions and
complicates her life, and tragedy ensues, threatening the stability of the
whole community. The first of his works set in Wessex, Hardy's novel
of swift passion and slow courtship is imbued with his evocative
descriptions of rural life and landscapes, and with unflinching honesty
about sexual relationships.

This edition, based on Hardy's original 1874 manuscript, is the complete
novel he never saw published, and restores its full candour and innovation.
Rosemarie Morgan's introduction discusses the history of its publication,
and the biblical and classical allusions that permeate the novel.

'Wonderful . . . a landscape which satisfies every stir of the imagination
and which ravishes the senses' Ronald Blythe

Edited with an introduction and notes by Rosemarie Morgan and
Shannon Russell

PENGUIN CLASSICS

MAURICE
E. M. FORSTER

'People were all around them, but with eyes that were intensely blue he whispered, "I love you"'

Maurice Hall is a young man who grows up confident in his privileged status and well aware of his role in society. Modest and generally conformist, he nevertheless finds himself increasingly attracted to his own sex. Through Clive, whom he encounters at Cambridge, and through Alec, the gamekeeper on Clive's country estate, Maurice gradually experiences a profound emotional and sexual awakening. A tale of passion, bravery and defiance, this intensely personal novel was completed in 1914 but remained unpublished until after Forster's death in 1970. Compellingly honest and beautifully written, it offers a powerful condemnation of the repressive attitudes of British society, and is at once a moving love story and an intimate tale of one man's erotic and political self-discovery.

The introduction, by David Leavitt, explores the significance of the novel in relation to Forster's own life and as a founding work of modern gay literature. This edition reproduces the Abinger text of the novel, and includes new notes, a chronology and further reading.

Edited with an introduction and notes by David Leavitt